Love Will Find A Way

Ellie Dean lives in a tiny hamlet set deep in the heart of the South Downs in Sussex, which has been her home for many years and where she raised her three children. She is the author of the Cliffehaven Series.

Also available by Ellie Dean

There'll be Blue Skies
Far From Home
Keep Smiling Through
Where the Heart Lies
Always in My Heart
All My Tomorrows
Some Lucky Day
While We're Apart
Sealed With a Loving Kiss
Sweet Memories of You
Shelter from the Storm
Until You Come Home
The Waiting Hours
With a Kiss and a Prayer
As the Sun Breaks Through
On a Turning Tide
With Hope and Love
Homecoming
A Place Called Home

Ellie
DEAN

Love Will Find A Way

PENGUIN BOOKS

PENGUIN BOOKS

UK | USA | Canada | Ireland | Australia
India | New Zealand | South Africa

Penguin Books is part of the Penguin Random House group of companies
whose addresses can be found at global.penguinrandomhouse.com

First published in Penguin Books 2024
001

Typeset in 11/12.5 pt Palatino LT Std
by Integra Software Services Pvt. Ltd, Pondicherry

Printed and bound in Great Britain by Clays Ltd, Elcograf S.p.A.

The authorised representative in the EEA is Penguin Random House Ireland,
Morrison Chambers, 32 Nassau Street, Dublin D02 YH68

A CIP catalogue record for this book is available from the British Library

ISBN: 978–1–804–94257–4

www.greenpenguin.co.uk

For Brett, Wayne and Nina. I'm so proud of you.

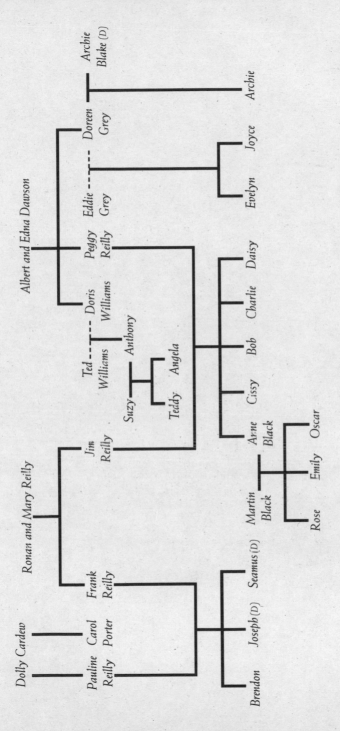

The Cliffehaven Family Tree

Dear Readers,

Another year has gone, and another book is now ready for you to read. When I started out on the Cliffehaven journey I never envisioned still writing about the Reilly family and the residents of that small seaside town all these years later. But Cliffehaven has become as beloved and familiar to me as my own family, and I've discovered there are still so many stories to be told, that for as long as you want to keep on reading them, I'm more than happy to write them. I've made many friends along the way – not least of all you, my readers, who have encouraged me to keep going and told me your own family stories of those who went through the war years. Thank you so much for taking my books to your heart, and for making the time to post reviews, send me messages on social media and keep faith in my work. It is a pleasure to offer *Love Will Find a Way* to you, and I do hope you enjoy the twists and turns of what is sadly an all-too-common story.

Until next year, I wish you all well and look forward to hearing from you.

Ellie Dean x

Acknowledgements

Writing is a solitary occupation, but no book is ever published without the dedicated efforts of many others. To that end, I wish to thank the terrific team at Cornerstone – Emily Griffin, Sarah Bance, Hope Butler, Jess Muscio and Laurie Ip Fung Chun who have made it their mission to help me produce the best possible book to offer my readers. I would also like to acknowledge the wonderful encouragement given to me by my French publisher, Jean-Daniel Belfond, and Jerome Pecheaux as well as their super team who produce and translate my Cliffehaven books. And to the editors, publicists and designers at my Dutch and Danish publishers. Last, but never least, thanks to my agent, Teresa Chris, for her unswerving loyalty and encouragement throughout the years we've been working together.

1

1946

It was a week before Christmas and from her vantage point on the hill above the town of Cliffehaven, the young woman watched preparations for the festive season, longing to be a part of them. She dared not leave her hiding place until she could be certain no one would see her. The time to go was fast approaching and, although she'd be returning home, she knew her world would never be the same again.

She refused to think about what the future might hold and forced herself to concentrate on the colourful scene being played out below. The shops had stayed open later than usual, and there was an excited bustle as people hunted for last-minute gifts, chatted on street corners, or bought bags of hot chestnuts from the man who'd set up his brazier outside the busy Crown pub. A school choir had assembled alongside the local brass band, and there was a sudden, expectant hush as their music teacher raised her baton.

Her gaze drifted to the children who stood in awe around the Christmas tree which had been erected outside the Town Hall some time ago. Its pretty lights twinkled in the early darkness of this winter's day like a beacon – torturing her with the memories of other Christmases and the promise of warmth and light, and sorely needed company. Although tempted to throw caution to the wind and go down there, she remained where she was, hunkered low in the deep shadows of the trees, her new-born baby asleep in her arms.

He'd come earlier than she'd expected, which was a blessing, for it meant there would be fewer awkward questions to answer when she returned home – as she'd promised – in time for the celebrations. She tucked the blanket firmly about the baby and nestled him within the folds of her coat as the sound of the brass band and choir drifted up to her. Their music was yet another reminder of Christmases past when life had been uncomplicated, and her future a bright and unchartered map.

The school choir was singing, 'Away in a Manger', and she wondered how they would react if they knew that a baby had already been born that night without fanfare, a crib for a bed or a star to mark his arrival – for this little one had come into the world in a dilapidated caravan that stank of mould, sheep and mice droppings.

The cold had now become unbearable and, fearing the baby might come to harm, she took one last look at the brightly lit, bustling town and got to her numbed feet before heading further uphill towards the caravan which had been her home for almost three weeks. The bright moon lit her way as her boots trampled the frosted grass and the hem of her coat snagged on the brambles and gorse which grew in wild abandon beneath the ancient trees that sheltered her makeshift home. She paused to catch her breath and looked up at the sky which was liberally sprinkled with stars. Tonight would be colder than ever, she realised, and soon there would be snow, so it was fortunate she was leaving.

The caravan had once been her childhood playground during the school holidays, but it had long been forgotten and abandoned once the shepherd had lost his life in the war and the flock had been sold. It sagged on shredded tyres, settling deeper each day into the soft earth as the windows and outer shell became greener with mould and lichen, and its delicate fabric swelled and buckled with damp. She'd taken much longer than she'd expected to find it. But she'd eventually come across it, well hidden in a deep fold of the hills, and now, as she stepped into the darkness of the sheltering trees, the only sounds she could hear were the rustle of the wind in the leaves and the distant hoot of a barn owl.

She tugged at the warped door and stepped onto the rickety floor which creaked beneath her slight weight. Although it had lain empty during the long war years, the caravan's interior still held the memory of lanolin and wool as well as the organic essence of soil and decomposition.

When she'd first set eyes on the wreck, she'd wondered if she was foolish to even contemplate setting up temporary home here, but accepting she had no other choice, she'd set to with a will to make it habitable. She'd dumped the stinking mattress and soiled bedding which had become a nest for vermin, tacked strips of old blanket over the windows to stop any light showing at night, and then scrubbed the interior from top to bottom.

She looked with some satisfaction at the results of her hard work, for it was almost homely with the blankets, eiderdown and sheet she'd brought with her draped on the planking bed and, once she'd lit the candles and kerosene heater, it felt quite snug; if one could ignore the blackness outside and the isolation which seemed to crowd in on her whenever she let herself think about it.

But she hadn't bargained on how cold it would become as the wind whistled through every crack and crevice and managed to penetrate even the thickest blanket – or how hard it would be to keep her resolve as the night sounds kept her awake, and the thought of scuttling spiders and rodents put her on edge. But for all its inconveniences and isolation, it had been the perfect hiding place, and she'd been immensely relieved to find it was still here.

She placed the baby on the bed and covered him in the eiderdown before lighting the candles she'd stuck in jam jars, and the small kerosene heater. The heater smelt horrid and soaked the thin walls in condensation, but it was better than nothing. He would wake soon and would need feeding, so she carefully measured the powdered milk, added the last of the fresh water she'd sneaked down to collect from Chalky White's well the night before last, and popped the feeding bottle into the saucepan of stale water to heat it up over the single gas ring.

As she waited for the water to simmer, she began to collect her few belongings and pack them into the holdall. There wasn't much as she was wearing almost every stitch of clothing she'd brought to ward off the cold, and she'd be leaving the bedding, heater and single-ring camping stove behind. Yet, as she packed, her thoughts kept returning to all that had happened here. It felt dreamlike now – almost surreal – but at the time it had been the most terrifying ordeal she'd ever had to face.

The days of waiting for him to arrive had seemed endless, but when the pains had started last night, and the terror of having to go through the birth on her own had set in, she'd been on the very brink of seeking help. But before she could pluck up courage, the labour had advanced too rapidly so she'd had to persevere on her own, praying desperately that nothing would go wrong – that through her panic and

4

selfish desire to keep him secret, her baby would not come to harm.

The very worst scenarios had flashed through her mind during that short, painfully hard labour. What if she died and no one found him? What if they both died? How would her loved ones deal with her mysterious disappearance? Who would ever think of looking for her here?

To her enormous relief, he'd arrived fairly quickly, and because she'd read every book she could find on the subject, she'd managed to deal with tying and cutting the cord, cleaning his airways and burying the afterbirth. But she hadn't counted on feeling so weak afterwards – hadn't realised how difficult it would be to keep them both clean and warm in the hours after his birth – or how utterly impossible it was to feel nothing for him. Which was why it was imperative she left tonight.

She finished packing and sank onto the hard planking she'd used as a bed, her gaze returning repeatedly to the baby beside her. He was beginning to stir, his tiny, mittened hands waving as his rosebud mouth began to pucker. His hair was surprisingly dark beneath the woollen cap, his skin pale and unmarked perfection under the layers of his knitted layette. She had no idea what colour his eyes were, for he'd yet to open them.

He was certainly sturdy enough to survive these brutal first hours, and that was probably because she'd been very careful to eat properly once she'd known she had no alternative but to see the pregnancy through. After all, she'd reasoned at the time, it wasn't his fault she'd been so stupid – so cowardly – so utterly incapable of making the right decision about anything.

He began to mewl and fuss, and she reached for the feeding bottle to test the heat of the formula milk on the back of her hand before changing his nappy, and dressing him once again in the layers of clothes she'd secretly bought from an out of town market. And then, with great reluctance, she cradled him in her arms so he could feed.

Her breasts ached with the need to feed him herself and tears pricked as she looked down at him. She didn't want to love him – couldn't bear the thought of getting to know his scent, or the way he felt in her arms. And yet . . . He was so easy to love – so perfect . . . And at this moment she was all he had in the world – and she was about to abandon him.

She blinked back the tears and then closed her eyes as her breasts wept with the milk her baby would never taste. She was being selfish and cruel, but he would be better off without her. He would be loved and cherished by parents who wanted him, and have the chance of a good life. Whereas she would return to her old life unencumbered by scandal and shame – and hopefully wiser from the experience and more clear-eyed in her choices.

Biting back on a sob, she knew she was only fooling herself – and that these last few precious moments would live with her for ever; the guilt a well-deserved punishment for the unforgivable sin she was about to commit.

He weighed heavier in her arms and she realised he'd finished feeding and was once more asleep. She dried her tears, wrapped him snugly in the blankets and then curled around him beneath the eiderdown to wait until she was certain Cliffehaven was sleeping.

She must have dozed off, for when she opened her eyes again, it was almost three in the morning – and dangerously close to the time when the town would begin to stir. She would have to hurry.

As the baby seemed to be sleeping peacefully, she left him on the bed while she switched off the heater and blew out the stubs of candle. Fastening the army surplus coat over the two cardigans, jumper and heavy-duty dungarees, she wound the scarf round her neck, pulled the knitted cap further down over her ears and picked up the baby in one gloved hand, the holdall in the other.

Stepping down from the caravan, she nudged the door shut with her heel and set off into the still and silent night, the cold bright stars accompanying a moon ringed by an ethereal halo. With a trembling breath, she hitched the baby closer to her chest, tightened her grip on the holdall and, without looking back, began the long trek over the hills to the track which would eventually lead her down into the sleeping town.

By the time she finally reached the stile at the end of the track, her legs were trembling from the effort it had taken to walk so far, and she was desperate to rest. But as she looked down the steep road towards the High Street, she became aware of the sounds coming from behind the high walls of the dairy. Alan Jenkins would be loading his drays, and soon he and his men would be leading the shires out of the yard to begin their rounds. There was no time to rest.

Pausing to catch her breath, she eased the baby to the other arm and flexed her stiff fingers before once again lifting the holdall. Frost glittered on the pavement and silvered the weeds growing by the factory estate fence, and she had to negotiate the icy patches carefully as she went down the hill.

Reaching the deserted High Street, she saw the Christmas tree lights had been switched off, and only a dim glow came from a solitary streetlamp outside Plummer's department store. All the shops were shuttered, the pavements deserted, and now the only lights she could see were a pale glimmer behind the curtains of Gloria's bedroom above the Crown, and the blue lamp outside the police station.

The thought of someone seeing her made her even more nervous, and it seemed her anxiety had been transmitted to the baby, for he began to mither and squirm. Fearing he was about to start crying, she hurried over the hump-backed bridge and headed into the labyrinth of alleyways that led off the High Street. She knew exactly where she was going and could only pray that the door hadn't been locked.

Her footsteps echoed as she entered the church grounds, but as she climbed the steps and reached for the heavy iron ring in the oak door she heard the stamp of horses' hooves ring out from beyond the bridge, and knew she'd almost run out of time.

Holding her breath, she twisted the iron ring and the door creaked open so loudly she was sure someone must have heard it. She froze momentarily and then slipped into the darkness that smelt of incense, cold stone and old hymn books, and gratefully dropped the cumbersome holdall onto a nearby pew.

The church was vast. Built in Victorian days, it had withstood two world wars and then seen the congregation dwindle, but at Christmas it became the hub of Cliffehaven with its ancient crib, special carol concerts, services and lively re-enactments of the Christmas story.

She felt the baby stir and stretch in her arms as she tiptoed down the long aisle towards the altar which had been dressed quite gloriously with red-berried holly, mistletoe, ivy and thick white candles. If he woke now, his cries would echo to the rafters and be heard in the surrounding houses. She jiggled him in her arms, hoping to still his fretting.

It seemed to work, but her heart was thudding painfully against her ribs as she paused at the steps and deliberately turned her gaze from the gold cross that hung above the altar. She needed no reminders that what she was doing was against everything she'd ever believed in, but she had no choice – really she didn't – and if God was as kindly as he was meant to be, then he'd surely understand and forgive her.

She turned from the altar towards the nativity tableau which, following a long-held tradition, was set up at the foot of the intricately carved pulpit. There was the stable, crudely made of wood off-cuts and straw thatch, but lovingly restored after many years of service, as were the painted wooden figures of Mary and Joseph, the three wise men and the shepherds with their miniature sheep. The crib at the centre was filled with straw in which lay a rather battered and ugly representation of the baby Jesus.

She bent down, and with a soft apology, lifted the effigy from the straw and placed it to one side before tenderly laying her own baby in its place. 'Forgive me,' she whispered as she placed the feeding bottle beside him, kissed his forehead and saw the sparkle of her tear on his downy cheek.

As if he understood that she was abandoning him, he opened his eyes, and meeting that accusing, clear blue gaze, she felt a pain so great it took her breath away.

'I'm sorry,' she sobbed. 'So very sorry. Please, please forgive me.' She backed away from those accusing eyes, and then was running down the aisle to snatch up her bag and make her escape.

The cold air and the reality of what she'd done hit her as the door-latch clicked shut behind her. Yet, on the point of rushing back to scoop him up and face the consequences, she heard the sound of approaching footsteps. Dashing from the doorway into the deeper shadows, she hid behind the town's war memorial and watched as a familiar figure strode towards the church doorway. She stifled her sobs as she felt a deep thankfulness that her baby would now be safe.

Blinded by her tears, and consumed with guilt, she picked up her bag and slunk away into the darkness as the first soft flakes of snow began to fall.

2

Bertram Grantley-Adams had pulled up the collar of his overcoat and tucked his woollen scarf more firmly about his neck for his early morning mission. With his Abercrombie hat tugged low and his hands encased in leather gloves, he'd maintained a brisk pace during his walk through the town which had kept him warm, the exercise sharpening his enthusiasm for the coming day. Once his church warden duties were accomplished, he planned to have breakfast at the golf club and then finish his Christmas shopping by collecting the pretty brooch from the jeweller's that he'd chosen for Cordelia.

The thought of her smile made his heart do a little extra skip as he carefully closed the church door behind him, switched on his torch and headed for the vestry. Cordelia Finch was a special lady, and although he was aware that she and everyone else at Beach View had nicknamed him 'Bertie Double-Barrelled', he knew it was meant affectionately, and it warmed his heart to know they cared for him. The only regret he had was that they hadn't met years ago, for Cordelia would have been a perfect wife.

His thoughts were interrupted by a twinge of arthritis in his ageing hip. It wasn't pleasant to be reminded that he was now in his eighties; winter seemed to stir up unwanted aches and pains which made life rather difficult at times, and on mornings like this, he thought longingly of the heat and dust of India where he'd spent many happy years in command of his beloved regiment.

Bertie had willingly taken on the role of church warden, for the early hours suited him and he liked to feel he was still a useful member of the community. He'd always been a light sleeper and firmly believed there should be no slacking, even in retirement. Yet as he switched on the vestry lights he could feel the chill of the old building settle around him, and the damp of the flagstone floor seep through his sturdy brogues. It was not a morning to linger.

He checked his watch and, with military precision, corrected the vestry clock which had the annoying habit of running at least five minutes fast every day. As he closed the glass over the dial he heard a distant mewling and gritted his teeth. 'That blasted cat's got in again,' he muttered. 'Goodness knows what sort of mess it's left for me to clean up this time.'

He switched on the main lights, marched purposefully out of the vestry and stood by the marble font in the hope he'd catch sight of the damned thing. His body might be crumbling, but there was nothing wrong with his hearing or his keen eyesight. He glared into every shadow and strained to hear the slightest movement, but there were myriad places it could be hiding, and as it moved like a silent streak of lightning, it was almost impossible to catch.

Bertie grimaced in annoyance. The blasted stray had proved to be quite feral on the two previous occasions he'd managed to corner it, so he was glad he was wearing stout gloves. However, it was his job to get rid of it, and the vicar would not be best pleased to find he'd been lacking in his duties.

He tensed as the mewling came again from somewhere near the pulpit. It must be in trouble, he thought, stealthily heading towards it, for it was unusual for it to make the slightest sound. But as he reached the front pew, poised to pounce, he came to an abrupt halt, scarcely believing what he was seeing. There was a real baby in the crib.

'Good Lord,' he breathed.

The baby waved its arms and legs about and gave a trembling wail that echoed to the high rafters and through the cold stone walls. Dressed head to foot in white knitted clothes and partially wrapped in a rather grubby blanket, it was clearly furious at being left there.

Bertie snapped out of his shock and quickly gathered the infant into his arms. 'There, there, little chap,' he soothed. 'No need for all that, don't you know. You're safe now.'

He tucked the blanket more tightly about the squalling scrap, retrieved the feeding bottle from beneath the crib and marched quickly back down the aisle. In all his years of military service, he'd never been faced with this sort of dilemma, and he wasn't at all sure what he should do. But this was no place for a baby.

Dithering on the steps, he hardly noticed the cat streaking past his feet as the church door banged shut behind him – but he did see the snow which was now coming down quite hard. Where to go? What to do? Hospital? Police? Vicarage? Beach View, or the midwife, Danuta?

He glanced at his watch. Five hundred hours was too early to go to Beach View; the vicar wouldn't appreciate being woken and probably wouldn't be much help anyway; and the hospital was too far away – as was Danuta. He'd go to the police station and ask Albert Williams's advice.

Bertie was astonished by the volume of the baby's cries as he sheltered it from the snow and hurried towards the police station. For something so tiny, it certainly had a good pair of lungs, and Bertram was sure it must have woken half the town by now. He jiggled the squalling mite in his arms to try and soothe it and decided it must be a boy – for surely no girl could make such a racket?

'By gad, little chap. You've the makings of a first-rate sergeant major,' he chuckled.

The police station was located in the large Town Hall building, with a separate door that led to a narrow reception area, with offices behind and cells in the basement. Bertie pushed through the door with the protesting infant to find his old pal, Sergeant Albert Williams, behind the reception counter.

'I'm jolly relieved you're on duty,' he shouted to the astonished man above the wailing. 'Any idea what I should do with this?'

The sergeant eyed him and the baby with growing horror. 'I'll get a WPC,' he said and made a hasty exit.

Bertie paced back and forth, disappointed that Albert had proved to be so unhelpful. He had rather hoped he could hand the baby over, make a statement and get on with his day. He really didn't have the time to be hanging about here – and the baby probably needed feeding – or changing – or . . . well, he didn't have a clue what it might need. He just wished it would stop bawling.

A door opened and a young woman bustled out looking very smart and capable in her police uniform. 'Oh, poor little mite,' she cooed, relieving him of his burden. 'He's very cold,' she said sternly, giving Bertram a baleful glare. 'Hungry too,' she added, taking charge of the feeding bottle.

'It's not my fault,' he blustered. 'I got him here as fast as I could.' But he found he was talking to himself, for the girl had gone and the baby's cries were now thankfully muffled by the closed door.

'You'll have to make a statement, Bertie,' said Sergeant Williams who'd miraculously appeared again now the coast was clear. He lifted the flap in the counter to allow him access to the inner sanctum, and led the way to an interview room.

Bertie's nose twitched at the stench of old cigarettes, sweat and vomit that permeated through the sharp tang of disinfectant, and gingerly sat down on the hard wooden chair.

'Sorry about the pong, Bertie,' said Albert cheerfully. 'The drunks and ne'er-do-wells must have drunk the town dry last night, because our cells are full.'

Bertie brushed the snow from his coat. 'Is this going to take long, Albert? Only I have to be somewhere, and the weather's closing in.'

Albert Williams grinned, for he knew Bertie's un- wavering morning routine. 'The golf club will still be serving breakfast by the time we're finished here. Let's get on with it, shall we?' He opened a notebook, licked the end of a pencil and laboriously wrote down Bertie's full name and address. 'So, tell me how you ended up with a baby at this time of the morning.'

He listened with growing astonishment as his old friend set the scene. 'There was no note? No sign of the mother?'

Bertie shook his head. 'Nothing. I just bundled it up and brought it straight here. I thought you'd be more experienced in such things.'

'I've been a copper in Cliffehaven for nigh on thirty years and it's the first abandoned baby that I know about,' muttered Albert, closing the notebook. 'No doubt the press will have a field day and will make a nuisance of themselves, but they'll have to be informed if we're to find the mother.' He grimaced at the thought and pushed back from the table. 'I'll get one of the other WPCs to type up your statement, and then you can sign it and be on your way.'

Bertie shifted on the uncomfortable chair. 'What will happen to him now? I assume it is a boy?'

'So WPC Jones informs me,' Albert replied. 'I expect I'll have to get in touch with the midwife, and if he doesn't need any medical care, he will probably be taken to the orphanage or handed over to the local authority.'

Bertie experienced a pang of distress which surprised him, for he hadn't realised how much the baby's welfare had already come to matter to him. 'Is the orphanage a good place?'

'I haven't heard anything bad about it,' muttered Albert. 'And I doubt he'll be there for long, anyway, because babies that young are soon snapped up for adoption.'

'Would you keep me posted on his progress, Albert? Only I feel sort of responsible for the little blighter,' Bertie admitted stiffly.

Albert grinned. 'You're getting soft in your old age, Bertie. But I'll see what I can do,' he replied, and left the room.

Bertie dug his hands in his pockets and tried to ignore the cold and the stench of the interview room. His own childhood experience of children's homes and so-called do-gooders had been far from pleasant, and he could only pray that things had improved over the intervening decades.

The picturesque, but draughty, weather-board cottages sat in a huddled line along a plateau in the steeply sloping shingle of Tamarisk Bay, their tar-papered roofs further insulated by a thick layer of moss and sea grasses. Sheltered on two sides by the hills rising in an arc around them, these rather basic dwellings were nevertheless fully exposed to the sea and the weather at the front, which made for uncomfortable living conditions when the temperature plummeted and winter set in with a vengeance.

The three-roomed shacks had been built almost a hundred years before to house the fishing families who'd once worked from this shore, but were now refurbished, with electricity, mains water, and even telephones. They were rented out to homeless returning servicemen and their families by Frank Reilly who lived in the most easterly one and ran his sizeable fishing fleet from nearby Cliffehaven's more sheltered beach.

Frank's grandparents had come from Ireland to Tamarisk Bay at the end of the eighteen hundreds, and in the ensuing years, his canny father, Ronan Reilly, had slowly taken over the fishing business and bought up the cottages once they'd been abandoned. Ronan had long since retired, handing over the business to Frank in return for a regular income to boost his pension; now Frank's son, Brendon, was the fourth generation of Reilly fishermen to make their living from the cold waters of the English Channel.

In the central cottage, Danuta snuggled into Stanislav's broad chest, reluctant to leave the warmth and comfort of the bed as the sea rolled against the shingle and ice frosted the inside of the window. She wasn't on duty at the Cliffehaven clinic for another two hours and was eager to savour every last minute she could before she had to brave the bitter cold and get dressed.

'You are going to be late,' Stanislav murmured in Polish against her hair.

'One more minute won't hurt,' she murmured. 'It's freezing out there.'

He shifted in the bed, causing a draught as his shoulders lifted the blankets. 'The stove must have gone out again,' he grumbled. He threw back the bedclothes and slid to the floor. 'Stay there while I light it.'

Danuta grabbed the bedclothes and huddled inside them to watch him hoist up his adapted pyjama trousers and use his powerful arms to swing his body through the bedroom door and into the other room. He was such a dear man and her heart swelled with love for him – but she did wish he'd hurry up and find them somewhere warmer and less cramped to live. But that was an argument for another day, and if she stayed in bed much longer, she really would be late.

She reached out for the underwear she'd left on a bedside chair and shivered at how cold it all felt as she wriggled into it beneath the blankets, and struggled to fasten the thick black stockings to her suspender belt. Once this was achieved, she took a deep breath and leapt out of bed to get quickly dressed in her dark blue nurse's uniform dress and cardigan. Slipping her stockinged feet into her sturdy walking shoes, she picked up Stan's dressing gown and prosthetic legs and went to see how he was getting on with the antiquated and troublesome stove.

'There, all warm in a minute,' he said, using his muscled arms again to swing into the low fireside chair. He shot her a beaming smile. 'I have put the kettle and porridge on.'

Danuta handed him his dressing gown, waited for him to put it on and then passed over the legs. She didn't offer to help him as Stanislav was very particular about doing things for himself, so she busied herself by laying the breakfast table and stirring the large pot of porridge on the stove. The porridge and tea would warm and set them up for the day, and by the looks of it, they'd need it, for the snow was coming down quite heavily and settling on the wild tamarisk that grew in the sand and chalk bank behind the cottage.

'We must try to find another place,' she said quietly in Polish. 'I know you like living here, but it's cold and too far from anywhere. If we get snowed in, I will not be able to tend my patients, and you will not be able to fly the cargo planes.'

'It's not as cold as Warsaw,' he muttered, concentrating on buckling his prosthetic legs firmly to the stumps of his thighs. He glanced up at her with a teasing light in his eyes. 'You've grown soft after living in England for so long and have forgotten what it is to go through a Polish winter.'

Danuta had a disturbing flash of a particular Polish winter – of trying to survive in that Warsaw basement as the Germans invaded her country. Stanislav was wrong. She would never forget the cold, the starvation, the terror imposed by the brutal Nazis, and the horror of having to bury her parents in iron-hard ground in the middle of a freezing night.

'That was then. This is now,' she said flatly.

He struggled to stand from the low chair and put his arms around her so he could nuzzle her neck. 'But I am happy here, *kotku*,' he murmured. 'It is our little love nest. Perfect for just us two.'

She smiled at his endearment. 'You can call me a kitten all you like, but it won't make me change my mind about this place.' She turned within his embrace and looked up at him. 'We talked about trying to adopt a baby,' she said quietly, 'and no authority will ever agree to it if we stay here.'

'I wish for this too, my *kotku*, but with so many without a home, it could be a long time before we can find somewhere else.' He softly kissed her brow. 'I will do my very best, Danuta, my love. But until things change, we must both learn to be patient.'

She knew he was right, but that didn't ease the yearning to have a child they could call their own. She rested her head against his chest and hugged him. 'I know,' she sighed. 'At least the low rent allows us to save up a deposit for when the time comes.'

Their conversation was rudely interrupted by the telephone's urgent jangling. As Stanislav was nearest, he reached for the receiver and Danuta quickly took the porridge off the hob to dole it out into bowls.

'I will tell her,' said Stanislav, replacing the receiver and sitting down heavily at the table. 'That was the police,' he said. 'There is a baby for you to see.'

'A baby? What have the police to do with a baby?'

Stanislav shrugged. 'I don't know. But Sergeant Williams said he wants you to check it over.'

Danuta frowned. 'Is the mother with the baby at the police station? Have they been involved in an accident – or is it a case of domestic violence?'

'I have no idea,' he replied, scooping the porridge into his mouth with relish.

Danuta gave a sigh of exasperation. 'I do wish you'd let me talk to him, Stan. It's very frustrating not to know the facts.'

'Sorry,' he mumbled. 'But Sergeant Williams was in a hurry and put the phone down before I could ask anything.'

Danuta didn't like the sound of this. She quickly finished her porridge and took a cautious slurp of the hot tea. 'I'd better not hang about then. If I've got to go there before I start my rounds, I'll be late to the clinic, and chasing the clock all day.'

'You must drive very carefully,' he said, glancing through the window. 'The snow is coming down even harder now, and the icy roads will be dangerous.'

The icy roads were the least of her worries as she had to get out of Tamarisk Bay first, and that could prove challenging at the best of times. She filled a Thermos with tea and reached for her gabardine mac which was warming near the stove. Winding a thick scarf round her neck, she pinned on her nurse's cap, pulled on her gloves and reached for her medical bag. Planting a kiss on Stan's lips, she caressed his unshaven cheek. 'I'll be careful, as long as you promise to do the same.'

'We'll probably be grounded until the weather lifts,' he replied. 'No one will fly in this.'

'If it looks as if the snow is settling in, pack some bags and make your way to Peggy's. She said we could always stay at Beach View if the weather threatened to close our way out.'

'Don't fuss,' he scolded softly. 'We will be just fine here. You'll see.'

Danuta didn't have time to argue, and there'd be no point anyway as once Stanislav had made up his mind, nothing would shift it. 'I'll see you this evening, then,' she said, kissing him again.

She hurried out of the cottage, her mind already going through the visits she had to make that day, and the mystery of the baby at the police station. Ducking her head against the windblown snow, she made her way up the steep slope to where they'd parked their cars in the lee of a gorse thicket.

Stan's specially adapted car was covered in snow, but her little Betsy had somehow avoided the worst of it, so she quickly cleared the windscreen and climbed in. Having dumped her medical bag on the passenger seat, she turned the key in the ignition, praying Betsy wouldn't let her down.

The neat black Austin was as reliable as ever and fired up immediately. With a sigh of relief, Danuta reversed away from the sheltering gorse, but as she turned towards the track, she was met by a whirlwind of snow.

With the wipers labouring to clear the windscreen, she switched on the heater in the hope it might actually warm the car's interior and demist the windows. Gripping the steering wheel tightly, she peered out anxiously and, with great caution, headed along the rutted chalk track which would take her over the hill to the valley road that led into Cliffehaven.

The wind rocked the little car as the snow was driven from the north-east to lie thick and heavy in the dips and hollows of the hills, and slowly weigh down the branches of the trees. It was probably quite beautiful to look at, but Danuta's gaze never deviated from the track which was becoming almost invisible. At the crest of the hill she felt the full force of the wind battering the side of the car, and she prayed that the hill she was about to negotiate wasn't too slippery.

Having reached the narrow country lane that ran past the Cliffe estate, she took a breath of relief. The snow wasn't lying so thickly here as it was sheltered by high walls and trees, but there were icy patches to negotiate, and in this strange half-light and deep shadow it was difficult to avoid them.

Eventually, she arrived at the police station and had to sit for a minute to unwind and loosen the tension knots in her neck and shoulders. She almost had to peel her fingers from the steering wheel, and her eyes ached from navigating her way through the blinding snow flurries. She had come through with no mishaps, but the prospect of the drive home later was not something she relished, and she could only pray that the sudden onslaught of snow would die out before then.

'Don't be such a goose,' she scolded herself as she clambered out of the car with her medical bag. 'You've driven in worse, and the snow will probably be gone by midday. After all, this is England, not outer Mongolia.'

She pushed her way through the doors of the police station to find Sergeant Williams sipping tea and reading a newspaper at his desk.

He looked up as the door clattered behind her and quickly opened the flap in the reception counter. 'Thanks for coming, Sister,' he said. 'It can't have been an easy drive in this weather.'

'It was not so bad,' she fibbed. 'Please, would you tell me about this baby? You did not give Stanislav many details on the telephone.'

'Bertie found him abandoned in the church and brought him in.'

'Bertie?' She wrinkled her brow as she thought about all the Berts, Alberts and Berties that lived in and around Cliffehaven. Yet the mention of the church brought a particular Bertie to mind. 'You don't mean Cordelia's Bertie Double-Barrelled?'

Albert grinned. 'That's the one. Proper put out he was an' all. I don't reckon he's ever been in charge of such a young 'un before.'

'Where's the baby now?'

'WPC Jenkins is looking after him in the canteen. Now he's been changed and fed he's fast asleep, which is a relief all round,' he added. 'Got a good set of lungs on him, that's for sure.'

'Any sign of the mother?' she asked as she followed him down the long corridor.

'I've sent my men out to knock on doors and ask if anyone saw or heard anything, but we've drawn a blank so far. Even Alan Jenkins saw nothing, and he's out at sparrow fart every day to deliver the milk. Whoever she is, she knew the right time to dump him and make a run for it.'

Danuta was not familiar with the phrase, 'sparrow fart', but let it go. She was more concerned about the mother who she doubted had just dumped her baby – but probably agonised over what she was doing and fled in tears.

'I wonder if she also knew that Bertie would be in the church at that time, so he wouldn't be left for too long in the cold,' she murmured. She paused at the door to the canteen and looked up at him. 'If so, then she must be local.'

'That was my thinking,' he said dourly. 'Better check on all your patients, Sister. Could be she's one of them.'

Danuta didn't think it was likely, for a girl in trouble wouldn't risk going to antenatal clinics for fear of being seen and losing her reputation. And she certainly wouldn't go to any doctor unless she was having complications. But whoever she was, she would need medical care, and someone to talk to.

Sergeant Williams pushed open the door to the almost deserted canteen and gestured at the young policewoman sitting at a nearby table with a baby in her arms. 'I'll leave you to it,' he muttered and stomped back to his tea and newspaper.

Danuta smiled down at the attractive girl in the smart uniform. 'Hello. I'm Sister Danuta, the midwife and district nurse.'

'Felicity Jenkins,' she replied and shot her a friendly grin. 'I've washed, fed and changed him and he's fast asleep now, so it would be a shame to wake him up.'

Danuta caught the soft lilt of Wales in the girl's voice and fleetingly wondered if she was any relation to Alan who owned the dairy. 'But it is necessary, Felicity. The mother was probably alone when she gave birth to him, and I must see he has come to no harm.'

She put down her medical bag and opened her arms to receive the baby, and the girl reluctantly handed him over.

'He's a *babi bach*,' Felicity murmured. 'The mother clearly did her best for him.'

Danuta didn't reply, preferring to form her own judgement. She carefully removed the blanket and asked Felicity to fold it on the table. When this was done, she placed the baby onto it.

Danuta gently manipulated his arms and legs to make sure there was nothing impeding their movement, and then checked that the umbilical cord was correctly tied – which it was – although with a length of string, rather than cotton. She dug into her bag for scissors and fine thread to correct the mistake, and then liberally dusted it with special talc.

Satisfied all was as it should be, she breathed on her stethoscope to warm it and then listened to his steady heartbeat. He felt warm to the touch and was a good colour and weight; he curled his toes when she ran a finger up his instep, and had a good grasp when she did the same with his palms.

He opened his eyes and looked up at her, his little arms and legs waving in anticipation of another feed. Felicity was right, thought Danuta. He was a healthy baby that had survived not only an unsupervised birth within the last twenty-four hours, but being abandoned in a cold church. Luck had certainly been on his side.

She lifted him into her arms and felt the all-too-familiar tug of yearning as she wrapped him once more in the blanket. He was adorable, and it would be all too easy to love him. But he was not her baby. She must close her heart and maintain a professional attitude if she was to do right by him. The mother was out there somewhere, and if she had any feelings at all for him, she must be plagued with guilt.

'I've made up another bottle if he gets hungry again.'

Felicity's voice broke the spell, and Danuta forced herself to concentrate on her duties. 'He is very well for one so young,' she said, resisting the urge to look into those lovely eyes again. 'But it is urgent we find his mother.'

'The local reporter has already been in. The story will be in today's late edition paper, along with his picture, and it will get into the mainstream papers by tonight. They decided to call him Noel,' the girl continued. 'It being so near to Christmas.'

Danuta didn't think he looked like a Noel, but as it was not her place to decide such things, she didn't comment. 'I suppose he will have to go to the orphanage until we can trace the mother.'

Felicity shook her head. 'The sergeant telephoned them, but they're full and can't take him,' she said. 'He'll either have to go to the hospital crèche or be fostered out. We certainly can't keep him here.'

This was a dilemma Danuta hadn't foreseen. 'You'd better give me that bottle. I'll keep him until I've sorted out something – which might mean handing him over to the adoption agencies. But I hope it does not come to that.'

Felicity handed over the bottle, then buttoned her jacket and smoothed the creases in her uniform skirt. 'I'm sure you'll have no bother,' she said, lightly running a finger over the baby's cheek. 'Who can resist such a *babi bach* at Christmas?'

Plenty of people, thought Danuta as she popped the bottle in her bag and carried the baby from the canteen. Families were already struggling to keep body and soul together in these straitened times, and with Christmas came visitors to fill up spare rooms; it was hardly likely there'd be somewhere for a baby who would need full-time care. The irony of the situation didn't escape her, for this little one wasn't the first to find there was no room for him at Christmas.

She sheltered the baby from the snow and settled him between pillows on the back seat of the car. Sliding in behind the steering wheel, she thought through all her options. The hospital nursery could only be temporary as it was so busy; the local social workers were inundated with needy families, and all the foster parents she knew were already looking after more children than usual – and Solly Goldman's crèche catered only for the children of those who worked in his factories.

Danuta looked at her watch. The local authority offices wouldn't be open for another three hours, but until then, there was only one place she could take him. She turned the key in the ignition and headed back down the High Street to Cliffehaven General.

3

At Beach View, it was barely light when Peggy Reilly went downstairs to her refurbished kitchen, yawning, then washed her hands in the Belfast sink and put the kettle on the hob. She'd been up half the night with poor little Daisy, who was feeling very sorry for herself and had proved to be a rather demanding patient. German measles had torn through the school like wildfire. Peggy had thought her five-year-old Daisy had managed to avoid it, but just as the school was about to close for the holidays, Daisy had woken the previous morning covered in the tell-tale rash.

Peggy tightened the belt on her thick dressing gown to ward off the chill and opened the curtains to stare in disbelief at the snow coming down. 'That's just about all I need today,' she sighed before prodding the range fire into surly life and adding a few more knobs of nutty slack to encourage it further. If the coalman didn't come as expected, she'd be hard pushed to cook anything, let alone heat the radiators. But at least there was the immersion heater for hot water, although it was an expensive way of going about things – especially if young Charlie forgot to turn it off when he'd finished in the bathroom.

She made the tea and let it mash in the pot in the faint hope the over-used leaves might actually look and taste like tea, and sat down at the table. Daisy's illness had caused a few problems, not least of all to Peggy's work schedule. She'd telephoned her boss,

Solly Goldman, as soon as the doctor had confirmed it was measles, to warn him of the situation and ask him for leave until Daisy recovered.

Thankfully, Solly wasn't a man to make a meal of things, and had agreed immediately to her shop-floor-manager, Florence Hillier, stepping temporarily into Peggy's shoes. Florence had proved to be reliable and loyal during the robbery at the factory, and had even gone that further mile by taking in Gracie Smith and her little boy as lodgers so they'd be safe from a vengeful Phil Warner – who was now in prison awaiting trial.

The second problem was rather more serious. Her permanent and much-loved lodger, Cordelia Finch, was over eighty, and although robust in spirit, was getting frail. It was imperative she kept Cordelia as isolated as possible from Daisy, one was never quite sure how these childhood illnesses might affect the elderly, which meant Peggy dared not leave the house in case Daisy needed something. However, it being so close to Christmas, there was a long list of shopping and last-minute gifts to be bought, which would now have to wait until her beloved husband Jim could be home long enough to babysit.

Peggy poured the tea into her favourite cup. It wasn't even as if she could rely on her son, Charlie, for Jack Smith had taken him on as assistant mechanic in his garage workshop for the grammar school holidays, and when he wasn't working, he was busy with rugby training, out with his pals, or swatting for his upcoming exams.

She sipped the tea and grimaced. It tasted like dishwater.

'You look all in, Peg,' Jim said as he came into the kitchen carrying three milk bottles dusted with snow.

'Why don't you go back to bed for a bit?' he murmured, kissing her cheek. 'I can see to breakfast.'

'I won't go back to sleep, Jim, so there's little point. I'll snatch a nap later – after all, I'm stuck at home all day.'

'I'm sorry I can't be much help,' he said, placing the bottles in the fridge before collecting a cup and pouring tea. 'But the British Legion is on duty every day of the year, and I'm lucky the brigadier has put me down for three days' leave over Christmas. I didn't expect it as I'm a new recruit, but it's probably because it's my first Christmas home since Daisy was born.'

'I just hope everything goes to plan,' she fretted. 'If the snow keeps up, it'll make it difficult for our Bob to get here from Somerset, and for Doreen to make it from Swansea. Even our Cissy might have problems travelling down from London. Which reminds me – she promised to telephone to firm up her arrangements, but I haven't heard from her for ages, and she always seems to be out when I ring. Her silence worries me. I do hope she isn't going to let us down again.'

'She knows how important it is to you, love, so of course she'll come,' soothed Jim. 'And you know what a busy life our daughter leads – she's probably just forgotten she'd said she'd ring.' He took a slurp of tea, curled his lip at the lack of taste, and left the table to put the large pot of porridge on the hob to warm through.

Peggy realised he was probably right. Their second daughter, Cissy, was scatty at the best of times, and now she had such an exciting life in London, thoughts of home rarely crossed her radar – unless she needed something. But to have gone so long without ringing was unusual, even for Cissy.

'I'll telephone the flat again later and leave a message if she's not there,' she said. 'Though it's unlikely any of those girls will be up and about before midday. They keep such late hours driving their taxis about the city.'

'Good idea,' muttered Jim, absent-mindedly stirring the porridge as he watched the snow settle on the roofs and garden walls. 'But I wouldn't let Cissy hear you call them taxis, Peggy. They're private hire limousines, if you please.'

'That's just a posh name for a taxi,' she replied, and giggled. 'Honestly, Jim, that daughter of ours has ideas above her station.'

'It was mixing with all the RAF toffs during the war that did it. If she'd gone to work in the armament factory it might have been a very different story.'

Peggy laughed. 'Armament factory? Our Cissy? You must be joking, Jim.'

He smiled ruefully. 'I know. Our little star of the back row of the chorus line always had her eye on bigger and better things, so we shouldn't be surprised that she's chosen the bright lights of London, and the society of debs and chinless wonders.'

He winked at her. 'You never know, Peg, she could end up marrying some toff with a title and really put your Doris's nose out of joint.'

'My sister's nose is permanently out of joint over something,' she replied, swiftly rescuing the porridge before it stuck to the pot. 'And if Cissy is daft enough to marry above her class, I just hope she remembers where she comes from and doesn't turn into another snob like Doris.'

All was quiet at the Crown after an extremely busy night in which a drunken fight had broken out and the police had been called. Gloria had been left with a terrible mess to clean up after closing time and hadn't climbed into bed until gone two o'clock. She had hoped to lie in this morning, but inexplicably, she'd woken at about five thinking she could hear a baby crying and had then found it impossible to settle again.

The Town Hall clock struck six and Gloria gave up on the idea of lounging about in bed and dressed quickly in warm underwear and a tight woollen dress. She spent some time plastering on her make-up before donning earrings, bracelets, high heels and a thick cardigan which she would remove the minute the pub opened. Her customers liked a flash of bosom and a curve or two on show, and dashing about behind the bar would keep her warm.

She went downstairs to fetch in the milk and found it had frozen to the point of pushing up the foil cap. Eyeing the snow without pleasure, she slammed the door on it and went into the kitchen to stir life into the fire, make a pot of tea and listen to the wireless. She curled her lip at the sound of Bing Crosby crooning about a white Christmas. Dreaming of such a thing was all very well, but the reality of being snowed in made life difficult, and when it turned to an icy slush, it became deadly to walk anywhere – especially in high-heeled shoes.

Realising she wasn't in the best of tempers, she lit a fag and plumped down into a kitchen chair to wait for the electric kettle to boil. She'd once loved Christmas, with all the gaudy decorations, the twinkling lights, the presents beneath a tree laden with baubles and tinsel, and the happy atmosphere stoked by alcohol and goodwill. But since her son had been killed in France, and her daughter-in-law had taken her grandchildren to live in Cornwall, the season had lost its appeal.

Her gloomy thoughts were interrupted by the telephone. Glancing at the clock, she wondered who on earth could be ringing her at this ungodly time of the morning, and steeled herself for what must surely be bad news.

'Gloria, it's Beryl.'

Hearing her younger sister's voice, she replied rather more sharply than she'd intended. 'Bloody hell, Beryl. What sort of time is this to be calling folk?'

'I'm sorry if I woke you, Glo. But I was wondering if my Sandra has been in touch.'

'Last I heard from her, she were planning to come down with you and her other 'alf for Christmas. That were a few weeks ago.'

'So, she hasn't phoned since?'

Gloria heard the wobble in her sister's voice and, with a degree of impatience, realised she was on the verge of tears. 'I just said so, didn't I? What's going on up there, Beryl? Why you getting yer knickers in a twist over Sandra?'

'I'm worried about her,' Beryl admitted fretfully. 'She's not been herself lately, and she and Graham had a big bust-up over a business trip she had to go on. He didn't like the thought of her going, but she said she had to as her boss relied on her and her job depended on it. He hasn't heard from her since, but from what she told me before she left, she's due back any day now.'

'There you go then. I don't understand what all the fuss is about, Beryl. Sandra is over twenty-one, with a bloody good job in those Inns of Court and no kids to worry about. Graham's always been a bit of fusspot, and just because she ain't there to iron his bleeding socks, it doesn't mean she's left him. Though I've always thought he were far too pernickety and stuck in his ways for someone as lively and bright as Sandra.'

'You don't think she could have gone off with another man, do you?' Beryl asked tremulously. 'I know Graham thinks she's been playing away.'

Gloria realised she'd spoken without thought for Beryl's delicate temperament. 'Nah, of course not,' she

33

said quickly. 'Graham's just naturally suspicious because he's got a young, pretty wife and likes keeping tabs on 'er. She's fought too hard to keep working after they were married and is far too sensible to be mucking him about. Graham might be dull, but they seem to rub along all right.'

Gloria stubbed out her cigarette and forced herself to stop being cross with her sister for being such a drip. 'If Sandra told you when she was due back, then I don't see why you're winding yerself up. All this ain't doing yer nerves any good, you know.'

'Yeah, I do, but I can't help it, Glo. Sandra and Andy are all I got since my Alf died, and you can't help worrying about yer kids, can yer?'

Gloria had a painful memory of the grave in which her brave, beautiful son lay.

Beryl seemed to realise how deeply that comment must have cut. 'Oh gawd, Glo, I didn't mean . . . I'm ever so sorry, love. Me and me big mouth.'

Gloria decided to change the subject. 'It's snowing here. Will you still be able to come down for Christmas?'

'That's the plan. It's snowing here too, but the forecast on the radio said it would clear up and probably not snow again until January. As long as Sandra comes home, we'll be catching the three o'clock on the twenty-third, and coming back to London the day after Boxing Day if that's all right.'

'Smashing,' said Gloria, pleased that she wouldn't be spending the holiday without her family as she had done throughout the war. 'Look, I gotta get on. If I don't hear from you before, I'll assume everything's turned out just fine. See you on the twenty-third.'

She replaced the receiver before Beryl could go off on one again, and gave a deep sigh. Her sister was as bad as Peggy Reilly with her fretting over everything, and since she'd been widowed, she was even worse. But she didn't have time to stand about here pondering her sister's determination to make a mountain out of every molehill; there were fires to be lit in the bar and the snug, shopping to do and food orders to pick up. If she didn't get on with it soon, it would be opening time, and before she knew it, the day would be over, the pub would be freezing, and her cupboards would be bare.

Peggy had made sure Jim and Charlie had left for their workplaces on time, and was now sitting on the hall chair, waiting for someone to answer the telephone at the Mayfair flat. Surely they couldn't all be out or asleep? It was past nine o'clock. She was about to give up when there was a click, and a sleepy voice recited the London number.

'Hello, Clarissa. This is Peggy Reilly. Is Cissy there?'

'Frightfully sorry, Peggy, but she's not.' The usually crystal-cut tones were rather rough around the edges, suggesting the young woman was likely suffering from a hangover or a very late night.

'It's a bit early for Cissy to be out and about,' said Peggy, suspecting she was lying.

'One of our most valued clients asked for an early pick-up,' Clarissa replied through a yawn. 'She'll be out with them all day.' She cleared her throat and there was the sound of a cigarette being lit. 'I could leave a note for her, I suppose.'

Peggy gritted her teeth in annoyance. 'Just tell her I called and would appreciate a ring back so we can discuss the arrangements for Christmas.'

Clarissa seemed to realise her attitude wasn't acceptable, and her tone became animated. 'Absolutely, of course I will, but I doubt she'll make it down there much before the day itself. We're booked solid, you see, and with one of the gels off with influenza, it does mean we're rather short on drivers.'

Peggy wasn't at all interested in Clarissa's staff problems. 'But she promised, Clarissa,' she said firmly. 'And I'm going to hold her to it as it's her father's first Christmas home for five years. Please make sure you pass that on to her, or I shall keep ringing until I *can* speak to her.'

'There's no need to get into such a bate, Peggy. Of course I'll tell her the minute she gets back. Look, it's been lovely chatting, but I really must have my bath and get dressed ready to enter the fray. Toodle pip, Peggy, and do have a jolly lovely Christmas.'

Peggy was about to reply when she realised the girl had hung up. 'Well, *really*,' she spluttered in annoyance. For all her money and class, Clarissa certainly lacked manners. She replaced the receiver and stomped back to the kitchen.

'Oh dear, you look out of sorts,' said Cordelia, who was sitting in the fireside chair, her arthritic hands snuggled beneath a blanket with a hot-water bottle. 'Cissy hasn't let you down again, has she?'

Peggy shook her head. 'She's out as usual, so I spoke to Clarissa who was half asleep and as witless as ever with her careless attitude and plummy voice. Honestly, Cordelia, I don't know how Cissy puts up with it. She'd drive me round the bend after five minutes.'

'Thankfully, you don't have to live with her, but I suspect Cissy is moulding herself into the same sort of young woman.' Cordelia gave a sigh. 'Which is a shame. I do miss our cheeky little girl with the stars in her eyes.'

'Those stars got dimmed after witnessing too much death and destruction at Cliffe aerodrome, Cordelia. The war made her grow up too quickly, and the crowd she ran with then has influenced her to such a degree I feel I'm losing her.'

'I'm sure you're not,' soothed Cordelia. 'She's had her head turned, that's all. She'll realise at some point how false that sort of life is and settle down to something more sensible, like Anne has.'

Peggy doubted it. Unlike her eldest daughter, Anne, Cissy had always had her head in the clouds. The life of a school teacher had never been her dream as it had for Anne – and the thought of settling down to family life in a small village had never crossed her mind.

'My girls are chalk and cheese, Cordelia,' she said sadly. 'And now Cissy's mixing with rich toffs and going to glittering parties and clubs in London, she must think she's fulfilling her destiny. Then there's the money she's making from her shared investment in the private hire company. She'd never give that up.'

She gave a sigh and was about to start the ironing when there was a knock at the front door. 'I wonder who that is so early?' she muttered. When she saw the man on the doorstep, she was delighted. 'Bertie! This is a lovely surprise. Come in.'

He took off his hat, brushed the snow from his shoulders and wiped his feet before stepping into the hall. 'I realise it's rather early, but something happened this morning, and I needed to talk to someone sensible.'

'Goodness me; that sounds very mysterious, Bertie.' Peggy relieved him of his hat, coat and gloves and led him into the kitchen.

'Hello, Cordelia,' he said, placing a gentle hand on her shoulder. 'Glad to see you're keeping warm. It's bitter out there and can't be doing your arthritis any good.'

'I'm fine as long as I stay indoors, Bertie. No need to fuss,' she replied calmly. She looked at him over her half-moon glasses as he sat opposite her. 'I suppose the snow put a stop to your usual morning round of golf?'

'It did indeed, my dear. But luckily they were still serving a hearty breakfast at the club, so I'm well set up for the day.'

Peggy set about making another pot of what didn't really pass as tea, then pulled out a kitchen chair and sat down. 'So, Bertie. What happened to you this morning to warrant this visit?'

He smoothed his neatly trimmed moustache. 'I found a baby,' he said dramatically.

'Good heavens,' breathed Cordelia. 'Where?'

'In the church.' Bertie embarked on his tale, and they listened in stunned silence until he reached the end.

'Was there no sign of the mother, Bertie?' Peggy fretted.

'The police are looking for her, but nothing as yet.'

'Oh, the poor girl must be frantic to do such a thing,' said Peggy. 'It was very lucky you were in the church so early to find him. He might have frozen to death in there.'

'Indeed,' he murmured. 'Sergeant Williams and I came to the conclusion that she must have known my church warden's routine and is therefore local. When I last spoke to him, he told me that Danuta had taken the infant to the hospital nursery as an interim measure, and that she would be going through her patient list to see if there's any clue as to who the mother might be.'

'I'd be surprised if there was,' said Cordelia. 'Abandoned babies aren't usually born to married mothers.'

'I agree,' said Peggy. 'Which means she probably kept it secret for nine months, and then went through the birth on her own. Poor little thing – and poor baby.'

She turned back to Bertie who was looking quite upset by it all. 'I suppose the press have been told?' At his nod, she gave a sigh. 'Then let's hope the mother changes her mind and comes forward.'

'It's what we all wish, Peggy,' Bertie said dolefully. 'But it's a rare occurrence, as I know rather too well.'

'Whatever do you mean, Bertie?' asked Cordelia, looking at him sharply.

He cleared his throat and stroked his moustache again before speaking. 'I was abandoned as a baby, Cordelia, and spent my formative years in orphanages and foster homes. To this day, I have no idea who my mother was, or why she had to leave me on that doorstep.'

He took a deep breath. 'One can only surmise that I was born out of wedlock and the shame and disgrace would have seen her out of work and probably banished from home by her family.' He shot them both a sad little smile. 'At least, that's my thinking,' he ended quietly.

'Oh, Bertie, I never dreamt . . .' Cordelia was close to tears as she reached across to place her hand on his. 'Why did you never tell me?'

He gave a shrug. 'It was a very long time ago and not something I've ever thought to talk about – until now.' He realised how deeply his shocking confession had affected both women.

'I do apologise, ladies, but please don't feel sorry for me,' he said hastily. 'Such an upbringing toughened me up, made me ambitious to beat the odds, and because of that, I've had a good and fulfilling life.'

Neither Peggy nor Cordelia looked convinced, so he hurried on. 'The army became my family, and although my career could have been hindered because of my unfortunate start, it didn't seem to make a ha'penny of difference. They looked after me very well and I rose steadily through the ranks until I had my own regiment.'

'You must miss army life dreadfully,' said Peggy, holding back her tears.

'Not so much now,' he admitted. 'I'm content to play my golf and the odd game of bridge, do my bit for the community and treat Cordelia to days out. And of course I'm a member of the Officers' Club, so regularly meet with old colleagues as well as new ones. My life is as organised now as it ever was, and I count myself lucky to still be fit and healthy enough to enjoy it.'

'And so you should, my dear man,' said Cordelia. 'But what is it that's really worrying you about this baby you found?'

He stared into the fire, deep in thought for a while before he rallied and became his usual brisk self. 'When I was small, orphanages – or workhouses – were often not very kind places. Oh, I know they were supposed to be, but behind the smiles there was, in some of those who looked after us, a meanness of spirit.'

He paused to consider his next words. 'It was the little things that could slowly wear one down, you see. There were few cuddles and no one-to-one attention because there were so many of us to look after, so it was a case of knuckling down and just getting on with things. But the times I hated most was when we had to line up for inspection by prospective parents.'

He stiffened his spine as he remembered those humiliating events when he'd always been passed over. It was all so long ago, but the rejections still had the power to wound. 'When one isn't chosen, it rather flags one's spirit, don't you know,' he said gruffly. 'Makes one feel less worthy.' He met Cordelia's sad gaze with determined defiance. 'But I survived, Cordelia, and am stronger for it.'

'Of course you are,' she replied softly. 'And what a fine man you've become.'

Bertie shrugged off her compliment even though it had warmed his heart. 'The point is, I have no wish for little Noel to experience any of the things I had to go through.'

'Things are different now,' said Peggy. 'The local authorities are getting more involved in the running of the foster homes.'

Bertie shook his head. 'Foster homes are all very well, but being paid to look after a child is not the same as taking them in through love. If Noel's mother cannot be found, or she rejects him, then I've a mind to approach the authorities and put myself down as his guardian. That way I can keep an eye on him, let him know there's someone watching out for him, and when he reaches maturity, there will be a sum of money to help him on his way.'

'Good, heavens, Bertie,' gasped Cordelia. 'That's exceedingly generous of you.'

'I have no one else to leave it to, Cordelia. And I like to think it will do a bit of good for another chap who found himself in my position.'

'Bless you, Bertie,' said Peggy, holding back a sob. 'That is such a lovely thing to do. But are you sure you're up to such a responsibility?'

'I might be getting on, Peggy, but I'm far from past it. The little lad needs all the help he can get, and I, for one, mean to see that he receives it.'

Peggy looked at Bertie through her tears, and realised that this lovely, elderly and very proud man meant every word, and that by sponsoring the abandoned baby he would find some recompense for his own loveless childhood.

4

Florence Hillier was delighted to take on the added responsibility of overall manager of the factory while Peggy was tending her sick child, but she was extremely miffed that Gracie had left it until the last minute to clock on at work. She didn't wait for her to hang up her coat but whisked her into the office so their conversation wouldn't be overheard by the nosy machinists who were already gossiping about Gracie's sudden and extended holiday.

'You've been away much longer than planned, Gracie,' she said flatly. 'You could at least have come into work on time this morning.'

'I'm sorry, Flo,' she said, hitching up the strap of the oversized dungarees she always favoured. 'But I needed to check on my Bobby first.'

'Bobby is absolutely fine. He went off to school quite happily this morning, and has been no trouble at all during your absence.' Florence folded her arms and eyed her young lodger. 'I know you needed to get away after that nasty to-do with Warren, but I had expected you back at least a week sooner than this.'

'I'm sorry, but I couldn't face returning at first,' Gracie replied, not quite meeting Florence's steady gaze. 'And then I got sick and couldn't travel. But I'm here now, and raring to go.' She eyed the untidy desk. 'Where's Peggy?'

Florence explained and then hurried on. 'As I shall be busy overseeing the day-to-day running of the business, I'd like you to take over as line manager.' She eyed the other woman from the scarf round her head to the layers of sweaters over the dungarees to the sensible shoes and thought how wan she looked. 'Do you think you're up to it, Gracie? You still look a bit peaky.'

'I had a bad tummy upset, and the train journey home went on endlessly because we had to keep stopping for frozen signals or something. But I'm fine now,' Gracie replied stoically. 'Does this promotion mean I'll get a pay rise?'

'You will. But you must understand it's only temporary.'

'Of course.' Gracie smiled. 'I could certainly do with the money just before Christmas. My savings didn't go very far in Margate.'

'Perhaps you should have come home sooner, then,' murmured Florence, her mind already occupied with things that needed seeing to. 'You'd better let the other machinists know you're in charge out there, and get on with some sewing. The factory will be shutting on Christmas Eve, and there are urgent orders to be filled before then as we won't open again until the new year, so there's no time to waste.'

Gracie saluted and shot her a cheeky grin. 'Yes, Sergeant.'

Florence chuckled. 'Get off with you. We'll catch up at home this evening.'

As Gracie hurried out of the office to hang up her coat and settled down to work at her sewing machine, Florence frowned. Gracie certainly didn't look the full ticket. It seemed that her time away hadn't really cleared the air for her after the trial, or resolved residual feelings of guilt and shame about her affair with that crook, Phil Warner, which had almost seen her charged with aiding and abetting a thief. In fact, she looked worse now than she had before she'd taken the leave owing to her – which didn't bode well.

Peggy had spent the day fretting over everything. She worried about Jim driving now the snow had become icy slush, thought constantly about the abandoned baby and the responsibility dear Bertie was thinking of taking on, and, following a short telephone conversation with Danuta, was concerned that she would get too involved in the baby's welfare, and then have her heart broken when he was put into care. On top of all that, Peggy was worn to a thread after dashing up and down the stairs to see to Daisy's needs, and repeatedly racing to answer the telephone in the vain hope it might be Cissy.

'I'm sorry to lay all this on you the minute you get home, Jim,' she said as he warmed his hands by the fire that evening. 'But at least the coalman came, so we can be warm.'

He put his arms round her and held her close. 'Glad to be of service, darling girl. It sounds as if you've had a tough old day.'

'Tougher than some,' she admitted. 'But I'm sure once Daisy is feeling better, things will get back onto a more even keel.' She looked up into his bright blue eyes. 'How was your day?'

'The driving conditions were difficult this morning, but most of the snow has gone now. It's the icy patches on the less-used country roads I had to watch out for. As for the rest of the day, it's just been my usual rounds, although I did manage to drop into Parkwood House to see Ernie for a few minutes.'

Ernie had fought alongside Jim in India and Burma, and sustained life-changing injuries during a particularly ferocious Japanese attack in which Peggy's Jim had also been wounded. Ernie's marriage hadn't survived and he'd been transferred down to the British Legion's superbly run care home for disabled servicemen where Jim had come across him again. 'How is he?' she asked.

'As well as can be expected – which doesn't mean much, unfortunately,' Jim replied sadly. 'The doctors are doing all they can, but . . .'

'Is there any hope he'll make some sort of recovery?'

Jim shook his head. 'Not really, Peg, and Ernie knows it. But he's a stubborn bugger and is fighting hard against the inevitable. He's beaten the odds by lasting this long, and I wouldn't be at all surprised if he's still with us this time next year.'

He drew back from her embrace and ran his fingers through his dark hair. 'If only I'd kept an eye on him during that attack. If only he hadn't tried to follow me up that bloody hill.'

'Stop it, Jim,' she said sharply. 'You'll torture yourself with all those if onlys. He's already said you weren't to blame, and knowing Ernie as we do, he would have gone his own way regardless of any order.' She cupped his cheek in her hand, her tone softening. 'What happened, happened, Jim, and unfortunately none of us can change that.'

Jim dipped his chin. 'I do know that, Peg, but even so . . .' He gave a deep sigh. 'He's stubborn and a pain in the rear end, but we've never been closer than we are now, and he's helped me so much these past few weeks. It just seems so unfair, that's all.'

'I agree,' she said softly. 'Life can be unfair. But you've helped him too, Jim. That letter he got the nurse to write to me spoke of how much he values your friendship, and what pleasure he's found in sharing those counselling sessions with you and reminiscing over your war stories and old pals. He wants those nightmares and flashbacks to be a thing of the past for both of you – as he also wants you to stop blaming yourself for what happened to him.'

She reached up and stroked his cheek. 'Let the past go, Jim, then you can both be at peace.'

He nodded and was about to speak again when Charlie slammed the back door and came thudding up the basement steps into the kitchen. 'I'm frozen solid,' he rasped, traipsing slush and mud across Peggy's clean lino to get to the range fire. 'The wind whips through Jack's workshop like nobody's business, and I can't feel my hands or my feet.'

Peggy closed the door to the basement to keep in the heat and eyed her handsome son whose hands were stained with grease, and his sodden boots streaked with mud. At almost sixteen, he was as tall and broad-shouldered as his father. 'You'd better get those boots off, and warm yourself in a bath before tea. I don't want you going down with something as well.'

'I've had measles, mumps and even chickenpox, but if I stay working at Jack's I'll probably go down with double pneumonia,' he moaned.

'It's an honest day's work, son,' said Jim, making way for him in front of the fire. 'No one ever said that earning a living was easy.'

Cordelia chose that moment to come into the kitchen. 'You wouldn't be moaning if you were out getting half-frozen playing rugby,' she observed tartly. 'Do move over a bit, Charlie, you're hogging the fire.'

He inched to one side so she could share the heat. 'Sorry, Grandma Cordy, but I really am chilled to the bone.'

'Well, there's a lovely rabbit stew in the oven. That'll warm you up,' she said with a twinkle in her eyes.

'Yuk. I'm fed up with rabbit stew. Can't Grandad catch a nice fat grouse again, or a couple of pigeons for a change?'

'Just be thankful Ron brings us anything,' said Cordelia sternly. 'It couldn't have been easy up in those hills today. He's no longer a young man, and even Harvey is showing his age now the winter has set in.'

'To be sure, that old lurcher will outlast us all,' said Jim brightly. 'And Da might be getting on, but I reckon he's fitter than all of us put together.' He lit a cigarette and sat down at the kitchen table. 'In fact, I quite miss having a dog in the house now he's gone to live with Da and Rosie. I wonder if . . .'

'Don't you go getting any ideas of bringing another dog into the house,' interrupted Peggy briskly, waving a wooden spoon at him. 'I have quite enough to do clearing up after you and Charlie without animals to look after as well.'

She put the pot of stew back into the warming oven and then turned to face Jim with her hands on her hips. 'Which reminds me. You'll need to put something over the hen house to keep those chickens warm, Jim, or we'll lose them.'

'Aye, I'll do it in the morning before I leave for work,' he replied. 'It's too dark now.'

'Please see that you do,' she said. 'Chalky won't be providing us with any more, and the eggs are a godsend while rationing is so tight.'

Jim lifted his hands in mock terror. 'All right, all right. Keep your wig on, Peggy. I said I'd do it, and I will – just not now.'

'If you two are going to have a row, I'm off for a bath,' said Charlie, making a hasty retreat into the hallway just as the telephone began to ring. 'I'll get it,' he shouted over his shoulder.

Peggy placed the wooden spoon on a saucer and went to the kitchen door in the hope it was Cissy on the line.

Charlie spotted her standing there and put his hand over the mouthpiece. 'It's my pal Paul about the rugby club Christmas party, Mum.'

The disappointment was sharp. 'Fine, but don't be on there for too long. I'm expecting a call from your sister.'

The evening dragged on for Peggy as the meal was eaten and cleared away, Charlie went to his top-floor room to study for his exams and Cordelia began to doze by the dwindling fire. Daisy had managed to eat a good portion of stew and was finally asleep, tucked up with her favourite doll, and Jim was reading the evening newspaper headlines about the abandoned baby.

'It looks like our Bertie is a hero,' he said, showing her the picture inset within the article. 'That church is as cold as the grave, and the poor little mite would have frozen to death if Bertie hadn't been so pedantic about his time-keeping.'

'I do worry about him though,' said Peggy, starting on the ironing. 'He really wants to sponsor that baby, but if it's adopted, I doubt the authorities will allow it.'

'There's little point in worrying, Peg. Things will sort themselves out regardless of how you feel,' he replied, turning to the back pages to check on the sport results.

It was almost nine o'clock when the telephone rang, and Peggy dashed into the hall to answer it.

'Hello, Mother,' Cissy drawled. 'Sorry I haven't rung earlier, but we've been rushed off our feet. Clarissa said you sounded rather fraught when you rang this morning. Whatever's so urgent?'

Peggy took a deep breath before answering. 'I haven't heard from you in weeks, Cissy,' she said carefully. 'I was starting to think you'd forgotten about us down here.'

'Mother, you were born a worrier,' she said dryly. 'Honestly, you are silly.'

'Silly or not, I'm your mother and as such have a right to fret about you. London is a dangerous place, and you're mixing with all sorts. I don't like the thought of you alone up there.'

Cissy's laugh was brittle. 'But I'm not alone, Mother. I'm sharing a flat with three other girls and hardly have a minute to myself. As for being dangerous in London – you don't know it as well as I do. I'm quite safe, I assure you.'

Her exasperation made Peggy sharper than she'd intended. 'But you haven't telephoned me for ages, Cissy, and you promised you'd let me know about our Christmas arrangements.'

'Oh, those,' she replied airily. 'I just forgot, sorry. But Christmas is our most profitable season, and to be honest, I've barely had time to think, let alone make travel arrangements.'

Peggy was more than miffed; she was steaming. 'I do hope you're not going to let me down like you did last year,' she snapped.

'Well, of course I'm coming,' soothed Cissy. 'I promised, didn't I?'

'You promised to telephone, but didn't,' retorted Peggy.

'Well, yes, but that's neither here nor there,' Cissy replied dismissively. 'I plan to catch the last train down on Christmas Eve, but I must return here after Boxing Day. We're fully booked right up to the New Year jollies.'

'You'd better book a seat on the train, then. It'll be very busy and you won't want to stand all the way down here.'

'Will do,' Cissy replied vaguely. Peggy wondered if she was even listening to her.

'How are you, anyway? Peggy asked.

'All tickety-boo, thanks. Sorry, Mother, but I can't chat. I'm expected elsewhere and am in danger of being terribly late.'

'As long as you're all right,' said Peggy, feeling sad that her daughter couldn't find the time to talk to her after such a long silence. 'I'll see you soon, then.'

'Give my love to everyone, won't you? Must dash. Bye.'

Peggy listened to the buzz of the disconnected line and could have wept. She replaced the receiver and plumped down onto the hall chair. Her own mother had said that children broke your heart, and if she'd needed any proof of that, she had it now – and the pain was a heavy, living thing settling into her very soul.

Cissy replaced the receiver in the cradle of the ornate white telephone, all too aware that Clarissa was watching her every move. She plastered on a smile even though her heart was breaking at having been so curt with the mother she adored. 'There, all done, Clarissa. She won't ring again.'

'I do hope not, Cissy,' the other woman drawled. 'It's all been tiresome having to fend her off with endless excuses for your absence.' Her cool blue gaze swept over Cissy with mild curiosity. 'I have to say, you still don't look yourself. Are you sure everything is all right?'

Cissy knew Clarissa's concern was more for the business than for her well-being, so forced a broader smile and reached for a cigarette from the onyx box on the coffee table. 'I'm just a little tired, Clarissa. These things rather take it out of one, don't you know,' she said blithely before lighting the cigarette and blowing smoke.

'Yes,' murmured Clarissa with a delicate shudder. 'I have heard it's a ghastly business all round.' She stubbed out her cigarette and got to her feet, her silk wrap swirling round her elegant figure and giving glimpses of expensive underwear and silk stockings. 'Harry will be here soon, so I'd better get ready. You know how my brother hates it when I keep him waiting.'

She bent to kiss the air in the region of Cissy's cheekbone. 'I hope you feel brighter tomorrow. We're booked solid and there's the party at the Ritz which you simply must attend. As our host is our wealthiest client he expects all of us to be there,' she said sternly before sweeping out of the room.

Knowing Harry could turn up at any minute, Cissy quickly stubbed out her own cigarette and dragged herself out of the deep cushions of the couch to gather up her holdall. She was in no mood to deal with Harry Corkendale tonight of all nights.

Hurrying into her luxuriously appointed bedroom, she closed and locked the door before sinking onto the bed. She was very grateful to Clarissa for the help she'd given over the past weeks, but she was exhausted by the lies she'd told, the act she'd had to keep up, and worst of all, the subterfuge she'd had to use to keep it all from her mother. The thought of being forced to continue the charade over Christmas when faced by a sharp-eyed Peggy was daunting – but there was no escape.

Danuta had been busy all day with antenatal clinic, deliveries and the general duties of a district nurse and midwife. However, her thoughts had kept returning to the baby she'd left at the hospital nursery, and the mother who had yet to be found.

Her visit to the local authority had proved to be brief and unsatisfactory. There was nowhere local that he could be fostered; the orphanage wasn't taking in any more children until well into the new year, and it was likely he'd have to be sent out of the area to another orphanage in Surrey.

Danuta had fretted over him endlessly, and had even wondered if she'd be allowed to take him home until things were resolved. However, she'd had to nip that idea firmly in the bud, as a short and rather heated conversation with Stanislav had made her see reason. The cottage at Tamarisk Bay was far from suitable for a new-born, and although Stan had been momentarily grounded from flying due to the weather, he couldn't possibly look after him properly while she was busy doing her district nurse rounds.

She left the hospital after her second visit of the day to reassure herself that he was thriving and, seeing a light blazing in the Camden Road factory office, decided she'd make a last-ditch attempt to save him from the social workers and the prospect of life in a distant orphanage, by going to see Solly Goldman.

It was almost nine o'clock, and although Solly was well into his late fifties, he was still in his office when she tapped on the door and stepped inside.

'Danuta! Come in, come in,' he boomed, rising from behind his desk and waving his cigar in welcome. He kissed her heartily on both cheeks and pressed her into a chair. '*Oy vey*, Danuta,' he exclaimed mournfully. 'You look half frozen, my dear. Let me get you a brandy.'

'I shouldn't really,' she protested weakly. 'I have to drive home, and Rachel told me the doctor warned you about over-indulging.'

'One little brandy will not hurt,' he said lightly and poured a hefty measure into two glasses. 'That will warm you,' he said, giving her a beaming smile before raising his glass to her. '*L'chaim.*'

'To life,' she replied and took a sip, relaxing as the warmth spread through her. She put the glass down and folded her gloved hands in her lap as she watched him settle his bulk in his large leather chair.

Solly was a big man in every sense, with a generous heart that was constantly being put at risk by his penchant for cigars, rich food and brandy. But he was a good man too, and well respected by his workforce as well as his peers. He and his wife Rachel were ardent fund-raisers for numerous charities, and had been a driving force in getting Jewish children out of Germany and safe from the Nazis. Yet Danuta knew there was a terrible sadness behind all these good works, for their own family members had disappeared during the crushing of the Warsaw ghetto, and with no children of their own to cherish, they gave their time and love to those who most needed it.

'Solly, we have been friends for some time, and I am hoping you will be able to help me.'

He sat forward and rested his forearms on the desk, curiosity clear in his expression. 'But of course I will help you if I can.'

Danuta told him about the baby. 'I don't like the thought of him being taken out of Cliffehaven and into another county. If the mother does come back – which I sincerely hope she will – then she won't know where to find him.'

As Solly remained silent, she looked down at her fingers which were knotted in her lap. 'And I've rather taken to him,' she admitted softly. 'He's a sweet baby.'

'It is natural to feel that way,' murmured Solly. 'My Rachel would too.'

She sat forward, her whole body tensed. 'Then would it be possible to let him come to your crèche until all other avenues have been exhausted? I would be willing to pay if the welfare people won't.'

He dipped his large head and gave a deep sigh. '*Oy vey*, Danuta, if only I could.'

'But he's a very tiny baby and wouldn't take up much space,' she pleaded.

'It's not that,' he said sorrowfully. 'But the factory will be closed over Christmas, and so will the crèche.' He must have seen how deeply his words had cut, for he reached across the desk and touched her arm. 'But of course, if it was at any other time, Rachel and I would have gladly helped.'

They both heard the light footsteps coming through the outer office to the doorway and looked up to see Rachel Goldman standing there.

'And what is it that we could have helped you with, Danuta darling?'

Danuta watched Rachel come into the room looking as elegant and beautiful as always, swathed in furs, with diamonds glinting in her ears and on her dainty fingers. As she stood to welcome her, she was swamped in a perfumed hug. 'It's so lovely to see you, Rachel,' she managed. 'I was just telling Solly about the abandoned baby.'

Rachel nodded. 'I saw the headlines on the newspaper stands earlier so, once I read through the article, I knew immediately I'd have to do something about it.' She gave them both a brilliant smile. 'Which is why I'm here.'

She eyed Danuta quizzically. 'I didn't realise you'd become involved, my dear, but of course as the local midwife it would be logical, I suppose.'

'It is her heart that is involved, Rachel, my love,' sighed Solly, giving her powdered cheek a loving kiss.

'But the crèche is closed over Christmas, so there is nothing I can do to help.'

Rachel smiled down at him then poured herself a small measure of brandy and took a sip. 'You can be very unimaginative at times, Solly Goldman,' she said with a teasing glint in her eye. 'Of course we can help.'

Danuta shifted to the edge of her chair. 'How?' she asked.

'By taking him home with us,' the older woman replied as if the answer was perfectly obvious.

'Really?' Danuta could hardly breathe.

Rachel smiled serenely and sat down in the other chair to take Danuta's hand. 'Yes, really. It will be lovely to have a baby in the house again now our little refugees have been found permanent homes, and although as Jews we don't celebrate Christmas, I think we can combine it with Hanukkah this year.'

Danuta looked at Solly who was staring at his wife as if he couldn't believe what he was hearing. 'How do you feel about that, Solly?' she asked, fearing the answer.

'I'm not sure,' he admitted. He looked at his lovely wife. 'It's a big responsibility, my darling. Are you certain you want to start all over again with one so young?'

'Solly, we have filled our home with other people's children for years. Why should this little one be any different? His story reminds me of Moses and how he was found in the bulrushes – and of course, of Jesus being born in a manger. It's Christmas, Solly, and this baby needs us to give him the love and care he deserves. We cannot turn our backs on him.'

'Rachel,' Solly murmured, his eyes warm with love for her. 'My darling Rachel. What would I ever do without your gentle wisdom to guide me?'

'You'd probably drink too much brandy and smoke too many cigars,' she replied, prodding him none too gently in his over-large stomach. She removed his brandy glass; reached for the cigar that was burning away in the ashtray, and stubbed it out.

'There are things we must do to prepare,' she said, getting purposefully to her feet, and buttoning up her coat. 'Danuta, you will have to guide me as to the correct way of getting permission to take him home, and then I will have to go shopping. It's a good thing Plummer's is still open.'

'Why does everything have to involve shopping?' Solly groaned theatrically. 'My poor wallet is under constant attack.'

Danuta smothered her giggles as Rachel told him to stop fussing and reached into his tailored jacket pocket to pull the wallet out and examine its contents. 'That should do for now,' she said, relieving the wallet of several notes, 'but I shall also need your cheque book.' She planted a soft kiss on his forehead before winking at Danuta.

Danuta noted that Solly's hangdog expression didn't quite disguise the gleam of happiness in his brown eyes, and knew that little Noel would be treated like a prince in their home. 'It's too late to set anything up now, but I can take you to the hospital so you can get to know him,' she said. 'And then first thing tomorrow we can go to the local authority.'

Rachel tutted and dug in her handbag, pulling out a tooled leather notebook with a tiny gold pen tucked into the spine. 'I've got an even better idea,' she said, handing the open book to Solly and pointing a bright red fingernail at a particular entry. 'That's Mark Friedman's home number. Ring him and tell him we'll be taking Noel home with us this evening.'

As Solly dutifully obeyed, Rachel turned to Danuta. 'Mark is involved with referrals for adoption and fostering and is a respected member of our synagogue.

He wouldn't dare refuse Solly anything after all he's done for him over the years.'

She swept into the outer office and connected to a second telephone line to ring the manager of Plummer's department store. 'Ah, Mr Dryden. This is Rachel Goldman. I know it's very late, but I have some urgent purchases to make that really cannot wait until morning.'

Danuta could only look on in admiration as money, connections and long-standing influence smoothed the path to little Noel's new start with the Goldmans.

Gracie Smith marvelled at how easy it had been to step back into the daily routine without anyone but Florence noticing how tired she was. A deep ache persisted low in her belly and she was still bleeding, which was worrying. But she'd smiled and joked and mucked in with the other machinists until her face grew stiff from the effort. The lies had come easily enough as she'd rehearsed her story so well, and no one seemed to notice it was all a sham.

It was when night fell and she kissed her little Bobby goodnight that the exhaustion and guilt weighed the heaviest. He was such a sweet, innocent little boy, and didn't deserve to have a wicked mother like her, but he must never know what she had done.

Tears pricked and she blinked them away. Her five-year-old Bobby was the most precious thing in her life, but every time she looked at him and kissed his soft cheek, she was forcibly reminded of what she'd done, and she knew that the guilt would remain with her always.

5

Thankful that the snow had all but melted away, Danuta drove home after what had been an exhausting and emotional day. There were no streetlights once she'd left Cliffhaven, and thick cloud hid the moon, so her only guide along the country lane and up the hill was the rather frail beam from her headlights.

She was low in spirit and aching with tiredness as she parked the little car next to Stan's larger one and clambered out. Retrieving her nursing bag, she switched on her torch to see her way down the treacherous slope to the path leading to her front door.

Stanislav must have been looking out for her, for she'd barely stepped beneath the porch when he threw open the door and dragged her inside and into his arms. 'I was very worried about you,' he said, holding her tightly and kissing her cheek. 'No one was answering the telephone at the clinic, and the doctor said you'd left a long time ago.'

She clung to him, glad of his love and strength. 'I'm sorry to have worried you, Stan. There was just so much going on today that I lost track of the time. I went to check on the baby after closing the clinic, and then popped into the factory to see if Solly could help.'

He stood back and looked down at her with a frown. 'How can Solomon Goldman help you, Danuta?'

'More than I ever could have hoped,' she replied. 'I'll tell you all about it once I've warmed up and had a cup of tea. It's bitter out there.'

'Of course, of course,' he murmured. He helped her off with her coat and scarf, steered her to the chair closest to the fire, and quickly refreshed the teapot. 'I have made vegetable and potato soup, and Frank gave me some fish to fry, so we will eat well tonight.'

'If I'd known I'd have gone to the chippy and brought some home to go with the fish.'

He smiled as he shook his head. 'They would have been cold by the time they'd got here. I will fry potatoes myself.'

Danuta was quite alarmed by this statement, for the last time he'd tried to fry anything he'd filled the house with oily black smoke and almost set the place on fire. 'Why don't we have the tea and soup first, and see how we feel? I can always cook the fish and potato tomorrow.'

'No.' His expression took on the familiar stubbornness she knew could herald an argument. 'I say I cook. So I cook.' He kissed the top of her head and plonked himself down in the chair opposite her.

She was too tired to argue, so she drank the tea and kept her fears to herself as she thawed out in the fire's heat.

They sat in harmonious silence as the fire crackled and the aroma of warming soup filled the little room. The tea was wonderfully strong as well as hot, and Danuta realised that Stanislav must have driven into town and bought a new packet.

'Tell me about the baby,' he said once he'd ladled out the soup, and waited for her to give her approval.

She didn't want to talk about Noel just yet. It made her too sad. 'This soup is lovely, Stan. Have you added spices?'

He nodded. 'It's how our cook used to make it in Poland. As a small boy, I liked to watch her do magic with the simplest of things from the garden.' He

59

grinned. 'Besides, the kitchen was always the warmest room in that big house, and the best place to be in the winter.'

She smiled back at him. 'Just like here.'

He cocked his head, his expression thoughtful. 'So. You were going to tell me about the baby and how Solomon has helped you.'

She drank a little more soup but found she'd lost her appetite, but as Stan had made such an effort to produce it, she didn't push the bowl away. She knotted her hands in her lap and watched the firelight glimmer on her engagement ring. 'The press have called him Noel, because it is almost Christmas,' she began. 'He's a little small, so probably premature by a couple of weeks. But he's a healthy, perfect baby any mother would be proud to have.'

She finally looked up to find he was watching her closely, and knew that he understood how difficult this was for her.

'He is in hospital nursery now?'

'That's where Solly and Rachel come in,' she replied. She went on to tell him how Rachel had taken over the situation. 'The influence they have is astonishing,' she said. 'Almost before I could draw breath, they'd arranged for him to come to them, and Rachel had bought most of the nursery department at Plummer's – which of course she had delivered before she got home.'

Stan chuckled. 'That Rachel is a hurricane. Poor Solly.'

Danuta sighed. 'There's nothing poor about either of them, and Solly is delighted to do Rachel's bidding. I think they're finding that big house a bit empty now the last of their refugees have left.'

'So what happened next?'

'We went to the hospital to find Mr Friedman waiting for us – he's involved in referrals for adoption and fostering, and a personal friend of the Goldmans. Rachel barely greeted him and went straight to the cot where Noel was sleeping.'

Danuta looked down, feeling the heat of shame rise from her neck into her face as she remembered the stab of unwarranted jealousy she'd felt towards Rachel as she'd gently taken possession of Noel and fussed over him.

'What's the matter, Danuta?' Stanislav asked quietly. 'You don't want him to be with the Goldmans?'

'It's not that,' she replied quickly. 'Noel couldn't be with anyone better suited to love and cherish and spoil him.' She closed her eyes as tears threatened. 'I just wish it could have been me bringing him home,' she whispered.

He hurried round the table and pulled her to him. 'I understand, my little one,' he murmured, stroking her rich brown hair. 'But one day there will be a baby for us – a baby that will be ours for ever. Noel would always be – how you say – on loan. He has a mother who might come back, and it would break your heart if you had to give him to her after you'd grown to love him. I do not want that.'

He kissed her cheeks. 'And even if she doesn't return, the authorities would never allow us to keep him here.'

She let him kiss away her tears, but he couldn't kiss away the ache in her heart. 'I'm so sorry I can't have your babies,' she managed raggedly. 'I wish things . . .'

He silenced her with another kiss. 'You will never again apologise for that,' he said firmly. 'What those SS brutes did to you was unforgivable. But I married you because I love you and want to share the rest of my life with you. And my heart is full because you agreed to take on this broken man, and have made him the happiest he has ever been.'

'Oh, Stan,' she sobbed as she fell back into his embrace. 'I love you so much.'

Without another word, Stanislav scooped her into his arms and carried her out of the kitchen into the bedroom where he tenderly pressed her down on the bed, covered her in kisses, and very slowly began to undress her.

It was after two in the morning and Ronan Reilly knew he shouldn't really have driven home, but what with the amount they'd had to drink at the Council's Christmas party, the freezing weather and Rosie's high-heeled shoes, it would have been impossible to walk.

He carefully negotiated his way through the gates onto the driveway of their Havelock Road home and gave a sigh of relief as he switched off the engine. 'We made it, Rosie,' he slurred. 'Though the Lord only knows how.'

Rosie was curled up in the passenger seat, her face almost buried in the fur collar of her coat. 'We are naughty,' she giggled, reaching to open the car door. 'But well done, Ron.'

He shoved his way out of the car and slammed the door, aware that the ground was heaving like the sea beneath his feet, and that the dogs were making a terrible racket inside the house. 'We'll have the neighbours complaining again,' he muttered, closing and bolting the high wooden gates as he glanced nervously at next door's upstairs windows.

'Ron, I need your help!' called Rosie. 'I can't seem to get out of the car.'

He grinned and stomped over to find her in fits of giggles as she tried to hold onto the door and push herself out of the low seat.

'Are your legs not working, Rosie?' he asked, admiring her shapely limbs which were waving about and showing rather a lot of delicious stocking top and thigh. 'To be sure, they're a sight for sore old eyes, darlin'.'

'Stop it, Ron,' she spluttered. 'Just get me out of this damned car before I catch a chill.'

He hoisted her out, steadied her while he closed the door and then kept hold of her as they weaved their way across the gravel to the porch. The dogs were making a terrible racket now and hurling themselves at the front door.

Rosie stumbled and knocked him off course momentarily. 'Steady there, wee girl, or you'll have us both over,' he rumbled.

On reaching the doorstep, he decided it might be best if he leaned Rosie against the wall while he tried to negotiate the tricky task of finding the lock and getting the key into it.

Rosie tottered alarmingly and almost fell off the low step. 'Whoops,' she giggled. 'Do hurry up, Ron. I'm freezing to death here.'

Ron was doing his best, but everything was blurred and there seemed to be two locks, neither of which would stay still. He stabbed the key in the general direction several times and missed as the dogs continued to bark frantically and scrabble on the door from inside the house.

'D'ya wan' me to do it?' slurred Rosie, leaning heavily against him and almost knocking the key from his hand.

Ron gritted his teeth and forced himself to concentrate. He glared at the lock and aimed the key towards the slot very carefully, finally managing to get it in. With a huge sigh of relief, he grabbed Rosie round the waist before she sank to the ground and opened the door.

The two lurchers came hurtling out and almost knocked them both down in their eagerness to welcome them home.

'My nylons!' shrieked Rosie. 'Down! Get down, the pair of you!'

Ron let go of Rosie, grabbed Monty and wrestled to get him and his sire, Harvey, back into the house. 'Ach, ye wee heathens. Quiet now, or we'll all be in trouble,' he hissed.

Rosie swayed on the doorstep but managed somehow to step into the house and lean against the hall table for support as she took off her shoes and fended off Monty who seemed intent upon licking her stockinged feet. 'Yuk, Monty, gerroff,' she muttered.

Having placated Monty with a vigorous pat on the head, she dug her feet into her comfortable slippers and removed her earrings. 'Do you think we'll get a bad reputation for coming in so late almost every night?' she asked, rubbing her earlobes where her earring clips had been pinching all evening.

Ron shut the front door, shooed the dogs ahead of them and took Rosie's arm to help her down the hallway into the sitting room.

Thinking they could get away with it, Harvey immediately claimed ownership of the armchair and his pup, Monty, jumped onto the couch.

Ron ordered both dogs to the floor. 'I'm thinking it's a bit late to be worrying about our reputations,' he replied, easing Rosie onto the couch. 'The neighbours already think we're beyond the pale.'

She looked up at him blearily and giggled. 'Oh dear. Do you think we'll be banished from the coffee morning and mothers' union brigade?'

He slumped down beside her. 'I suspect we already have been,' he chuckled.

'Their loss,' she replied, rolling away from him and managing to get to her feet without falling over. 'I really do need the lav. Make us some tea, will you?'

Ron watched her stagger away and tried to gather enough strength to lever himself off the comfortable couch. But the dogs had other ideas, and before he knew it he was swamped by furry bodies, cold noses and long, slobbering tongues.

'Gerroff,' he groaned, pushing them away. 'It's too late at night for that, and this is my new and very expensive dinner suit you're trampling all over.'

Harvey and Monty sat on the floor looking suitably repentant as Ron hauled himself to his feet and managed to take off his overcoat and white silk scarf. He had a hat somewhere, but he couldn't for the life of him think where he'd left it.

The dogs followed him out into the hall in the hope they might get some extra food, and sat panting in anticipation as he placed his coat and scarf on the hall stand, picked up Rosie's coat from the floor, and then paused to listen at the downstairs cloakroom door to make sure she was all right.

Heading for the kitchen, Ron switched on the light and stood for a moment trying to remember why he'd come in here. He felt Harvey nudge his thigh, noted the empty bowls and decided he'd better let them out for a few minutes as they'd been shut in since early evening.

They didn't stay in the garden long, and had mercifully not discovered any cats or squirrels to bark at, so he reached for the tin of food he'd opened earlier. 'To be sure, you'll be eating us out of house and home, ye wee gannets,' he muttered, forking out the mess into their bowls and wrinkling his nose at the smell. Lord only knew what they put in the stuff, but as the dogs didn't seem to care and it was cheap and not rationed, he shouldn't complain.

He'd only just remembered that he was supposed to be making tea when he heard a noise in the hall and peeked out to see Rosie making her slow and rather unsteady way up the stairs. And as she reached the halfway landing, he caught a tantalising flash of stocking top from beneath the swirl of her black silk cocktail dress.

All thoughts of tea were instantly dismissed. Ron switched off the light, shut the kitchen door on the dogs and hurried after her.

Neither of them was feeling the full ticket the following morning, so Ron left Rosie curled beneath the bedcovers as he washed in the bathroom and prepared for the day. It was still dark outside as he dressed in his usual corduroy trousers, moth-eaten jumper and warm shirt, so he didn't bother to shave or run a comb through his hair. There wouldn't be anyone about at this hour to see him, and the dogs didn't care a jot how he looked.

He let the animals out into the back garden while he made a pot of tea and retrieved his pipe and tobacco from his overcoat pocket. Once the tea had brewed to his satisfaction, he listened for any sign that Rosie might be stirring, and as there was none, took the tea into the sitting room and sank into the couch. He would have a pipe with his tea, and then take the dogs for a quick walk around the recreation ground. He certainly wouldn't be going into the hills today since it felt as if a platoon of heavy-footed drummers had taken up residence in his head.

All was still quiet as he pulled on his poacher's coat and grubby cap and let himself and the dogs out of the house – only just remembering to take a key as

Rosie had decided it was unsafe to leave one under the doormat.

The streets were almost deserted, with only the milkman and postman doing their rounds, and a straggle of women traipsing towards Solly's large factory in Camden Road to begin their day shifts. He strode out with the dogs running ahead of him, feeling the cold air slice away the thunder in his head.

The recreation ground was situated beyond the small, gated Havelock Gardens which had given its name to the road in which he lived, and stretched northward beneath the folds of the eastern hills for several acres until it met the line of trees that shielded the elegant Victorian villas which were slowly being turned into apartments.

Because of the season, the rugby posts had been erected on one side of the playing field that was marked out in front of the pavilion which served as club house and store for the local rugby, football and cricket clubs.

The dogs immediately shot off to investigate the undergrowth and water the goalposts before snuffling about in the hope they might find something to chase. Ron walked around the circumference of the field, his thoughts drifting to Christmas and the family gathering planned at Beach View. Peggy already had her hands full with Daisy being unwell, and with so many of them expected over the two days, she'd be hard pressed to get everything ready. Perhaps he should go up to see Chalky soon and ask if he had a decent-sized chicken he could buy – or better still, a couple or three ducks. The thought made his mouth water.

'I say. It's Reilly, isn't it?'

Ron turned slowly at the sound of the booming, plummy voice, recognising his pompous neighbour, Archibald Chapman, immediately. He eyed the Hitler moustache and the yappy Pekingese dog that was prancing about on the end of a lead. 'It's *Mr* Reilly,' he replied firmly.

'Well, it's not good enough,' the man blustered.

'Really? What isn't?' he asked, knowing full well but refusing to give an inch.

The officious little man lifted his many chins, his moustache and heavy eyebrows bristling. 'The noise you make at all hours of the night. My wife was most disturbed, and poor little Fifi was a nervous wreck.'

Ron eyed the hairy Fifi which was bug-eyed and yapping so hard it was becoming quite hoarse. 'Well now, I'm sorry if we disturbed you. To be sure, we'll try to be quieter next time.'

'One rather hopes there will not be a next time,' Chapman replied crossly, gathering the small dog into his arms as Harvey and Monty came rushing over to see what was happening.

He held the dog higher as Harvey sniffed the air beneath that fluffy tail. 'And will you *please* keep your dogs under control? Poor Fifi is far too delicate for such ruffians, and the Smythes' Persian cat is now terrified to even leave the house.'

'That cat comes into our garden and digs up my vegetable plot to use as a lavatory. If my dogs see it, they quite rightly chase it off – as do I.' Ron clicked his fingers to bring his dogs to heel and then dug his pipe out of his pocket. 'And my dogs won't harm that ball of yapping fluff. They're just curious to know what it is.'

'Well, *really*,' Chapman huffed. 'Just see to it, Reilly, or I'm warning you, I shall telephone my friend the Chief Constable if there is any more trouble from you or your wolf pack. Havelock Road used to be a pleasant place to live, with decent, quiet families who conducted themselves with decorum.'

Ron said nothing as the man paused to draw breath, and was fascinated to see the colour rise in his face as he worked himself up to deliver a final tongue-lashing.

'You're nothing but a *rabble*, sir. *An absolute shower!*'

Ron grinned as he watched him stomp off. He'd been called a great many things during his lifetime, but 'an absolute shower'? What on earth was that supposed to mean? He shrugged. Whatever it meant, it was clearly supposed to be an insult.

It's all water off a duck's back, really, he thought as he filled his pipe and got it going satisfactorily. Yet he'd been clearly labelled as 'not the right sort' by the likes of the Chapmans and Smythes – and probably the rest of the snobs that lived in Havelock Road – so he'd better get home and warn Rosie there could be trouble.

His good mood was spoilt, and he brusquely ordered the dogs to remain at heel as he trudged home to Rosie in the hope she'd see the funny side of this morning's altercation. But he had a nasty feeling she wouldn't.

Daisy's temperature had come down, the rash was less angry, and she seemed a little better today, although her eyes continued to be sensitive to the light and she was grizzly. Peggy kept the curtains closed and used the gentle beam from the nursery night-light to help Daisy take a dose of her medicine and then eat some porridge to take away the taste.

'I'm thirsty, Mummy,' she complained. 'Want some juice.'

Peggy was grateful to the Ministry of Food for the free orange juice she received each week for Daisy, and it certainly seemed to help soothe the child's sore throat. 'There; is that better?' she asked, gently tucking the dark baby curls behind Daisy's ears.

Daisy nodded and slid back under the covers with her doll, Amelia. 'Melia tired now, Mummy. She wants to sleep.'

Peggy tucked the sheet and blankets firmly over the small shoulders and softly kissed her brow. Her baby girl had been very poorly these past couple of days, but the doctor had said that sleep was a good cure, and she'd certainly got a lot of that. She tiptoed out of the room, leaving the door ajar, and quietly went into the bathroom to get ready for her day.

Dressed in tailored grey slacks and knitted lavender-blue twinset, Peggy applied her make-up, and then dabbed a drop of scent on her wrists and neck. The exquisite bottle of perfume had been a gift from Jim upon his return home from Burma, and she loved it, for it was like being surrounded by tropical flowers. It was probably expensive too, so she was very careful about how much she used. Although it was really for special occasions, she'd decided today would be one such occasion as she was going to be escaping the house for a while.

Slipping on her high heels, she grabbed her over-coat, hat and handbag from the bedroom, and went downstairs to the kitchen to find the usual morning chaos in full flow.

The wireless seemed to have been turned up to full volume as it blared out music from the Broadway shows; the kettle was whistling, and everyone was talking at once as the toast began to burn. She dashed in, turned the radio down and rescued the toast and kettle.

'For goodness' sake,' she hissed. 'Isn't anyone paying attention to anything this morning?'

'Sorry, love, we were discussing this abandoned baby,' said Jim, coming from the table to take charge of the toast and hastily scrape off the burnt bits.

'It's in all the papers, Mum,' said Charlie. 'And look what's happened now!'

'Has the mother turned up? Who is she?' Peggy forgot the kettle and went to look at the front page of the newspaper Charlie was waving at her.

ABANDONED BABY TAKEN IN BY PROMINENT LOCAL COUPLE

The bold headline appeared above a photograph of Rachel and Solomon Goldman smiling down at the baby in Rachel's arms.

'Good heavens,' she breathed, sinking into a chair. 'How on earth did they get involved?'

'If you read the piece, you'll find out,' said Cordelia rather waspishly. 'I bet that will put poor Bertie's nose out of joint.'

'I really don't see why it should,' replied Peggy, scanning the article quickly. 'Noel will be safe with them, and probably be spoilt rotten into the bargain; and surely it's far better than being sent to some ghastly children's home.'

'Of course it is,' Cordelia replied. 'It's just that Bertie feels responsible because he was the one to find him, and now the Goldmans have rather stolen his thunder.'

Cordelia looked up at Jim who was about to put the scraped toast on her plate. 'No thank you. I prefer not to eat carbon for my breakfast.'

'Goodness, you're in a funny mood this morning, Grandma Cordy,' said Charlie. 'Whatever's the matter?'

'There's nothing funny about arthritis,' she snapped. 'As you'll find out when you're as old as me.' She carefully lifted her teacup in both hands and took a sip before clattering it back into the saucer with a grimace. 'The tea gets worse every day,' she grumbled.

71

Peggy put the newspaper aside and decided the best thing was to ignore the grumbling and make her a hot-water bottle for her poor hands, as she was clearly suffering this morning.

'You're looking very smart, Peg,' said Jim, eyeing her up and down with admiration. 'And I can smell my perfume too.' He frowned and looked at her more keenly. 'Do you want to tell me where you're going?'

She filled the bottle and tucked it into a tea towel before folding it in the blanket Cordelia had over her lap, and giving the old woman a wink. 'Well, Jim,' she said, turning to face him. 'Not that it's any real business of yours, but I'm going shopping.'

'Oh yes?' His expression and his tone revealed he didn't believe her.

'Yes,' she said, trying hard not to giggle. 'And before you say another word, think on, Jim Reilly, or there will be trouble.'

'I never said anything,' he protested. 'I was just . . .'

'I know what you were just doing,' she retorted, 'and I won't stand for it, do you hear?'

'Oh, Peg, don't be like that,' he wheedled, sitting down next to her and taking her hand. 'It's just you look so pretty this morning, and . . . and . . .'

She patted his face and giggled. 'Lawks, Jim, you're so easy to wind up. I'm just off shopping, that's all. Not running away with a fancy man.'

'I never thought . . .'

Peggy raised an eyebrow. 'Oh yes, you did. Now shut up and eat before your breakfast gets cold.'

'But what about Daisy?'

'Rosie's coming in to look after her.' She sipped the tea and had to agree with Cordelia – it really wasn't worth the effort. 'I shall be popping into the factory as well – just to check that Florence is coping all right and Gracie got back safely from her break.'

Jim ate some porridge, clearly deep in thought. 'Don't you think it's time you gave up that job, Peg?' he said at last. 'I earn enough to keep us both, and with Daisy being still so young, she needs you at home more – especially during the school holidays.'

'We've had this discussion before,' she replied mildly, 'and I refuse to have it again until I'm good and ready to make any changes.' She held him in her steady gaze. 'I enjoy what I do and I'm good at it, Jim. So let it rest, eh?'

He gave up the argument with poor grace and finished his breakfast in silence.

Charlie finished stuffing down his porridge then slathered two slices of bread with jam and margarine and made a sandwich, which he wrapped in paper and shoved into his coat pocket. 'Well, I'm off to work,' he said, pulling on the tweed cap his grandfather had given him on his last birthday, and wrapping a knitted scarf round his neck. 'And can everyone please be in a better mood when I come home tonight? I'm fed up with you all getting snappy with each other.'

Having made his speech, he pecked his mother on the cheek, waved goodbye to the others and slammed out of the kitchen to thud down the steps to the basement and slam the back door behind him.

Peggy closed her eyes at every slam and bang, and gave a sigh. 'There are days when I think I still have Rita and Ivy back in the house. Why is it the young feel they have to crash through doors?'

'In too much of a hurry,' said Cordelia gruffly. 'Which reminds me, we haven't heard from those two imps lately. I do hope they're all right.'

'I'm sure they are, Cordelia, they're probably too busy getting on with their new lives to sit down and write to us very often.'

Jim returned to the kitchen in his hat and coat, and carrying his briefcase. He bent to kiss Peggy. 'Sorry about earlier,' he murmured. 'It was just a surprise to see you all dressed up after getting used to you being in a dressing gown half the day.'

Peggy bridled; she'd never spent half a day in a dressing gown. But she let the remark go and kissed him back. 'Have a good day. And if you see Ernie, send him my warmest regards.'

'I'll do that. Maybe, if Rosie could babysit again, you'd come with me to visit him. I know he'd like to see you.'

'That's a lovely idea,' she murmured, although the thought of visiting a dying man at any time was depressing – and even more so at Christmas. However, Ernie deserved better of her, and she felt ashamed of her uncharitable thoughts. 'Try and arrange it, and I'll sort something out with Rosie.'

He nodded cheerfully and hurried through the hall and out through the front door to the British Legion car parked outside.

As the front door closed behind Jim, Peggy heard the back door open and Rosie call out. 'Only me!'

Her light footsteps ran up the concrete steps and the door flew open to reveal a rather dishevelled platinum blonde dressed in slacks, boots and a belted gabardine mac. 'Sorry if I'm late, but Ron and I rather overdid it last night at the Council bash.'

Peggy grinned at her best friend. 'You're not at all late,' she soothed. 'But you do look a bit fraught, so sit and have a fag while you simmer down.'

'Thanks, Peg,' she said, plumping into a chair. 'Sorry for bursting in on you like this, Cordelia. I have to admit,' she said, lighting a cigarette, 'that it's been quite a morning already – and frankly I could do without it after last night.'

'Oh dear,' chuckled Peggy. 'Was it that bad?'

'Actually, it was a good night, but we both drank far too much. The problem was this morning. I've got a thick head, and according to Ron, the neighbours are complaining about the noise we made coming home.' She broke into a fit of giggles. 'You'll never guess what old Chapman called Ron.'

'A pain in the neck? A rogue?' piped up Cordelia.

'Oh, far worse than that, Cordy. He called him a rabble and an absolute shower.'

Cordelia sniffed. 'Rather apt if you ask me.'

'I'll tell him you said so,' Rosie responded dryly. 'But he is rather put out, Peggy, and worried that if Chapman does report us to the Chief Constable, it will harm my standing on the Council.'

'I thought you and the Chief Constable were old pals? Couldn't you use your influence there?'

Rosie waved her cigarette about. 'Well, of course I could, but I'm not telling Ron that, am I?'

'Why ever not?' frowned Peggy.

Rosie shot her a cheeky grin. 'It might make him better behaved. It certainly taught me a lesson to hear what the rest of those snobs think about us. I've always been careful in the past about drinking, as you know, Peg, but there won't be quite so many shenanigans in the future, I can assure you.'

'So you were both rowdy last night?'

Rosie pulled a face. 'I suppose we were, but it was the dogs that really did it. They set up a fearful racket when they heard us come home, and then Ron couldn't get the key in the door and they just went on and on.'

Peggy laughed. 'I can just picture it. My goodness, Rosie, you really did have a good night, didn't you?'

'Rather too good if the truth be told,' she admitted, scrabbling in her handbag. 'I bought a bottle of Camp Coffee on the way here,' she declared, placing it firmly on the table between them. 'I'm in need of something stronger than tea today.'

Peggy frowned. 'But you'll be all right looking after Daisy?'

'Once I've had a large cup of that I can deal with anything,' Rosie declared.

Sandra Fortescue had already endured one long train journey and now she sat on an overcrowded bus, clutching the holdall on her lap as she contended with the dull headache that had plagued her since waking that morning. As the bus trundled through the London suburbs, she kept her gaze fixed on the grimy window to shut herself off from the other passengers. Her thoughts churned over the inevitable confrontation with her husband, Graham, that awaited her on arrival. The knowledge that every turn of the wheels on the bus brought her closer to the tree-lined street she'd called home for seven years made her feel nauseous and her pulse raced as she struggled to breathe.

As the bus stopped and started and rattled its way through the familiar streets, she became aware that the woman across the aisle was watching her with some concern, so with a great effort, she managed to control the rising panic by taking a deep breath and clutching the holdall even tighter. She shot the woman a tight smile and turned once more towards the window and saw the fear reflected in her blue eyes and wan face, and that she was now only two stops from home.

Would Graham be there waiting for her? She hoped not, for she'd planned her arrival to coincide with his accountancy office hours – he was a stickler for time-keeping and had never been late. She really wasn't ready to face him – feeling ill and completely wrung out, she just wanted to crawl into bed, pull up the covers and hide from the world.

At thirty-two, Graham was five years older than her, and still possessed the boyish good looks that had attracted her seven years earlier when they'd met at a party. The attraction had been mutual, and their whirlwind love affair had seen them married within months of meeting and moving into the large Victorian villa he'd bought as an investment in leafy Kew. Despite their coming from very different backgrounds – and his parents being disappointed in his choice of wife – they'd been happy. Or at least they had until it became clear there would be no children, and Graham had been adamant in his refusal to even discuss adoption, let alone fostering.

Sandra blinked back tears, determined not to make a show of herself in front of all these strangers who pressed in around her. She'd always wanted children – a baby to hold and love, a little person to watch over and cherish – and she wouldn't have cared if it had been another woman's child. The stark knowledge that all her dreams of motherhood had been shattered had caused untold misery and pain. Graham had been unsympathetic – his love-making brief and unsatisfactory, almost as if it was a duty expected of him. And so, in a moment of madness, she'd given in to the persistent charms of her very married boss, Simon Dandridge KC, seeking solace and the fleeting comfort of being close to someone who didn't make her feel useless. He'd taught her how much she'd been missing with Graham, for Simon was a skilled and generous lover who'd taken his time and allowed her to reciprocate – even to the point of initiating the intimacy.

In hindsight, of course, she could see their rather sordid affair for what it was, and bitterly regretted being so weak and unfaithful. But it was she who had been left to suffer the consequences and to find another post in a different Inns of Court. Although her future

77

there with Margot Jameson KC was not in doubt, she couldn't say the same about her personal life.

A tear rolled down her cheek and she hastily swiped it away. The bus was approaching her stop and she grabbed her small suitcase from the rack then pushed past the man standing in the aisle and pulled the cord, ringing the bell to get off.

The quiet, tree-lined street was almost deserted as she stepped down from the bus, and she stood for a moment to gather her courage for the short walk home. She felt frail and queasy, her body aching for respite after her tortuous journey, but it was the dread of having to face Graham with the decision she'd made that truly weighed her down. She could picture him now – eagerly welcoming her home, his soft hazel eyes lighting up, but not quite hiding the suspicions that haunted him every time she went away for work. They'd had the most fearsome row before she'd left with Margot for the trial in Manchester, and it had taken every ounce of her courage to stand her ground and fulfil her obligations to her new boss. Would Graham still be harbouring his resentment? She hoped not, for it would make what she had to do next even more difficult.

It took a tremendous effort, but she knew there could be no turning back. The die had been cast, her guilt undeniable – and she would need to call on the courage which had seen her through the last few weeks to get her through whatever was to come.

She took a deep breath, lifted her chin in defiance and began to walk down the pavement, her high heels clacking on the uneven slabs. At twenty-seven, she looked every inch the ambitious legal secretary and wife of a successful London accountant, dressed as she was in her good overcoat and smart little hat, her fair hair neatly styled in gentle waves that framed her heart-shaped face. How shocked any observer would be if they could see beyond all that and realise her life with Graham was nothing but a sham.

Sandra's pulse was racing and her mouth was dry as she approached their large Victorian villa. She was hoping that all the businessmen would have left for their offices and their wives would be busy ferrying their children to the nearby private school or preparing for one of their interminable coffee mornings. However, as she reached the gateway to their home she felt a stab of alarm and came to an abrupt halt. Graham's car was parked in the driveway.

Her legs threatened to collapse beneath her as she gripped the gatepost and stared at the car. It was too soon to face him and she wasn't sure that she could listen to the soft words he would use to belittle and undermine her. She'd rehearsed many times over what she had to say to him, and yet she didn't feel well enough to deal with the fall-out.

Sandra was tempted to flee but she reminded herself that her tough upbringing in the East End had given her the tools to be strong-minded and resourceful, even though those attributes had been worn away over the years of her marriage. Whatever happened next, she had no option but to see it through. Graham was a pedantic, practical man who liked an ordered life unhindered by any sort of complications, and although she'd be testing him to the limit, she'd have to face him sooner or later and deal with the consequences. Better to get it over and done with. Besides, he could be looking out for her and might have already seen her, so there really was no turning back.

Taking a deep breath, she gripped her luggage, crunched over the gravel and let herself into the spacious hall.

'Hello?' she called tentatively. 'I'm home.'

Graham came hurrying from the kitchen at the back of the house, his gangly figure unusually attired in corduroy trousers, a baggy gardening sweater and slippers. His thick brown hair was dishevelled and he was unshaven, but his boyish face was wreathed in relief as he swamped her in an embrace. 'I've been so worried about you, Sandra. Why didn't you telephone me while you were away?'

She momentarily leaned into his strong embrace for the comfort and sense of security it had once offered, but it was too tempting to give in to that familiar, treacherous warmth, and she pulled away.

He looked down at her, his expression puzzled, hazel eyes full of hurt. 'Sandra? Are you ill? You look terrible, and your lipstick is smeared. I do wish you'd give up this ridiculous idea of working. It's quite unnecessary and it clearly isn't doing you any good.'

Unable to look him in the eye, she concentrated on pulling off her gloves, determined not to be drawn into the age-old argument. 'I caught a stomach bug while I was away, and haven't got over it yet,' she said. 'But I wish you hadn't worried. I did tell you I had to go to Manchester for the Rex versus Roper trial. And warned you I could be away for some time.'

Graham's lips thinned. 'I know, and I accept you were busy, but I expected you to find the time to ring me, Sandra.' His gaze was steady and accusing.

'Margot Jameson is a hard taskmistress,' she said, turning away to take off her hat and coat and tidy her hair – which didn't need tidying. 'When she's prosecuting, I'm expected to have everything to hand so she and her junior are well prepared. It's my job to go through the transcripts and type up all her notes as well as take dictation. It's usually well past midnight before I get to bed.'

'As long as it's your own bed and not Dandridge's,' he said flatly. 'I'm not stupid, Sandra. I've guessed what's going on.'

She turned and braced herself to look into his face, knowing his suspicions were eating him up. 'I know you're not stupid, Graham, and that's why I've decided to clear the air between us.' She took a breath. 'I'm sorry, but . . .'

'Don't, Sandra,' he interrupted. The colour had drained from his face and his eyes were like flint. 'Whatever it is you wish to say, I don't want to hear it. Not now. Not ever.'

She would have reached for his hand, but he'd stuck them in his trouser pockets and was standing like a statue before her, clearly bracing himself for what was coming. The fear of what she was about to do made it hard to speak – but it had to be done if she was ever to be free.

'It's got to be now, Graham,' she said raggedly. 'Neither of us can ignore this any longer, no matter how much we might want things to be different.'

He shook his head, his expression obdurate. 'Our marriage is worth fighting for, and although you've clearly lost your way and had your silly head turned, I will not allow that womanising rotter Dandridge to destroy it.'

His tone was harsh, his abhorrence for Simon clear in every word – and yet his eyes were fearful. Sandra wished she didn't have to hurt him, but she couldn't go on pretending all was well in their marriage – not because Graham wasn't a faithful husband, or that she didn't appreciate all he'd done for her – but because she'd finally realised what sort of a man he was, and she could no longer trust him. And no marriage could survive the loss of trust.

She folded her arms tightly about her waist and battled to keep her nerve. 'You were right about me and Simon,' she said. 'But I want you to know that I deeply regret the affair, and the hurt it has caused you.'

'Apologies mean nothing after the event, Sandra,' he said coldly. 'How long has it been going on?' His expression was unforgiving, his tone edged with hurt and anger.

'About six months,' she replied, forcing herself to meet his steely gaze.

A pulse beat rapidly in his jaw. 'And are you planning to leave me for him?'

'It's well and truly over,' she admitted. 'In fact, I never want to see or hear from him again. Although I love my new job with Margot, I've asked for some time off to think about the future. Which is why I think it would be best if I moved out.'

Graham was clearly struggling to keep his emotions in check. 'But I love you, Sandra,' he managed. 'And I thought that once your affair had run its course, you'd realise you loved me and want to mend our marriage.'

She dipped her chin. 'It's too late, Graham,' she said. 'Once the trust between us is broken, the damage is done, and you'll always be wondering where I am and who with. As much as we both might wish it to be otherwise, our marriage can never truly be the same again.'

She steeled herself to meet his arctic gaze. 'It's probably best if I move out to a hotel or something so we both can think this through and keep things civil.' She took a deep breath and dared to say the words she knew would enrage him. 'But I want a divorce, Graham.'

'No,' he broke in, his face flushed with anger as he grasped her arms. 'I won't divorce you, Sandra;

neither will I accept that our marriage is over. You're unwell and emotional, and not thinking straight – and of course you mustn't move out. It's Christmas, and the hotels are full – and we're expected down at your Aunt Gloria's.'

Ever the practical man, she thought bitterly. God forbid we break the routine. Yet somehow it was oddly reassuring amid the turmoil she'd caused.

He tugged at her arm, which was still tightly folded round her waist. 'At least stay with me until we come back from Cliffehaven,' he begged. 'We can make our marriage work now Dandridge is out of the picture.'

She felt the strength in his fingers as he grasped her hands, and was tempted to relent – to give in, as she always had when he was like this. But that wasn't possible. 'It won't work, Graham,' she replied, her voice breaking. 'Really it won't.'

'It will,' he replied earnestly, grasping her hands against his heart. 'Please, Sandra. I'll give you all the space you need, and I understand you'll want time to think things through properly once you're feeling better, because this has come as a terrible shock to me, and I will need time too. But it doesn't mean we have to give up on our marriage just like that. We can work together as we've always done, see this through and hopefully have a stronger marriage because of it.'

She knew then that this was going to be harder than she'd imagined. If she left now Christmas would be ruined – not only for Graham, but for her recently widowed mother. And there would be questions – so many questions she couldn't possibly answer without destroying everything. However, if she stayed she'd be forced to contend with Graham's remorseless persuasion to see things his way – and she didn't know if she was strong enough to do that.

'So, what do you say, Sandra? Will you stay until after Christmas?'

'I don't know,' she murmured. 'It will be difficult.'

His eyes were once again filled with suspicion. 'Is Dandridge waiting for you somewhere? Was this demand for a divorce and space a ruse so you could run off with him?'

She snatched her hands from his grasp. 'No,' she said firmly. 'I've told you. It's been over for several months, and as far as I know, he's prosecuting at a trial in the Old Bailey – but you clearly don't trust me and never will again, so it's kinder to both of us if I leave now and start divorce proceedings.'

She stood quaking before him as he regarded her for a long, silent moment, his expression unreadable. 'You're right about the trust, Sandra,' he said eventually. 'But despite everything, I'm determined to overcome it. I'm not too proud to beg. Please stay.'

'It won't do either of us any good, Graham,' she replied. 'What's done is done, and no matter how much you deny it, things can never be the same. At least with me gone, we'll manage to salvage something, even if it's only a civilised parting of the ways.'

Graham dug his hands into his trouser pockets. 'I thought you loved me,' he said quietly. 'That if I gave you everything you wanted you'd see how right we are together, and how much you need me. This house, the elocution lessons and advice on social etiquette were all to help you fit in here. Which is what I thought you wanted.'

It was as if he'd heard nothing of what she'd said previously, and the suggestion that he'd moulded her to fit into his world was just another example of how he'd been able to manipulate her – never through violence, but through the endless drip-feed of logical persuasion that she'd had no way of fighting until now.

He gave a deep sigh. 'I understand why you fell for him. He's more sophisticated and ambitious than me – wealthier too,' he said morosely. 'Dandridge, rot his soul, can offer you far more than I ever could.'

Sandra had heard enough. 'I really think I should leave, Graham. This is only going to lead to an argument, and I don't feel well enough to deal with any more today.'

Graham stilled her hand as she reached for the telephone to call a taxi. 'I don't want to fight with you, Sandra, but I can't let you leave like this when you're clearly not in your right mind. If you promise to stay, I will give you all the time and space you need to think things through, and I won't mention any of this again until you're ready to talk.'

She really was feeling quite ill and didn't have the strength to argue, so she reluctantly nodded. 'All right, but I'll move into the spare room.'

The gleam of victory in his eyes told her that once again she'd crumbled to his will, but now the first step had been taken towards severing the ties, she would have to find the strength to see her plan through to the bitter end.

6

Peggy loved Christmas; loved the bustle and noise and the sight of smiling faces, happy children, and tinsel everywhere. The large tree outside the Town Hall was fairly bristling with baubles and fairy lights, and the band from the Sally Army was revving up to bring the true spirit of Christmas to the crowds of people swirling along the pavements in the hope they'd put a penny or two in their collection tins.

Peggy stood outside Plummer's department store and took it all in. She could smell the pine from the tree and the delicious aroma of roasting chestnuts on a brazier; and could feel the lightness in the atmosphere as people chattered and laughed and looked in the brightly dressed shop windows. It seemed everyone was determined to have the best Christmas despite the gloom of rationing, the lack of housing, and the countrywide tightening of belts.

She hitched up her heavy shopping bag and was about to explore the department store for something special to give Cordelia when a familiar and rather raucous voice stilled her.

'Oy, Peggy! Hang on a minute, mate!'

She grinned at the startling sight of Gloria decked out in an eye-wateringly tight red dress beneath a vivid green short coat, with tinsel in her dyed blonde hair and what looked like gold tree decorations strung round her neck and hanging from her ears. 'Hello, Gloria. My goodness! You're looking very . . . Very festive.'

'You gotta make the effort, don't ya?' she replied, patting her hair and making her many bracelets jangle. 'How you keeping, Peg? I hear your Daisy's gone down with the measles.'

'The doctor said she won't be infectious for much longer. Which is a relief,' she said, 'because it looks as if we'll still be able to get together for Christmas. I've had the devil's own job keeping Cordelia away from her, and then there's Anne's little Oscar. He's only a few weeks old, and the consequences of him catching it could be awful.'

Gloria nodded sagely, making her earrings swing. 'Your Anne's lucky 'er Rose didn't get it. I 'eard it went through the school like a dose of salts.'

Before Peggy could comment, Gloria caught sight of a woman staring at her in what could only be described as horrified disgust. She jutted out her chin and snarled, 'You got a problem, lady?'

The startled woman hurried away and Gloria blew a raspberry. 'Silly cow,' she muttered before turning her attention back to Peggy. 'I suppose you got a houseful coming?'

Peggy was relieved Gloria hadn't started a fight, and glad to change the subject. 'If the weather doesn't close in. What about you?'

'Me sister Beryl's coming down with her Sandra, and Sandra's husband, Graham.' Gloria pulled a face. 'Graham's a few years older than our Sandra and can be a bit of a wet weekend, but if you get a few drinks inside him, he livens up to tepid, if you know what I mean.' She nudged Peggy in the ribs as she winked a heavily made-up eye.

'Oh, it'll be lovely to see Sandra again,' Peggy said. 'She was such a lively little thing when she used to come down to stay with you during the holidays. I remember she and Cissy used to get up to all sorts of mischief, but it seems like years since I last saw her.'

'It were back in the summer of 'thirty-nine after war was declared and before the bombing started in earnest. She married Graham the following spring, and although it was all a bit hasty, they seem happy enough.' Gloria grinned. 'I'm looking forward to seeing 'er and me sister too, though Beryl's inclined to fret about everything from the crackers to the amount of coal on the fire. Still, Christmas ain't the same without family, no matter what they're like.'

Peggy detected wistfulness in Gloria's tone and felt a pang of sympathy. 'It takes a lot of organising, though, doesn't it? Especially when no one bothers to ring back to confirm anything,' she said, still miffed about Cissy. 'Over two weeks I've tried to get hold of that daughter of mine, and only got to speak to her yesterday – and that conversation lasted all of five minutes.'

'Kids, eh?' Gloria rolled her eyes. 'They just don't think, do they? Beryl had the same problem with her Sandra. Heard nothing from her for weeks, and then just turns up and wonders what all the fuss was about.'

Gloria heaved a sigh so great it almost exposed her entire bosom above the low neckline of her dress. 'Honestly, Peg, Graham thought she'd run off with some other man, and Beryl was – as usual – on the brink of a nervous breakdown. But it turns out she were only on a business trip and didn't think she needed to phone home.'

'Were we as thoughtless at that age?' asked Peggy.

'Probably,' muttered Gloria. 'Youth and common sense rarely go 'and in 'and.'

She swamped Peggy in a heavily scented embrace. 'Have a good one, Peg, and if you feel like a drink, you know you're always welcome at the Crown.'

Peggy liked Gloria but had no intention of setting foot in the Crown as it had such a bad reputation. She watched with some amusement as Gloria tottered away on her high heels, seemingly unaware of the scathing looks of the women and the leers of the men as she cut a swathe through the crowds. For all her raucous ways, Peggy rather admired Gloria, as she possessed a great spirit and fortitude despite her many troubles. And she knew that beneath all that heaving bosom and gaudy jewellery, there beat a generous and loving heart.

She turned away and acknowledged the salute of the liveried doorman as she pushed through the new revolving doors of the department store, her thoughts still on Gloria. How sad it was to suddenly become aware of how lonely she must have been all these past Christmases once her son had been killed and her daughter-in-law had taken the grandchildren to live miles away. And how remiss she had been as a friend not to have realised that and done something about it.

With that thought, she made a beeline for the make-up counter, picked out the brightest red lipstick and the bluest eye-shadow, and got them gift-wrapped. Gloria would love them, and it would, in a small way, atone for her own thoughtlessness.

Two hours later, she'd loaded up the car with her shopping, chatted to Fred the Fish and Alf the butcher and secured a lovely bit of ham as well as some slivers of salmon which had cost an arm and a leg but would be a special treat on a special day. She'd get Jim to pick up the turkey on Christmas Eve.

Now she was stepping through the door of the Anchor to find Ruby and Brenda busy behind the bar and almost every seat taken by weary housewives laden with bags of shopping. She smiled inwardly as she saw Dr Darwin sitting to one side of the bar, his warm brown eyes following Ruby's every move. Easing her way through the crush, she waited patiently at the other end of the bar for Ruby to spot her.

'Auntie Peggy! How lovely to see you.' Ruby came to give her a big hug. 'How's everyone at Beach View?'

Peggy grinned as she noted the girl's sparkling eyes and animated face. 'Apart from Daisy having the measles, we're all fine,' she said. 'And it looks as if you are too.'

Ruby shrugged. 'No point in moping, is there? I got a pub to run, so there ain't no time for feeling sorry for meself.'

Peggy patted her hand. 'You don't have to pretend with me, Ruby,' she said quietly. 'How are you really?'

The smile faded. 'I'm coping, Peg, it's all I can do. But Mum's at peace and out of pain, so I've gotta learn to get on with things.'

Peggy nodded. 'Yes, it's hard to lose a parent, but you're made of strong stuff, Ruby, you'll get through this.'

'D'ya wanna drink while yer 'ere?' Ruby asked, darting a glance across to Brenda who was struggling to cope behind the bar.

Peggy shook her head. 'I just popped in to see how you were and to remind you that Christmas dinner will be served at one.' She shot a glance towards Dr Darwin. 'That's unless you've made other arrangements,' she teased.

Ruby laughed. 'You just can't help yourself, can you? Christmas is a time for family, and you're the only family I got, Auntie Peg, so of course I'm coming.' She hugged her again. 'I'd better get on, sorry.'

'Me too, but if Alastair finds himself at a loose end on the day, he'd be very welcome to join us.'

'He's just a friend,' said Ruby firmly. 'So you can knock those ideas straight out yer head.'

Peggy chuckled, kissed her cheek and hurried out to her car, glad Ruby seemed to be coping after the sudden and very painful loss of her mother, Ethel. The funeral had been forlorn as very few had turned up, but at least Ethel had had the chance to reconcile with the daughter who'd always loved her despite everything.

She climbed into the car, ready now to check on Florence and Gracie. Driving through the factory gates, she realised it must be lunchtime, for she could see the crowd through the fogged windows of the canteen.

She parked the car in her designated spot by Solly's second factory, then made sure her hat was firmly tethered by its decorative pin, dabbed some powder on her nose and refreshed her lipstick. It was important to look as if she was in charge, even if she was taking an enforced sabbatical. Grabbing her handbag, she climbed out of the car and her spirits sank as she saw Doris waiting for her. 'Hello, Doris.'

'You're looking very smart for once,' said her elder sister, eyeing her from dinky hat to polished shoes. 'Where are you off to?'

Peggy swore silently that she wouldn't take umbrage. 'I've been shopping,' she replied, taking in the twinset, pleated skirt and triple row of pearls beneath the lustrous fur coat. Doris was now in her fifties but carried her age well, and as usual, looked as if she'd just stepped out of a beauty parlour. 'You don't look too shabby yourself.'

Doris patted her freshly permed and artfully coloured hair. 'It doesn't hurt to take pride in one's appearance,' she said smugly.

'And you do it so well,' retorted Peggy with a touch of cattiness that seemed to go over Doris's head.

Her sister leaned closer, her face alight with curiosity. 'I say. What's all this about the abandoned baby? I understand Bertie actually found it, and now Rachel and Solly have taken it in. Do you have any inkling as to who the mother might be?'

'I know as much as you,' said Peggy coolly. 'But whoever she is, she must be in hell right now.'

'She deserves to be,' snapped Doris. 'How any woman could do that . . . It's a disgrace – and in a respectable place like Cliffehaven too!'

Peggy really didn't want to prolong this unpleasant conversation, for the wind was bitter and Doris was getting on her nerves. 'Are Anthony and Suzy coming with the children for Christmas?' she asked, hoping to change the subject.

'Of course they are,' Doris said, dismissing the subject with an impatient wave of her hand. 'You don't think it could be one of the women here, do you?' Her gaze swept across the deserted forecourts. 'It might very well be, you know. There are some girls here with very loose morals, and I've seen how they carry on. It's quite disgraceful.'

'If I didn't know you better, Doris White, I'd suspect you were enjoying the scandal,' said Peggy dryly. She pulled her scrappy fur scarf tighter about her neck and turned towards the factory. 'I'll see you all on Boxing Day,' she said over her shoulder before stepping through the door and shutting it firmly behind her.

She stood and let the familiar scents and sights of the factory floor calm her down. Doris always wound her up like a clock, and it infuriated Peggy that she couldn't learn to take it on the chin and not react. She headed across the deserted factory floor to her office where Florence appeared to be hard at work during her dinner hour. Peggy tapped on the door and walked in.

Florence shot to her feet looking flustered. 'Peggy,' she gasped. 'I wasn't expecting to see you today.'

'I've only popped in to see how you're doing,' she soothed before sitting in the visitor's chair and warming her hands by the two-bar electric fire. 'I hope you've given yourself time to have a proper lunch, Flo. You won't get far without some food inside you now it's so cold.'

'I usually bring in a sandwich and a flask of soup at lunchtime, so I can work in here in peace,' Florence replied briskly. 'I find that's quite filling enough.' She shuffled the papers on her desk. 'Do you want to see the order books and time sheets?'

Peggy shook her head. 'I'm confident you're dealing with them in your usual efficient way.' She sat back in the chair. 'I really came in to ask if there were any problems you wanted to discuss, and to find out how Gracie is getting on.'

Florence smiled, which made her look much younger than her forty-odd years. 'There are the usual minor squabbles amongst the machinists, and some tomfoolery involving a couple of the younger lads in the loading bay. But they've been dealt with.'

'And Gracie? I take it she *is* back?'

Florence bit her lip and began to fiddle with a pencil. 'She's back all right, and proving to be very good with the other machinists. She also has a sharp eye when it comes to suspected pilfering, which is commendable. But . . .'

Peggy sat forward. 'What's the matter, Flo?'

'She hasn't been very well since returning, and although I tried to persuade her to stay in bed for a couple of days, she's insisted upon coming in.' Florence shrugged. 'I can't say I blame her, for I suspect her time away cost more than she'd expected, and she needs the money.'

'Then it's understandable – especially in the lead-up to Christmas – and with her little boy no doubt expecting something from Santa. But is her ill health affecting her work?'

Florence shook her head. 'Not really. It's all this gossip about the abandoned baby that's upsetting her. I've found her in the toilets in tears on two occasions, and could barely console her.'

'That's odd behaviour, even for a soft-hearted soul like Gracie,' Peggy murmured, her thoughts going into a dangerous whirl of suspicion.

'To be fair, Peggy, I think all that to-do with Warner knocked the stuffing out of her, and when she got that tummy bug in Margate, it completely wiped her out. I'm hoping the long break over Christmas will put her to rights again.'

'If she's that poorly she should see a doctor,' said Peggy.

Florence shook her head. 'Refuses to even discuss the idea.'

'Silly girl,' Peggy sighed before looking sharply at Florence. 'You don't think there's something more serious going on with Gracie, do you?'

'Well, she's not pregnant, if that's what you're thinking,' replied Florence flatly. 'She had to borrow my packet of sanitary towels until she could get to the shops this lunchtime.'

'Well, that's a relief.' Peggy pulled on her gloves and picked up her handbag. 'If you have any further worries about Gracie, then please let me know. And keep your ear to the ground, Flo. This lot like to gossip; and someone somewhere knows whose baby was abandoned – and whoever it is will need medical attention and a shoulder to cry on.'

'I'm sure it's none of our girls,' said Florence firmly. 'The majority are too old and the rest are married or in steady relationships.'

'Even so,' murmured Peggy. 'There are a lot of women working on this factory estate, and truth has a way of rising to the surface once the gossips get going. That lot out there probably know more than you think.'

She shook off the dark suspicions over Gracie and smiled as she headed for the door. 'I'll leave you to it, Flo. And well done for keeping the place in such good order. Solly's delighted with the way you're handling things.'

Doris returned from the melee in the canteen feeling quite put out after her short run-in with Peggy and the battle she'd had to get lunch. It had been an absolute scrum in the canteen and the raucous noise was at such a pitch she'd barely been able to make herself heard.

She carefully carried the two covered plates of hot food up the wooden staircase to the estate management office and was relieved that her husband was waiting there to open the door for her. 'Thank you, John,' she murmured, placing the plates on table mats so they wouldn't mark her highly polished desk.

She took the metal covers from the dishes and eyed the dollop of shepherd's pie with little pleasure. 'It's not the most appetising of meals, but I suppose it's better than nothing,' she sighed.

'Let's eat before it gets any colder,' he said, closing the window that overlooked the estate and sitting opposite her to unfold the pristine white linen napkin Doris insisted they use at mealtimes, even in the office.

Doris lifted a forkful of the food to her mouth and grimaced. 'Cheap meat, barely cooked onions, no other vegetables, and the potatoes are so old they're watery. But then I shouldn't be surprised. The standards in that kitchen are hardly first class – and let's be honest,

John, the customers wouldn't know any better, would they?' she said, wrinkling her nose.

John put down his fork and reached across the desk for her hand, his blue eyes concerned in his handsome face. 'Darling, you really should learn to be more charitable,' he said sadly. 'The cooks do their best with what they have, and for some, it's the only hot meal they'll have today, and they're grateful for it.'

Doris realised she'd said the wrong thing and tried to make light of it. 'I didn't mean to sound unkind,' she said quickly. 'And of course I realise we're lucky compared to so many others. But surely the cooks could be a bit more inventive?'

John picked up his fork again to stab at the food, but instead of continuing with his lunch, he held Doris's gaze. 'I overheard what you said to Peggy,' he said quietly. 'Do you really feel that way about the poor girl who abandoned her baby?'

'I speak as I find,' she replied, concentrating on swirling her fork in the meat and potato mess, trying to make up her mind whether to risk eating it. 'Whoever she is should be locked up. And I wouldn't mind betting she's one of those little tarts in the canteen.'

John's fork clattered on to the cheap china plate. 'Enough, Doris.' His quiet voice held icy command.

Startled, she looked up and saw something in his eyes that made her feel suddenly wary. 'Well, you did ask.'

His face was a mask of dislike as he leaned towards her, and his voice was low with barely contained anger. 'I said enough. Before you do any more damage, Doris.'

She abandoned the food, trapped by his glare and unable to think.

'Whoever that poor girl is, she deserves our pity and understanding,' he said into the heavy silence. 'I detest gossip and salacious rumour, and am shocked that my wife – of all people – should take such vicious delight in another's tragic circumstances.'

Doris couldn't speak for shock.

'I heard the rumours about you and chose to ignore them,' he continued, 'but it seems I should have listened more carefully and taken heed.'

'But they were just spiteful gossip spread by people I'd fallen out with,' she protested raggedly. 'Truly they were.'

He shook his head, the sun gleaming through the office window on to his silvery hair, his expression sorrowful. 'No, Doris. You're uncharitable and spiteful – and the worst kind of snob. You treat your sister and our lovely daughter-in-law as if they're beneath you, and when someone is in trouble – like that poor girl – you positively revel in it.'

Speechless and now very much afraid, Doris could only watch as he pushed back from the desk and reached for his coat and hat. She looked up at him as he stood tall and straight like the retired colonel that he was, and then, without another word, left the office.

Doris shot out of her chair but was too proud to call after him as he went down the steps to stride away across the forecourt and through the gates, his gaze firmly fixed ahead. The tears fell unheeded down her perfectly made-up face as he disappeared from sight, and for the first time since they'd met, she wasn't at all sure if he would ever forgive her.

'Oh, John,' she sobbed. 'I'm sorry. So sorry. I didn't realise how strongly you felt, and . . .' Distraught and afraid, she collapsed back into the chair, angrily swiped the dishes with their barely touched meal from the desk and buried her face in her hands.

7

As the sun had come out and the rain had held off, Ron decided to take the dogs into the hills to visit his old pal Chalky White. The thought of those ducks had stayed with him all morning, and if Chalky wouldn't oblige, then he'd have to risk sneaking into the Cliffe estate to nab a couple of Lord Cliffe's – although he didn't really fancy it.

It was a long, hilly walk to Chalky's smallholding, but it felt good to stretch his legs, and the dogs were delighted to be able to race about. Although he noticed with some concern that Harvey was finding it more difficult these days to keep up with his pup Monty. Ron calculated that Harvey had to be at least fourteen now, so he was faring well, considering the vet had said he had a heart murmur, but it wouldn't hurt to keep a judicious eye on him.

He reached the top of the hill and looked down at the brick-and-thatched farmhouse standing within a half-circle of trees that sheltered it from the wind that often blew through the long, narrow valley. It was a pleasant vista on this cold, bright day, and Ron had always enjoyed coming here.

Chalky had planted a huge vegetable plot next to the large chicken coop, and at the base of the valley, there was a murky duck pond surrounded by reeds and sheltered by a weeping willow. The stinking piggery was set well away from the house, and half a dozen goats were frolicking within a high-fenced pen.

It seemed Chalky had started a new enterprise, for he'd never had that many goats before.

Ron's gaze drifted over the many barns, sheds and outhouses. He knew that Chalky had turned the largest barn into a workshop to mend and store his machinery and tools, and the second one to butcher his pigs and smoke the bacon. The third and smallest was well camouflaged behind a false wall in the house, and it was here he conducted his illegal brewing enterprise, which produced various lethal concoctions that blew your head off if you weren't careful.

Ron grinned and began the steady descent to the farmhouse, the dogs racing ahead of him in the expectation of getting their usual juicy ham bone. The sun was surprisingly warm for the time of year, and as he got further into the valley, he noticed the wind had dropped and it felt almost spring-like.

Chalky appeared in the doorway of his farmhouse and watched Ron's approach, arms folded. Slight of figure but surprisingly sturdy for a man already well into his seventies, he was in his usual garb of gumboots, dungarees and layers of ancient cardigans. He had the weathered face of an outdoors man which enhanced sharp blue eyes, and his mop of snow-white hair which drifted like a cloud from beneath a filthy peaked cap.

'If it's bacon you're after, you're too late,' he said once Ron was within earshot. 'I sold it all to Alf.'

'That's no way to greet an old pal,' said Ron, shaking his roughened hand. 'It's nearly Christmas, and to be sure I'm thirsty after that long walk.'

Chalky rolled his eyes. 'I thought my brew didn't agree with you?'

'It agrees with me very well,' replied Ron, taking off his cap and wiping the sweat from his brow with his coat sleeve. 'So how about it?'

'All right. As it's nearly Christmas, I suppose,' Chalky said gloomily, turning back into the house.

Ron plonked himself down at the big wooden table on the rough patio outside the kitchen window and frowned. It was most unlike Chalky to be long-faced – especially as he'd sold all his meat to Alf and probably made a tidy profit.

Chalky returned with two large glasses of his home-made brew and placed them on the table before digging out a couple of bones from his filthy trouser pockets for the dogs. He plumped down on the bench and raised his glass to Ron. 'Happy Christmas.'

'And the same to you.' Ron took a glug of Chalky's infamous plum vodka and didn't have to wait long for the burn to make its way down his gullet into his belly and up into his head. 'Whoa,' he gasped. 'That's good stuff,' he managed hoarsely. 'Certainly has a hell of a kick. You wouldn't fancy selling me a couple of bottles, would you? To be sure it would get any party going.'

'You can have a couple to take home, Ron. No charge.'

Chalky never gave anything for free – especially his plum vodka. Ron gaped. 'Are you feeling all right, old son? Not had a knock to the head recently?'

Chalky shrugged and stared out over his vegetable plot. 'Was there something you wanted, Ron? Only I have to be somewhere before it gets dark.'

'There was, aye. But I'm more concerned about you. Has something happened, old pal?'

'You could say that,' Chalky murmured, expertly rolling a cigarette. 'But what are you after? The chickens on offer are all spoken for, most of the vegetables will be going to the greengrocer in the morning, and I only have enough chicken feed to last me through until New Year.'

'Ducks,' said Ron, realising his friend was reluctant to talk about whatever was worrying him. 'I'd like to buy three or four ducks.'

Chalky raised an eyebrow. 'There's not much meat on a duck – not enough to feed your enormous brood, anyway. Haven't Jim and Peggy got a turkey or capon ordered?'

Ron bit his lip. He hadn't thought to ask them. 'Not sure,' he muttered. The vodka was already making him a little light-headed. 'But I'll take the ducks off your hands anyway. They'll always come in useful,' he declared, as if he was doing his pal a favour.

'I'll *sell* you four,' said Chalky evenly. 'They bred well this year, so you can have them at half what Alf would charge.'

Ron put down the glass and regarded his friend with deep concern. 'Chalky, we've known each other since we were in short trousers – and you have never *ever* sold me anything on the cheap, let alone given stuff away. What the heck is wrong with you today?'

'I've got things on my mind,' he said, his gaze slipping away.

'What things? Is it the wife? She's not come back, has she?'

Chalky took his time to light his smoke. 'Nah, she's gone and won't be back, thank goodness.' He finally looked Ron in the eye. 'It's something else, but I don't know if I should tell you cos it's not very pleasant and could cause me a lot of trouble.'

'Chalky, we shared the hell of the trenches. Surely nothing can be worse than that?'

'Aye, maybe. But it's difficult, you see. The police will have to get involved, and well . . . Things could become awkward if they start to dig around here.'

'Dig?' Ron took a deeper swig of the vodka and felt it go straight to his head. 'You haven't found a body, have you?'

'Don't be daft, Ron. Of course I haven't.' Chalky dragged on his cigarette and watched the curl of smoke get caught in the light breeze that was now stirring through the valley.

Ron watched him, trying to read his thoughts and failing.

'Do you remember Wilf Hallam?' Chalky asked after a long silence.

'To be sure, that's a name from the past. But of course I do. He was old man Watkins's shepherd. Got killed at Monte Casino.' Ron frowned. 'What about him?'

'I found something today that's been worrying me ever since. And I don't know what to do about it.'

'To do with Wilf?'

Chalky shook his head. 'To do with the caravan Wilf used during lambing season.'

'Blooming heck – I'd assumed old Watkins had got rid of it years ago,' muttered Ron.

'It seems he didn't, and I'd forgotten about it too until I came across it by accident this morning.'

Getting a story out of Chalky was like pulling teeth, thought Ron impatiently. 'But I seem to remember it was on Watkins's land. You took a bit of a risk going up there, my old son. That new owner of the Watkins's place wouldn't be best pleased to catch you trespassing – he's a suspicious bugger at the best of times, by all accounts, and very handy with a shotgun. What were you doing up there in the first place?'

Chalky blew out a stream of smoke in a long sigh. 'One of my blasted goats got out of the pen, so I went looking for it. Ruddy nuisance they are – forever escaping.'

'Yes, yes, and?' Ron urged impatiently.

'I heard it bleating up on what was Watkins's top field and went to investigate. Stupid thing had gone into a thick copse of trees and got entangled in some baling wire that was trapped in a gorse bush. And there was the caravan, sinking on its arse and falling to bits.'

Ron dug out his pipe in frustration. 'I really don't see where this is leading, Chalky. But do get on with it – I have to be home by six and it's already midday.'

The older man eyed him dolefully. 'Sarcasm is the lowest form of wit, Ron,' he said quietly. 'If you'd shut up for five minutes I'll tell you where this leads – and it's straight to the door of the police station.'

'So you did find a body,' said Ron.

'No. I found where that lass gave birth to the baby she abandoned.'

Ron gaped at him. 'How the hell can you know that?'

Chalky's gaze drifted once more across his land. 'The scent of birthing stays with you after all the years I've helped bring animals into the world, Ron, and there was no mistaking it. There was other evidence too, but I won't go into that.' He shook his head mournfully. 'How she knew about that caravan is a complete mystery.'

Ron pondered on this as he filled and lit his pipe. 'The consensus of opinion in Cliffehaven is that she must be local,' he said thoughtfully. 'And after what you've found, it sounds as if they're right.'

As Chalky remained silent, Ron watched the sweet-smelling pipe smoke drift into the air. 'All the older kids knew about that caravan before the war, and once lambing was over it became a popular meeting place far from parental interference during the summer. Whoever it was hiding there didn't have to have a very long memory.'

'Your Cissy was certainly one of them,' said Chalky, 'and even Anne was up here on a few occasions with Gloria's niece, Sandra, and little Gracie.' He shook his head at the memory. 'In fact, most of the Cliffehaven kids had been messing about up there at one time or another according to what Wilf told me.'

'Makes you wonder, eh?' murmured Ron, his thoughts drifting to those long summer days between the wars when his granddaughters disappeared for hours with their friends and rarely made it home before dark. 'But how long had she been hiding there? It can't have been pleasant if the caravan is falling apart.'

'She'd set it up quite well, I'll give her that,' Chalky replied. 'I found a cooking ring and paraffin heater as well as a pile of mucky bedding and dirty nappies. There were books too. Medical books, so she came prepared.'

'It was a very brave thing to do,' said Ron. 'She must have been terrified.'

'It was bloody foolish,' snapped Chalky. 'She could have set fire to the whole shebang, cos there were stubs of candles all over the shop, a gas canister, and a third of a tin of paraffin left open right in the middle of it all. The fumes alone could have killed them both.'

'You'll have to tell Bert Williams, Chalky.'

'I really don't want to involve the police, Ron. You know how nosy they can get.'

'Bert is fully aware of all your dodges, Chalky, and won't do anything about them unless you get careless and give him no option but to run you in. And as the caravan is not on your land, the police have no reason to start poking about here.'

Chalky didn't look convinced, so Ron hurried on to persuade him to see sense. 'It's your civic duty, Chalky, and as the still is well hidden, there's nothing else they can find.' He looked at Chalky sharply, and saw the colour rise in his cheeks. 'Or is there?'

Chalky stubbed out his smoke in a chipped saucer and sank his chin to his chest. 'There's a couple of mutton carcasses I was about to butcher. Questions could be asked,' he said, avoiding Ron's gaze.

'Oh,' said Ron, fully understanding the situation. 'In that case things could get tricky.'

'So what should I do, Ron?'

He finished the glass of home-made vodka and puffed on his pipe as he sat staring across the small-holding, deep in thought. 'There's only one thing you can do,' he said eventually. 'Butcher those sheep today and get them down to Alf who'll gladly take them off your hands no questions asked. Then go to see Bert Williams.'

'I was hoping for a good price,' Chalky moaned. 'And if Alf smells a rat, he'll pay far less than they're worth and I'll lose all me profits.'

Ron tutted with annoyance. 'If they were nicked in the first place they cost you nothing, Chalky – so anything you get from Alf will be a profit. In fact,' he added slyly, 'I could take a couple of joints off you if it would help.'

Chalky laughed for the first time that day. 'I might have known you'd jump in at the merest sniff of a deal to be done.'

'All's fair in love and sheep rustling,' said Ron with a wink.

Chalky knew when he was beaten, so he finished his drink in one large gulp and stood up. 'In that case you can help with the butchering. The quicker it's done the better.'

Ron grinned. The day had turned out far better than he ever could have hoped.

Doris had finally stopped crying, and used her pent-up emotions to clear away the mess she'd made with the revolting shepherd's pie. In her fit of temper she'd actually broken one of the plates, but as they were cheap she didn't think it really mattered, so she dumped the shards in the waste basket along with the mess of meat and potato. She certainly had no intention of taking the other plate and covers back to the canteen, for she was quite frazzled, and the last thing she needed today was to be the subject of tittle-tattle.

Having returned the office to its usual pristine state, she'd repaired her make-up, noting that her eyes were still red and puffy. And then she'd waited. But as the lonely day had worn on and it turned dark, she was forced to accept that John wasn't coming back.

Heartsick and with her head pounding and her eyes stinging with unshed tears, she turned off the heater and the light, switched on her torch and locked the door, then carefully made her way down the wooden staircase. The factory had closed by now, everything was deserted and eerily silent as she hurried away, heading for Mafeking Terrace and home in the desperate hope he would be waiting there for her.

The two bungalows which they'd converted into one splendid detached house were in darkness, and although his car was still parked at the kerbside where he'd left it this morning, that didn't necessarily mean he was at home. As she entered the spacious hall, her heart began to thud in dread at the silence which greeted her.

Surely he didn't mean to punish her by not coming home at all? But where could he go? Neither the golf club nor the officers' club had accommodation, and the only place with rooms still to let was the Crown. She knew John well enough to be certain he'd never go there, and she was also fairly sure he wouldn't have gone to Beach View – despite the fact that Peggy would probably side with him over their disagreement. John might be angry with her, but he'd never dream of airing his private grievances to anyone outside this house – not even Peggy.

Still in the dark, she slipped out of her shoes and used the reflected glow of the streetlamp through the glass of the front door to place her fur coat on a padded hanger in the cupboard under the sweeping staircase. With her handbag and gloves on the telephone table, she decided to check on the bedroom. Perhaps he had come home and fallen asleep in their bed.

The luxurious carpet muffled her footsteps as she climbed the stairs and went into their room. The soft glow of the wall-lights showed a neatly made but empty bed, and she took a trembling breath to ward off the return of tears. Padding into the connecting dressing room, she saw that nothing had been disturbed and all his clothes were still in his wardrobe. At least it seemed he hadn't planned to move out.

She put her hat on the dressing-table stool, dug her feet into her slippers and contemplated crawling into bed. But it was still too early to retire, and she was feeling too sorry for herself to be able to sleep, so after checking the spare bedroom, she went back downstairs to the kitchen.

The pot of stew she'd prepared that morning was still sitting on top of the cooker waiting to be heated through for supper. But she had no appetite, and if John was planning to stay out all night there was no point in heating it up. She reached instead for the bottle of gin she kept in an overhead cupboard and poured a generous measure before adding the merest splash of tonic water.

The drink went straight to her head, for she'd eaten nothing since breakfast. She took another gulp anyway before lighting a cigarette and plumping down on a kitchen chair. It was a small act of defiance, which she knew was rather silly, but she was getting cross now. John shouldn't have been listening in to her conversation with Peggy – neither had he given her a chance to explain why she felt as she did – and although her words might have been a little harsh, he really was taking things too far. After all, he'd asked her opinion, and she'd only told him the truth as she saw it. There was absolutely no excuse for him to be playing games. Feeling she was perfectly justified to be angry with him, she finished the drink and poured another.

It was now almost nine o'clock, and in place of the anger and self-pity there dawned a fear that he was so disgusted with her he'd decided not to come home at all. For all she knew, he could have had an accident or been taken ill. But she was letting her imagination run away with her.

Doris pushed away from the kitchen table feeling cross again. The kitchen was cold, the chairs not comfortable enough to sit in them for long; she'd light the fire in the sitting room, have another drink and listen to the wireless. If there was still no sign of him by ten, she'd go to bed – and to hell with him.

She was a little unsteady on her feet as she carried the glass across the hall and reached round the partially open door for the sitting-room light switch.

The shock of seeing him stretched out in his chair looking quite dead made her drop the glass and it shattered into a million pieces on the parquet floor. 'John!' she shrieked, rushing to his side to grab his lifeless hand and shake it. 'John!'

He slowly opened his eyes and blearily regarded her in utter confusion. 'Wha'sh'iit?' he slurred. 'Wha'sh'a'matta?'

Doris burst into tears and slapped him on the arm. 'You're not dead,' she yelled, hitting him again. 'How dare you let me think you were?'

John blinked and tried to make sense of what was going on as she hit him for the third time. 'Ow,' he protested, rubbing his arm. 'That hurt.'

'It serves you right,' she sobbed.

He struggled to sit up in the chair but it seemed to take too much effort, so he gave up and slumped back into the cushions. 'I'm sorry,' he muttered. 'Had too much whisky at the club. Mush have fallen asleep.'

Doris was still in shock, and although she was tremendously relieved to have him home, she was absolutely furious with him for being drunk. She folded her arms and glared down at him as he tried to focus on her. 'I've spent all day in tears after those horrid things you said to me – and all the while I thought you were planning to leave me – you were drinking at the bloody club.'

'Ish quiet there,' he managed, his eyes drooping wearily as his chin dipped to his chest. 'Had losh to think about.'

'And did you find the solution at the bottom of the whisky glass?' she snapped.

A deep snore was his only reply.

Doris watched him, her emotions in turmoil. She'd never seen him like this before and hated it. He was home at least, but her frustration was at boiling point, because he was in no fit state to hold an intelligent conversation so they could clear the air.

She stomped off to collect a cloth and the dustpan and brush to mop away the spilled drink and clear up the shattered glass. With everything tidied away, she fetched a blanket and tucked it round him before turning off the light and closing the sitting-room door. He'd have one heck of a hangover in the morning, which would serve him right.

Climbing the stairs to their bedroom, she was forced to acknowledge a harsh truth. John was not a man who would easily forgive – that had been proven when he'd cut himself off entirely from his vindictive son – and if she wanted her marriage to succeed, then she would have to rein in her class prejudices and be careful to keep her less than charitable opinions to herself. The events of today had been a stark warning, and one she would have to heed at all costs. It would be difficult and often frustrating, for she'd never flinched from saying what she thought, but she loved John with a deep and abiding passion and didn't want to lose him.

It was after ten when Ron finally arrived home with the dogs and Rosie seemed far from pleased to see any of them. 'I've a good mind to give your dinner to the dogs,' she said crossly. 'Though I see they've brought their own,' she added, eyeing the chewed meat bones they'd dropped on the parquet floor. 'Where the hell have you been until this time of night?'

Ron decided to use all his native Irish charm to get her out of her bad mood. 'Now, Rosie, me darlin', I know I'm late, but to be sure there's a very good reason for it,' he said. 'And to prove it, I've brought you a wee present.' He dug deep into his poacher's coat pockets and drew out a blood-stained parcel wrapped in newspaper and tightly bound with garden twine.

She eyed it suspiciously as both dogs whined and sniffed eagerly at what Ron was holding out to her. 'What is it?'

'A mutton joint. Freshly butchered and all ready for the pot,' he said, shooting her a beaming smile. 'Compliments of our old pal, Chalky.'

She folded her arms and eyed him with even deeper suspicion. 'Chalky doesn't keep sheep,' she said evenly.

'He's diversified,' he replied airily, holding the parcel out of reach of the dogs' noses. 'There are more goats up there now as well, and he's trying to make cheese.'

Rosie rolled her eyes. 'Now I've heard it all,' she sighed. 'You'd better put that in the fridge before it bleeds all over my polished floor, and clear up these bones. Then you can explain why you're so late.'

Ron was aware of her following him into the kitchen and silently watching his every move as he stowed the meat in the fridge and chucked the chewed bones into the side garden. She was making him nervous. 'A cup of tea would go down a treat,' he said, scooping dog food into bowls and topping up their water.

'When you've told me the whole story,' she replied, her expression warning him of a brewing storm.

He gave the dogs their food, then pulled out a kitchen chair and sat down still fully dressed in cap and poacher's coat. 'Chalky had to go and see Bert Williams,' he began.

A delicate eyebrow rose. 'Sergeant Bert Williams? Why?'

'Because he discovered the place the girl had been hiding when she had her baby,' he replied. 'If you stop asking questions, Rosie, the tale will be told a lot quicker.'

The storm clouds remained in her eyes for quite a while, but as the story of his day unfolded, they were replaced by a look of understanding and a deep sadness. 'That poor girl,' she sighed. 'She must have been petrified. The risks she took don't bear thinking about.'

'Well, I managed to persuade Chalky to see sense, and went with him to the police station to give him some moral support.'

Rosie burst out laughing. 'Moral support? You? The pair of you are as bad as each other, and Bert Williams isn't much better with him turning a blind eye to all the black market deals Chalky gets up to with Alf.'

Ron was quite hurt she should think so little of him and his pals. 'He's my oldest friend, and we were doing the right thing,' he protested.

Rosie nodded and grinned. 'Of course you were, and now all the evidence of his sheep stealing has been divided up between us and Alf, he has little to fear.' She paused on the brink of giggles. 'Unless they find his still.'

'Ah, that reminds me,' said Ron, digging into his coat's deep pocket. 'He gave me a couple of bottles of wine as a Christmas present, and four cheap ducks, which I dropped off with Peggy before coming home.'

'Well, well, aren't we all lucky?' she asked, her mouth twitching with humour as she eyed the two bottles on the table. 'Peggy gets duck, I get mutton and that so-called wine will probably addle our brains.'

Ron was puzzled that she wasn't better pleased, but in fear of breaking the improved mood, he stayed silent – it was something he'd learnt to do since marrying Rosie.

She leaned forward and reached for his hand over the table. 'You know that's not really wine, don't you, Ron? It's *slivovica* – a plum vodka popular in the Balkans, and quite lethal.'

'Oh, I didn't know that,' he said with studied innocence. 'Can I have my dinner now? Only I'm starving.'

She blew him a kiss and went into a fit of giggles as she fetched his dinner plate from the cooling oven. It was mutton stew.

In every conversation she overheard during the next few days, there was talk of her baby and almost lascivious speculation on the heartless tart of a mother who'd abandoned him. The voices of the few who sympathised were drowned out by those taking on the roles of judge and jury, suggesting she should be horsewhipped and thrown into jail for the rest of her life. She'd never realised how viciously cruel people could be, and as the newspapers screamed their headlines and the police ordered her to come forward, she hid her terrible secret in growing fear.

Life had become intolerable, and now she could hardly bear to walk down the street, for the newspaper stands were full of pictures of her baby, and there seemed to be no escape from the awful reminders of what she'd done. Yet she'd painted on her smile, pretended to be as horrified as everyone else, and kept up the awful charade even though she was dying inside.

Her mind was overwhelmed by it all, but there were physical repercussions she had not expected, and she'd had to tightly bind her breasts to stop the milk seeping through her clothes – and she was still bleeding, which was very worrying. She also ached in every fibre of her body, and although she was exhausted at the end of each long day, sleep had proved almost impossible.

As the bedside clock ticked away she lay staring into the darkness and thinking of the newspaper reports she'd pored over earlier. He would be loved by the Goldmans, for they were good-hearted, generous people, and they would make sure he went to a loving family. There could be no going back, no changing of heart, for he really would be better off without her.

And yet deep in her soul she would always carry the memory of those few precious hours she'd had with him and be burdened by the agonising guilt of what she had done.

8

Albert Williams had been the sergeant in charge of Cliffehaven's police station for some years. He was a widower of long-standing, and when he wasn't visiting his lady friend of many years, he preferred to spend his time at the station rather than in the soulless flat provided by the constabulary. It was warm there, and companionable, with a good canteen so he didn't even have the bother of cooking. What he would do once he was retired, he didn't know. Policing had been his life and he had no hobbies or interests outside it, no children or grandchildren – and his lady friend certainly wouldn't want him getting under her feet. His only hope was that HQ would forget about him so he could stay on. Although ever the optimist, Albert knew that it was a forlorn hope.

He'd listened to Chalky tell his story, and then made him make a statement and sign it before letting him and Ron leave the police station. He knew both men very well indeed and was fairly certain there was more behind Chalky's tale than he was letting on, because they'd both looked far too shifty. But he'd let it pass as he had far more important things to do this evening than dig into their murky goings-on. The CID force in the county town were already showing too much interest in the missing girl, and it would be a feather in his cap if he was the one to find her – proof, if any was needed, that he was still up to the job of policing

Cliffehaven and deserving of the promotion he'd been denied for so long.

It was after ten by the time he and the two young constables reached the distant farmhouse now owned by the dour Bill Arkwright and his sour-faced wife. Having parked the police car in the farmyard, he ordered the two constables to check their torches were working, arm themselves with evidence bags, and then wait until he'd explained their visit to the Arkwrights.

After a good deal of arguing from both Arkwright and his wife, Albert, drawing on every ounce of his authority, ordered them to help with his enquiries or risk arrest for hindering a police investigation.

Arkwright had eventually given in despite his wife's shrill complaints, and grumpily pulled on his coat and cap and tugged on mud-encrusted wellingtons. Muttering under his breath, he led them at a brisk pace across the undulating fields in the pitch-black night guided only by the light of their torches.

'White shouldn't have been on my land in the first place,' he grumbled, negotiating the stile that led into the top field. 'I've had my suspicions he's been stealing my sheep too,' he continued sourly. 'Two went missing yesterday, and they aren't the first.'

'If you have evidence of that,' said Albert, 'then perhaps I can do something about it.'

Arkwright's expression was grim in the torchlight. 'I can hardly show you evidence when he's already pinched them, and probably slaughtered and sold them into the bloody bargain,' he snapped.

Albert grinned in the darkness. Chalky was a cunning old so-and-so, but he'd have to watch it if he really was making off with Arkwright's sheep. The man was not someone to rub up the wrong way, and he suspected he was quite capable of taking the law into his own hands given half a chance.

Arkwright finally came to a standstill and shone the torch over the dilapidated wire and post fence that sagged close to a copse. 'From what you say, it should be in there somewhere, though I've never noticed it.'

Albert wasn't built for tramping hills at speed and was so out of breath he could barely speak. 'Thank you, Mr Arkwright,' he panted.

'Can't say it's been a pleasure,' he muttered.

'We'll take it from here,' Albert managed. 'But please keep this to yourself. I'm sure you don't want the press and half of Cliffehaven up here disturbing your sheep.'

The man glared before nodding. 'I'll get back to the wife then,' he said before stomping off.

Albert didn't envy him, and wondered if living with such a harridan was the reason behind his grumpiness. He shook off the thought and set his mind to the business in hand.

'Shine your torches over there and mind your step,' he ordered the two young constables. 'I can see baling wire hooked into the gorse, and that broken fence could be lethal as it's held together with barbed wire. There are probably rabbit holes too, and we don't want any twisted ankles this far from civilisation.'

The three of them carefully picked their way over the fallen fence posts and strips of barbed wire, and found they had to push their way through the damp and clinging undergrowth. Stumbling over fallen branches and cursing loudly as brambles snagged their coats, they eventually found what they'd been looking for.

The wreck of the caravan looked quite eerie as the torchlight danced over it, and they all jumped as a flock of roosting crows suddenly took flight with caws of alarm.

Albert shivered and quickly pulled himself together, unwilling to let the youngsters see how unnerved he was by the darkness and the isolation. Despite having lived in this neck of the woods for so long, he'd never been one to enjoy the outdoors – least of all in total darkness with the lord only knew what lurking in the long grass. How any girl had had the nerve to hide out here for more than a day was beyond him.

He pulled on his gloves, ordering the others to do the same, and then led the way around the encroaching gorse to the caravan door. It creaked alarmingly as he tried to open it, and then, without warning, came loose from its remaining rusty hinge with a mighty crack and crashed to the ground, just missing his boots and shins.

The noise disturbed something hiding in the undergrowth, and as it flashed past them, Albert thought he glimpsed the furry body and long tail of an enormous rat.

He fought to slow his racing heart and appear calm. He couldn't let the side down now. Yet his shaking hand betrayed him as he tried to keep the beam of his torch steady on the interior of the caravan.

'Bloody hell,' he muttered, wrinkling his nose at the reek of paraffin and other unpleasant pongs. He eyed the mess of bedding and the state of the floor, and realised he was too heavy to go any further on for fear of the whole damned thing collapsing and bringing the ruin down on his head.

He sized up his two constables and picked the skinniest. 'Come on, Granger. In you go. Just tread carefully and don't touch anything without your gloves on. Apart from the fact you might catch something nasty, you could contaminate any evidence.'

PC Granger didn't look too happy as he stepped warily inside and flashed his torch around. 'Do you reckon there could be more rats, Sarge?' he asked nervously.

'Don't worry about them,' Albert replied airily – although he suspected there very well might be. 'Just get on with it.'

'But what do you want me to do, Sarge?'

'Search under the bed and in that cupboard, then gather everything up and hand it out to PC Morgan so he can bag it for forensics – and then search the place inside and out for any clues as to who she might be.'

It didn't take long to clear the caravan of everything the girl had left behind, and having vainly searched everywhere, Albert called a halt. 'That's enough,' he said. 'It's too dark to see anything properly, and we could be trampling over things we shouldn't. We'll make the place secure for the night and come back tomorrow.'

'How do we do that, Sarge?' asked Morgan.

'You're to stay here on watch,' said Albert. 'I don't trust Arkwright not to come and tear the place down. And once the news gets out about this – which it will – we'll have all the nosy parkers and the press up here getting in the way.'

'All night, Sarge?' The young man's Adam's apple bobbed in his skinny neck as he peered round nervously into the darkness. 'On me own?'

'Well, I'm not holding your hand, Morgan,' Albert retorted. 'Chin up, lad,' he said, thumping him on the shoulder. 'I'll send reinforcements first light along with a sniffer dog to see if it can track where she's been.'

'But we don't have a sniffer dog, Sarge,' said Granger.

'Then it's up to me to find one, isn't it? Come on, Granger, we've wasted enough time as it is.' Albert took charge of the large paper bags in which the books and heater had been stowed, leaving PC Granger to carry the rest.

'Try and stay alert, Morgan, and if Arkwright shows his ugly face, warn him I will arrest him if he so much as touches that heap of old plywood.'

Albert tightened his grip on the evidence bag and headed for the stile with Granger trailing behind him. He was looking forward to getting back to civilisation at the police station for a well-earned cup of tea and a hot fish and chip supper straight from the fryer at Dawson's chippy. But first he had to make an important telephone call.

Ron had just switched off the wireless and they were about to go to bed when the telephone rang. He hurried to answer it, exchanging a worried glance with Rosie – any call at this time of night usually meant trouble.

Rosie stood in the doorway to the hall to listen to Ron's side of the conversation and breathed a sigh of relief upon realising there hadn't been some family calamity. She took their empty cocoa mugs into the kitchen to wash them, and then topped up the dogs' water bowls.

'Well,' said Ron from the doorway. 'To be sure, that's grand, so it is.'

'I take it he hasn't decided to arrest you for anything,' she replied dryly. 'So what was so urgent he had to ring you at this time of night?'

'He wants me to be at the police station before first light with the dogs. They've been up to the caravan and the girl has definitely been living there, so they need my dogs to try and sniff out her trail.'

'I really can't see what good that will do,' Rosie replied thoughtfully. 'Once she came down into town we know she went to the church. But from there? I doubt even Harvey could pick up her trail once she's in the town.'

'Well, it's worth a try,' Ron muttered. 'He has a good nose, and he's found people before.' He grinned. 'I had to negotiate a wee bit, but Albert promised to pay thirty bob for our time.'

'Quite right too,' she replied, reaching down to pat Harvey's soft head. 'He's a clever boy, and well worth the money.' She looked back up at Ron. 'We'd better get to bed if you have to be out so early.'

There was a gleam in his eye as he slipped his arm round her waist. 'You read my thoughts exactly, wee Rosie.'

Ron left the house at five-thirty the following morning, the dogs happily trotting at his heels as they headed up the deserted High Street to the police station. It was still dark, for the winter days were very short, and although the clocks had been put back, it would be at least another hour before the sky began to lighten. Ron didn't mind early mornings – in fact, they were his favourite time of day – and it seemed both dogs were eager for the adventure.

Albert met them outside the police station with a sturdy young policeman who had a large paper bag in his arms. 'Glad you're prompt, Ron,' he said, indicating to his colleague that the bag should be dumped in the back of the police van. 'This is PC Aston. He'll be taking over watch until the caravan can be removed. I've left young Morgan up there for now, and he's probably frozen stiff, as well as scared of his own shadow. It's a creepy place, Ron. I certainly don't envy him.'

Ron nodded a greeting to the younger man who he recognised as being one of the rugby boys. 'Aye, but the girl stuck it out, didn't she? Had to have some guts to do that, don't you think?'

He waited for Aston to climb into the van and shooed the dogs in after him before sliding into the passenger seat. 'Is that our breakfast?' he asked hopefully, eyeing the paper bag in the footwell that was emitting the delicious aroma of hot sausage roll.

'It's for Morgan. There are flasks of tea too, but we'll have them once we get up there. I've heard good things about your Harvey, Ron, so I hope he's still able to sniff things out.'

Harvey's nose poked between their shoulders and sniffed the air, ears pricked as he licked his lips.

'He can smell whatever's in that paper bag all right,' said Ron with a chuckle, and dug into his deep coat pocket for the biscuits he always carried. Placating both dogs with the treats, he ordered them to stop lolling all over PC Aston, and then sat back to enjoy the ride.

Albert was a careful driver and so it took a while to negotiate the steep main road into the rolling hills, but they eventually arrived at the farmhouse and came to a halt by one of the more isolated barns. 'I don't want Arkwright interfering,' said Albert, 'so best not to wake him.'

They clambered out of the van with the dogs eagerly leaping about them. Albert fetched the food and Thermos flasks and handed them to Ron. 'Hold those while I get the blanket out of the boot.'

Harvey and Monty were far too interested in the paper bag of food, so Ron shoved it deep into his poacher's coat pocket. 'Will ye behave, ye heathens? he hissed. 'To be sure, ye have a job to do, so concentrate, or none of us will be paid.'

Albert pulled the evidence sack from the boot, handed it to Aston and took charge of one of the heavy-duty torches before leading the way out of the farmyard.

Ron clicked his fingers and the dogs stayed at his heels as if sensing something was up and it was important they behave. He followed Albert and Aston across the rough field where a few sheep were quietly dozing, and waited for the dogs to get over the stile.

The world was in monochrome, for the sky was now pearly grey, the air so still and bitterly cold he could see the mist of his breath, and that of the panting animals. Deep shadows lay in the ruts and folds of the fields, pooling beneath the stands of wind-sculpted trees and frosted grass, and somewhere close by a robin was welcoming the dawn.

'There it is,' said Albert, pointing.

Ron ordered the dogs to sit and wait as he shone his torch over the lethal barbed wire and the gorse decorated with more wire. 'I'm not letting my dogs go in there,' he said firmly. 'Their feet will get cut to ribbons.'

'Well, they're not going to do much good here, are they, Ron?' replied an exasperated Albert. 'You'll have to carry them in if you're going to be so fussy.'

Ron glowered at Albert – the man should have been more caring about his dogs. He tucked the Thermos into another of his pockets and lifted Harvey into his strong arms. 'Aston, you take Monty. He's lighter, but more inclined to wriggle,' he ordered.

Once he'd made certain both dogs were securely held, he hitched Harvey on to his hip and made his way over the barbed wire and through the tangle of undergrowth and gorse.

Harvey dangled like a dead weight beneath his arm and snorted with disgust at having to be carried, but Monty seemed to be enjoying himself and as the younger man carried him over his shoulders, he kept licking his face.

As Ron caught sight of the caravan, his heart filled with pity for the wee girl who'd hidden away here. How terrified she must have been to go to such lengths to avoid discovery. He stepped round the final gorse bush and came face to face with the young policeman, who looked scared out of his wits.

'No need to be alarmed, fella. We've brought you breakfast.'

The boy relaxed and gave a sickly grin when he saw PC Aston and his sergeant. 'Nothing to report, Sarge,' he said, the colour slowly returning to his face. 'But I'm frozen solid and starving.'

Ron and Aston gently lowered the dogs to the ground and they immediately went to hunt in the undergrowth, no doubt scenting rats and mice and all manner of things.

'To heel, the pair of you,' barked Ron.

Harvey pricked his ears and came immediately, but Monty was still engrossed in something he'd come across amongst the nettles.

'Heel, I said. Now, Monty!'

The young dog reluctantly left his treasure hunt to slink towards him and sit remorsefully at his feet, amber eyes pleading for clemency.

'That's better.' Ron glared at them both. 'You have a job to do, so behave.'

Albert had given Morgan his sausage roll and flask of tea, and was now drawing out a grubby blanket from the evidence sack. 'They need to get the scent of her from this. Hopefully, we'll be able to trace her way out of here and where she went after leaving the church.'

Both dogs seemed to realise it was their turn to show what they could do when not distracted by other things, for they sat, tongues lolling, eyes bright, tails wagging, as they watched Albert approach with the blanket.

'Hold it right over their noses, Albert,' said Ron.

Harvey and Monty buried their noses in the blanket, and before anyone had time to pour the tea from the flasks, they were off.

'Aston, you stay here,' shouted Albert. 'Morgan, go back to the farmhouse and drive the van to the church. We'll meet you there.'

Ron and Albert set off behind the dogs, but within minutes they were already some distance away. Ron watched as Harvey and Monty put their noses to the ground and weaved back and forth following the scent of the girl. They paused for a while on the steep slope overlooking the town and went round in circles as if they'd lost her, but then picked up the scent again and went haring down towards the chalk farm track.

Ron glowed with pride as the animals raced down the track and danced impatiently at the gate at the bottom which was too high for them to jump. 'Good boys,' he praised, giving them both a hearty pat. 'Let them smell the blanket again, Albert, so they don't get confused with all the other scents once we get into the town.'

Once the dogs had had a fresh sniff at the blanket, Ron opened the gate and they bounded down the steep hill past the dairy and the factory estate and over the hump-backed bridge. Without faltering, they followed the invisible trail and turned into the High Street, making straight for the church.

Ron grinned, for he could hear Albert wheezing behind him as he tried to keep up.

'To be sure, Albert, you've been behind that desk for too long,' he teased as he waited for him.

'I don't usually have to go hiking at sparrow fart,' he panted, bending over and resting his hands on his knees to try and catch his breath. 'Shouldn't you be keeping those dogs in your sights, Ron? They could be anywhere by now.'

'They'll be at the church waiting for us,' he replied, digging into his coat pocket for his pipe and roll of tobacco. 'There's no hurry.'

Albert didn't look convinced, but he was glad to wait until Ron had filled and lit his pipe before they had to start walking again.

And as Ron had said, there were the dogs, sitting on the church steps at the feet of a clearly confused Bertie Double-Barrelled. 'I say,' he said once they were in earshot. 'I did wonder what these two were doing out alone at this time of the morning. I was about to take them across to the police station, but I see that won't be necessary now.'

'It's all in hand, Bertie,' said Albert pompously. 'You carry on with your warden duties. We'll take care of things now.'

Bertie was about to let himself into the church when Albert grasped his shoulder. 'Keep schtum about this, Bertie. Don't want half the town finding out what we're up to.' He tapped the side of his nose and winked.

'But what exactly *are* you up to?' asked a puzzled Bertie.

'We're tracking the girl to see if we can find where she went. The dogs have got a good scent so far and we're just hoping they don't lose it from here on.'

'Ah. Jolly good show. Carry on.' Bertie went into the church and shut the door.

'Silly old duffer,' mumbled Albert. 'Still thinks he's on the parade ground.'

'To be sure, he's a fine wee man,' retorted Ron, 'and I'll not be having you making fun of him, Albert. Now, let the beasts have a good long sniff of that blanket again and see where they take us.'

The dogs eagerly picked up the scent and followed it to the war memorial, then put their noses to the ground and trotted through the garden of remembrance. They followed a narrow lane which ran between the houses and slowly climbed towards the hills again.

Albert groaned. 'Don't tell me we're going back up there.'

'It looks like it,' said Ron. 'I'll go ahead if you want to stay here. If they find anything or lose the scent, I'll come back for you.'

'Well, if you're sure,' he murmured, sinking gratefully on to someone's garden wall. 'In fact, I might go and see where Morgan's got to with the van.'

Ron nodded, suspecting Albert was actually planning to sneak back to the station to warm up and drink his tea. He strode out up the rough lane. It was quite an adventure really, and now the sun was rising, the day was promising to be beautiful, if rather cold.

He kept the dogs within his sight and tried to work out where the girl had been heading. The station was behind him, the nearest bus stop several miles away on the main road to Seahaven, and if she was local, why hadn't she headed for home? Someone must have missed her unless she'd made up a damned good story to cover her absence.

It was a puzzle. The general thought was that she was local, and as it didn't look as if she'd gone straight home, then perhaps she'd arranged for someone to wait for her up here – or had she hidden a car somewhere? Thumbing a lift probably wasn't on her agenda as she wouldn't have wanted to risk being seen until she was well away from Cliffehaven, and at that hour of the morning there wouldn't have been much passing traffic. But if the dogs were still following the right scent – and he had to hope they were – then all that lay ahead of them was more hills, the track down to Tamarisk Bay, the main road to Seahaven and the county town.

His heart was thudding as he made the long, steep climb, and he had to pause to catch his breath as he reached the top. It seemed he was getting out of condition, for not so long ago he'd tackled this hill with ease. 'To be sure, Ronan, you're showing your age, old fella,' he panted mournfully.

The sound of excited barking snapped him from his thoughts, and he shielded his eyes from the glare of the rising sun to try and make out where it was coming from. And then he saw Harvey galloping towards him looking very pleased with himself.

Harvey gave a commanding bark and shot back to where Monty was dancing about, waiting for him halfway down the hill.

Ron frowned and slowly followed him, wondering what on earth they'd found to make them so excited. If it was a rabbit warren or a dead badger they'd dug up, he wouldn't be best pleased after all the effort it had taken to get this far.

However, as he drew nearer, he saw that both dogs were sitting by a natural grassy bowl in the side of the hill. Sheltered by gorse and half hidden by a mound of flints and chalk shards, it was unremarkable and unlikely to cause curiosity to any passing walker.

Both dogs got to their feet, tails wagging and tongues lolling, so Ron fed them another dog biscuit from his pocket and ordered them to sit while he went to inspect what they'd found. On looking closer, it was clear that the flints and lumps of chalk had been carefully stacked to hide the deep hollow which lay at the back of the grassy bowl and beneath the roots of the wild gorse.

Having removed them, he sat back on his heels and regarded the pile of grubby clothes which had been stuffed in there. Knowing not to touch them, he found a stick to prod them apart and discovered an old army greatcoat; a stained pair of corduroy dungarees that could only fit a boy or a young woman; three sweaters; a woolly hat and, last but not least, a sturdy pair of walking boots that looked as if they'd done a good deal of service. 'Well, well, well,' he murmured. 'You *were* prepared, weren't you?'

He turned to give each dog a good deal of praise and a thorough pat before giving them another biscuit. 'It's a grand job you've done, boys. Well done.' He got to his feet. 'Now you sit and guard that lot while I get Albert up here. It might take a while, so have another biscuit while you wait.'

The biscuits went down with alacrity, and the dogs settled with their noses on their paws to wait for his return.

Doris woke that Saturday morning to the delicious aroma of frying bacon and the sound of John moving about downstairs. She climbed out of bed, still suffering from the aftermath of too many gins and the previous day's drama, but tremendously relieved that life seemed to have returned to normal.

Taking off the hairnet that kept her permed hair in order during the night, she drew on her warm dressing gown and slippers, quickly used the bathroom and went downstairs, praying that John was in a better frame of mind and not inclined to drag up yesterday's fall-out. If he did, she decided, she would remind him that coming home drunk and incapable was hardly saintly, and not at all what she expected of him.

John had washed and shaved and was dressed in his usual weekend attire of smart slacks, shirt and sweater, over which he'd donned her frilly apron which she found quite endearing.

As she entered the kitchen, he shot her a rueful smile and then lifted the rashers of bacon from the pan and placed them on plates he was warming beneath the eye-level grill. 'I thought we could both do with a decent breakfast,' he said, breaking eggs into the pan and avoiding her gaze.

'That sounds wonderful and smells delicious,' she replied, sitting at the small kitchen table where the pot of tea was waiting to be poured. She noted that he'd made no move to kiss her like he usually did every morning but accepted that he was probably as embarrassed as she after last night. She didn't really know what to say to him since he seemed as unwilling as she was to broach the subject, so remained silent as she filled their cups and added a dash of milk.

John turned from the stove and placed the plates of bacon, egg, tomato and fried bread on the table before sitting down. He kept his gaze fixed on the table. 'I don't think either of us needs – or wants – to return to the distressing events of yesterday,' he said softly. 'It's a new day, and I for one would like to begin again.'

'Me too,' she replied, reaching for his hand.

He finally looked at her and gave her fingers a loving squeeze. 'Good,' he murmured before picking up his knife and fork. 'Tuck in before it gets cold, and then I thought we could go into town to finish our Christmas shopping and perhaps pop into Plummer's for a late lunch. Have you any idea what to buy for the grandchildren?'

Doris's heart was full of thankfulness that the rocky moment in their marriage seemed to be over. 'Toys, probably,' she replied before tucking into the delicious breakfast. 'And, of course, some little things for their stockings. They'll expect Santa to visit even though they're away from home.'

'It will be lovely to see them again after so long,' he said. 'I wish for both our sakes that they didn't live so far away.'

'Anthony has to go where his work is,' she replied, 'but I agree, I do wish we had more to do with our grandchildren. Peggy's very lucky in that respect, really,' she added wistfully.

'Talking of Peggy, I'm reminded that we promised to take sherry and mince pies on Boxing Day. Have you got that in hand, dearest?'

Her heart sang at his endearment. 'Oh, yes, my love,' she murmured. 'All in hand.'

Peggy was having a similar conversation with Jim as they ate their cereal and toast in the kitchen. 'I've spent an absolute fortune on Daisy and the other children, so I've warned Anne there will only be token presents for her and Martin,' she said. 'The trouble is, there's so little choice of things to buy in the shops, and what there is, is expensive or takes numerous ration stamps.'

'It is a problem,' Jim agreed. 'Especially as there are so many of us now. Have you heard from Doreen? Is she still coming with her three?'

'Yes, and I've warned her too that there won't be much in the way of presents for her if the girls and little Archie are to have something nice.'

'I really do think that it's getting to the stage where the adults go without,' he replied, slathering margarine on his toast. 'Christmas is for children, after all.'

'Oh no,' retorted a horrified Peggy. 'Christmas wouldn't be the same if there weren't presents all round, and I'm sure Charlie and Bob would be as devastated as darling Cordelia if they got nothing at all.'

'Well, I hope you don't go overboard and spend too much,' he muttered. 'January is just around the corner and all the bills will be coming in thick and fast.'

'I've saved a fair bit from my wages,' she said, 'so no one has to go short.'

He grinned at her over the table. 'So what did you get me, then?'

She giggled. 'That would be telling.'

'Good heavens,' muttered Cordelia as she came into the room and propped her walking stick over the back of a chair. 'Billing and cooing at this time of the morning is a bit much.' She plonked herself down on the chair and grinned. 'Nice to see it though,' she added.

'Good morning to you, Cordy,' said Jim with a twinkle in his eyes. 'You seem to be in fine fettle this morning. Are you all ready for Christmas?'

'Bertie's taking me shopping later,' she replied, struggling to lift the teapot and giving up. 'Would you mind, Jim? Only my hands aren't cooperating this morning.'

Jim poured out the tea and then went to make a hot-water bottle for her arthritic hands. 'You'll have to make sure you keep your gloves on and wrap up well, Cordy. It was quite bitter out there when I covered up the hen house. In fact, I was thinking it might be a good idea to have them indoors for the winter as there are only two now.'

Peggy stared at him in astonishment. 'And where exactly would you put them?'

'I thought the basement,' he said blithely. 'I could rig up something from that spare wood Da's keeping in his shed at Havelock Road, to keep them comfortable, warm and laying.'

'Over my dead body,' Peggy replied fiercely. 'My lovely laundry room and extra bathroom are sacrosanct, and not to be polluted by hen's feathers, poo and straw bedding. I had enough of all that when Ron kept his blasted ferrets in his bedroom.'

'Fair enough,' he replied with a shrug. 'But if you want them to survive, they can't stay out there.'

'I don't see why not. The other chickens got through the winters as well as the bombs and air raids, and I'm sure Chalky didn't cosset those two. They stay where they are, Jim, and that's an end to it.'

'Well, it seems the situation is back to normal as you're both arguing,' said Cordelia tartly. 'How is Daisy this morning?'

'Much better and starting to want to get out of bed more often,' Peggy replied. 'I'll probably bring her downstairs later while you're out with Bertie as the rash is almost gone and the doctor says she's no longer infectious.'

'Well, that's good,' Cordelia said. 'I've missed having her around.' She eyed the empty chair. 'Charlie out already? It's a bit early for him, isn't it?'

'Jack's got a rush job on so he's helping out before he goes off to rugby practice,' Jim replied. 'Then he's off with his pals to the cinema.'

Jim grinned as he wrapped the hot-water bottle in a tea towel and placed it on her knees. 'I get the feeling there's a girl he's interested in. Her name keeps cropping up in conversations.'

'Yes, I've noticed that too,' said Peggy. 'It's probably time you had a talk with him, Jim. Man to man, if you know what I mean. We don't want any slip-ups.'

Jim looked uncomfortable. 'I'm sure he knows enough about the birds and bees without me having to do that,' he protested.

'It's not the birds and bees I'm worried about,' she replied. 'It's youthful high spirits and untapped passions. You and I both know where that leads, Jim Reilly.' She shot him a meaningful look.

Jim squirmed in his chair. 'Yes, well, all right. But what do I say? Where do I even start, Peg? I didn't have to do it with Bob, and he seems to be coping without my guidance.'

'You were in Burma and he was in Somerset when that conversation should have taken place,' said Peggy evenly. 'I've no doubt that living on a farm taught him all he needed to know, and Auntie Vi probably filled in the rest.'

'Is he still coming for Christmas?' asked Cordelia hopefully.

'I haven't heard anything to the contrary, but Auntie Vi won't be with him which is a shame. She's crippled with arthritis now and finds travelling too difficult.'

'So how many are we actually feeding over the holiday, Peg?' asked Jim, clearly relieved to change the subject.

'Christmas Day is the five of us plus Bertie Double-Barrelled, Bob, Cissy, Doreen, her two girls and little Archie – who probably isn't that little any more. I've also asked Ruby and Jack Smith to join us for lunch, and Ron and Rosie will come in the afternoon. Martin and Anne are spending the day at home and will be with us on Boxing Day with their three, as will Doris and John, Suzy, Anthony and the two little ones.' She bit her lip. 'I think that's everyone.'

'It sounds as if we're feeding a ruddy army,' muttered Jim. 'God help us with all those children rampaging about the house. And where's all the food coming from?'

'Bob's bringing a joint of beef, sausages, pickles, a can of cream, and two of Vi's gorgeous Christmas puddings. Doreen is bringing ham, cheese, port and savoury biscuits, and Ruby's providing a small keg of beer and a bottle of gin. Cissy promised to bring down a proper iced cake, but I've ordered one from the bakery just in case she forgets. Neither will go to waste, I'm sure.'

She took a breath and studied the long list she'd made. 'Doris is bringing sherry and mince pies – I have no idea if Suzy will also donate to the cause, but I'd be surprised if she didn't. I've also ordered a turkey, and Ron gave me four ducks as well as a huge lump of mutton which I've made into a stew that will do us until Christmas Eve.'

Jim gave a low whistle. 'Well, you certainly seem organised, Peg, my love,' he murmured. 'You'd have been a whizz as an army caterer, and that's a fact.'

Peggy just smiled and didn't let on that she was frazzled by all the organisation it was taking, and fretting over whether she really ought to buy another Christmas pudding – if there were any to still be had this close to Christmas.

9

Sandra had moved into their spare bedroom which, thankfully, had a lock and key so she wouldn't be forced to confront her husband and his insidious determination to change her mind about the divorce. The nasty bout of food poisoning she'd caught while away still lingered, and combined with the stress of trying to be free from her marriage, she was left feeling completely washed out. Over the following days she'd avoided Graham by staying in the room until he'd left the house, and then spent long hours wandering the streets of London with her thoughts and emotions in turmoil. Returning late at night to slip into the single bed and lie exhausted but unable to sleep, she suspected Graham was also awake on the other side of the wall.

Graham had kept his promise and said nothing about her decision to file for divorce, but it was clear that he was doing his utmost to change her mind, with his sad eyes haunting her every time they passed each other on the landing or in the hall, and little notes left outside her bedroom door with a single rose or a sprig of heather. Yet she couldn't allow herself to weaken as she'd done so many times before, for the life-changing decision Margot had helped her make was something she was now determined to stick to.

His reproachful looks and deep sighs made her feel absolutely wretched, but she had no doubt that she was doing the right thing – especially after what she'd learnt the previous day. There was much to organise if she was to carry out her plan, but Christmas was fast approaching, so everything had to be put on hold, which was utterly frustrating. She just hoped that once they'd all returned from Aunt Gloria's she would be more clear-headed and physically capable of seeing things through.

It was now two days before Christmas, and they would be meeting her mother, Beryl, at the station for the journey down to Gloria's later that morning. Sandra was dreading it, for although she'd spoken regularly to her mother on the telephone, she'd managed to avoid seeing her, knowing that her mother's nose for trouble would be twitching the instant she laid eyes on her. Yet it couldn't be avoided – much like the newspapers that came thudding through the letter box each morning with their distressing stories and photographs of the abandoned baby.

She finished packing and eyed her reflection in the long mirror behind the bedroom door. The corset was a bit too tight but it sculpted the curve of her hips beneath the oatmeal woollen dress and made her look svelte. The short fur jacket was a deep brown which would set the dress off nicely, and she'd chosen brown high-heeled pumps to match. Fake pearls in her ears and in a single string round her neck finished off the look. With her fair hair freshly set at her favourite City salon, she looked remarkably well considering the terrible state she was in. Giving a sigh, she picked up her jacket, handbag and gloves, and carried her case downstairs to the hall.

Graham was busy in the kitchen that looked out over the back garden. He turned from the stove with a determinedly cheery smile. 'All set? I've done us boiled eggs and toast. I didn't think you'd want anything too heavy before as you don't travel well on trains.'

'That's thoughtful, thanks,' she said coolly, sitting at the table. Her gaze fell on the newspaper which lay open to yet another article about the baby – the sweet little motherless baby. It was all far too painful, so she folded the paper and shoved it to one side.

'You're looking lovely this morning,' said Graham, placing the two boiled eggs and toast on the table before sitting down to tuck in.

Sandra felt far from lovely but accepted the compliment with a brief nod.

'I see the papers are still trying to find that girl,' he said, dipping a finger of buttered toast into the egg's runny core.

Sandra really didn't want to discuss it, but Graham seemed to be obsessed by the story. She kept her expression noncommittal and her tone cool. 'You'd think they had more important things to report. Surely it's old news by now?'

Graham reached for the folded newspaper and opened it out on the table between them. 'There are new leads as to who she might be,' he said. 'And look, Sandra – look where she'd been hiding. Isn't that the old caravan you used to play in?'

She gave the black and white photograph of the rotting caravan a quick glance and skimmed quickly over the one of the baby being held in Rachel Goldman's arms, and was unable to answer.

But Graham seemed determined to fill the silence and air his opinions. 'I really can't understand any woman leaving her baby like that,' he said before biting into his toast. 'She must have had a very serious reason for doing such a desperate thing, don't you think?'

Sandra noted the vicarious gleam in his eyes and concentrated on eating her breakfast. 'I agree,' she murmured, 'and no doubt, if and when she's found, it will all be explained.' She reached for her cup of tea, noted how unsteady her hand was and gave up on the idea.

'You don't seem to be very touched by the story, Sandra,' he said, his steady gaze holding her. 'I would have thought you'd at least feel something for the baby if not for the poor girl. After all, my love, it does rather bring home the fact that we shall never have a baby of our own, but that girl, for whatever reason, has simply walked away from hers as if it meant nothing.'

Sandra's stomach clenched and it was as if icy fingers were running down her spine. She felt far more than Graham could ever imagine, and it was all she could do not to scream at him. 'I very much doubt she just walked away,' she managed. 'And of course I feel for them both. What woman wouldn't?'

'It'll be interesting to hear what the local opinions are,' mused Graham, returning to his boiled egg. 'It says in the paper that Ronan Reilly and his dogs were the ones to find the clothes she'd hidden. I wonder if they held any clues that the newspapers haven't released?'

Sandra's stomach rebelled and she pushed back from the table to dash to the downstairs cloakroom, and only just made it in time.

'Sandra? Sandra, whatever's the matter? Have I said something to upset you?'

'Go away, Graham,' she managed before her stomach heaved once more. 'Just go away and shut up about that girl. I don't want to hear any more about it.' She slammed the door shut and was violently ill again.

It was six in the morning and Cissy was feeling ghastly. She dragged herself out of bed, caught sight of her face in the ornate dressing-table mirror and quickly turned away. The late-night parties, troubled dreams, and long days of negotiating the hellish traffic in the city were taking their toll after the ordeal she'd already suffered. And to top it all, Clarissa and the others were beginning to complain that she wasn't pulling her weight. In fact, there had been several cutting and hurtful remarks, which she'd felt had been most unfair considering they all knew why she'd been away – and had colluded to keep it secret.

The recurring thought that perhaps her time in London was coming to an end, and she should think about cashing in her investment to find something else to do far from this catty bunch, was something she didn't want to dwell on this morning – although in the past few weeks the idea had certainly become ever more enticing.

She opened the door and padded barefoot across the deserted sitting room to the hallway to collect the morning newspaper and, without looking at the headlines, went into her en suite and turned the gold taps until the hot water was gushing into the deep marble bath. Perching on a padded stool, she added sweet-smelling pink bath salts and let her thoughts wander as the bath filled.

Knowing it was important to at least pretend she was fully recovered, and placate the others, she'd been reluctantly coerced into chauffeuring one of their most demanding clients around London today before driving her to her country pile in Surrey. It would mean an early start and a very late night back, but that suited her as she could avoid yet another party and prepare herself for the dreaded journey down to Cliffehaven the next morning.

Cissy turned off the taps, tested the fragrant water with a toe, and then slid into the bath with a sigh of pleasure. It was still very early, so she could soak for a while, peruse the headlines and get herself into the right frame of mind to be able to deal with the ridiculously rich American woman who'd snared herself a titled husband and was spending millions on bringing his rambling ruin of a country mansion back to its former glory.

Still, she thought, it shouldn't be too arduous, as she'd probably spend most of her time waiting outside Harrods, John Lewis and Selfridges, before carting her off to the Ritz for lunch and later, to Browns for afternoon tea. The routine was the same for most wealthy Americans, it seemed, but at least the old trout tipped generously and wouldn't insist upon driving past Buck House in the hope of seeing someone royal, as she'd already dined with the King twice.

Feeling rather more cheerful after that inner rant, she plucked the newspaper from the padded stool and glanced over the headlines which showed a photograph of the Nazi doctors who were standing trial at Nuremberg. A shorter piece discussed which car was the most prestigious between the Rolls and the Bentley, and the advertisements were for a particular brand of cigarette that was supposed to be good for the heart and lungs, and another extolling the virtues of Pears soap.

Cissy flicked through the thin pages until she caught sight of a narrow column down one side of an inner page. She discarded the rest of the paper and tried to read what it said beneath the photograph of the dilapidated caravan and the clothing that had been found by her grandfather in the hills, but her hands were shaking so badly, she could barely make out the words.

Tossing the flimsy sheet across the bathroom, she watched it settle on to the floor. She'd hoped that all the fuss would have died down by now, but it seemed that even the London dailies were still running with it, though thankfully off the front page.

She slid down into the soothing hot water and closed her eyes. Considering what she'd gone through and how fragile she was feeling, the constant and upsetting coverage was too much. And the knowledge that by tomorrow night she'd be in Cliffehaven and probably have to hear all about it – endlessly – was almost enough to make her change her mind about going. But she had to face it out, act the part that was almost becoming second nature – and hope to any god that might be watching that her mother never found out the truth.

Gracie was really frightened now. The bleeding wouldn't stop, the dull pains in her lower belly were intensifying, and no matter how many times she washed, there was a horrid smell she simply couldn't get rid of. She managed to get out of bed and stagger to the bathroom at the end of the hall. Something was very wrong, but she dared not confide in Flo who was already asking too many questions about her lingering ill health, or risk going to see the doctor. She could only be thankful that Peggy Reilly wasn't coming into the factory every day, for her eyes missed nothing and she wouldn't be so easily fobbed off.

It took a tremendous effort to wash and dress in her usual dungarees and sweaters, but having made herself look as presentable as possible, she went to find Flo and little Bobby who were eating breakfast. She avoided Flo's worried gaze and kissed the brown curls on her small son's head before dredging up the brightest smile she could muster.

'Are you looking forward to school today?'

Bobby nodded, his face alight with excitement. 'Santa's coming,' he breathed.

'Well, isn't that exciting?' Gracie managed as she sat down at the table and took a welcome slurp of hot tea. 'What do you think he'll bring you?'

'I hope it's a kite,' he said, his eyes shining. 'A big red kite with a long yellow tail.' He stuffed some porridge into his mouth and quickly swallowed it. 'If he does bring me a kite, will you teach me how to fly it?'

'Of course I will,' she replied. 'And I'm sure Auntie Flo would love to come with us too.' She kept her smile fixed as she turned to Flo. 'Isn't that right?'

'Indeed I would,' she replied, her eyes still questioning. 'But if Bobby isn't going to be late for Santa, you'd better get a move on, Gracie.'

'Oh, goodness,' she breathed after glancing at the kitchen clock. 'Come on, Bobby, finish your porridge quickly while I find my coat and bag.'

She ignored the gnawing pain in her belly and the swirling in her head as she hurried into the narrow hallway to get her outdoor shoes and overcoat. Bundling up against the cold that was icing the inside of the windows, she turned to help her son. Ramming a woolly hat over his ears and tying the knitted scarf around his neck, she helped him with his gloves and reached for the latch.

'I'll see you at the factory, Flo,' she called over her shoulder, and quickly shut the door.

It was bitterly cold, with everything covered in sparkling frost which she might have thought pretty if she hadn't been in such awful pain. She held on to Bobby's hand as they headed for Camden Road and the junior school. Pausing by the gate, she had to lean against the railings as the world seemed to be tilting beneath her feet and making her giddy.

'Are you all right, Gracie?' asked one of the other mothers with concern.

'I'm fine, really,' she replied, shooting her a forced smile. 'Just missed breakfast.' She gave Bobby a hug and a kiss. 'Have a lovely day, sweetheart,' she murmured before he ran off to join his friends.

'Are you sure you're all right?' the other woman persisted.

Gracie blinked to try and keep her in focus. 'I'm fine, really.' She hurried away before the woman could ask any more questions.

She managed to stagger back the way she'd come and negotiate the labyrinth of narrow alleyways that led to Flo's spacious ground-floor flat. The pain was worse now, stabbing at her insides and making her gasp.

She stumbled to the back door, praying that Flo had already left for the factory, but the world was tilting and whirling, and she could barely see to put her key in the lock. Staggering like a drunk, she knocked against the dustbin and the metal lid fell to the brick path with an ear-shattering clang before somehow getting under her feet just as the world spun out of control. She fell, her breath punched from her lungs as she hit the unyielding ground.

'Gracie? Oh, lawks, Gracie. I knew you weren't right. Let me get you inside.'

Gracie couldn't move and was almost bent double with pain as she lay helplessly on the icy ground. 'I'll be all right in a minute,' she moaned.

'Stuff and nonsense. You're far from all right,' snapped Florence in a tone that brooked no argument. She put her hands beneath Gracie's armpits and lifted her to her feet.

The dagger of agony made Gracie cry out, and her legs buckled beneath her.

Florence hauled her up again and carried her into the flat, slamming the door behind her before the nosy neighbours started to twitch their curtains. 'It's a good thing you don't weigh much, Gracie,' she panted, awkwardly settling her on to the couch.

Gracie struggled to sit up. 'There's blood, Flo,' she sobbed, feeling it warm and sticky on her thighs. 'It'll stain the couch.'

'Don't worry about that.' Florence gently eased her back and put a cushion under her knees. 'Stay there. I'm phoning the doctor.'

'No! No, please. Not the doctor,' she pleaded in panic.

Florence eyed her thoughtfully. 'What have you done, Gracie?' Her voice was low, her gaze penetrating.

Gracie looked away and shook her head. 'I can't tell you,' she whispered before once again curling into the awful stabbing pains.

Florence was silent for a long moment and then took a shuddering breath. 'I'll telephone the factory to let Mavis know I won't be in, and then I'm calling Sister Danuta. I get the feeling she'll know what all this is about.'

Gracie stayed curled in a miserable huddle, knowing that her secret was about to come out, but unable to do anything about it. The pain was all-consuming now, but the fear of perhaps dying and leaving Bobby alone in the world was far greater than the fear of what would happen to her when her unforgivable sin was discovered.

'Sister Danuta is evidently round at one of our neighbours. I'll pop out and get her,' said Florence, returning to the tiny sitting room with an armful of blankets. Tucking them over and around Gracie, she placed the back of her hand on her forehead. 'Good grief, Gracie, you're burning up. Why the hell have you left it so long without saying anything?'

The tears streamed down Gracie's hot little face. 'Because I was frightened you'd throw me and Bobby out,' she sobbed.

Florence stroked back the damp hair from her forehead. 'Why ever would I do that, you silly girl?' she murmured. 'Oh, Gracie. If only you'd confided in me. I would have helped, and made sure you didn't have to go through all this on your own.'

Gracie frowned. 'I don't understand,' she whispered.

'I've been suspicious ever since you got back, and put two and two together.' Florence pulled on her coat and lit the gas fire. 'No more talking now,' she soothed. 'I'm off to find Danuta.'

Danuta had just finished bandaging old Mr Grey's leg ulcers when there was a knock on the door. 'That's probably Fred. You sit and drink the tea I made you.' She smiled at the old man in the hope he'd smile back, but he was his usual grumpy self and didn't oblige.

She made her way carefully around the piles of old newspapers and bags of assorted rubbish Mr Grey refused to throw away and went to the door, expecting to see his neighbour, Fred, who came in each morning to keep him company. But it was a tall, attractive woman in her forties, looking very agitated.

'Can I help you?' she asked with a frown.

'I'm Florence Hillier,' the woman explained quickly. 'I live in the next block with Gracie Smith and her small boy. Gracie needs you urgently.'

'What's the matter?'

'I can't explain on the doorstep,' replied Florence, catching sight of Fred ambling towards them. 'But I assure you, it's urgent.'

'I have finished here, so I'll just get my bag.'

Danuta hurried back indoors, packed her medical bag and said goodbye to Mr Grey and Fred who were settling down to have a good old moan and put the world to rights. She closed the door behind her and saw Florence Hillier anxiously shuffling from one foot to the other by the garden gate.

Florence set off immediately when she saw Danuta come out of the flat. She set a rapid pace as she strode down the narrow road, and Danuta had to almost run to keep up with her. It was only when the other woman suddenly turned in through a gate and hesitated at the front door that Danuta was able to speak to her.

'What has happened to your friend? She has had an accident?'

'No accident,' Florence replied agitatedly. She lowered her voice and spoke rapidly. 'But something's very wrong – has been for a week now – and I suspect she's had an abortion.'

Danuta stared at her as the words sank in. 'That is a serious assumption. What makes you think such a thing?'

Florence wrung her hands. 'She's been away for almost three weeks, bursts into tears every time the abandoned baby is mentioned, and hasn't been at all well ever since she came home.'

Danuta absorbed this information, the alarm rising. 'Do you know if she is bleeding heavily?'

Florence nodded. 'She admitted to it this morning and is in a very bad way. I wanted to call the doctor but she absolutely refuses to see him.' Tears glistened in her eyes. 'But she needs medical help, Danuta, and I didn't know who else to call.'

Danuta nodded, her thoughts in turmoil as Florence unlocked the door. If this Gracie Smith had really had an abortion, then she would indeed need help, but first it was most important to establish the facts and find out exactly what was going on.

She followed Florence into the narrow, dingy hall, and was led into a warm sitting room crammed with large furniture. One look at the shivering girl curled up in blankets told her that she was indeed very ill. She slipped off her gabardine mac and woollen scarf, and set them aside on a nearby armchair.

'Florence, would you please fetch me a bowl of hot water, some soap and a towel and then stay in the other room while I examine her?'

Florence hurried away, and once the door between them was shut, Danuta approached the girl on the couch and squatted down to ease the blanket below the girl's chin so she could see her properly. She looked far worse than Danuta had first thought. 'Hello, Gracie. I'm Danuta the district nurse,' she said calmly. 'And I am here to help you.'

Frightened, bloodshot grey eyes regarded her as she touched her hot forehead, and then felt for the pulse in her slender wrist. 'You have high temperature, and your pulse is too rapid,' Danuta murmured. 'Are you in a lot of pain?'

The girl nodded and placed her hands over her lower abdomen. 'Sharp, awful pains, and losing lots of blood,' she managed before bursting into tears.

Florence came in with the bowl and towel and placed them on the floor beside Danuta, shooting a worried look at Gracie, then went back to the other room, shutting the door firmly behind her.

Danuta washed her hands thoroughly before drying them. 'Let me examine you, Gracie. I will be very gentle, but it is necessary to find out what is happening to you.'

Gracie held the blankets tightly to her. 'I know Flo's worried, but it isn't what she thinks, honest it isn't,' she sobbed.

Danuta held her gaze for a long moment, her thoughts going into directions she really didn't want to follow. 'All right, Gracie, I believe you,' she replied eventually. 'But I still have to examine you. Can you remove your clothes from the waist down, or do you need help?'

'I can do it,' she said between sobs. 'But it's not very nice down there, and I must have made a terrible mess on the couch.' She struggled beneath the blankets and finally flopped back into the cushions.

Danuta switched on the standard lamp so she could see better and asked Gracie to raise her knees. It took less than a minute to learn the truth, and the realisation made her want to weep with pity and utter frustration.

She eased the girl's knees down and covered her again in the blankets. 'I will have to telephone the doctor, Gracie. I'm sorry, but I cannot help you on my own.'

Gracie sat bolt upright and grabbed her hand. 'No! No doctor! Only you – please, only you, Danuta,' she pleaded.

Danuta's heart ached as she looked into Gracie's distraught little face. 'I know what you've done, Gracie, and it's left you with a very bad infection,' she said quietly.

'Can't you give me some pills, or something?'

Danuta shook her head. 'I can clean you up and make you more comfortable, but the infection could have spread further, and only a doctor can deal with that and prescribe the correct treatment. If this is not dealt with very soon, it might mean you have to lose your womb. At worst, you could die.'

The silence between them was heavy with foreboding.

'You must think of your little boy,' Danuta urged. 'What is his name?'

'Bobby,' she replied, her voice small and frightened, her big grey eyes filled with terror.

'Bobby does not want to lose his mother, Gracie. It is for his sake you must get proper treatment.'

'But . . . I can't – I can't let the doctor see. He'll report me to the authorities, and they'll take my Bobby away.'

'I doubt they would do that,' Danuta soothed, even though she knew it would have to be reported sooner rather than later.

'What will happen to me?' Gracie whimpered as the pain ripped through her.

'You'll be given the very best medical care once Dr Darwin has seen you and arranged for you to go into hospital,' said Danuta.

Flo came into the room at that moment with a second basin of water. 'Oh, Gracie, you silly, silly girl. Why didn't you say something to me before it got to this stage?'

'I was too ashamed,' she admitted, the tears rolling down her face. 'And terrified you'd chuck me and Bobby on to the streets.' She broke into almost hysterical sobs as the agonising pains shot through her.

'It is best you go back to the kitchen, Florence. I will do what I can for her now, but she needs to be in hospital where they'll conduct the right procedure and prescribe the appropriate medicines.'

Florence nodded, squeezed Gracie's hand and then left the room.

Danuta carefully washed Gracie and made her as comfortable as possible. She finally stepped back from the couch and reached for her coat. 'I will go and speak to the doctor, and make arrangement for you to be admitted to hospital,' she said solemnly. 'It is the only possible way you will recover from this.'

Gracie pulled the blanket over her head and keened with anguish.

Danuta gave the narrow shoulder a gentle squeeze of comfort, picked up her bag and went to tell Florence to stay with her until she returned. Letting herself out of the house minutes later, she hurried to her car and climbed in, but then just sat there staring out, her mind reeling from all she'd witnessed.

She realised that this was a defining moment in her career as a midwife and district nurse. She would have risked keeping quiet and doing all she could for Gracie if there weren't other factors involved and the risk to her health wasn't so great. But she really had no choice but to seek Dr Darwin's help – and he in turn would have to inform the authorities.

It meant that patient confidentiality couldn't be kept, and that would mean mistrust not only from Gracie, but from her other patients who until this moment had come to her with their most private secrets and fears. Danuta had worked hard to gain their trust, but once word of this got out, as it surely would, it would do untold damage not only to Gracie, but to her own reputation.

She snapped out of her thoughts and turned the key in the ignition. She had a job to do and sitting here worrying about her career and reputation wasn't doing Gracie any good at all.

10

Peggy had a very busy day ahead of her, so she'd risen early to finish preparing the spare rooms before everyone woke and started demanding breakfast. She'd decided that Bob could go into the single bedroom off the entrance hall that she and Jim had shared when Beach View was being run as a boarding house, and that Cissy could have her old bedroom which was between Cordelia's and Daisy's on the first floor, which left the large family room at the top of the house next to Charlie for Doreen, her two girls and Archie the toddler. Jim had already brought the cot down from the attic and put it together – albeit with a great deal of swearing – so it was just a case of making the beds and giving each room a jolly good sweep and dust.

She had just finished the big room under the eaves when Charlie wandered in and eyed it all with little appreciation. 'I think I might move out to Grandad and Rosie's,' he said with a frown. 'If Doreen's lot are as bad as Anne's were when they stayed here, I won't get any peace.'

'I'm sure they won't be,' Peggy soothed. 'And besides, you won't be swotting over Christmas, so I really don't know why you're complaining.'

'How long are they staying for?' he asked with his habitual early morning gloominess.

'Only for a week.' She smiled up at him, tempted to ruffle his dark hair, but managing to resist. 'If they do prove to be noisy, I suspect your father will join you at

Ron's, but it would be a pity, because it's very rare to have all my family around me.'

He nodded, dug his hands into his trouser pockets and thudded down the stairs.

Peggy clucked her tongue, then picked up the broom and basket of cleaning materials to follow him down to the first-floor landing. She could hear Jim snoring which made her smile, for he was sleeping much better since having those sessions with Ernie's doctor, and the only time he'd come close to losing control was on Guy Fawkes night when someone had let off a series of very loud bangers in the street outside that had sent him cowering down into the basement.

It didn't take long to prepare Cissy's room, and she gave a smile of pleasure at the thought of her coming home again. This room had been put to good use once Cissy had joined the WAAFs, for Suzy, Fran and Danuta had slept in here at one time or another, but it had been Jane and Sarah Fuller from Singapore who'd last occupied it, and they were now married and living in America.

The thought of her numerous evacuee chicks warmed her as she went down to the hall. All of them were married now, and although some of them lived on the other side of the world, they kept in touch with letters and cards, and sometimes little gifts which she treasured.

Peggy made up the bed for Bob, smoothed the eiderdown, and gave the pillows an extra plumping. It would be wonderful to have Bob home, even though it wouldn't be for very long, and she was eager to hear all about the girl he was courting, and how he was getting on with managing Vi's dairy farm. His few letters were woefully short on any real news, but she had to accept that although she had no real idea of what he was getting up to down in Somerset, at least he did actually bother to write occasionally.

She ran a duster over the chest of drawers, and then quickly swept the floor and replaced the rag rugs she'd given a good shake out of the window. At least there wasn't a draught howling beneath the door now she'd got Jim to tack a thick excluder to the bottom of it.

The telephone rang and, as always, she dreaded the thought it might be Cissy ringing to say she wasn't coming. 'Hello?' she asked tentatively.

'Hello, Mrs Reilly, this is Mavis Fuller.'

Peggy frowned, for she could hear the sound of the sewing machines in the background. Mavis was one of her senior machinists and had no business to be using the office telephone. 'Hello, Mavis. Is there a problem at the factory?'

'Well, I'm not sure,' she said hesitantly. 'There was no sign of Florence this morning, so I had to go up to Colonel White's office to get the keys to let everyone in. I'd only just got my coat off when Florence telephoned to say that neither she nor Gracie would be in this morning, and would I keep an eye on things for her.'

Peggy's frown deepened, for Mavis was now in charge of the factory keys which gave her access to her office, which was most irregular. And what on earth was Florence up to? 'Did she say what was keeping them home, Mavis?'

'Not really anything specific,' Mavis replied hesitantly. 'She just said something had happened which she had to see to, but she'd try to come in before we closed tonight for the Christmas holidays.'

Peggy's thoughts were in a whirl at this startling news. 'I see. Well, thank you for letting me know, Mavis. Are you sure you can cope? Or should I come in?'

'I've been here long enough to know the routine, Mrs Reilly, and if Florence doesn't make it in before we shut, I'll lock up and pop the keys through Colonel White's office letter box.'

'Thank you, Mavis. I might drop in anyway just to wish everyone a happy Christmas, but if there are any problems at all, you're to ring me immediately.'

Mavis thanked her and disconnected the call.

Peggy replaced the receiver and sniffed the air. 'Charlie, the toast is burning,' she shouted, hurrying into the kitchen to find it deserted.

With a sigh, she snatched up the blackened toast and threw it in the bin below the sink. Opening the door to the basement to let the smoke out, she saw the back door was open, so hurried down to find Charlie feeding the two hens. 'Thanks for doing that,' she said, 'but next time do try and concentrate on one thing at a time. Your toast is burnt and my kitchen stinks of it.'

Without waiting for a reply, she hurried back indoors and headed straight for the telephone. She urgently needed to speak to Florence to find out exactly what was going on, and if it had anything to do with Gracie, who still hadn't recovered from whatever ailed her since returning from her break. She dialled the number and heard the engaged tone, which was frustrating, so had no choice but to leave it for a bit before trying again.

Pacing the hall floor, she bit her lip as she wondered if she should tell Solly that Mavis was now in sole charge. Mavis was a middle-aged, reliable housewife and an old hand at a machine and quite popular with the other women – but was she made of the right stuff to be in charge, and could she be trusted with the keys to the office, the personnel files and the safe?

Turning back to the telephone, she knew she needed to speak to Florence to find out exactly what was going on before she went any further, and if she couldn't get hold of her, she'd have to go round there, and then up to the factory to take up the reins. A disaster just before Christmas had to be avoided at all costs, for there were numerous orders to fill, to package and to despatch by lunchtime if they were to arrive at their destination before everything closed down tomorrow night.

The engaged tone greeted her again, so she disconnected and rang through to the local exchange where her one-time evacuee chick, April Wilson, was now on duty. 'April, can you check a line for me, please? I'm trying to get through to Florence Hillier and keep getting the engaged tone.'

'Of course, Aunt Peggy. Just a minute.'

Peggy fidgeted as she waited, the sense that something was very wrong at Flo's house growing by the minute.

'There's no one on the line, Aunt Peggy. The receiver must have been knocked off its cradle, and no one's noticed,' said April.

'Thanks, love. And I hope you have a really lovely Christmas.'

'The same to you, Aunt Peggy. I expect you're snowed under as usual, but it'll be super to have the family around you again after so long.'

Peggy really didn't have time to chat. 'Yes, it will. Bye, April.' Feeling guilty at having cut the girl off so abruptly, she ripped off her apron and headscarf and hurried into the kitchen.

Charlie was stuffing his face with porridge while the rest bubbled in the pot on the hob. She rescued the pot and reached for her coat and scarf. 'I have to go out, Charlie,' she said, kicking off her slippers and digging her feet into her ankle boots. 'Will you warn your father I might be late for our visit to Ernie, but say that I'll do my best to get back in time? It would also be really helpful if you could take charge of Daisy until your dad gets up as she's back to her usual lively self, and I don't want her disturbing him.'

'Do I have to?' he moaned.

'Yes. You do,' she retorted, pulling on her gloves.

'What's so urgent you've got to go out at this time of the morning, Mum?'

'It's probably something and nothing, but I need to check on someone,' she replied, reaching for her handbag and cigarettes.

To avoid further questions, she hurried out of the back door into the frosty early morning. The garden path was slippery, but the rutted lane that ran between the backs of the houses was iron-hard, so she picked up her pace and headed for Flo's flat, the sense of urgency growing with every step.

She had negotiated the labyrinth of twittens that led off Camden Road and was just approaching the rear of the telephone exchange when she heard the screeching of tyres on tarmac and the roar of a racing engine. The sense of impending trouble deepened and as she reached the street where Flo lived, she saw the back of Dr Darwin's car disappear at speed towards the High Street – and Flo huddled with Danuta by the gate.

Flo turned ashen when she caught sight of Peggy. 'I meant to ring you,' she stuttered. 'But with everything that's happened this morning . . .'

'What's going on, Flo? I've had Mavis on the telephone already.'

'It is Gracie,' said Danuta who was looking unusually flustered. 'Please, Mamma Peggy, you will come inside while I explain.'

Peggy felt something akin to dread but, aware of watching neighbours, said nothing as she followed the two young women into the dimly lit hall. She waited for Flo to close the door before saying what was on her mind. 'There was more to Gracie's ill health than you were letting on, wasn't there?' she asked Flo.

Florence glanced at Danuta as if seeking permission to speak, and at her nod seemed to brace herself before revealing what had happened that morning. She told Peggy about Gracie collapsing, about the fever and the heavy bleeding. 'I could see immediately that she was in a great deal of pain,' she said. 'So I called the surgery and asked for Danuta, who luckily was only a few doors away.'

'But I saw Alistair's car driving off,' Peggy broke in.

Danuta nodded solemnly. 'I asked Dr Darwin to attend as I was concerned by the amount of blood she was losing and her high temperature. He confirmed that she has a serious internal infection, and has taken her to hospital where she will have a dilation and curettage procedure. If all goes well, she should be home again for bed rest by tomorrow night.'

Peggy knew what a D&C was and eyed them both suspiciously. 'I get the feeling there's more to this than you're telling.'

'Not at all,' protested Florence quickly. 'She has an infection, which probably set in while she was in Margate, but thinking it would clear up on its own, the silly girl did nothing about it. Now it's really set in, Dr Darwin decided that hospital was the only answer.'

Peggy nodded, relieved that everyone had acted swiftly once they realised what was going on with Gracie.

Florence dug her hands into her trouser pockets. 'As I'm not needed here until it's time to pick Bobby up, I'll get to the factory and relieve Mavis. I'm sorry to have worried you, Peggy.'

Peggy smiled. 'All's well that ends well, I suppose. You did the right thing, Florence, though I would have appreciated a telephone call first thing to warn me of what was happening.' She turned to open the door. 'I'd offer to give you a lift up there, but the car's at home. I'll pop in later, and no doubt Solly will too, as he'll have your Christmas bonuses to hand out. I'll ring him when I get back home to keep him up to date.'

'Thanks, Peggy, but I need to clean up here first, and a bit of exercise and cold air is just what I need after this morning's dramas.'

'I must get on with my rounds,' said Danuta, following Peggy down the slippery path. 'We will see you on Boxing Day, Mamma Peggy.'

'Yes, of course,' Peggy murmured, distracted by the suspicious thoughts that were still plaguing her. She caught Danuta's arm before she could open her car door. 'Why did Alastair take her in his car instead of waiting for the ambulance?'

'He decided there was no time to waste as she was bleeding very heavily,' she replied, her expression giving nothing away.

Peggy regarded Danuta evenly. 'I'll pop in at visiting time this evening, then, and make sure she has everything she needs.'

Danuta shook her head. 'She will not be allowed visitors tonight,' she replied. 'And Florence packed her a bag with everything she will need. Please do not worry, Mamma Peggy. She's in very safe hands.' She yanked open the car door, climbed in and was driving off before Peggy could say another word.

Peggy watched the little car disappear and turned back towards Beach View. 'I have no doubt Gracie is in safe hands,' she murmured to herself, 'but if I was a betting woman, I'd lay odds he hasn't taken her to the General.'

As she made her way home, Peggy went over everything that had been said – or rather, avoided being said – by those two young women, and although it all sounded logical, she had a feeling that there was far more to the story than they'd been willing to reveal. And it seemed that Alastair Darwin was part of this conspiracy of silence. It was very worrying to realise that not even Danuta trusted her enough to tell her the truth, but that truth had to be very ugly indeed – and she really didn't want to believe it of little Gracie.

She walked along the twitten and paused at her back gate. If her suspicions were right, then Danuta and Alastair were risking not only their careers, but their reputations and everything they'd worked so hard for. It was an unbelievably foolish thing to do, and she could only pray the truth never came out.

She took a deep breath, plastered on a smile and let herself into the house. As she climbed the concrete steps to the kitchen she could hear excited voices and laughter, and with hope in her heart that Cissy had arrived early, she opened the door to the delicious aroma of mince pies cooking in the oven.

One glance told her there was no Cissy, but there was a great pile of parcels – mostly unwrapped – in the centre of the kitchen table. 'My goodness,' she breathed. 'It looks as if Christmas has come early.'

'My nieces in Canada sent an enormous jar of sweet mincemeat for the pies, so I thought I'd get on and make some,' said Cordelia, her eyes twinkling with delight behind her half-moon glasses. 'There's also a tin of ham from Rita and Pete in Australia, along with a huge tin of IXL apricot jam, packets of dried fruit, and little presents for everyone.'

Peggy hung up her coat and scarf and then toed off her boots to leave them under the table. 'Oh dear, everyone is being so generous; it makes the poor bits and pieces I sent abroad look very mean in comparison.'

'Don't mind about that,' said Jim, looking flushed from the heat of the oven as he checked on the mince pies. 'Sarah and Jane sent oranges, nuts, dates and chocolate! I've had the devil's own job to stop this lot tucking in.'

'Oranges,' sighed Peggy, looking at them longingly as he placed the fruit bowl amongst the parcels. 'I can't remember the last time I tasted an orange.'

'I can,' said Cordelia. 'It was halfway through the war, and Bertie and I won it at that charity bridge game we had up at the posh house with the big glass conservatory.'

Peggy sat down and let Daisy clamber on to her lap, though she was getting a bit big for it really. 'Yes, I remember now, Cordy. We sat and looked at it for at least an hour before we carefully divided it up so everyone had a piece.'

Jim placed the mince pies on to a wire tray to cool. 'We'll have those when we get back from seeing Ernie,' he said. He wagged a playful finger at Charlie. 'And there're two each, so if you decide to tuck in before we get back, I expect to see the rest still here, young man.'

Charlie rolled his eyes and was about to reply when the telephone rang. 'I'll get it,' he said, jumping to his feet.

Peggy and Jim exchanged a knowing glance, for Charlie seemed to be glued to the telephone these days and they both suspected it was because of a certain girl. 'I do hope you remember to have that talk before we have a houseful,' she said quietly.

'I said I would,' he muttered. 'And I will tonight if he's at home. The trouble is he's so rarely here, it's like trying to herd cats.'

Peggy began to comb through all the luxuries she couldn't possibly have found in England, and was almost in tears at the loving generosity of her darling

160

chicks. Apart from Rita and Peter's contribution to Christmas, there was a case of wine from Fran and her husband; a box of gorgeous bottled pickles and wedges of cheese from Mary's family farm; and an enormous box of chocolate-coated biscuits from Ivy which had a card on it saying it was from Harrods of all places. And in amongst it all were little gifts beautifully wrapped in colourful paper for each of them.

'Mum,' said Charlie, returning to the kitchen. 'It's Auntie Doreen, and it's not good news, I'm afraid.'

Peggy had had enough bad news today, but she set Daisy on to her feet and hurried into the hall. 'Doreen? What's the matter?'

'Oh, Peg, I'm really sorry to let you down,' she said fretfully at the other end of the line in Swansea. 'The girls woke up this morning covered in spots and the doctor has just confirmed it's chickenpox of all things. And Archie isn't looking too clever either, so I suspect he'll go down with it any minute.'

'Oh, Doreen, that is such a shame, I was so looking forward to having you here after so long. I've missed you, little sister.'

Doreen sounded as if she was on the brink of tears. 'I miss you too, Peg, and I was really looking forward to it as well. And so excited about seeing all the work you've had done on the old place, and to meet up with Bob and Jim and all the rest. But the girls aren't well enough to travel and with Archie probably brewing as well . . .'

'It's rotten timing, Dor, but as I've only just got Daisy through the measles, I do understand.'

'How is everyone? Is Cissy still coming? Anne's new baby looks very bonny in those pictures you sent.'

'Oscar is cuddly and smiley – the perfect baby,' Peggy replied warmly. 'Jim's much better and sleeping well; Charlie is growing like a weed – as is Daisy;

Cordelia's a little more frail but Christmas seems to perk her up, and Doris is Doris. Bob writes that he's now half an inch taller than his father, and Cissy – well, she's a law unto herself these days, and I rarely hear from her.'

'That's sad about Cissy,' sighed Doreen. 'But then she flew the nest when she joined the WAAFs, and although it must be hard for you, she always was independent-minded, Peg.'

'Yes, I know, but it's not easy to let go of them, Dor, as you'll find out when your two get to that age.'

'God forbid,' she replied. 'They're difficult enough to please already and they haven't even left school yet. I'm pinning my hopes on little Archie to stay home and look after his aged mother,' she added with a chuckle.

Peggy giggled. 'Best of luck with that. If he's anything like my Bob and Charlie, you won't see him for dust once he's found girls and finished school.'

'Thank goodness that's years away yet. I'm determined to enjoy him being my baby for as long as I can.'

'You're sounding quite chirpy, Dor. Got a new man in your life to replace the bearded wonder who never got round to writing his best-selling book?'

Doreen laughed. 'No fear. I have enough to contend with looking after myself and the three kids without all that. Look, Peg, I'm in a phone box, so I can't speak for much longer as I'm running out of coins and this is long-distance. Give everyone my love, won't you? And a big kiss and hug for your Jim and Ron. They're the only men I need in my life for now.'

Peggy laughed. 'Of course I will, but why are you in a phone box? I'd have thought it was easier to ring from the school office.'

'The school's closed for the Christmas break, and I don't have a phone in our flat.' She was interrupted by the pips going. 'Happy Christmas, Peg. Love to all, and I hope to make it to you in the new . . .'

Peggy sighed with disappointment as the line went dead. She hadn't seen Doreen for a year and she missed her very much, for she had a great sense of humour and was good fun to have around. But at least there wouldn't be any falling-out with Doris this year. So many other Christmases had turned into a battleground, with Peggy caught as referee and peacemaker.

The trouble was that Doris and Doreen were chalk and cheese, and there was nothing Doreen enjoyed more than tweaking Doris's nose about her high ideas and snobbish outlook – and Doris delighted in being scathing about the fact Doreen hadn't married Archie's father and was living what she thought of as a rather rackety life down in Swansea.

The fact that Archie's father had been killed in the Blitz before they could marry was neither here nor there with Doris, and as for a rackety lifestyle – Doreen was a secretary at a boys' private school, and as far as Peggy knew, her social life was restricted by the fact she had three demanding children and most of the masters were of retirement age.

She returned to the kitchen and explained to the others why Doreen wouldn't be coming before sitting down to catch her breath.

'You've been running about like a mad thing all morning, Peg,' said Jim, placing a cup of tea in front of her. 'Drink that and try to relax for a bit.'

She smiled up at him. 'Thanks, love.' She looked at the dark tan tea and took a pleasurable sip. 'Aah,' she breathed. 'Now that's what I call proper tea.'

'I nipped to the shops while you were out earlier.' He sat down, moved the packing boxes and brown paper to one side of the table and lit a cigarette. 'We don't have to leave for Ernie's until eleven, so anything you want doing, just ask me or Charlie. I don't want you frazzled before the celebrations even start.'

Peggy raised an eyebrow and tried not to giggle. She'd been frazzled since the beginning of December with all the organising, present-buying and wrapping; the card-writing, decorating and cleaning the house from top to bottom between her shifts at work. But she knew that once Christmas dinner was on the table and her loved ones were around her, she would be able to draw breath, relax, and start to enjoy herself.

11

Jim could see that something was worrying his Peggy, but he knew she wouldn't tell him what it was until she was good and ready, and there was no point in questioning her. He sat at the kitchen table and watched as she sipped her tea, thinking how lovely she was, and how hard she'd worked to ensure that this Christmas would be the best yet. And it would be; he'd make sure of that.

He grinned as Daisy bounced about on his knee, clutching her beloved Amelia rag doll and babbling on about Father Christmas and what he might put in the stocking that was hanging on the dining-room mantelpiece. 'What if he brings an elephant?' he teased. 'Where on earth would we put it?'

Her big brown eyes looked back at him with some scorn. 'Don't be silly, Daddy. Santa lives in the North Pole – our teacher said – and ephelants live in Africa.'

'That's me told, then,' he chuckled. 'Perhaps he'll bring a polar bear instead. It will certainly feel at home in this cold weather.'

She rolled her eyes and gave a sigh which told him she wasn't amused and then continued to chatter on to anyone who cared to listen.

He tuned her out and eyed the bowl of oranges, the pretty wrapping paper and the discarded boxes, brown paper and string that would need to be safely stored away to be used again. Oranges had been ten a penny out in the tropics, as had bananas, pineapple, and many other exotic fruits, so he wouldn't take one morsel of orange as he wanted his family to enjoy them to the full. It was such a delight to see how excited they were about the gifts that before the war had been staples of the Christmas table, and he was glad he'd done his bit by helping Cordelia with those mince pies – the aroma was making his mouth water.

He leaned his cheek against Daisy's dark curls. She'd been a new-born baby five years ago, so tiny and sweet – and a very big surprise as she hadn't been planned. In hindsight, the time since seemed to have flown, but in reality it had crawled while he'd been in India and Burma, yearning to be home.

Unlike Christmases in England, it had always been steaming hot in the tropics, with the monsoon rains mingling with his sweat and making life even more uncomfortable. What with the mud, the snakes, the mosquitoes and the Japs to contend with, there was little joy in celebrating something so far removed from a traditional Christmas.

Two had been spent deep in the jungle fighting for his life – the day passing with little or no recognition as none of them had time to think about it, and it was hardly the moment to celebrate anything. Two others had been spent under canvas, still deep in the jungle, drinking as much beer as possible and eating wild turkey shot by one of the Gurkhas, and great mounds of roast potatoes. Raucous games had followed, he remembered, but the hangovers the next day had been so bad their officers had decided to shock them out of it by making them go out in a cloudburst to do physical jerks in the cloying mud.

His last Christmas abroad had been in Singapore, which had been much more civilised. He'd attended the double wedding of Sarah and her sister Jane, danced with Elsa Bristow and Sylvia Fuller in the ballroom at Raffles, and got roaring drunk with Jumbo and the rest of his platoon before they'd got their tickets home. That final day when the barracks were emptying fast and the trucks had come to take the others to the docks had made him feel abandoned, but he'd never forget Jumbo in his kilt, red hair gleaming in the bright sunlight as he played those bloody bagpipes until the truck disappeared into the glare.

'You look as if you're miles away, Dad,' said Charlie, nudging him.

He dragged his mind back to the present. 'Just thinking about how much it means to be home at last,' he replied. He eased Daisy off his knee. 'I think I'll put on another jumper; it's cold in here.'

'It isn't, Dad. In fact, it's lovely and warm.' He eyed the thick sweater beneath the even thicker cardigan. 'You must still be acclimatising.'

The memories of those days in the sun were still with him. 'I expect so,' he murmured before leaving the kitchen to run upstairs to the bedroom.

He crossed to the bay window and looked out over the rooftops to the narrow view now afforded him by the loss of the houses directly in front. He could see the sea, steely grey and flecked with white beneath a lowering sky in which seabirds hovered and swooped; the rusting remains of the old pier where he'd taken Peggy dancing during their courting days; and part of the promenade which stretched from the western green hills to the chalk cliffs in the east.

Jim discovered to his amazement that even from this distance he could hear the screeching gulls; the distant discordant song of the wind in the fishing boat saillines; and the rhythmic breath of the rolling waves as they broke against the shingle beach. There was plenty of movement and sound, but the colour had been leached from the scene by the cold and the wind and the black clouds that were scudding across the sky to cast their shadows on the water.

Shivering, he stripped off the cardigan and pulled open a drawer to find another sweater which he tugged over his head before donning the cardigan again. The cold seemed to have got into his bones, and he wondered if he'd ever get used to it after so long in the tropics. It was a shame, he mused, that his body couldn't have stored all that heat like a radiator so he could switch it on when he needed it.

With a wry smile, he dug his hands into his cardigan pockets and returned to the window. The English seaside was far removed from the vibrant colours of the Far East with its green palm trees bearing exotic fruit, white sands, coral reefs, and calm turquoise seas that were warm and silky against sunburnt skin. And strangely enough, he missed it – missed the sights and sounds, even the smells – but most of all he missed the camaraderie of the men he'd fought alongside and got drunk with; and the knowledge that he was a part of something bigger than all of them – but together they'd prevail.

He touched his damaged earlobe and felt the fading scar on his cheek. He had to remind himself that it was safe here – he didn't have to remain permanently on guard against a murderous enemy.

'I wondered where you'd got to,' said Peggy, coming into the room. 'Are you all right, Jim?'

He quickly dismissed his sombre thoughts and put his arms round her to kiss her. 'I'm absolutely fine, wee girl. Just thinking what a lucky man I am, that's all.'

'Well, as long as you're not going into one of your horrid dark days,' she murmured, cupping his scarred cheek with her hand. 'I do worry about you, Jim.'

'You worry enough for the entire population of England,' he teased, kissing her again. He gently slapped her bottom. 'We'd best get going or we'll be late visiting Ernie.'

Danuta was finding it very hard to concentrate as she went on her rounds and helped at the antenatal clinic. Alastair had acted promptly, and whisked Gracie off to the cottage hospital in the hope she'd remain more anonymous there. But he'd warned Danuta that he would eventually have to report her to the authorities.

Danuta knew he was doing the right thing, but that didn't make her feel any easier about it, and as she weighed babies and checked on new mothers, her thoughts kept returning to Gracie. The cottage hospital was a few miles out of Cliffehaven, on the edge of a tiny hamlet surrounded by farmland. It was well equipped and fully staffed, and Gracie would be seen immediately, and after the procedure would be given a room of her own in which to recover. If Alastair had taken her to Cliffehaven General, it would have been a very different story, for women who'd had any sort of obstetric treatment were placed on the maternity ward. It was a cruel situation to be in, surrounded by newly delivered mothers and their babies.

Danuta finished at the clinic, and as she was due a half-hour break, she decided to go down to the seafront to try and clear her head. She wrapped her woollen scarf round her neck, pulled up the collar of her gabardine coat and climbed out of the car. The wind was tremendous and she had to hold on to her hat and lean into it as she made her way down to the promenade and into one of the elegant refurbished Victorian shelters.

The sea was icy blue and green, the waves like sleek, glassy leviathans rolling into shore to break upon the shingle in white spume which was caught by the wind and whipped into the air. Gulls huddled in the hollows of the shingle, their backs to the wind, their heads tucked beneath their wings as others swooped and screeched overhead.

Danuta dug her hands in her pockets and watched them for a while before turning her attention to the fishing boats which had been tethered well out of reach of the high-tide line beneath the chalk cliffs to the east. She could hear the discordant clatter of the wind in the rigging, and the occasional shout of one of the fishermen who were battening everything down on their boats. They clearly expected the weather to worsen.

'Hello, Danuta.'

Startled, she looked up to find Alastair standing there, bundled up in a thick coat and university scarf. 'It is done?' she asked.

He nodded and sat down next to her. 'The surgeon phoned half an hour ago. She's still asleep, but the infection was so deeply entrenched, he had to do a full hysterectomy. He's prescribed strong antibiotics in the hope the sepsis will clear. But the next forty-eight hours will be crucial, Danuta. She's a very sick girl.'

'And did you report her?'

His expression was grim. 'Not yet. I thought it best to wait until we know if she will recover fully. If she doesn't make it – well, that's another matter.'

His brown eyes regarded her solemnly. 'I bear the girl no malice, Danuta, and I certainly don't blame you for wanting to keep what she did secret. But if we don't report these things, other girls could be encouraged to take the same life-endangering risks.'

Danuta took a deep breath of the salty air and let it out slowly in a sigh. 'It's just so sad. What will happen to Gracie now?'

'She'll have to stay in hospital until the infection is well and truly under control – and that could take some time. Gracie is underweight and the infection has weakened her immune system. Having had the hysterectomy as well, she really does have a fight on her hands to get through this.'

'Poor girl,' she sighed tremulously. 'Thank goodness Florence is willing to look after little Bobby – though whether she'll still feel the same if . . .'

Alastair put his gloved hand on Danuta's arm. 'That's a battle for another day, Danuta. Let's deal with this one first.'

'Thank you, Alastair. It's good to know I can rely on you.'

He tucked his chin into his scarf and watched the waves breaking on the shore. 'I just wish our antiquated laws had been brought up to date.' He sighed. 'There was talk before the war of making abortion legal in certain circumstances. It's time for change, Danuta, and we in the medical profession need to get our voices heard, so that girls like Gracie don't have to resort to making their own arrangements.' He got to his feet and smiled down at her. 'Sorry for sounding off like that.'

She stood and dug her hands in her pockets. 'How did you know I would be here?'

His smile warmed his eyes and made him look less careworn. 'I often come down here to blow the cobwebs away, and when I saw your car, I realised you'd want to know how things went today. I hope you don't mind?'

She smiled back at him. 'Of course I don't. We all need to talk of these things, for it cannot be done at home, or anywhere outside the surgery.' She glanced at her watch. 'I didn't realise the time,' she gasped. 'I must get on with my rounds.'

Alastair tucked her hand into the crook of his sturdy arm. 'You might need to hold on to me,' he said. 'You're such a slip of a thing, this wind could blow you away.'

She laughed. 'Thank you, Alastair. You are a gentle-man just like my Stanislav.'

Peggy had changed into her neat two-piece navy skirt and jacket, with a lavender wool twinset and a dark blue hat. She'd carefully applied make-up, brushed her hair and donned her fake pearl earrings and neck-lace, determined to look her best for this long-promised visit to Parkwood, and she was glad she'd done so, for Jim had taken her to the British Legion's head office first to introduce her to his boss, Colonel Harry Field.

'He's a nice old boy, isn't he?' she said as they drove away and headed along the coast road. 'A real gent.'

'He certainly is,' agreed Jim. 'And very under-standing. He takes an interest in all the men we're caring for as well as those of us who work for the charity. You only have to count the number of parcels I've stowed in the boot to know that.'

'Has he really given something to every patient at Parkwood?'

'Aye, that he has,' he replied. 'But just try and re-member, Peggy, they aren't patients at Parkwood, they're residents.'

Peggy made a mental note of this, and then sat back in the passenger seat to enjoy this rare outing with her darling Jim. She was relaxed and feeling quite fancy-free for a change, as Charlie had taken Daisy to Ron's for the morning, and Bertie Double-Barrelled was treating Cordelia to lunch at the Officers' Club after they'd finished shopping. The only fly in the ointment was the continued niggle over what was going on with Gracie.

Determined to set aside all her worries for the next few hours, she concentrated on the wide, almost empty road ahead and the beauty of the rolling, forested hills on one side and the churning sea on the other. The sun was low in the sky, but between the scudding clouds its rays shone down to touch the silvery water of the English Channel and to gild the wings of the seabirds that swarmed above the chalk cliffs.

Seahaven was a strange sort of place, she mused, catching sight of the hotel by the cliff edge, the endless rows of bungalows huddled together, and the parade of rather dowdy shops. It wasn't really big enough to call a proper town, and yet it was larger than a village, but whoever had come up with the idea of building that eyesore of a church should have been shot. She sniffed in disapproval at the crooked cross on the roof and the acres of glass and concrete that were about as inspiring as a factory unit.

'I'm glad we don't live here,' she said, casting a disapproving eye over the ramshackle pub fronting the main road. 'It's a nothing sort of place, and you can't even get down to the beach without risking life and limb on those crumbling steps.'

'I agree. But there are plans for a lot more housing here. Prefabs, probably, but at least they'll provide for some of the families who are living on the streets at the moment.'

'That's what's going up behind the station at Cliffehaven. Rosie told me the Council finally passed the plans the other week. She'd been hoping for more permanent housing there, but with so many shortages and not much money, it's the best the Council can do for now.'

Jim turned off the main road to head into the countryside, and they sat in contented silence as they passed the ranked lines of neat brick bungalows, a playing field and school. Reaching the end of the narrow country lane, Jim steered the car between the imposing pillars of the gateway to the Parkwood estate and slowly followed the sweeping gravel driveway lined with trees before drawing to a halt and letting the engine idle.

'Look over there, Peg,' he murmured.

Beyond the lychgate she could see a small flint church with a peg-tiled roof, its origin clear in the crenellated Norman tower at its northern end. At the top of the tower was a delicate wrought-iron cross above a weather vane depicting a shepherd and his sheep, and set within the flint was a clock that must have stopped because the hands were at half-past six. The ancient building was protected by trees, some of which still clung to their autumnal golds, reds and bronzes which shone like beacons on this gloomy day.

'Oh, how perfectly lovely,' Peggy breathed. 'Can we go inside?'

'We're running a bit late, Peg, but if we have time after seeing Ernie, I'm sure no one will mind if we have a nose round.'

He put the car in gear and they moved on down the driveway, the tyres crunching on the freshly raked gravel. 'The little chapel was built to be a private place of worship for the family who once owned the estate. It's quite plain inside, but that's part of its charm really,' he said. They left the deep shadows of the overhanging trees and were rewarded with their first view of the old mansion.

'Oh, my goodness,' Peggy exclaimed, taking in the towers and turrets, the long, elegant windows overlooking the manicured gardens, and the graceful flights of steps leading from the driveway to the sweeping terrace. 'I know you said it was very grand, but I never imagined it would be so . . . so magnificent.'

'By all accounts, it was far from magnificent when the Legion was gifted it in the will of the last owner,' said Jim, parking by the fountain. 'A lot of money went into restoring it and making it fit for purpose. Thankfully, the donations poured in and there were enough valuable things left in the house that could be sold to raise the rest.'

He climbed out of the car and dragged the large hessian sack from the boot. Swinging it over one shoulder, he waited for Peggy to admire the fountain, and then led her up the steps to the deserted terrace. 'It's too cold for sitting out here now, but in the summer, this terrace is jam-packed,' he said.

Peggy stood and gazed out over the sweeping lawns to the surrounding trees, the distant view of the hills and fields, and the tennis courts. There were stone benches placed in arbours; rose beds; hydrangea hedges; a croquet lawn set out with hoops; and great stone urns placed every few feet along the terrace balustrade. They were empty now, but she could just imagine how glorious they must look and smell when filled with flowers during the spring and summer.

'Come on, Peg. I need to get this lot under the tree while everybody's occupied elsewhere.' He hitched the heavy sack once more on to his shoulder and led the way through the French doors into the reception hall.

Peggy gasped as she took in the grandeur of the old mansion. A bank of lifts had been sympathetically installed to one side of the sweeping oak staircase which gleamed from centuries of polish; an enormous crystal chandelier hung from the ornate ceiling where plaster cherubs peeked from behind garlands of roses and entwined vines; and the wooden floor glowed honey-warm beneath the enormous Christmas tree that stood in the centre of the hall. Fairy lights and tinsel competed with the reflected fire of the crystal chandelier and twinkled in the delicately spun glass baubles – and on the topmost branch sat a golden star.

'It makes our tree look very small and shabby,' said Peggy, craning her neck to look at the star and the prisms of light shooting from the chandelier. 'But it smells wonderful, doesn't it?' She reached out her gloved hand to touch the exquisite glass baubles. 'And these really are quite marvellous.'

'They were donated years ago by one of the veterans of the first shout,' Jim told her, busily placing the parcels beneath the tree. 'He was a glass-blower by trade before he lost his hands at Verdun, and on his return home, he simply shut his shop and donated his entire stock to the Legion.'

Peggy examined the intricate patterns etched on the glass. 'How sad,' she said with a sigh.

Jim folded up the sack and stuffed it in the pocket of his overcoat before putting his arm round Peggy's shoulders. 'There are a lot of sad stories in here, Peg, but they're rarely told, so I don't want you feeling blue today – none of the men in here would thank you.' He grinned. 'Especially Ernie, who can get grumpy at the drop of a hat – but pay no mind to it, Peg. It's all for show really.'

'I'll try to remember that,' she replied, briefly resting her head on his shoulder.

Jim led the way through deserted corridors, the sound of voices and laughter coming from behind the closed doors.

'Where is everyone?' she asked.

'In the bar, I suspect. This lot enjoy a drink or three.' He paused at a door and looked down at her. 'Ready?'

Peggy nodded, but her pulse was racing and she knew it would be a struggle to hide the emotions she would surely feel when she came face to face with the man she remembered as so vital from before the war.

'Who's that?' came the voice in answer to Jim's knock.

Jim pushed the door open just far enough to look round it. 'It's me, you miserable bugger. I hope you're decent, because I've brought Peggy with me.'

'I'm about as decent as I'll ever be,' Ernie replied. 'Get in here and shut that bloody door. You're causing a draught.'

Jim grinned at Peggy. 'I did warn you he's touchy,' he said before opening the door and ushering her inside. 'Ernie, you remember my Peggy, don't you?' he said cheerfully.

Peggy hesitated by the door, taking in the pale, skeletal figure strapped from shoulder to ankle in a high-backed, padded wheelchair. Despite everything Jim had told her, it was still a terrible shock to see how old and helpless he looked beside her robust Jim. Her gaze travelled from his withered legs to the oxygen tank beside the chair, to the clawed hands lying limply in his lap, and up to his face where she met his cool, mocking gaze.

Utterly ashamed of herself, she moved quickly towards him. 'Hello, Ernie. Long time no see,' she managed.

'You're probably wishing you didn't have to see me at all,' he replied, the mocking glint still in his jaundiced eyes. 'It's not the prettiest sight, is it? But I'm glad you came, Peggy,' he added breathlessly. 'It's good to see you're still as fetching as ever. Jim, you're a lucky man.' He reached for the oxygen mask and fumbled it over his mouth and nose.

'Don't I know it.' Jim smiled at Peggy and patted the seat of the chair next to him to encourage her to sit.

'I don't get many visitors,' grumbled Ernie from behind the mask. 'So you'll have to excuse me if I sound a bit rude.'

'You've always been rude, Ernie,' said Jim. 'Why change the habits of a lifetime?'

Ernie shot him a grin from behind the oxygen mask. 'That's why I like you, Jim Reilly. You're a man after my own heart and never afraid to say what you think.' He let the mask drop to his concave chest, and the teasing light dimmed in his eyes. 'I got a letter from Maureen yesterday.'

'Was that good or bad?' asked Jim, watching him closely.

'Doesn't make much difference to me either way,' he said flatly. 'I'm done for, so anything she has to say is water off a duck's arse.' He glanced across at Peggy to see if his language had offended her and then took a couple of breaths from the oxygen mask. 'She's met some man, and wants a divorce so she can marry him.'

'Oh, Ernie,' breathed Peggy. 'I'm so sorry to hear that.'

'Don't be, Peggy. I'm no use to her, so why keep her tied to me? I've asked Larry to find me a lawyer so I can get the ball rolling – though I'll probably be gone before it all goes through. Either way, she'll be free.'

Despite his cavalier attitude towards his wife, Peggy saw the single tear slowly roll down his face and her heart ached for him. She reached out to gently take the clawed hand, unable to express her feelings, but hoping her touch would be a small comfort.

'Well, aren't you the cheerful one,' said Jim, rather too brightly. 'Is there any more bad news to tell us, or is that it?'

Ernie's grin was almost impish as he looked back at Jim. 'The ladies of the WI are coming tonight to sing to us, and I've taken rather a fancy to a certain Mrs Molly Carter.' He moved his hands to indicate her generous figure. 'Quite a little smasher, and if I'm good, she might even give me a second glimpse of her stocking tops.'

Peggy burst out laughing and Jim chuckled. 'You sly old sod. Trust you to find the one woman in the WI who's young and bold enough to dare show you anything, much less a stocking top.'

Ernie's chuckle was stopped by a fit of coughing. 'Special privileges in this place, Jim,' he managed eventually. 'I get to see quite a lot of things as long as I keep my hands to myself.'

From that moment on the tension eased in Peggy, and as the men chatted and joked, she joined in occasionally and was warmed by the deep friendship they shared. The language was a bit ripe at times, but she could ignore that in the knowledge that their visit was cheering Ernie up and making a difference to what must be very long days stuck in that awful chair. The atmosphere and the camaraderie between the men must surely buoy both their spirits, and that was something to be grateful for.

12

'I really don't think I can face travelling all that way,' Sandra said. 'Why don't you go with Mum, and I'll follow on tomorrow if I'm feeling better.'

'I'm not going without you,' said Graham. 'And we can't possibly cancel so late in the day. My parents are already upset that we're not going to them as usual, and your Aunt Gloria will have organised everything down to the last table napkin. She'll be devastated if she's left on her own at Christmas again. Then there's your mother. How do you think she'll feel if we leave her to travel down there on her own?'

'You're not being very sympathetic, Graham,' she replied. 'I feel rotten, and all you're worried about is what other people will think.'

His lips thinned, and she could see he was fighting to keep his patience. 'Those other people are your family, Sandra, and I care about what they think of me, even if you don't. I don't know what's got into you these past few days, but you've not been yourself ever since you came home from Manchester.'

'Well, I'm sorry about that, Graham,' she snapped. 'But you did insist I stay with you until after Christmas, so I'm afraid you're just going to have to put up with it.'

'I'm sorry too,' he replied softly. 'Sorry you're feeling rotten, and sorry for sounding uncaring.' He put his arm round her shoulder. 'Do you want me to ring the doctor?'

She shook her head and eased away from his arm. 'It's probably just a chill or the tummy bug I got in Manchester lingering on. It'll pass,' she said lightly. 'But it would probably be best if we continue to sleep in separate room once we're down at Gloria's.'

'Well, if you're still sick, I suppose that's logical. But I really don't understand why you won't let me call the doctor.'

'As I said, it's not serious enough to bother with a doctor, so please just drop it, Graham.' She ran up the stairs before he could reply.

Reaching the sanctuary of the bathroom, she eyed her reflection and hated what she saw: a mean, spiteful, bad-tempered woman who was in danger of losing control of her senses.

She cleaned her teeth, combed her hair and repaired her make-up. Feeling marginally better, she caught sight of her reflection again and grimaced. Her skin was pale, there were dark shadows beneath her blue eyes and new lines creasing her forehead. She looked how she felt – old, sick to the heart, and utterly exhausted by the stress of it all.

'Buck up, Sandra,' she muttered. 'You've got to see this through, so stick to the plan and let's get this damned holiday over and done with before I go mad.'

'Who are you talking to?'

She whirled round to find Graham lurking at the bathroom door. 'I do wish you wouldn't creep up on me like that. It's unnerving.'

His sad eyes regarded her before he turned away. 'I'll wait for you downstairs, then. We're already late because of you shilly-shallying, so don't be long.'

Sandra took a deep breath, praying she wouldn't be sick again, and swallowed a couple of aspirin. She didn't like travelling by train at the best of times, but she had a nasty feeling that today's journey down to Cliffehaven would be the hardest yet.

Graham was waiting for her behind the wheel of their car. Dapper in a three-piece pinstripe suit with a watch and chain tucked into the waistcoat pocket, he looked ready for a day in the office rather than a jaunt down to the seaside for Christmas. He was wearing his driving gloves, and his overcoat was neatly folded on the back seat with his black fedora placed on top. 'Everything is in the boot,' he said as she climbed in.

'Did you remember the presents?'

'Of course.' He regarded her coolly. 'Are you feeling a bit better?'

'I'm not about to throw up all over your car if that's what you mean,' she replied waspishly. 'Just get on with it, Graham. Mum will be wondering where we've got to.'

Graham clearly didn't appreciate being spoken to in this way. He gripped the steering wheel and drove in tight-lipped silence through the London suburbs, following the Thames until they reached the devastated East End and the ugly block of flats Beryl had been moved into by the Council after her terraced house had been blown to smithereens by a German doodlebug.

'It still astonishes me that she stays here when she could be far more comfortable in the little house I wanted to buy for her,' he said.

'It was a kind thought, Graham, but she wouldn't feel comfortable our side of the city, and besides, all her friends are here,' Sandra said. 'Since losing Dad, she's relied on them as much as us, so please don't start badgering her to move again.'

'You go in and fetch her while I take the car round to the lock-up garage. If we don't hurry, we'll miss the train and have to wait another hour for the next one.'

Sandra walked towards the low-rise block of flats and pushed the buzzer for the second-floor flat. 'It's me, Mum,' she said when her mother's voice came back to her through the intercom. 'Are you ready? Only we're running a bit late.'

'Oh, dear, oh dear, I was hoping you'd have time to come up. Only I've got a lovely surprise for you.'

'Bring it down with you, then. Only Graham's already fussing about missing the train, and I'm not in the mood for another argument.'

She paced back and forth, glancing repeatedly through the glass doors at the bank of lifts for any sign that Beryl was on her way. However, when the lift door opened and her mother stepped out with her brother, Andy, his wife, Ivy, and a pushchair in tow, she wasn't as pleased as she normally would have been. 'Not today, please not now,' she muttered before plastering on a smile.

'Andy, Ivy,' she called brightly before giving them both a brief hug, and a blown kiss to the rather snotty-nosed toddler in the pushchair. 'How lovely to see you. I wish you'd let me know you'd be here; I would have made sure to come earlier – as it is, we're running late, and we still need to get our tickets.' She saw her mother looking at her strangely and realised she was gabbling.

Ivy's brown eyes regarded her with some amusement. 'Blimey, Sandra, it's usually me what's late for everything. Me and Andy was just saying we wondered what were keeping you.'

'Yeah, it ain't like you, gel,' said Andy, looking at her more closely. 'What's up, mate? You ain't the full ticket by the looks of yer.'

She regarded her tall, handsome brother, and grimaced. 'I've got a bit of a tummy bug,' she replied, 'and almost didn't make it here at all. But you're looking good, the pair of you,' she added brightly. 'Life seems to be treating you well.'

'Good, yeah, real good thanks,' he replied. 'The London Fire Service is much more demanding than the set-up down in Cliffehaven, but they're a great bunch of blokes to work with, and we've got the flat just how we want it.'

Sandra turned to her mother and carefully embraced her while planting a kiss on her cheek. 'You look lovely, Mum,' she said, admiring the smart matching coat and dress, and the felt hat covered in fake mistletoe and holly berries. 'New outfit?'

Beryl's penetrating gaze was full of questions. 'I bought it down the market, special like for Christmas. Are you all right, Sandra? Only you look a bit rough, and you're clearly not in the best of tempers.'

'She's got a tummy bug,' said Ivy helpfully. 'Probably something she ate when she were away on her posh job.'

'That'll be it,' said Sandra, desperate to end this conversation and be on the move. 'You got everything, Mum? Remembered to put your keys in your handbag? Don't want you locking yourself out again, do we?'

'I'm not senile, Sandra,' she huffed. 'There's no need to talk to me as if I'm five.'

'Sorry, Mum,' she said, blushing. 'Oh, look, here's Graham. We'd better get going.'

'I'm giving you a lift to the station,' said Andy. 'It's too far for Mum to walk with her bad knee, and you don't look like you'd manage it either,' he said, giving her a cheeky smile.

'That's very kind of you, Andrew,' said Graham who was loaded down by two suitcases and a large, heavy holdall. 'It'll certainly save me having to lug this lot down the road. Sandra seems to think she needs to bring her entire wardrobe for a few days away.'

Once everything was stowed in the boot of Andy's car along with the pushchair, Ivy held the toddler on her lap as he drove them the short distance through heavy traffic to the local station and then helped Graham to unload it all and find a trolley.

'We got this for yer,' said Ivy, handing over a beautifully wrapped present. 'Andy got a Christmas bonus and took me shopping in Harrods of all places, but you're to promise you won't open it until the day.' She didn't wait for an answer but dug into her capacious handbag and gave Sandra a pile of envelopes. 'These cards are for everyone at Beach View, as well as Rita's dad, Jack, Ron and Rosie – and of course Ruby. I thought I'd save on stamps as you're going down there.'

Sandra placed everything in the holdall and drew out a box tied with red ribbon, and a smaller gift of a teddy bear wrapped in paper covered in Santas. 'These are for you and the little one,' she said, shooting a quick glance at the sweet, chubby toddler perched on Ivy's hip. 'Have a lovely Christmas, both of you, and I'll make sure your cards get to the right people.'

'Oh, we will,' breathed Ivy, her brown eyes sparkling. 'Me and Andy are expecting again. Ain't that grand?'

Sandra could barely smile through the agonising shock of Ivy's announcement. 'Congratulations,' she managed, fighting back a wave of jealousy as she gave the girl a brief hug. It was so unfair that Ivy could get pregnant so easily and think nothing of it when . . .

Graham was clearly taken aback too as he shook hands with Andy and awkwardly kissed the air above Ivy's cheek.

Ivy seemed to realise that her announcement had upset them both, for she gasped and put her hand over her mouth. 'I'm ever so sorry for blurting it out like that,' she said, her eyes full of concern. 'It was so thoughtless of me when I know how 'ard it is for you not being able to 'ave kids of yer own. But you can share ours, can't they, Andy?' She looked up, beseeching him to help her out.

'I'm sorry, mate,' said Andy, clamping a meaty hand on Graham's rigid shoulder. 'Ivy never has learnt to keep her gob shut.'

'It's lovely news, though, isn't it?' trilled Beryl.

'It is indeed,' replied Graham stiffly before grabbing hold of the trolley handle. 'Come along, Sandra,' he snapped. 'The train is due to leave in precisely seven minutes.'

Relieved the awful moment was over, Sandra blew a kiss to her brother and sister-in-law, took her mother's arm and steered her through the entrance and past the booking office where Graham was buying the tickets and out to the platform. Their train was puffing smoke as the porters slammed carriage doors, and the guard prepared to wave his flag and blow his whistle.

Graham came dashing out of the booking hall to chivvy her along and help them both up the step into the train. Taking charge of her suitcase, she left the rest for him to carry, and then led the way down the narrow corridor to the nearest carriage which luckily was empty.

Graham huffed and puffed as he stowed the cases and bags on the luggage rack above their heads, then took off his coat, used his handkerchief to flap away any dust from the seats and sat down. 'I didn't think we'd make it after you took so long to get ready,' he told Sandra reproachfully, before opening his newspaper to the financial section.

She ignored the barb and focused on settling her mother by the window with a magazine, then unfastened her fur jacket and sat opposite her. Her stomach was rumbling, but at least she wasn't feeling sick, and the carriage was lovely and warm after the icy chill outside. The guard blew his whistle and the train began to laboriously chug away from the platform.

The little scene with Ivy and Andy had shaken her to the core, but the real test was to come.

Cissy was having a bitch of a day, and it wasn't even lunchtime yet. Her passenger hadn't stopped complaining from the moment she'd picked her up from the Savoy Hotel. According to Lulabelle, the standards at the Savoy had slipped; the service in Texan hotels was far better; the limousine wasn't warm enough; the leather seats were too slippery; and the perfume Cissy wore was making her sneeze.

Cissy tried to oblige by opening the window, but that only drew further complaints about draughts and exhaust fumes, so she gritted her teeth and closed it again.

The traffic in central London was at its worst, and they got caught in endless hold-ups before they'd even reached Harrods. The commissionaire in his smart livery and top hat helped the woman out before informing Cissy that she couldn't park there and would have to drive round until her passenger was ready to be picked up.

As the blasted woman had already disappeared into the emporium without a backward glance, and Cissy had absolutely no idea how long she planned to be in there, she'd driven off bad-temperedly and almost ploughed straight into the side of a Rolls-Royce. Slamming on the brakes and missing the Roller's wing by a gnat's whisker, she hit her head on the windscreen and was then shouted at by the chauffeur of the Rolls.

It was the last straw. With a howl of anguish, she burst into tears and turned off into the first road she came to then screeched into a gap between a delivery van and an Austin. Unfortunately, it wasn't a space at all but the entrance to a very smart apartment building, and she was forced to move on by an irate chauffeur in another blasted Rolls-Royce.

Seething now, Cissy was tempted to just drive back to her flat, dump the car and head for Cliffehaven. She'd had it with London and its traffic and was fed up to the back teeth with rude chauffeurs, unhelpful doormen and Lulabelle bloody Lady Muck.

It seemed to take for ever before she found a place to park legally, and once she'd finally calmed down, repaired her make-up and had a cigarette, she steeled herself to join the fray again. As it was almost lunchtime and plump Lulabelle never missed a meal, she headed back to Harrods to find her already on the front step with a laden bellboy at her side, and clearly in a furious temper as she berated the hapless commissionaire.

Cissy leapt out of the limousine. 'I'm so sorry you've been kept waiting,' she said politely. 'But the traffic is simply too much today.' She nodded to the bellboy. 'Pop those into the boot, please.' She opened the rear door for Lulabelle. 'Don't worry, I'll soon get you to your luncheon engagement at the Ritz.'

Barely mollified, Lulabelle adjusted her luxurious mink wrap around her bejewelled neck, handed pound notes to the bellboy and commissionaire and slid on to the back seat with a bad-tempered scowl at Cissy.

Cissy knew better than to engage her in any small talk, so drove in silence to the Ritz, where, thankfully, there was a space for her to park and wait. Another liveried doorman rushed to help Lulabelle out of the car, and she sashayed through the hotel doors as if she owned the place – which she probably could afford to do with her daddy's oil billions, thought Cissy sourly.

She sat in the limousine and watched the bustle of pedestrians on the pavements and the snarl of traffic which filled the air with exhaust fumes, and heard the cacophony of blaring horns mixed with angry shouts and the clanging of the passing trams. Everyone was in a hurry to get somewhere, jostling, barging, side-stepping, eyes front and focused only on their destination. There wasn't much joy in it all, she thought, just a frantic sort of fever to find the right gift and keep the tills ringing in the shops.

Cissy lit a cigarette and watched another limousine park in front of her, the chauffeur leaping out to open the door and hand his overdressed, bejewelled and very fat passenger over to the concierge. It was at moments like this that she missed the peace and tranquillity of Cliffehaven, with its clean, crisp air and friendly faces. Money still talked, of course, but it was done discreetly, and really, she thought, eyeing the woman's jewellery, wearing diamonds in the middle of the day was very common.

'Good grief,' she sighed. 'I'm beginning to sound like Clarissa.' Yet she felt a little better tempered after that bit of cattiness. She sat smoking and watching the melee around her until she realised she rather urgently needed to find a loo.

Climbing out of the Bentley, she caught the eye of the doorman, and knew she wouldn't get past him to use the luxurious powder rooms inside, so hurried down to her favourite Italian café on the next corner to use theirs. The aroma of freshly ground coffee was enticing, and as Lulabelle usually took at least two hours over luncheon, she was tempted to stay for a while in the warmth to savour the delicious scents of garlic and herbs and olive oil. Restraining herself, she paid for her coffee and wished the owner, Vito, a happy Christmas, then strolled back to the limousine.

To her horror, Lulabelle was already sitting in the back, her expression thunderous. 'I pay y'all to wait,' she said in her Texan drawl. 'Now move your butt, missy, and get me outta here.'

Lulabelle must have had another falling-out with her friend over their luncheon. Holding back a rude rejoinder, Cissy slid into the driver's seat and eyed her passenger in the rear-view mirror. 'Where do you wish me to take you?'

'Claridge's. And step on it.'

It was only a short tube ride from here, but of course Lulabelle couldn't possibly be expected to use public transport like normal people, and wear out her expensive shoes by actually walking in them, thought Cissy crossly. She gritted her teeth, pulled out into the traffic and was immediately caught in a snarl-up. With horns blaring all round her, drivers gesticulating and shouting, and the horse-drawn coal merchant's dray getting in everyone's way, it was complete mayhem.

'You can see how it is, Your Ladyship. It might be quicker to walk,' she said over her shoulder.

'Y'all getting paid to drive me, missy,' she replied sourly. 'So drive.'

Cissy took a deep breath, keeping an eye open for the smallest gap in the traffic. She was getting a headache and needed to eat something and lie in a darkened room for at least an hour – but she'd invested all her savings in this private hire business and was earning good money from it, so there was little choice but to put up with demanding clients and the impossible London traffic which seemed to get worse by the month.

Inching the Bentley along the road towards Berkeley Square, surrounded by blaring horns and clouds of exhaust fumes, Cissy's thoughts turned again to

Cliffehaven. After more than a year in London, life here suddenly didn't seem as alluring as it once had.

Peggy was surprised at how much she'd enjoyed the visit to Parkwood. She'd expected it to be a gloomy sort of place filled with sad people, but had found everyone Jim introduced her to in high spirits, the staff really caring, and the house itself very beautiful. They'd said goodbye to Ernie when it was clear he needed to rest, and after a drink and sandwich in the bar with some of the residents, had driven down to the little church.

The day was already closing in, with storm clouds darkening the sky. Peggy held Jim's arm as they walked through the lychgate and down the narrow path that was slippery with fallen leaves. The church door opened silently on well-oiled hinges and Jim turned on the lights, bringing the lovely stained-glass window alive with colour.

As Jim had warned, it was quite austere inside, with rows of dark pews, a lectern carved into the shape of an eagle with spread wings and a choir stall and pulpit simply made from the same oak as the rafters that soared overhead. The floor was roughly hewn stone, worn in places by the tread of many generations of worshippers, and the standards of regiments past and present hung above plaster wall plaques commemorating those who'd died on the estate. Peggy looked around her and felt at peace. She could understand why the men found solace here, and was glad she'd come.

'I need to pop into the factory to make sure everything is running smoothly,' Peggy told Jim as they headed back to Cliffehaven. 'There was a bit of a to-do this morning with Florence.'

'I wondered why you'd gone out so early.' Jim glanced across at her, hoping for an explanation.

Peggy wasn't about to enlighten him. 'After that, we'd better go to Ron's and pick up Daisy. Charlie will be on the rugby field by now, and she'll be ready for her afternoon nap.'

They came down the hill and were about to turn off over the hump-backed bridge when they saw Gloria wrapped in a fake leopard fur coat tottering across the road with a holdall, followed by Beryl, Graham and Sandra. Jim tooted the horn and they all turned to wave before hurrying towards the Crown.

'I have to say,' murmured Peggy, 'they don't look very happy to be here. I do hope they haven't all fallen out already.'

'They're probably just tired after the journey, and this weather isn't helping,' replied Jim. 'And you know what Gloria's like – she speaks her mind and to hell with people's feelings.'

Peggy knew he was right and decided not to voice her worry that Sandra had looked unwell, and Graham down in the mouth. She waited for Jim to park the car by the factory. 'I shouldn't be long,' she said, climbing out and heading quickly for the door before the wind blew her hat off.

The machinists were clearly not in the mood for doing any work, but as it was almost four o'clock, it was hardly surprising. She smiled and nodded and greeted each one as she headed for the office, noting some wore tinsel in their hair or round their necks, and others had donned silly paper hats.

'I'm not staying,' she said to Florence as she entered the office. 'I just wanted to see if everything is all right here.'

'Mr Goldman came in about an hour ago with the Christmas bonuses, so no one's in the mood to go back to work,' Florence replied. 'I'm thinking of closing earlier than usual as all the orders have been filled and despatched, and there doesn't seem much point in keeping everyone here. Besides, I have to go and fetch Bobby from school in half an hour, and I daren't be late.'

'Have you heard how Gracie is?'

Florence nodded. 'The infection turned out to be more serious than we'd thought,' she said solemnly. 'They had to perform a hysterectomy, so she'll be in for some time.'

'Oh, no,' breathed Peggy. 'Poor Gracie. But how will you cope with Bobby?'

'He's a good child and very little bother. If I can manage this lot here, I'm sure I can cope with one small boy.' Florence smiled to ease Peggy's concern. 'Once she's well enough I'll take him in to visit, and of course I'll do all I can to make sure Bobby has a lovely Christmas.'

'She's not at the General, is she?'

Florence couldn't meet her gaze. 'Dr Darwin thought it best to take her to the cottage hospital. She's very poorly, Peggy, and will get much more focused attention there with a room all to herself instead of on the maternity ward.'

She took a breath and began to clear the paperwork on her desk. 'Danuta will be visiting her regularly and has promised to keep me informed about her progress and when we'll be allowed to visit. But I suspect it won't be for a while.'

All of Peggy's suspicions were aroused by this bit of news, but she kept them to herself. This was clearly not the time for the sort of questions she wanted to ask – and she doubted Florence would tell her anything, anyway. 'Well, I'm just thankful that Gracie's being so well looked after. Will you let me know when I can visit her?'

'Of course I will.'

Peggy dug into her handbag and pulled out a small gift. 'I'm glad I thought to bring this in the circumstances,' she murmured. 'It's for Bobby.'

'That's very kind of you, Peggy, and thank you for being so understanding about this morning.'

Peggy smiled. 'You've proved to be a very good friend to Gracie by taking her in when she had all that bother with Warner, and looking after Bobby while she was away. I hope she appreciates it, Florence.' She glanced down at the machinists through the office window. 'You might as well dismiss the staff and lock up so you won't be late to pick up Bobby. Drop the keys through Colonel White's office letter box. I'll let the cleaners in on the twenty-ninth so the place will be in good order for when we open again on the second.'

She gave Florence a brief hug. 'Try and have a happy Christmas, Florence, but if you need me for anything, you know where I am.'

13

'Right,' said Gloria, closing the front door behind her and dumping the holdall on to the floor. 'We've got two hours before I've got to open up, so let's have a drink to celebrate.'

'I'd prefer a cup of tea,' said Beryl.

'I wouldn't mind a whisky,' said Graham, rubbing his hands in anticipation before turning to Sandra with an obsequious smile. 'What about you, dear?'

'I don't feel well,' she replied truthfully. 'I think I'll go up to rest for a bit.'

'Well, you're a cheerful lot,' snapped Gloria, shrugging off her fake fur and slinging it over the newel post before putting her hands on her hips and glaring at them. 'I've had wet weekends that were brighter. What's the matter with you all?'

'I dunno,' said Beryl. 'Graham's been tight-lipped ever since they come to fetch me, and Sandra's in a funny mood altogether.'

'I told you, Mum. I'm not feeling well,' said Sandra, huddling into her fur jacket.

Gloria regarded her for a moment. 'You'd better go and lie down then,' she said. 'I've put you and Graham in the double at the back, and Beryl, you're in the single next to me.'

'I'd prefer to go into the other single,' said Sandra, avoiding meeting Graham's furious gaze. 'I don't sleep well when I'm feeling poorly, and Graham is like a bear with a sore head if he doesn't get his eight hours in.'

Gloria gave an exasperated sigh. 'You'll have to make up the bed then. I hope you're feeling better by tonight, because we're having a party in the bar.' She turned away. 'I'll stick the kettle on. Come on, Graham, let me get you that whisky. You look like you need it.'

Sandra hadn't been lying when she'd said she wasn't feeling well. The tensions of the day were already making themselves felt, but the return to Cliffehaven was even harder to bear, and now she had a thudding headache.

She slowly went upstairs to the small single bedroom that overlooked the pub's back yard and the narrow lanes and alleyways that threaded their way through the lines of Victorian villas. This room was where she'd spent the long summer holidays when she was small, summers when the days seemed to stretch for ever, when life was simple and she'd spent hours playing in the streets and hills with Cissy, Gracie and Anne and the other children. And in particular, it was in here last summer that she'd dismissed her doubts about marrying Graham, just as the ugliness of war was darkening all their lives.

Not wanting to dwell on these memories, she dumped her case on the floor and went to find a couple of aspirin from the bathroom and the bedlinen in the airing cupboard on the landing. At least she'd bought some time for herself, and as Gloria had agreed to her being in here, she could lock the door and continue to avoid sleeping with Graham.

The journey down had passed in frosty silence. Graham had read his newspaper from end to end, and her mother had buried her nose in her magazine – clearly in a huff because neither of them was particularly keen to share in her delight at Ivy's latest pregnancy.

The train had chuffed and puffed and rattled along, making the carriages sway and jolt as they crossed over junctions and headed further south. Other passengers had occupied the empty seats in their carriage, so any intimate conversation was thankfully out of the question.

Sandra had spent the ninety-minute journey staring out of the grimy window at the fields and villages they passed, watching the smoke and sparks from the engine get scattered by the wind. But as they'd drawn nearer to Cliffehaven and the scenery became hauntingly familiar, Beryl put down her magazine, and Sandra became all too aware of her puzzled gaze as it drifted from her to the grim-faced Graham and back again. There would be a confrontation before the day was out, and Sandra had mentally braced herself to face it.

With the bed made, she locked the door and drew the curtains against the darkness that had fallen outside. Still wrapped in her fur jacket, she settled on the bed beneath a blanket and closed her eyes. She would get through this.

Cissy's day hadn't improved. Following her lunch at Claridge's, Lulabelle demanded to be taken to Bond Street, and after that to a dressmaker in Sloane Square, before afternoon tea in Mayfair. The traffic was still bad, but as darkness fell and the rain began to bucket down, driving became hazardous with cars skidding on the wet tarmac, and deep puddles being formed in the potholes by blocked drains.

Cissy peered through the misted windscreen at the glare of headlights as the wipers battled to clear away the heavy rain and dirty water that was being thrown up by the wheels of passing buses and vans. Delivery boys on bicycles risked life and limb by weaving through the traffic at breakneck speed, and pedestrians dashed out from the pavements without a care for oncoming traffic.

Lulabelle of course complained about the weather and the puddles on the pavement when she had to dash from car to emporium, and then had the nerve to blame Cissy for frightening the life out of her when a delivery boy on a bicycle suddenly swerved in front of the Bentley, making Cissy brake so sharply her passenger had almost been thrown to the floor.

Cissy apologised profusely, kept her sour thoughts to herself and soldiered on towards Savile Row where the narrow streets were almost entirely jammed by limousines dropping and picking up their wealthy clients. But it seemed the parking gods were at last on her side, for she managed to nip into a space left by another Bentley outside the bespoke tailor's. There was no doorman here, so she quickly opened her umbrella to help Lulabelle out and was left without a word of thanks to watch her march inside to collect the new suit she'd ordered for her husband.

Cissy knew that if she dared move the car she'd never get another space, so she sat stony-faced behind the wheel, glaring at everyone as the wipers laboured on the fogged windscreen and everything became a blur in the bright moving lights.

Lulabelle eventually came out of the tailors followed by several young men carrying boxes and, as she sat impatiently in the warmth of the limousine, Cissy hurried to open the boot which was already jam-packed with her shopping.

Cissy gave up when it became impossible to cram anything more into the space. She asked the porters to carry the excess parcels into the car and, not wanting to inconvenience Lulabelle further by surrounding her with her purchases, had them stacked on the floor in front of the passenger seat. Having achieved this and been soaked through into the bargain, she got behind the wheel.

'Where would you like me to take you now?' she asked, dreading the thought of returning to the mayhem of Regent Street or Piccadilly.

Lulabelle looked over her powder compact, the tiny powder puff poised above her sharp little nose. 'Y'all can take me home now. I've done with London,' she drawled.

'You and me both,' breathed Cissy wholeheartedly.

The journey out of the brightly lit city took an age, but eventually she could put her foot down and they were motoring along, unimpeded, through the wide and almost empty streets of the suburbs. Into the darkness of the narrow countryside lanes, they passed through small villages where lights showed briefly from cottage windows and roadside inns, and then on through miles of unlit farmland to the vast estate that was home to Lulabelle and her titled husband.

It was all a far cry from Texas, Cissy guessed as she drove between the vast pillars topped by bronze stags. She headed up the gravelled drive towards the well-lit mansion and drew to a halt at the foot of the elegant steps leading up to the imposing front door. It opened and within seconds there were servants running towards the car beneath umbrellas.

Lulabelle hurried out of the car without her customary invitation to a light supper in the servants' quarters, and disappeared indoors. Cissy opened her own umbrella and went to organise the unpacking of the boot and the passenger footwell. Once Lulabelle's purchases were being carried indoors, Cissy got behind the wheel and, with a sigh of relief, drove round the turning circle and headed back to London.

She was now feeling quite faint from hunger as the sandwiches she'd brought had been eaten hours ago, and the flask of tea was empty. She began to look out for one of the inns she'd passed earlier, hoping they provided food as well as alcohol – though it was unlikely, especially this far out.

The rain was still bucketing down, the twin beams from her headlights cutting through a darkness so profound she had no idea what was on the other side of the hedges that lined the narrow road. She dared to open her window an inch to try and get rid of the mist on the windscreen, but the wind blew the rain into the car so she quickly shut it again.

She'd driven about eight miles when the car began to behave strangely. It was coughing and spluttering, and no matter what gear she chose, it seemed to be losing power. She felt the first tremor of panic as she pressed her foot on the accelerator and it made no difference. And then, to her horror, she saw that the headlights were beginning to flicker on and off.

'Oh lawks, now what?' she groaned, stamping her foot on the accelerator and changing down to first gear in the hope the car would do as she wanted. But with a final cough and judder, the engine died; the lights went out, and the car slid silently along the road until it came to a gentle upward slope and stopped entirely.

The panic was now very real. Cissy yanked on the handbrake, repeatedly turned the ignition key and pumped her foot hard on the accelerator. But there wasn't even a splutter of life in the engine or the lights. Her fear made her fumble as she reached into the glove box for the torch she always carried, but when she switched it on so she could look at the dashboard, the answer to her predicament was all too clear. The petrol gauge was on empty.

Cissy let out a stream of curses and hurried through the teeming rain to get the can of petrol she always kept in the boot. It wasn't there. She slammed the boot shut and burst into tears as the events of the whole ghastly day overwhelmed her. 'I don't believe it,' she sobbed, clambering back into the car. 'I just can't believe I didn't put it in there. What on *earth* am I going to do now?'

She sat there, the tears coursing down her face as she stared at the petrol gauge as if she could somehow magically will it to show at least a drop of fuel. Trying to remember the last time she'd seen the petrol can, she realised she *had* checked it was there when she'd set off this morning. The only explanation for its disappearance was that the men from the tailors must have taken it out when they'd loaded in Lulabelle's shopping, and forgotten to put it back.

Yet she only had herself to blame, for although she was being badgered by Lulabelle and in a tearing hurry to get the awful day over, she should have checked on it before she'd driven away, and also filled up during one of Lulabelle's long absences. To always check and never risk running out of fuel had been the first lesson that had been drummed into her at Cliffe Aerodrome when she'd been a WAAF, and now she was paying the price for letting herself become distracted and careless.

She sank back into the leather seat and swiped away her tears. Driving around London always used more petrol – she'd known that – and she'd experienced several close calls by leaving it very late to fill up when she'd had the chance – but without that can to save her, she was well and truly stuck.

She stared miserably out of the window into the empty darkness surrounding her. She was miles from the Surrey estate, and even if she wasn't, she'd be damned if she'd walk back there to ask for help – which meant she'd have to walk until she found an inn, or a village – or someone who could get her out of this bind. But that could be even more miles away, and the rain was now drumming on the roof so hard she could barely think straight.

Lighting a cigarette, she decided to stay in the car in the hope she could flag down a passing motorist. But an hour and two cigarettes later she was feeling quite nauseous, her head felt as if it was in a vice, and she was again in desperate need of a pee. There had been no passing cars, no tractor, not even a hardy pedestrian.

She flashed the torch over the dashboard clock, but that too had stopped. Her wristwatch told her it was almost ten, and soon the inns would be closing and people would be going to bed. She had no option but to get out and walk in the hope that civilisation – or what passed for it here in the middle of nowhere – was just around the next corner.

Thankful she'd thought to bring it, she dragged on her lightweight raincoat, grabbed her bag and umbrella and stepped out of the car into the driving rain. Attempting to open her umbrella, it was immediately blown inside out and snatched from her hand to disappear over the nearest hedge. Miserable and soaked through already, she locked the car, switched on the torch and began to walk down the road.

As much as she would have liked to stay locked in her room for the rest of the day, Sandra knew she couldn't. Her mother and Graham had both knocked and rattled the knob, asking how she was and if she needed anything. Now her Aunt Gloria was banging on it, refusing to leave until she opened up. She reluctantly climbed off the bed to face the music.

'It's about time,' Gloria snapped, arms folded beneath her vast bosom. 'You've 'ad yer mum and Graham worried sick. What's up with yer, gel?'

'I got food poisoning when I was away for work,' she replied, avoiding Gloria's penetrating glare. 'I'm still feeling the effects.'

'You'd better see the doc, then,' Gloria replied flatly. 'I'll ring through and get 'im out 'ere to give yer the once-over.'

'I don't need to see a doctor,' she said firmly. 'I'll be fine by morning, really I will.'

Gloria eyed her solemnly. 'Let's hope so, gel, cos I got things planned, and if this is really about you and Graham falling out, I ain't having it, you hear?'

'We haven't fallen out,' she muttered, her gaze fixed firmly on the floor.

'Yeah, and I'm the Queen of Sheba,' retorted Gloria, pushing her way in to shut the door behind her and therefore bar Sandra's escape. 'Something's up between you, and I ain't leaving 'ere until you tell me what's going on.'

Sandra was cornered and realised she would have to tell Gloria part of the truth if she was to be mollified. But Gloria was daunting to say the least when she was in this mood, and Sandra had to gather her courage before she could reply.

'I told Graham I'd been having an affair,' she said quietly. 'And asked him for a divorce. But he refuses point blank to give me one and has insisted we stay together until at least after Christmas.'

The heavily made-up eyes widened. 'Bloody hell, Sandra. You've only been married five minutes. No wonder he's wandering about like a lost soul.'

'It's seven years, actually,' she replied defiantly.

'Huh,' Gloria grunted. 'That's five minutes in the scheme of things, gel. You're suffering from the seven-year itch, that's all. You'll get over it,' she said with a dismissive wave of her hand. 'But you've been a bloody fool, Sandra, risking yer marriage by having an affair. Who was it? That fancy barrister you used to work for, I suppose?'

Sandra could only nod in the searchlight glare of her aunt's gaze. For all of her twenty-seven years, it was as if she was five again and caught doing something naughty – and Aunt Gloria was not a woman to rub up the wrong way.

'I see, so it's all been a bit of fun, 'as it? Or is 'e offering to marry yer?'

Sandra dipped her chin and miserably admitted he was already married, and that the affair was well and truly over.

Gloria gave a deep sigh and pulled Sandra into a tight embrace. 'I know it's 'ard, love, but you gotta put all that behind yer and work on yer marriage. Graham's a good bloke who went against his family to marry yer, and he's proved to be a proper diamond. I know he can't give yer kids, but yer luckier than most what come out of the East End, Sandra. You just remember that and 'old on to 'im, cos you ain't gonna find another like 'im, that's fer sure.'

She gave Sandra an extra squeeze and then suddenly pulled away, her expression hardening. 'I don't get to 'ave Christmas with me family very often, and I don't want you spoiling it – you hear? Now, fix yer make-up and hair and put on a smile and a pretty frock. There's a party starting downstairs, and you're going to bloody well enjoy it.'

As Gloria swept out of the room Sandra sagged against the brass bedstead. A party was the last thing she needed, but it seemed she had no choice in the matter. However, Gloria was bound to tell her mother about her affair, so no doubt she'd get another earful before the night was out – and Graham would be positively fuming about her airing her scandalous behaviour to Gloria. It was all too exhausting, really, but then that was the price she had to pay for the mess she'd got herself into.

Danuta was drooping with fatigue as she parked her little car and traipsed down the steep hill to where Stanislav was waiting for her at the front door. She walked into his encircling arms and gave a sigh of pleasure. 'It's so lovely to finally be home.'

He closed the door and with his arm about her shoulders, gently steered her into the tiny kitchen which was warmed by the roaring fire in the stove. 'It is very late. You come and sit down,' he said in Polish. 'I am heating the soup and the last of the vegetable stew, but first you must have a drink of vodka to raise your spirits.'

She dragged off her sodden raincoat and nurse's hat and kicked off her shoes. 'I'd rather have a cup of tea, Stan. I'm half frozen from all the running about I've had to do today, and there has barely been a moment to stop for tea.'

He eyed her with concern before putting the kettle on the hob. 'It was very bad? What happened?'

'Unfortunately, I can't really tell you very much, but yes, it hasn't been a happy day. I had one patient very early this morning who could have died because she stupidly ignored all the warning signs, so I had to call the doctor, and he took her straight to hospital. Thankfully, there is a chance she will get better – but it will take time. Then I had a young woman who went into premature labour with her first baby, and although I tried to revive him, and got the doctor out again, he was too small and weak to survive.'

She took a breath and let it out on a long sigh. 'Then there was the usual clinic and the everyday tussle of trying to persuade some of my pensioners to wash more thoroughly and eat properly. That's about it really.'

He bent to kiss her cheek. 'I'm sorry it has been such a sad day,' he murmured.

She kissed him back and reached for the mug of tea he'd placed on the table. 'This will revive me,' she murmured before taking a sip. The fragrant tea was strong and very sweet, and she dreaded to think how many spoons of rationed tea and sugar had gone into it, but it was what she needed and she felt very grateful to have it.

'I'm sorry for sounding so gloomy, Stan, but it hasn't all been bad today,' she said eventually. 'I popped in on Rachel Goldman earlier. Noel is thriving, and Rachel is positively radiant with joy at being permitted to care for him. I think she's rather hoping the mother doesn't turn up so she can keep him – but I doubt the authorities will allow it as they are both in their sixties now.'

'I have heard there are many children orphaned by the war, or put into care because the parents cannot look after them. Perhaps Rachel and Solomon will get their wish. You said yourself, they are well connected and rich – and experts at getting what they want.'

She regarded him with love and knew her eyes were gleaming with the suppressed excitement she'd been holding on to all day. 'Speaking of which, there is a possibility we might be moving out of here soon.'

He sat down with a thump on the other chair. 'How is this to be?'

Danuta smiled. 'Rachel is very good at getting people to talk to her, and before I knew it, I was telling her about our plans to adopt, and the difficulty of finding somewhere more suitable to raise a baby.'

Stanislav sat forward, his expression eager. 'She can help us?'

Danuta held up a warning hand. 'Maybe, but we must not get too excited, Stan, because nothing is certain yet.'

He brushed off her warning with a wave of his large hand. 'Tell me how this might happen, Danuta.'

She finished the cup of tea and poured another before replying as she was half afraid to even speak of it in case their hopes were dashed. 'A much older friend of theirs has a semi-detached house at the end of Elms Avenue, where the surgery is. Rachel told me that since his wife died, he's finding it difficult to manage the stairs and keep the house and garden in good order. She also told me in confidence that he really isn't looking after himself properly either, and there is some concern for his health.'

She paused to smile at Stanislav. 'This I know, because he is one of my patients.'

'Go on, go on,' he chivvied impatiently.

'Rachel has managed to persuade him to look for something smaller which he can manage, and she was considering buying the house from him as an investment to rent out.'

'But we agreed it would be good for us to buy, and not pay rent any more,' he said gloomily. 'I don't see that this will help.'

'It might,' she said, shooting him a grin. 'Because Rachel has advised him not to put the house on the market until he finds somewhere else to live, and has promised me she'll shelve her idea of buying it if we want to put in an offer first.'

'Those houses in Elms Avenue are very big and probably worth a lot of money,' he replied, shaking his head. 'The price will be too much for us, even with our savings, so I wouldn't get your hopes up, Danuta, my love.'

She gave a sigh. 'I know, but it's a lovely dream, isn't it? And you never know, Stan, the price might not be out of our reach if the bank agrees to top up our savings by lending us the rest.'

She drank the cooling tea and stared down at the tea leaves left in the bottom of the mug. 'I wish I could tell fortunes like the *babcie* back in Warsaw,' she murmured. 'It would be nice to know if we ever will move out of here.'

He took the mug from her and peered into its depths. 'I don't need grandmothers to see that supper, vodka and then making beautiful love to you in our bed is *our* fortune,' he said, dumping his mug in the sink before wrapping her in his arms. 'And you are my treasure – worth more than gold and large houses in Elms Avenue.'

Cissy trudged on in the darkness, the needles of wind-driven rain stabbing her face and soaking right through her clothes to numb her skin. The wavering beam of the torch followed the deserted country lane for what seemed like miles, while all around her there was silence but for the wind making the branches creak and the rattle of the rain in the hedgerows.

After all the years she'd been out in the hills at night with her grandfather Ron, Cissy had never been afraid of the dark and certainly didn't believe in ghosts, but this was alien territory and anything was possible. Telling herself to stop imagining things, she put her head down and picked up her pace, but when a vixen suddenly gave a blood-curdling scream close by, her heart missed a beat and she almost dropped the torch in fright.

'It's a fox,' she muttered. 'It's the countryside. She's probably more scared of me than I am of her. Just keep walking.'

She had no idea how far she'd walked, but her stockings were ruined, there was a blister forming on her heel, and she was so cold and wet she'd lost the feeling in her hands and face. If she didn't find shelter soon she'd die of exposure out here. She flashed the torch into the hedgerows on either side, and up the spreading branches of the almost naked trees. She would have to keep going.

Then she heard a distant noise – the unmistakable sound of an approaching car. With her heart pounding, she stepped into the middle of the road and waited until she saw twin headlights coming round a bend and heading straight for her at speed.

She waved her torch frantically and began to yell. 'Help! Help! Stop. Please stop!'

The headlights bore down on her, and she was poised to leap out of the way when the driver stamped on the brakes and the tyres squealed against the tarmac as the impetus of its speed sent the car sliding towards her. It came to a halt inches from her legs.

'What the *hell* do you think you're doing?' the driver roared as he climbed out of the sports car and strode towards her.

He was a big man and towered over her. She looked up into his furious face and burst into tears. 'I'm so sorry, but my car's broken down and I've walked for miles to try and find help.'

He glared down at her and snorted in disdain. 'Typical bloody woman,' he barked. 'Run out of petrol, I suppose?'

'Well, yes,' she admitted tearfully. 'Will you please help me? I really don't think I can walk any further.'

He eyed her from sodden shoes to wet and clinging clothes and up to her hair which was now plastered to her head and smeared in tendrils across her wet and frozen face. He gave a sigh. 'Apologies for shouting,' he said in a gentler tone, 'but you gave me a bloody fright. Thought I was about to flatten you.'

He held out his hand. 'Jonathan Meyers, landowner of this parish, and already rather late for an appointment. But glad to help a lady in distress if I can.'

'Cissy Reilly,' she replied, her hand feeling very small as it was enveloped in his large paw.

'Come on then. Let's get you in the car before we both drown.'

Cissy slid into the warmth and comfort of the little sports car and tried to control the shivers that wracked her frozen body. 'This is very kind of you,' she managed through chattering teeth. 'My car is somewhere back there.'

'Lucky for you I'm going in that direction and always carry a can of petrol,' he replied, putting the car in gear and heading off at speed. 'Do you have far to go?'

'Mayfair,' she replied, folding her arms tightly round her waist in an attempt to control her shivering and garner some of the warmth from the car's heater.

'You're a long way from home,' he said. 'What on earth are you doing all the way out here?'

Cissy told him the full story of her awful day, and was rather put out when he gave a bark of laughter. 'It isn't funny,' she muttered.

'Indeed it isn't,' he replied, still clearly amused. 'But if you will get involved with our Texan firebrand, you should always expect life to get difficult.'

They rounded a series of bends and the headlights suddenly picked up the Bentley looking very forlorn at the roadside. He slowed to a halt beside it. 'You stay in the car while I fill her up, and then I suggest you come to my place and dry off before you get pneumonia.'

He didn't wait for a reply but climbed out of the car which was really too small for such a large man, fetched the can from the boot and strode over to the Bentley.

Cissy could think of nothing she'd like more than to be warm and dry again, but could she trust this man? Then again, she didn't fancy driving all the way back to Mayfair in these soaking clothes.

She watched, still shivering, as he emptied the can into the Bentley's tank, checked the tyres and headed back to her. He was in his forties, she guessed, well dressed in country tweeds, sturdy brogues and a long, shoulder-caped waterproof coat that reminded her a bit of the ones depicted in the Sherlock Holmes stories. He certainly looked and sounded respectable, but then so had Clarissa's brother – and he'd proved to be an absolute rotter.

'There we are, all done,' he said after returning the can to the boot and climbing back behind the wheel. 'Now look here, Cissy Reilly, you're clearly frozen to the bone, and I really can't have you driving all that way in such a state. I realise you don't know anything about me, but I can assure you that I'm quite honourable – my wife sees to that,' he added with a grin which made him suddenly rather attractive. 'She's at home, so why don't you jump into the Bentley while I turn my car round, and follow me there?'

Cissy was tempted, for it did make sense. 'Your wife is at home? You promise?'

'I promise faithfully,' he said, hand on heart. 'Go on, get in your car and I'll escort you there before I carry on to my appointment. Flora will look after you – she's very good with waifs and strays.'

Cissy decided she'd risk it, so ran to the Bentley, unlocked it and climbed in before following him until they reached a gateway that led to a large farmhouse set some distance back from the road. She drove towards the house, noting the lights behind the curtains and the smoke coming from the chimney.

Jonathan introduced her to his wife, explained the circumstances and left again almost immediately. Flora Meyers was plump and motherly and seemingly unfazed by having a stranger foisted upon her at this time of night. She took charge of Cissy without any fuss, providing a hot bath, warm dressing gown and towels, and a plate of delicious and very welcome beef stew. The house was cosy beneath the low oak beams, the delicious smell of stew emanated from the large farmhouse kitchen, and the bathtub was deep. Having soaked for a while, and washed her hair, Cissy wrapped herself in the dressing gown and padded downstairs to the kitchen where her clothes were steaming on an airer in front of a huge range.

Three hours later, warm, fed and feeling very much better, she finally arrived back at the flat she shared in Mayfair. It was now almost three in the morning, but all the lights were on and she could hear voices in the sitting room, which wasn't unusual as her friends rarely went to bed before dawn. She'd already discarded the ruined stockings but kept her coat on as her clothes were still a bit damp, very wrinkled and unpleasantly clinging. Kicking off her mud-stained, wrecked shoes, she padded barefoot into the drawing room to find all three women glaring at her.

'It's about time you turned up,' said Clarissa. 'Where the hell have you been?'

Cissy was about to explain, but Clarissa cut through her words. 'Actually, I don't want to know,' she snapped. 'We've had some serious complaints about you and your disgraceful behaviour today. Not only that, Lulabelle has been talking to her friends and you've lost us at least another two of our most important clients.'

'But I . . .'

'There are no excuses, Cecily,' she ploughed on. 'This business relies on word of mouth and customer satisfaction. We have our reputation to think of – and today you have let all of us down.'

Cissy wasn't having that. 'Now, just a minute, Clarissa, you know how difficult Lulabelle can be,' she protested. 'It was why you dumped her on me in the first place. And the traffic was appalling. It really wasn't my fault things . . .'

'Enough!' Clarissa cut the air with her hand. 'We're done with having to bail you out of trouble every five minutes. Your contract with us will be terminated and your investment returned to you along with any other monies still owing.'

'You can't do that,' breathed a shocked Cissy.

'I think you'll find we can,' drawled Jacintha, who was lounging on the couch. 'We've had our lawyers look into it, and the papers will be delivered by courier later this morning.'

'You seem to have worked it all out very efficiently,' Cissy snapped. 'Are you also planning to dump me on the doorstep until the courier arrives?'

Annabelle, who'd been silent so far, got to her feet and reached for the jade cigarette box on the coffee table. 'There's no need for histrionics, Cecily,' she said. 'Of course you may sleep here for what's left of the night. But you'll have to clear out all your things by nine as my sister Alicia is joining the company and will be moving in before luncheon.'

Cissy folded her arms and fought to keep her temper. 'I see. So I'm supposed to just take this decision of yours without a fair hearing or a fight? How very convenient for you all that Alicia has suddenly come up with the money to invest when she's been pleading poverty for months. But I'm sure my lawyer will find something in that contract to stop you from doing this.'

'Oh, do have some pride, Cecily,' sighed Clarissa. 'We did our best for you, and even helped you out with that little problem you had recently, but even you must admit you never truly fitted in comfortably with our set.'

'Your brother didn't help in that matter,' she retorted, glaring at Clarissa.

'My brother was at fault, I agree – which is why that little problem you had was dealt with at my not inconsiderable expense.' She fitted a cigarette into a long ivory holder and, after lighting it, snapped the gold lighter shut. Her blue eyes were arctic.

'Your unfortunate indiscretion will remain our secret as long as you accept the situation and take the money. There should be more than enough for you to set yourself up quite nicely in more rustic surroundings – which I'm sure you'll find suits you better.'

Cissy saw the smirks the three women exchanged, and knew she was beaten. *What absolute bitches you all are*, she thought as she stared at them, seeing them as they really were for the first time. Smug, superior women who regarded themselves as entitled to ride roughshod over those they considered to be lesser mortals, and who'd now very firmly closed ranks.

She'd always suspected her tenure as their business partner would last only until they found someone else to take over her investment, and as Alicia had somehow stumped up the money, Lulabelle had provided the perfect excuse to get rid of her. But she was finding it almost impossible to absorb the fact that they'd turned their backs on her so brutally; that she was now homeless, friendless and out of a job.

She squared her shoulders and lifted her chin, determined not to lower herself further in their eyes by telling them what she thought of them, and marched into the bedroom, closing the door softly behind her even though she really wanted to slam it so hard it would rock the entire building and send it crashing down to smash their snooty, self-satisfied faces to a pulp.

She leaned against the door and slid to the floor as tears of anger and frustration streamed down her face. The unfairness of it all made her want to scream. Yet, as she buried her face in her hands, she knew she was meant to hear the loud, catty remarks and shrieks of cruel laughter coming from the other side of the door. They weren't her friends – never had been. Her life in London had turned into a nightmare, and now it was over.

14

It was almost eight o'clock on Christmas Eve morning and Peggy was in the dining room, helping Daisy put the last bits of tinsel and the few remaining baubles on the large Christmas tree that Jim had set up in the bay window. She watched the radiant little girl drape the tinsel round the lower branches, and marvelled once again how the magic of Christmas brought so much pleasure at that age.

Peggy gazed around the room, satisfied with her preparations. The floor had been waxed, a fire laid in the hearth, and the mantelpiece laden with gold tinsel from which hung Daisy's red cloth stocking awaiting Santa's visit tonight. She'd almost finished dressing the table and it looked lovely with her mother's white damask cloth, and her own handmade red napkins.

There were shop-bought crackers this year, and although the cutlery was as mismatched as the numerous chairs, it really didn't matter. She'd placed her mother's silver candlesticks down the middle and had almost finished making the centrepiece of holly, ivy and mistletoe. Jim and Ron had checked that the old gramophone still worked, and Charlie had insisted upon stringing paper chains across the ceiling, so it all looked very festive.

'Can we open the presents now?' Daisy asked hopefully, her gaze fixed to the collection of mysterious packages piled by her mother's feet.

'Not until tomorrow, darling. You know that. But let's put these under the tree for now, and then you can help me finish off the table centrepiece with that lovely red ribbon I bought yesterday.'

Daisy took the brightly wrapped parcels and stuffed them higgledy-piggledy with the others. 'Santa won't forget to come, will he?' she asked with an anxious frown.

'Santa never forgets, Daisy. Of course he'll come.' Peggy heard the sound of a car drawing up outside. 'That must be Daddy. I hope he's remembered to pick up everything on my list, because the shops will be shutting at noon.'

Daisy squeezed past the tree to look out of the window. 'It's not Daddy,' she said. 'But the man looks like Charlie, and he has a lady with him. A very pretty lady in a red coat, and with long golden hair like a princess.'

Intrigued, Peggy went to the window. 'Oh, my goodness,' she breathed, catching sight of the tall, slender girl climbing the front steps beside her very grown-up son. 'It's your big brother Bob, and that must be Pippa.'

'Who's Pippa?'

'She's Bob's friend, Daisy,' she replied in panic, quickly whipping off her apron and checking her appearance in the mirror above the mantelpiece as the sound of the front door knocker resounded through the house. 'Come on, we can't leave them out on the doorstep.'

Hurrying into the hall, she threw open the door. 'Bob,' she exclaimed, flinging her arms about him and giving him a huge hug. 'Oh, Bob, it's so wonderful to see you.'

He grinned back at her, unable to return her embrace as he was loaded down with bags. 'Mum, this is

Pippa,' he said, standing to one side so she could meet the girl who was shyly lurking on the step behind him. 'I know I should have warned you, but it was all rather last minute and . . .'

'It's lovely to meet you at last, Pippa, and you're very welcome,' said Peggy warmly. She shook the girl's hand, noting how soft it was, and came to the conclusion that Pippa did not work on her parents' farm as she'd been led to believe. 'Come in out of the cold, both of you. You must be exhausted after that long journey and frozen to the marrow.'

Bob waited for Pippa to enter the hall and then followed. 'Luckily the car has an efficient heater, and we stopped several times along the way to stretch our legs,' he said in the West Country burr he'd picked up during his long years in Somerset.

He put down the heavy bags and squatted in front of Daisy. 'How are you, squirt?' he asked, ruffling her curls and dislodging her ribbon. 'My goodness, you're a big girl now, aren't you – and going to school, too, I hear?'

'I'm not a squirt,' she protested. 'I'm Daisy.'

Bob laughed. 'Well, Daisy, I'm your big brother, Bob, and if I say you're a squirt, then that's what you are.' He tickled her to make her laugh, and then hoisted her into his strong arms. 'Say hello to Pippa, and then you can help me unpack some of these bags.

Daisy eyed Pippa with open curiosity. 'Hello,' she said. 'You've got a funny name.'

Pippa and Bob laughed, but Peggy didn't find it so amusing. 'That's rude, Daisy. Apologise.'

'It's all right, really, Mrs Reilly,' said Pippa, 'I don't mind.' She leaned towards Daisy. 'My name is actually Philippa,' she confided in the same soft Somerset burr, 'but I prefer Pip or Pippa, because it's short and sweet – just like you.' She gently poked Daisy's tummy and made her giggle again.

Daisy reached out to touch the long, shining fair hair that fell over Pippa's shoulders almost to her waist. 'Are you a princess?' she asked in awe.

Pippa giggled. 'I wish I was, but I'm just a girl who lives on a farm and works as a receptionist in a vet's practice while I'm at university.'

'That's enough questions for now.' Bob put Daisy back on her feet and picked up the bags. 'I'll drop this lot into the kitchen and go back to the car for the rest.'

'Goodness,' breathed Peggy. 'It sounds as if you've brought half of Somerset with you.'

His grin made him look even more like his father. 'Half of Somerset, and a huge hamper from Swansea. Auntie Doreen telephoned me very early yesterday morning to let me know she'd managed to get the things she was planning to bring down on the milk train to Bristol. I dropped in to Bristol to pick it up on the way here.'

With that, he strode into the deserted kitchen and dumped the heavy bags on to the kitchen table. 'Where is everybody?'

'Cordelia's still upstairs and your father has taken Charlie with him to fetch the last of my food orders and deliver presents to your grandad and Doris. They should be back any minute.'

Daisy clambered on to a chair to explore the bags' contents.

'Take your coat off and get warm, Pippa,' Peggy said, easing a protesting Daisy away from the enticing bags. 'I'll make us all a nice cup of tea. Have you had breakfast?'

Pippa had shed the lovely red woollen coat and was now warming her hands by the fire. 'Yes, we stayed in a hotel last night and ate before we set off again.' She hesitated, as if suddenly unsure of herself. 'It's very kind of you to let me stay at such short notice, Mrs Reilly. I did tell Bob he should warn you I was coming.'

Peggy silently noted they'd stayed in a hotel, but let it pass for the moment. 'I'm delighted to have you, and as you and my Bob are clearly very good friends, then please call me Peggy, or Aunt Peggy if you'd prefer. We don't stand on ceremony in this house.'

She waited in hope that Pippa would clarify her relationship with Bob, and explain why this visit was all so last minute, but the moment was broken by him slamming the front door behind himself and entering the kitchen laden with a huge hamper and a bulging hessian sack.

'Auntie Doreen said to put the cheese in the fridge straight away, and to keep the port somewhere warm,' he said to his mother. Turning to Daisy, he smiled as he shed his scarf, gloves and thick overcoat to sling them over the nearest chair. 'Do you want to help me put these presents under the tree?'

Daisy clapped her hands and danced from one foot to the other. 'Yes, please. Can Pippa come too?'

He shot a glance at his girl who blushed prettily and nodded.

Peggy's heart was full as she watched them troop back into the hall. Bob had become his own man, and Pippa seemed to be friendly as well as pretty, with her long fair hair, blue eyes and clear skin. The relationship must be far more serious than she'd thought, for he wouldn't have brought her home for Christmas if she'd been just a friend or passing fancy – and certainly wouldn't have stayed in a hotel overnight with her.

She gave a deep sigh and began to unpack the hamper. The years were flying by too fast and she'd missed so much of his growing up, what with the war, and his decision to stay down in Somerset to manage the farm which he would one day inherit from Violet. But he was here now, and she was determined to make the most of the time she had with him.

She placed the cheese in the fridge and eyed the bags on the table, her mind already racing ahead to the sleeping arrangements. Pippa would have to go in the room off the hallway instead of Bob, and he would be better off upstairs in Charlie's spare bed, which would leave the other attic room free in case anyone else wanted to stay over. Cissy could stay in her room as planned – if she put in an appearance.

Peggy bit her lip as a worrying thought occurred to her. Pippa's parents would surely expect her to keep an ear out for tiptoeing along corridors and landings in the night – though she hoped things hadn't gone that far – and that Bob was sensible enough not to attempt anything here. But just in case, she decided she'd keep her bedroom door ajar as long as the girl slept under her roof.

Sandra had managed to avoid being alone with her mother or Graham, both of whom had spent the evening glaring at her as she'd helped Gloria behind the bar and joined in with the singing and dancing that carried on until very late. There had been the inevitable fight over some girl, and two women had got into a hair-pulling, clawing brawl over a spilled drink, but Gloria had managed both incidents with practised expertise; a strong right arm and a voice that could shatter eardrums.

She'd slipped away unseen as Gloria herded her customers out of the bar and into the street at closing time. Quickly using the bathroom at the other end of the landing, she'd locked the bedroom door behind her and prepared for bed. She was stone-cold sober and utterly exhausted from the stress of keeping things to herself while battling with her stomach upset.

Waking later than usual that Christmas Eve morning, she reached for her dressing gown and climbed out of bed to use the bathroom, but upon opening her door, found her mother sitting outside it on a kitchen chair – and clearly fully prepared to have her say.

'For goodness' sake, Mum,' she sighed. 'I need the loo, and I really don't have anything more to say to you than you already know from Gloria.'

'That's as maybe,' she replied, her expression grim as she got to her feet and folded her arms. 'But we *are* going to talk, Sandra. And I won't be put off any longer.'

Sandra clenched her jaw. Wrapping her dressing gown more firmly about herself, she snatched up her washbag and stomped to the bathroom.

She deliberately took her time, and once she'd gathered up the nerve to face her mother again, went back to her room to find her sitting on the edge of the bed. Closing the door, she folded her arms and waited in stony silence for the diatribe that was about to come.

Beryl didn't disappoint. 'You're a bloody fool,' she snapped. 'What on earth did you think you were doing by risking everything for that toff you worked for? He ain't never going to leave 'is wife, yer know. He got what 'e wanted when you slept with him, you silly gel. And I bet he's already lining up another easy-goer to keep 'im happy once he's tired of you. And 'e will get tired of yer, Sandra; men like 'im always do once the novelty wears off.'

Sandra didn't bother to interrupt and tell her the affair was over – there would be no point as her mother just went on and on – and on.

'And another thing,' Beryl continued, barely pausing for breath. 'What's Graham done to deserve all this? That's what I'd like to know. He might not be able to give yer kids, but that man loves you; he's given you a posh house in a very smart part of town – AND he went against his family to marry you, for gawd's sake, and this is how you repay him – by asking him for a divorce.'

Beryl folded her arms, her face a picture of fury. 'Well, his family were right, weren't they? You ain't good enough fer 'im. I never felt so ashamed in my life. Gawd knows what yer poor father would 'ave made of all this.' She pulled a handkerchief from her cardigan sleeve and made a show of drying her eyes.

'Have you quite finished?' asked Sandra quietly. 'Because I'm getting cold and need to get dressed.'

Beryl's hand struck Sandra's cheek with the lightning speed of a cobra. 'Speak to me like that again, and I'll slap the other side even harder,' she snapped. 'Just because you're twenty-seven and full of airs and bleedin' graces don't mean you can give me lip, gel. You ain't too big to slap. In fact, you're a bleedin' disgrace altogether.'

Tears threatened to fall as Sandra felt the stinging heat of the slap and the deep barb of every word, and it was all she could do to fight back the desperate need to tell her mother the whole truth and be done with this awful charade.

'I'm sorry,' she managed. 'Just please don't keep on. I know I done – did wrong – but yelling and slapping me ain't – isn't going to change anything.'

'Then you'd better pull yerself together and put things right with yer husband before any more damage is done,' retorted Beryl. 'What you need is a kid to keep you at 'ome and together. Talk to 'im again about adoption, Sandra. He'll agree to it now, I'm sure.'

'That's where you're wrong, Mum,' she said flatly. 'Graham refuses to adopt another man's child, cos according to him, not knowing where it came from could bring endless trouble and complications, and Graham doesn't like complications – not when they upset his very orderly life. And you can't use kids to mend a marriage. It's not fair on the kid.'

Her mother's expression brooked no argument. 'Either way, you two need to talk and clear the air, before this goes too far. A man can only take so much, and once 'e's broken, you ain't getting 'im back. So be warned.'

'I will,' she promised aloud. But her internal voice was screaming, 'You don't know the half of it! And if you did you wouldn't keep on!'

It was now almost nine o'clock on Christmas Eve morning. Cissy hadn't slept but had spent the past few hours packing her belongings into suitcases and a holdall. She had lived in London for just over a year, and couldn't believe how much she'd accumulated – and how so little of it would suit her new life in Cliffehaven or wherever she'd end up next.

Thrift had been a byword when she'd been growing up, and it was a lesson she'd learnt well and stood by, so she'd saved hard during her time in London, but when she had spent money, she'd done it wisely by choosing well-made clothes that would last, and the odd piece of jewellery that would keep its value. The ballgowns, cocktail dresses, fancy shoes, evening jackets and numerous handbags were all second-hand and had been picked up for a song at a discreet little place off Bond Street that only a few canny women knew about.

Having discarded two ballgowns and three pairs of shoes, she crammed everything else into her two large suitcases before filling the holdall with toiletries, night-wear, velvet rolls of dress jewellery, and the small gifts she'd bought for her family. It was only then that she remembered she'd promised to take a cake home, but it was too late now – and her mother probably wouldn't be too surprised.

Feeling a headache coming on and in desperate need of sleep, she sank on to the bed and eyed the room she'd once loved. For all its grandeur, it now felt like a hotel room, and before this day was over, there would be another girl sleeping here. It was strange to have no regrets about leaving this place she'd once considered to be a dream fulfilled. But she must focus now on the coming days – days in which she'd be walking a tightrope of half-truths and down-right lies.

Unable to relax despite her exhaustion, she stripped off the clothes that had been ruined the night before and, leaving them in a heap on the floor, washed for the last time in the bathroom, took two aspirins to ward off the headache, and got dressed. Pulling on fresh underwear, she stepped into comfortable dark brown slacks, a cream silk shirt and a long, soft mohair sweater the colour of caramel. Low-heeled brown T-bar shoes and a brown overcoat trimmed with a mink collar completed her outfit.

After carefully applying her make-up to disguise the ravages of the past twenty-four hours, she put pearl studs in her ears and gold bangles round her wrists. She regarded her reflection in the long mirror behind the door, nodded with satisfaction and re-turned to the bedroom.

She picked up the two cases and carried them through the deserted sitting room to the hall and then returned for the holdall. Nothing stirred in the flat, and the only sound she could hear was the early traffic outside and the clink of bottles rattling on the milk-man's delivery cart. She paused by one of the long couches, noting the full ashtrays, the empty bottles, and carelessly discarded shoes on the floor where a mink stole lay forlorn and forgotten. The poor cleaning woman would have to sort out the mess – as she did every day – and Cissy hoped they would give her a good Christmas bonus on top of her meagre wages.

She took the holdall into the hall and picked up the telephone receiver to order a taxi. As she finished the call there was a discreet knock on the door.

The courier was tall and broad, dressed all in black, with a face that reminded her of a disgruntled bulldog. 'Miss Cecily Reilly?' he asked, without taking off his bowler hat. At her nod, he handed her an envelope. 'Please read that and then sign this other document.'

Cissy tore the envelope open to find a single sheet of thick creamy paper with the solicitor's company name emblazoned in black ink at the top. She read through to the end. 'Where's the money owing to me?'

'You must sign this first,' he replied, his expression stony.

She looked at what he'd handed her. It was an agreement to accept the sum in lieu of her investment, and further monies due to her through her partnership. In signing the document, she was giving up any rights to the private hire limousine company or its future monies, and promising that she would not contact any of the other shareholders from that day on.

Cissy was not her father's daughter for nothing. 'I need to know how much money it is before I sign any-thing,' she said, giving him her best smile. 'After all, I do have some idea of what they owe me, and I just need to be certain it's all there.'

He looked down his nose at her. 'I can assure you, miss, the firm's accountant has gone through the figures. We are a reputable establishment, and the correct sum has been calculated.'

'Let me see it then.' She held out her hand and maintained eye contact.

His gaze was unfriendly, but it seemed he was as keen as she to get this unpleasant business over and done with. He reached into an inside pocket of his coat and drew out a flat brown envelope which he grudgingly handed over.

Cissy would have preferred cash, but she pulled out the cheque and read the figures which were actually rather better than she'd expected. 'How do I know this won't be stopped before it can be cleared into my account?'

'As I said before, miss,' he said evenly, 'we are an old, established family firm and I do not like your insinuation that we are fraudulent.'

'You might not be, but I wouldn't trust those witches that pay you.' She saw the taxi draw up to the kerb and gave a sigh. 'I suppose I'm just going to have to trust you.' She signed his bit of paper and slipped the envelope into her handbag.

He took the signed document, tapped the brim of his bowler hat with a forefinger and walked hurriedly past the taxi driver who was coming up the path.

'You all right, miss?' he asked.

'Fine, thank you,' she replied, shooting him a smile. 'There are these two cases and the holdall. And before we go to the station, I shall need you to wait while I drop into Barclays Bank.'

'Right you are, miss. Hop in, I'll get this lot loaded up.'

Cissy sat impatiently while he drove through the London streets to her branch of Barclays. It was a good thing the banks were open this morning – a few more hours, and they would be closed until January, and she certainly didn't trust that bitch Clarissa to keep her part of the bargain.

Reaching the bank, she hurried up the steps to find there were long queues at all the tellers' windows, so turned wide-eyed and smiling to the assistant manager she'd flirted happily with during the year and a half she'd been coming here, and who was busy talking to one of the clerks. 'Excuse me, Mr Robson, I'm sorry to butt in, but it's a matter of urgency.'

'Yes, Miss Reilly. Always a pleasure to help.' He grinned back at her, clearly quite smitten.

'I have this cheque, you see, and it is rather urgent that it goes through before the end of business today.' She leaned towards him, batted her eyelashes and lowered her voice. 'I know it is a lot to ask, but if I don't cash it, I shall really be struggling over Christmas, and my parents are expecting me home.'

He actually blushed, which almost made her giggle – but he took the cheque, asked her to wait and then disappeared through a door next to the main desk.

Cissy kept checking her watch, hoping and praying he wouldn't be long, for there was a train she had to catch and she didn't fancy hanging around London for another hour and a half for the next one.

'All done,' he said quietly on his return. 'Although I did have to pull a few strings with the manager as it's an unusual request.'

'But the money is now in my account? They can't cancel the cheque?'

He smiled and shook his head.

'Oh, thank you,' she breathed. 'You are so kind.' She lightly kissed his cheek, deepening his blush. 'Happy Christmas, Mr Robson,' she said before dashing out of the bank and into the taxi.

Peggy had warned Jim that the shops would be closing at noon, and so he and Charlie picked up the turkey and bacon early from Alf the butcher, and the cake from the baker, before delivering the presents to his father and Rosie in Havelock Road. They had of course stopped for a glass of hot punch to catch up on Ron and Rosie's latest run-in with their neighbour, and Albert Williams's failure to find the missing mother.

It seemed that the neighbour was still complaining about the dogs, and poor Albert was staring retirement in the face as a new man was being brought in to take over in the new year. There was still no clue as to who the baby's mother might be, and the search for her had been set aside over Christmas.

Having left Ron's in a happy mood, they delivered cards to Doris – who luckily was out – as well as more cards and little presents to Kitty and the other fliers who shared an extended house set in a narrow, rutted lane on the hillside above the factory estate. Several sherries later, Jim was driving back up the High Street.

'Daisy's really looking forward to coming into town tonight,' he said, after popping more cards into letter boxes. 'She loves seeing the tree all lit, and Alan Jenkins all togged up as Santa on his sleigh. Just like you and the others did at that age. It's become a bit of a tradition, really, so I expect Anne and Martin will be there with their kids too. And if Bob and Cissy make it down in time, it'll be a real family gathering.'

'Ah, well,' said Charlie hesitantly.

Jim took his eyes off the road to glance across at his son. 'Well, what?'

'There's this party tonight, and I sort of said I'd take Christine,' he muttered.

'Oh, I see. So this girl and a party is more important than Christmas Eve with your family?'

'Don't be like that, Dad,' Charlie sighed. 'I'll be home for the rest of the time, and I did promise I'd take her to the party.'

Jim pulled the car up outside the fish and chip shop. 'I'll get us some chips to warm us up while we talk about it,' he said, getting out of the car before Charlie could reply.

Returning minutes later, he handed over two portions of chips wrapped in newspaper. 'Hold on to those while I park down on the seafront.'

'Dad, there isn't anything to talk about, really there isn't. It's just a party at a friend's house.'

Jim didn't reply until he'd parked facing the sea. 'Which friend?' he asked, taking his portion of chips and digging in.

'Tom Chester. You don't know him,' Charlie replied, blowing on a chip before popping it into his mouth.

It was like pulling hen's teeth. 'So, where does this Tom live?'

'Out towards Seahaven,' Charlie managed around the very hot chip.

Jim ate his chips and looked out at the cold grey waves rolling in like glass to break on the shingle. He'd managed to avoid having 'the talk' with Charlie, but now realised that the dreaded moment had come. 'Will Tom's parents be there?'

Charlie shrugged and kept his gaze firmly fixed on the sea. 'He didn't say, but I expect so,' he replied.

'And this Christine – her parents have given permission for her to go to this party with you?'

'Well, yeah, of course.'

Jim ate another chip which burnt his mouth and made it impossible to speak for a moment. 'How old is she, Charlie?'

'Sixteen.'

A dangerous age, thought Jim. *Too young to understand the passions that can rage through them at that age, but old enough to want to experiment.* He could remember it all too well. 'Look, son, I know we're both going to find this awkward but there are things we need to talk about.'

Charlie looked at him in horror. 'I don't need the birds and bees talk, Dad. We did all that our first term in sixth form.'

'The mechanics and science of it, maybe,' Jim ploughed on. 'But there's more to it than that – like loving the person, making sure they're comfortable with it all and . . .'

'Stop, Dad,' Charlie broke in. 'This is so embarrassing. Please stop.'

'It's not easy for me either,' Jim replied, 'but I'd be failing in my duties as a father if I didn't say something.' He rushed on. 'This Christine is still very young – you both are – and your mother and me understand how things can quickly get out of hand when beer and excitement are involved. But the consequences can ruin your life, son. And we don't want that for you when you have such a bright future ahead.'

'I do know, Dad. And me and Chris haven't . . . haven't . . . well, you know. Her dad's terrifying, and it would be more than my life's worth to do anything to upset him.'

'Good for him. But there will come a time, son – perhaps not with Christine – that you'll find someone and go that extra step. Taking precautions is vital if you don't want to end up with some girl in the family way – and the barber always has what he calls "something for the weekend", if you know what I mean.'

Charlie went scarlet and squirmed in his seat. 'Yeah. I do. Can we go home now?'

Jim grinned and softly laid his fist against his son's freshly shaven cheek. 'Lecture over, Charlie, I promise. But let's finish our chips first and get prepared for the chaos that's bound to greet us back at Beach View.'

Charlie grinned back and finally relaxed.

15

Doris had finished the last of her shopping just as the High Street began to close at lunchtime. Relieved that she'd managed to find everything on her list and that her larder was fully stocked for the week ahead, she drove back to Mafeking Terrace to unload the car and prepare for Anthony and Suzy's arrival.

The house looked lovely now the decorations were up and the tree was glittering with lights, tinsel and glass baubles in the corner of her large, elegant dining room. She'd laid the fire in preparation for tomorrow, and the table was already dressed quite elaborately for Christmas dinner, but this evening they would eat in the kitchen and use the small sitting room on the other side of the hall as it was cosier once the fire was lit in there. The guest bedroom and bathroom which, before the conversion, had once been John's bedroom and sitting room were all made up, and she'd readied the smallest bedroom for Teddy and Angela with a single bed and cot.

She carried her shopping in and put everything away before wrapping the last few gifts and opening the card that someone had dropped through the letter box. Seeing it was from Peggy, she smiled and placed the card on the mantelpiece with all the others. They'd received quite a few, which was gratifying, and she was delighted that so many of Cliffehaven's most worthy from the golf club and officers' club had sent their greetings. It just went to show that she and John were moving in the right circles – although she'd never say that to him as he'd probably call her a snob.

Realising that time was passing, she finished laying the kitchen table for their evening's meal and remembered to put a cushion on Teddy's chair so he could reach his food more easily. She'd cleaned the high chair she'd bought at a jumble sale the year before so baby Angela could join in the fun, and there were red cloth stockings hanging by the fire in the dining room to be filled tonight after the children were in bed.

She should have felt relaxed and happy that her darling Anthony would soon be here with her beloved grandchildren, but in fact she was quite tense. She'd never really taken to Suzy, and she found it hard to be at ease with her, although she didn't really know why, as there was nothing actually wrong with the girl, and Anthony seemed happily married to her.

And then there was the situation with John. He might have said he wanted to forget the distressing falling-out they'd had the other day, and he had put up a good pretence of having done just that – but she'd noticed a coolness that crept into his eyes occasionally, and a sense of him distancing himself, which upset her terribly.

She so wanted him to love her the way he had before that awful day up in the office, and she'd tried very hard to make him believe that she really regretted what she'd said and was determined never to air those views again. But the stress of having to watch what she said all the time was beginning to tell on her. She had the feeling that the damage had been done, and it would take a long time before he truly forgave her.

Her gloomy thoughts were scattered by the sound of a car pulling up outside. Hurrying to the door, she waved excitedly from the doorstep to welcome her son and his lovely family. *Remember to be nice to Suzy*, she thought, as she watched her climb out of the car with little Angela in her arms.

'Suzy, how lovely to see you,' she said with all the enthusiasm she could muster. 'Come in and get warm. You must all be frozen after that long journey, although that gorgeous fur coat is surely helping.'

'Hello, Doris,' said Suzy, giving her a broad, happy smile. 'The fur's an early Christmas present from Anthony. Would you like to take Angela while I help him unload the car?'

Doris wondered how Anthony could afford such an expensive coat but kept her thoughts to herself. 'I'd be delighted to have her.' She took the little girl into her arms and nuzzled her sweet face. 'Hello, darling, welcome to Grandma's house. Now where's that brother of yours, eh?'

Teddy came running down the path to throw his arms round Doris's legs. 'Hello, Grandma,' he shouted, his face alight with excitement. 'Is Santa here yet?'

Doris laughed and bent to stroke his fair curls. 'He'll be here later while you're asleep. Come on in and let's see if I can find you both a nice bit of cake and a warm drink.'

Anthony and Suzy eventually followed them into the kitchen which was cosy from the stove. He put down the many bags and gave his mother a hug. 'It's lovely to see you again, Mother. I'm just sorry we can't get down more often.'

She softly patted his face and looked at him in adoration. 'Well, you're here now, so let's enjoy the time we have together. John should be home soon, and I've planned an early supper so we can take the children down to see the tree lights and listen to the band. Peggy and her lot will be down there, so it will be a real family occasion.'

'Indeed it will,' said Anthony, helping himself to a large slice of Victoria sponge as Suzy saw to the children. 'Are they going ahead with the children's service in light of what that girl did?'

'Of course they are,' she replied. 'Nothing is allowed to break the Christmas tradition, and that baby was only there a matter of minutes, thanks to Bertie's impeccable timekeeping.'

'Who do you think the mother is?' asked Suzy as she held the cup for Angela to drink the milky tea.

Doris was about to reply when she suddenly became aware of John coming through the front door to stand in the hall and listen. 'There are rumours, of course, but no one really has any idea,' she replied. 'Whoever she is, I hope someone is looking after her. One can't imagine what must have driven her to make such a decision.'

John came into the room and smiled down at Doris, then kissed Suzie's cheek and shook Anthony's hand. 'I see the clan's all here,' he said cheerfully. 'Let's have a glass of champagne to get us all in the mood for a wonderful Christmas.'

Doris felt warmth in her heart for the first time since their falling-out. Maybe it was going to be all right after all.

Cissy was relieved when the other people sharing her carriage left early on in the journey, for the quiet meant she could spend the time planning how she would tell the family that she'd been sacked from her business partnership and was now homeless. But that was actually the least of her worries in many ways. As the scenery became ever more familiar and the train chugged along the spur line to Cliffehaven, her heart began to thud so hard that she thought it was about to break through her chest.

She could barely breathe as the train slowed and then drew to a screeching halt. There was no going back now, and nowhere else to run to, so she fumbled to drag her large cases from the luggage rack, pulled the leather strap to open the window and leaned out to push down the door handle.

Putting her cases on the platform, she reached in for the holdall, slammed the door shut and looked at the deserted platform with its single light glowing in the early gloom above the exit. Gone were the days of porters, the waiting room, booking office and the friendly smile of Uncle Stan who'd been stationmaster here since Noah built his ark. She stood feeling isolated and lost as the train pulled out.

'Looking for a taxi, miss?'

The deep voice had come out of the shadows beyond the confines of the station. 'Yes, please,' she called back. 'But I will need help with my luggage.'

'It's a good thing you've got me, then isn't it, Sis?'

'Bob! Oh lawks, how big are you?' she squealed as he grabbed her by the waist and swung her off her feet. 'Put me down, you great lummox,' she laughed, holding tightly to his sturdy arms. 'You're making me giddy, and I'll lose my hat.'

He set her back on her feet and grinned down at her. 'You're shorter than I remember,' he said, 'and far too skinny after all that high living in London.'

She smothered a giggle and slapped his arm. 'You sound like a proper Farmer Giles from Somerset, but as your big sister, I'd like to remind you that I'm owed some respect, Robert Reilly. I'm neither skinny nor short. You just grew bigger than Dad, and you're certainly giving him and Charlie a run for their money in the wide-shoulder stakes.'

'Ooh argh,' he teased, waggling his dark eyebrows. 'Still a bossy-boots, then.'

Still smiling, she pulled the fur collar closer to her neck. 'I hope you've got a car,' she shivered, 'because I don't fancy lugging this lot all the way home.'

'Your carriage awaits, me lady,' he said with an even more pronounced Somerset burr, tugging his forelock, before grabbing the cases. 'This way.'

'Goodness, you have gone up in the world,' she said, admiring the large black saloon. 'I thought you farmers were always pleading poverty.'

'It's Auntie Vi's,' he said, dumping her luggage in the large boot before opening the door for her. 'She doesn't drive much so she lent it to us to come down here in comfort.'

Cissy looked at him sharply. 'Us?'

'Me and Pippa.' He made the car rock on its chassis as he sank into the driving seat. 'And before you ask, yes, she's my girlfriend; no, we're not engaged or secretly married; and yes, her parents know where she is; and no, we aren't sleeping together.'

Cissy chuckled. 'Well, as the Americans say, "Hold the front page." Thanks for the information, Bob, but have you told Mum all this?'

Bob's cheeky grin reminded Cissy of the little boy he'd once been. 'She's probably grilling Pippa right now, so we'd better get back and rescue her.' He turned the key in the ignition and switched the headlights on. 'Oh, and another thing – mind what you say to Charlie. He told me that Dad gave him the birds and bees talk this afternoon because he's going to some house party with a girl, so he's not in the best of moods.'

Cissy groaned. 'Lawks, how embarrassing. Poor Charlie. I remember when Mum had that talk with me and Anne. We were giggling for ages afterwards, because we neither of us really understood what on earth she'd been going on about.'

'Charlie knows more than he lets on,' said Bob, steering the car away from the station. 'We had a chat before he left Somerset, but as he'd grown up on the farm, there wasn't much he didn't already know or guess.'

Cissy buried her chin in her fur collar and regarded the bright displays in the shop windows as they went down the almost deserted High Street. The tree outside the Town Hall looked festive, though the lights hadn't been switched on yet, and Gloria had gone overboard on the decorations as usual with a vast wreath of holly and red ribbon on the front door and strings of paper chains and lights in every window.

'I suppose we'll be coming back into town for the ceremony around the tree, and then the service in the church?' she murmured.

'It's a family tradition, Cissy, you know that, and your life won't be worth living if you don't take part. Charlie's already in the doghouse because he's off to his party.'

Cissy bit her lip and stayed silent, her thoughts in a whirl as Bob drove along Camden Road towards Beach View. She really didn't fancy standing about in the cold listening to the Sally Army band, and certainly didn't want to go to the service in that church – but if she tried to get out of it, there would be questions, and they were to be avoided at all costs.

'Here we are – home, sweet home,' said Bob, parking the car at the kerb in Beach View Terrace. 'I have to say, Cissy, you've brought a heck of a lot of luggage with you. Are you planning to stay on after Christmas?'

'I like to pack everything – just in case it's needed,' she replied vaguely. 'What I want to know is how you knew I'd be on that train?' She was desperate to avoid further questions.

'I didn't, but Mum asked me to drive to the station every hour just in case, so that when you did arrive, you wouldn't have to walk home.' He turned and looked at her with concern. 'Are you all right, Sis? Only you're very pale, and you don't look as if you've slept or even eaten properly for weeks.'

239

'I'm fine,' she fibbed. 'As for sleeping, there isn't much chance of that in London when there are parties every night and fussy clients to ferry about all day.' To avoid further questions, she reluctantly opened the door and climbed out to look up at Beach View.

It was the only real home she'd known, and after her grandfather, Ron, and Uncle Frank had done the refurbishments, the ugly scars of war had been erased. The stucco was fresh white, the glass replaced in the windows; the front door was a lovely dark blue above the repaired concrete steps. There were new lanterns set in the low pillars at the foot of the steps, and she could see a brightly lit Christmas tree in the bay window of the dining room.

In that moment she wondered why she'd been in such a hurry to leave this place when it had offered so much love and comfort and held such fond, happy memories. Now she was back, older – probably not much wiser – and deeply troubled. Would there still be love and shelter here once her family knew the truth? She very much hoped so – but it certainly wasn't guaranteed.

'Something's eating at you, Cissy. I can tell,' said Bob softly. 'What happened in London?'

'Things I'm not yet ready to talk about, Bob,' she said on a sigh. 'And please don't say anything to Mum, she'll only worry.' She took the holdall and smiled up at him with deep affection. 'Thanks for asking, though.'

'Well, when you're ready to talk, I'm happy to listen, Sis. A problem shared and all that . . .'

She nodded, unable to speak as she battled to keep her emotions in check. Grasping the handles of the bag, she plodded up the steps and waited for Bob to unlock the front door. As she stepped into the familiar hall, she could hear Daisy chattering, Cordelia giggling, and the clatter of pots and pans coming from the

kitchen. Her heart was thudding again, making it difficult to breathe as she stood there, every second feeling
like a minute as she clutched her large handbag to her
chest and steeled herself to face her mother.

Peggy came dashing into the hall to throw her arms
around her. 'Cissy, you came! Oh, darling, it's so lovely
to have you home.'

Cissy tearfully leaned into the embrace, breathing in
the scent of her, and revelling in the warmth she'd
missed for so long. 'I said I would come,' she said,
drawing back. 'I wouldn't dare miss a Beach View
Christmas, would I?' she joked weakly.

Peggy regarded her with a frown. 'Are you all right,
Cissy? Only you look very washed-out, darling, and
you seem to be bundled up in layer upon layer of
clothing. Have you lost weight?'

Cissy avoided her mother's gaze and pulled her
thick overcoat more firmly over her chest. 'I had a
nasty bout of the flu not long ago and have felt the cold
ever since,' she said. 'No doubt one of your famous
cups of tea will put me to rights.'

Peggy caught her hand as she was about to head to
the kitchen. 'Are you sure that's all, Cissy?' Her voice
was quiet, her gaze penetrating and full of questions.

'Of course it is,' she said dismissively. 'Honestly,
Mum, you do worry needlessly.' She eased from her
staying hand and quickly headed for the kitchen.
'Hello, everyone,' she said brightly as she posed in the
doorway. 'I've arrived!'

'Trust you to make a grand entrance, my wee girl,'
said Jim, leaping out of his chair to wrap her in his
arms. 'My little Cissy is still the star of the show.'

Peggy followed Bob into the kitchen and silently
watched her daughter kiss and hug her father, Charlie,
Daisy and Cordelia before prettily greeting Pippa, and
settling down by the fire for a gossip. Cissy was

certainly putting on a star performance, but something was wrong behind that bright smile and brittle laughter. She was too thin and pale – and then there were those big suitcases in the hall. Something had happened in London to cause this change in her darling girl, and Peggy had a nasty feeling that whatever it was, it had broken her daughter's heart.

Sandra had spent most of the morning keeping busy so she didn't have time to dwell on things, or be left alone with a sullen Graham. She'd helped her mother and Gloria ready the bar for the midday session, and then cleaned up the mess afterwards. Once she'd finished making the mince pies and preparing the vegetables in readiness for the following day, she'd waited for her mother and aunt to get stuck into the sherry with Graham, and then pulled on her hat, coat and walking shoes and escaped.

Living on the outskirts of London and working in the City, she'd missed the sight, sound and scent of the sea, and although it was bitterly cold down on the front, she found it invigorating and restorative. She walked from east to west, noting the bomb craters, the missing houses and hotels which had been turned to rubble, and the children playing amongst the debris in search of treasured shrapnel and bits of planes, just as they did in London.

She stood for a while watching the waves splashing against the last rusting remains of the pier as the memories flooded back. She'd spent many happy hours on there with Cissy and Anne and her other Cliffehaven friends, riding the carousel which had stood at the far end, and attending the summer shows with her parents and the Reillys in the big theatre with its glass domed roof, orchestra pit, and red velvet seats. Cissy had been part of the troupe that performed there, and she remembered she'd been envious of her vivacity and lack of stage-fright as she'd high-kicked and sung in the chorus, all gussied up in heavy make-up, sequins, feathers and fishnet stockings.

Sandra smiled at the memory. Cissy was younger than her by a few years, but she'd always led her into mischief and certainly had what the old Jewish traders called chutzpah. It was little wonder that she'd left Cliffehaven for the bright lights of London, for a girl like Cissy was meant to live life to the full – and according to Aunt Gloria, she was now a partner in a very swanky private chauffeur business based in Mayfair, and no doubt being wined and dined at all the very best places London had to offer.

She sighed. Although she'd escaped the East End by sheer hard work and elocution lessons to end up with a responsible job at the Inns of Court – and although she was married to a respectable man who'd given her a home and status to be proud of – she hadn't achieved much with her life really.

Turning her back on the boats and the tall white cliffs, she began to stroll towards the hills that rolled gently down to the shingle beach. The Victorian shelters had been repaired quickly after the war to encourage the return of the holidaymakers who'd arrived in their droves. It all looked rather forlorn now the deckchairs and parasols had been stowed away for the winter. The little wooden kiosk at the western end of the promenade had been boarded up too, so there was no chance of a cup of tea, but if the Lilac Tearooms was open, she would be able to sit in there for a bit and get warm before she had to face her family again.

The bell above the door tinkled as she stepped inside to be greeted by the hum of happy chatter and the delicious scent of coffee and fresh baking. There was a table free by the window, so she sat down, unwound her scarf and unbuttoned her coat before ordering a pot of tea and a scone with jam and cream. The walk had made her hungry for the first time in ages, and she was looking forward to being able to relax and enjoy these few moments of peace.

There was a fire in the Victorian hearth, and tinsel round the mirror above it, with paper chains strung between the oak beams of the ceiling. A tiny Christmas tree stood on the front windowsill with a sign wishing everyone a joyful yuletide, and each table was covered with a red and white gingham cloth, a sprig of red-berried holly jammed into a tiny pot at the centre.

Her order arrived and she poured the tea, adding milk and a few grains of sugar. It was utter bliss to be alone and to savour a cup of decent tea for a change.

'Hello, Sandra. Mum said you were down. Do you mind if I join you?'

Sandra's fleeting annoyance at being disturbed fled as she saw Cissy Reilly standing next to her. 'Of course I don't mind,' she said, quickly getting to her feet to welcome her with a kiss on her cold cheek.

And then she looked more closely at her childhood friend and realised all was not well with her. 'My goodness, Cissy,' she stammered. 'I was only just thinking about you.'

Cissy's answering smile was wan. 'All good things, I hope,' she replied, divesting herself of her overcoat to reveal layers of what looked like very expensive knitwear masking a bony frame.

Sandra felt another pang of concern at how drawn and thin her friend looked but didn't remark upon it as she probably didn't appear especially bright herself. 'Of course, all good things.' She waited for Cissy to settle at the other side of the table. 'It's lovely to see you after so long,' she murmured. 'How are you?'

'Fine, thanks,' Cissy replied, shooting Sandra a brittle smile that didn't quite hide her feelings.

Sandra decided to keep things light for the moment, for it was clear that Cissy was troubled with something but unwilling to talk about it. 'I don't know about you, Cissy, but I'm escaping for a bit. Aunt Gloria can be a bit too much at times,' she admitted ruefully, 'and when she and Mum get together over the sherry, it's even worse.'

'So can my lot,' Cissy replied after ordering tea and a crumpet with jam. 'Mum's dashing about like a whirlwind and Dad's moaning about the cold; Daisy's overexcited, Charlie's itching to be off to some party and Bob's brought home a girlfriend who's so over-whelmed by us all she can hardly put two words together.'

'Poor girl,' murmured Sandra. 'I remember how it was when Graham took me to meet his parents at their posh place in Twickenham.' She pulled a face. 'Coming from the East End, I went down like a lead balloon, of course, and once it was clear they didn't approve, I clammed up and stopped trying to impress them – which made Graham difficult to live with for the next two days. At least your parents aren't stuck-up, and I'm sure your mum will make sure she fits in all right.'

'Yeah, Mum's good at putting people at ease.' Cissy paused while the waitress served her tea and buttered crumpet. 'So, how long are you down for?' she asked as she poured the tea.

'We go back after Boxing Day. Graham has to be in his office on the twenty-eighth.' She shrugged and shot Cissy a wry grin. 'No peace for the wicked – or busy accountants. What about you? I hear you're making pots of money in London, so I suspect you won't be staying long down here.'

'I'll stay until after New Year,' said Cissy, loading the buttery crumpet with jam. 'London's lost its sparkle after the mayhem leading up to Christmas. You really wouldn't believe how some of our clients demand the impossible, and then blame you when you can't make it happen.'

Sandra caught the sharpness in Cissy's tone and wondered if her work was the root cause of her unhappiness. 'I was always surprised you never continued with your stage career,' she said. 'You were ever so good in those shows on the pier.'

Cissy chuckled. 'No, I wasn't, and those dreams got knocked out of me when I joined the WAAFs and ended up driving wing commanders about during air raids up at Cliffe Aerodrome. I had to grow up fast – as I expect you did.'

Sandra nodded as she finished a mouthful of delicious scone, cream and jam. 'I worked at the Inns of Court all the way through, but put in the hours at night fire-watching and digging people out of burning buildings. Graham had a cushy desk job with the Treasury, but I saw some terrible things – especially when the whole of the East End went up in flames.'

They drank their tea and ate their treats in silence, united by their experiences of the war, and the childhood months they'd shared during Sandra's summer and Christmas visits. However, the newspaper lying on the table next to them with its photograph of that caravan made them both aware of the subject neither of them wanted to broach, for the caravan up in the hills had been a part of those childhood memories, and was now tainted by what had happened since.

Sandra finished her tea and scone and sat back with a contented sigh. 'I suppose I'd better get back or Graham will be sending out a search party. Are you going to the tree ceremony later?'

'It's more than my life's worth to miss it,' Cissy replied, 'though I really don't think I can sit through the vicar droning on.'

'Me neither. After all, it is for the little ones, and church doesn't really have the same meaning for me that it once did.'

'Nor me,' said Cissy. She leaned forward across the table, her face suddenly animated. 'Shall we sneak off and meet at the Anchor instead, then?'

'Yes, let's,' said Sandra and grinned. 'Though there'll be hell to pay after. But we've got a lot of catching up to do, and I'll be with the family all day tomorrow and Boxing Day, so they can't moan.'

Cissy grinned back. 'It's quite like old times, isn't it? Us bunking off?'

Sandra giggled. 'At least boys aren't involved this time, and you won't insist we act out some silly play you've dreamt up and make me and Gracie dress in costumes you borrowed from the theatre. I seem to remember you were always the heroine and Gracie and I were the villains.'

They shared a smile as the memories united them and the years they'd been apart felt as if they were only hours. And then Cissy gave a gasp. 'I almost forgot,' she breathed. 'Mum told me that Gracie's been taken really ill and is in hospital. She didn't go into much detail – but it's women's trouble by the sound of it.'

'Oh, no, poor Gracie. Will it mean she'll be in over Christmas?'

Cissy nodded. 'It sounds as if she will. Her little boy is being looked after by the woman they lodge with, but it does seem horribly unfair after all she's been through.'

Sandra gave a sigh. 'Gracie's had a lot to contend with since her husband was killed in the war and their home was bombed. I do hope she pulls through this.'

'It's all a bit touch and go, according to Mum, but if she does pull through enough for visitors, I think we should try to get to see her. It might boost her a bit to see old faces again.'

Sandra grinned. 'Less of the old, if you don't mind. But yes, I agree to visiting if we can. We all go back a long way, and it sounds as if she needs all the support she can get.'

Having decided on this, they stood, paid their bills and wrapped up again against the cold before going outside.

'Ta ta for now,' said Cissy, giving Sandra's hand a brief squeeze. 'See you in the Anchor at six.'

Sandra watched her walk away and then headed up the High Street towards the Crown. Cissy appeared to be as bright and vivacious as ever, but there was something different about her, and she wondered if Cissy's life in London really was as good as everyone thought, or if there was another reason behind the sadness in her eyes – but then perhaps it was only a reflection of her own unhappiness that she'd seen.

16

Gracie opened her eyes and tried to work out where she was. She felt light-headed and as weak as a kitten, and when she tried to move against the pillows the dull ache in her belly became a ball of fire.

'Don't try and sit up, Gracie,' murmured Danuta. 'You're in the cottage hospital and have had an operation.'

Gracie looked about her and saw the needle in the back of her hand which led to a drip hanging above the bed. 'What happened?' she rasped. 'Who brought me here?'

As Danuta went through the events of the previous day and gently explained about the severity of the infection which had led to a hysterectomy, she tried to take it all in. But her thoughts were muddled and she was so tired her eyelids felt as if they were made of lead. 'Does that mean no more babies?' she managed.

'Yes,' said Danuta softly. 'I'm afraid it does. I'm so sorry, Gracie, but there was nothing else they could do – and it probably saved your life.'

The tears ran hot down her face. 'And Bobby? Where's my Bobby?'

'He's safely at home with Florence,' soothed Danuta. 'And if the doctor thinks you're strong enough for visitors, he will come to see you tomorrow.'

'But it's Christmas and . . . Bobby's stocking . . .' Gracie tried to fight the waves of sleep that washed over her, but they were too strong – too powerful – and she was only vaguely aware of Danuta drawing the bedclothes over her shoulder and stroking back her hair before oblivion returned.

Peggy had managed to coax Pippa into telling her about her parents, and had discovered they'd decided to go to Cornwall to her mother's much older sister for Christmas. As Pippa didn't really get on with the elderly woman who lived in a tiny house filled with the stray cats she'd taken in, her father had agreed she could accompany Bob to Cliffehaven on the proviso that they both behaved themselves.

Peggy rather liked the girl, not only because she was clearly in love with Bob, but because beneath that shy exterior, she was ambitious. Pippa had confided in her that she was studying to be a vet and her part-time work as a receptionist at a local vet's practice was not only helping to pay for her university but giving her hands-on experience of how a practice ran.

They had spent a pleasant half-hour chatting while Bob and Jim erected a sturdier shelter over the chicken coop, and Charlie went upstairs to get ready for his party. But Peggy's mind was still troubled over Cissy, for the girl had left the house in almost indecent haste after taking all her bags up to her room.

It was a huge relief to see that her girl looked a little brighter on her return from her walk, and Peggy was delighted to hear that she'd caught up with Sandra, for the two girls had known each other since they were toddlers playing with their buckets and spades in the sand. However, the time was fast approaching for the start of the tree ceremony, so Peggy didn't get the chance to delve into what was clearly troubling her daughter.

She chivvied Daisy into her coat, hat and shoes, and while Pippa helped her with her mittens, Peggy took the opportunity to dab on some powder and a dash of lipstick. Dressed and ready to go, she looked round for Charlie.

'He slipped out while you were busy with Daisy,' said Jim. 'Don't worry, Peg. He's had the talk. He'll be fine.'

'Let us hope so,' she muttered, distracted by Cordelia calling to her from the hall. 'What is it, Cordy?' she asked, hurrying to her.

'I'll wait here for Bertie,' she said, settling on the hall chair. 'He's driving me there and back as I can't manage the walk any more. But do you think you could help me with my gloves? I'm all fingers and thumbs, rather like Daisy.'

'Of course,' she replied softly. With great gentleness, she eased the knitted gloves over the arthritic fingers, and then pulled the woolly hat more snugly over Cordelia's ears. 'Are you sure you'll be all right standing about in the cold, Cordy? I don't want you getting pneumonia.'

Cordelia's eyes twinkled from behind her reading glasses. 'I'm tougher than I look, Peggy, dear. Don't worry about me.'

Peggy hid the fact that she always worried about Cordelia by shooting her a loving smile. 'Are you planning on reading anything? Only if you're not, it's probably best to put those glasses in your handbag. You don't want to lose them, do you?'

'Silly old me,' she tutted, reaching to pluck them from her nose. 'I forgot I was wearing them.'

The knock on the front door heralded the arrival of Bertie, who was, as usual, looking very dapper in his Abercrombie hat, thick scarf and tailored dark navy overcoat. 'Good evening,' he said with a smile to Peggy before he lifted Cordelia's hand to his lips. 'You are looking very fetching, my dear,' he murmured. 'Are you ready to leave?'

Cordelia giggled and blushed. 'Silly man,' she teased. 'I don't look anything of the sort, but thank you for the compliment.'

Peggy watched as he carefully guided her down the front steps to the car, and then settled her in the passenger seat with a rug over her knees. 'They really are the perfect Derby and Joan, aren't they?' murmured Cissy, who'd come to stand beside her.

Peggy nodded, her heart full. 'I hope that will be me and your dad in the future.'

Cissy chuckled. 'You already are,' she replied, hugging her arm. 'A right old pair of lovebirds, if ever I saw one.'

Peggy turned to face her, noting the shadows under her haunted eyes that the thick make-up couldn't disguise. 'And what about you, Cissy? Is there someone special in your life?'

Cissy moved away to collect her scarf and hat, and kept her back to Peggy as she pulled them on. 'Not at the moment,' she said shortly. 'We'd better go, or we'll be late.'

Peggy was about to pursue the subject but was halted by Jim and the others streaming into the hall with a clatter and babble of chatter and laughter. Frustrated by yet another missed chance to talk to Cissy alone, she buttoned up her coat, tied the woollen scarf firmly about her neck and squashed her felt hat down over her ears. Looking up at Jim, she saw the love in his eyes and knew that whatever was going on with Cissy, she would deal with it quietly and calmly so it wouldn't spoil his first Christmas home.

'Right, you lot. Off we go,' Jim said, and picked up Daisy to swing her on to his shoulders. 'Hang on tight, Daisy, and try not to knock off my hat.'

Cissy hurried down the freshly gritted steps, closely followed by Bob and Pippa who were holding hands and laughing into one another's eyes. Peggy waited until Jim had negotiated the steps with Daisy on his shoulders, and then clicked the door shut behind her before tucking her hand into the crook of his arm.

They walked swiftly across the main road as the wind whipped at the waves and blew up the hill to chill exposed skin and make eyes and noses water. Frost glittered like snow on rooftops, and Camden Road looked lovely with the shop window displays and the decorations in every window. Then, as they turned the corner and saw the High Street, they gasped in delight.

Within the last few hours the Council workmen had strung coloured lights across the street, and every lamppost bore a cardboard cut-out of Santa or one of his reindeer. A large crowd had gathered around the tree, and the Salvation Army Band was just striking up to play carols from the Town Hall steps. The town crier looked resplendent in his bright red cape and black tricorn hat, as did the mayor in his scarlet robes and glittering chain of office.

'To be sure, Bertie came well prepared,' murmured Jim, nodding towards Cordelia and Bertie who were now sitting on canvas chairs in front of the Crown, well wrapped up against the cold in a thick blanket.

'Once a soldier, always a soldier, bless him,' she replied, eyeing the pair of them sitting side by side. 'He even thought to bring a flask of something to keep out the cold,' she added. 'I hope there isn't too much alcohol in it, or you'll have to carry her upstairs tonight.'

'Ach, she weighs nothing,' he said, lifting Daisy from his shoulders. He set her down so she could run about with the other children. 'And at her age, does it really matter if she gets a bit tipsy, Peg?'

'Probably not,' she agreed before turning to hug their daughter Anne, who'd just arrived with her husband, Martin, and their two little girls, Rose and Emily. Having embraced them all and satisfied herself that they were well and happy, she turned her attention to the baby in the pram. 'How's my darling little Oscar doing?' she asked, peeking into the pram for a glimpse of her newest grandchild.

'He's been an absolute horror all day and is finally asleep, so please don't disturb him, Mum.' Anne looked round at the milling crowd as her girls ran off to join their little friends. 'It's a good turnout,' she said. 'And is that Sandra with our Cissy? Goodness, I haven't seen either of them for ages – I must go and say hello.'

Peggy watched as Anne wheeled the pram over the road towards the two girls who were standing outside the Crown with what looked like glasses of steaming hot mulled wine. It was interesting to see the three of them all grown-up after the years they'd played together on the beach and up in the hills, and she wondered if any of them had much in common now their lives had turned out so differently. Yet it seemed they had a lot to talk about as Sandra and Cissy peeked into the pram and chattered away.

Her attention was then drawn to Gloria, who was emerging from the pub looking resplendent in green and scarlet, a crown of tinsel perched on her heavily lacquered blonde hair. She was laden with glasses for the mulled wine she was selling from the small stall she'd set up on the pavement.

'I could do with one of those,' Peggy said, nudging Jim's arm.

'I think we all could,' said Martin, digging his gloved hands into his coat pocket. 'It's jolly chilly out here.'

The two men headed for Gloria's stall, and looking round, Peggy caught sight of Florence who was holding little Bobby's hand while she chatted to one of the factory machinists. Peggy waited until the women drifted apart and went to speak to her quietly beneath the hubbub of the brass band and the milling crowd. 'How is Gracie?'

'Sister Danuta popped in just before I left to tell me she's woken up finally but is still very groggy and heavily sedated. There's a chance they'll allow me and Bobby to visit tomorrow, so it looks like she might pull through.'

'Oh,' Peggy sighed. 'That is such a relief.' She smiled down at the five-year-old boy whose face was alight with excitement as he tugged at Florence's hand, clearly desperate to join the other children who were racing about with balloons tied to string. 'Then let's hope everything turns out all right for young Bobby's sake. Give her my love if you get to see her, and please let me know when I can visit.'

Florence nodded, wished her a happy Christmas and headed for Gloria's stall which was now selling toffee apples as well as mulled wine.

Jim and Martin returned with the drinks and, after waving hello to Danuta and Stanislav who'd just arrived with the other members of the air-freight team, Peggy cupped her gloved hands around the warm glass and breathed in the delicious aroma of the mulled wine. Now she was hopeful that Gracie would be all right, she could attempt to set aside her worries over Cissy, relax and enjoy the evening, for she had her Jim home at last, and was surrounded by friends and family.

'I see you're making the most of Gloria's hooch,' teased Rosie, coming to slip her hand into the crook of Peggy's arm. 'I wouldn't drink too much of it, though; knowing Gloria, it's probably lethal, and you could end up being taken home in a wheelbarrow.'

Peggy laughed. 'That would be a sight, wouldn't it?' She gave her friend's hand a squeeze and admired the earrings sparkling from within the swirls of platinum hair, the flawless complexion, fur coat and expensive-looking handbag. 'You look marvellous,' she breathed. 'How *do* you do it?'

Rosie giggled. 'Clever make-up, a glass of champagne before leaving the house, and the love of a good man.'

Peggy grinned at the implication that despite being married for a year, their honeymoon was far from over. 'Oh, I see.' She glanced across at Ron, who seemed to have made an effort to look smart for once in his overcoat and fedora, and even the dogs looked as if they'd been brushed. 'I have to say, Rosie, you both look well on it, whatever it is. How on earth did you manage to get him looking so smart?'

'Ah, that would be telling.' She tapped the side of her dainty nose, her blue eyes full of humour. 'I see Ron's already found the mulled wine. I think I'll join him before the mayor starts his speech and bores us all to death. Will I see you later in the Anchor?'

'Probably not, sadly. Daisy and the other children will need to be put to bed, but Jim and the others will probably call in. Aren't you coming to the church?'

Rosie shook her head. 'Trying to get Ron into a church is a non-starter, and the service is for the children really. Besides, it's more fun in the pub – and a whole lot warmer.'

Peggy grinned. 'I'll see you tomorrow then.' She was about to go over to Cordelia and Bertie when she heard her sister calling her name. Turning, she saw Doris advancing on her with great determination, and braced herself.

'Peggy, there you are,' said Doris, rather unnecessarily. 'Thank you for the card. I'm sorry I wasn't in when you called, but I've been up to my ears preparing everything for the family's arrival.' She glanced around to make sure she couldn't be overheard. 'Suzy is wearing the most exquisite fur coat,' she breathed. 'Poor Anthony must have worked his fingers to the bone to fork out for it.'

'Lucky girl,' murmured Peggy without any envy. 'And Anthony can't be that poor, as he holds quite a high government position. Where are they? I'd love to catch up with Suzy.'

'Oh, they're about somewhere with John,' Doris said vaguely. 'I see Ron's looking fairly respectable for once,' she murmured. 'It must be Rosie's influence.'

'Are you all set for tomorrow?' Peggy wanted to change the subject before Doris wound her up.

'Oh, yes,' she replied smugly. 'Harrods delivered my order two days ago and I finished all my other shopping this morning.' She looked down her nose at the scrap of moth-eaten fur Peggy had round the collar of her faded navy blue coat, and made a show of stroking her mink coat with her gloved hand. 'It's a great pity you didn't accept my offer of my spare fur coat, Peggy. It's so much smarter and warmer than that old thing you insist upon wearing.'

'It suits me just fine, thanks, Doris. Now, if you don't mind, I'm off to get another glass of this delicious mulled wine.'

Doris sniffed and was about to make a cutting remark, so Peggy shot off before she had time to even open her mouth.

The crowd milled and swirled around her, the noise rising in anticipation as the time approached for the mayor to turn on the lights and begin the countdown for the town crier's proclamation, and the arrival of Father Christmas. The children were getting overexcited; the mulled wine and toffee apples were proving as popular as the hot chestnuts from the nearby brazier; and a group of older boys was huddling surreptitiously to share what looked suspiciously like a bottle of gin – and in the middle of it all were Cordelia and Bertie, snug and comfortable in their garden chairs, sharing a thick blanket and the contents of a large Thermos.

She stood next to her childhood friend outside the Crown and tried her hardest to feel a part of the scene, but it was not to be, for the burden she carried isolated her from the noise and general gaiety, the chill in her heart having very little to do with the cold weather.

As her friend chattered on with Anne, her gaze kept returning to the baby who was snug beneath the blankets in his pram, tiny mittened fists beneath his chin, a curl of dark hair just peeking from beneath the knitted cap. It could have been her baby – but of course it wasn't – and she fervently hoped she could get through these next few days without making it obvious that she was perilously close to falling apart from sheer stress.

She breathed a silent sigh of relief when Anne left to find Martin and her other children and was about to suggest getting another glass of mulled wine when she saw Rachel Solomon walking towards them, pushing a pram, her face alight with happiness.

Her heart hammering and her pulse thundering in her ears, she tried to edge away, but her back was to the wall and she was hemmed in on all sides, so she had no choice but to stand and face her. Then she felt her friend stiffen at her side and glance towards her with a frown. Why would she react in such a way to the sight of Rachel and that pram?

But there was no time to ask, for Rachel was standing right in front of her – greeting them both – folding the blankets back tenderly to show them the sleeping baby.

'Isn't he just perfect?' Rachel sighed. 'See how long his lashes are. *Oy vey*, the girls will be envious of such beauty. And he's so good – a real little cherub – an angel sent to us as Moses was delivered from the river. What a precious gift he is.'

As her friend bent over the pram and made all the right noises, she found she couldn't speak or move, transfixed by the sight of him. Rachel was right, he was perfect in every way. But Rachel was watching her, frowning and puzzled as the crowd and the noise began to close in on her.

'I'm sorry, Rachel,' she managed hoarsely. 'But I won't get too close as I'm not feeling the full ticket. In fact, I feel rather faint, so if you'll excuse me . . .'

Before Rachel could reply, she'd shoved her way through the crowds towards the door of the Crown. But instead of going inside, she headed down the alleyway to lose herself in the deep shadows cast by the surrounding buildings. Her legs almost gave way, and she had to lean against a wall to fight for control of her rebelling stomach. Her heart was beating so hard she had to fight for breath.

Ron had been sent by Gloria to fetch the crates of mixers from her back yard as the bar staff were running low. He was about to carry them inside when he overheard his granddaughter, Cissy, and her friend engaged in a very odd conversation. Intrigued, he set aside the crates and moved closer to the wall that divided the yard from the alleyway so he could hear better.

'Are you all right?' asked Sandra.

'I don't feel at all well,' Cissy replied.

'Then let me take you into the pub.'

'It's too noisy in there and I need to get away from the crowds and the crush. I'll be all right in a minute – really I will.'

'Are you sure that's all? Because you've been acting strangely ever since Anne came to show us Oscar, and when Rachel turned up you went as white as a sheet.'

'You weren't exactly relaxed either,' Cissy retorted. 'I felt you flinch and stiffen beside me, and all that cooing didn't fool me for a second.'

'I flinched because I thought you were about to drop in a dead faint and was preparing to catch you. As for cooing over the baby, Rachel expected it, and as you seemed to be struck dumb, I didn't want to disappoint her.'

There was silence between them as the noise ebbed and flowed from the High Street to echo from the roof-tops, and the town crier announced the mayor's speech. Ron pressed closer to the wall, his suspicions mounting.

'Let's find somewhere warm where we can talk,' said Sandra.

'I don't want to talk. I have nothing to say.'

Sandra's voice was so low Ron could barely hear it. 'I think you do. In fact, we both do. I know you, Cissy. I suspect that, like me, you're in trouble and it's eating you up. Aren't you?'

'How did you guess?' Cissy rasped.

'Because I've known you for ever, and I see the same haunted eyes in my mirror every morning. We told each other everything as children, and even in those years leading up to our twenties. We might have been apart for six years and gone our separate ways, but it feels like it was only yesterday.'

Ron tensed as both girls fell silent, and he wondered if they'd decided to walk out of earshot, and he'd be left not knowing what it was all about. But to his great relief, Sandra spoke again.

'The last time I was down here we met up at that caravan, just before war had been declared. Back then, we trusted our secrets were safe with one another, and neither of us ever judged the rights and wrongs of those much more innocent misdemeanours. I'm hoping the same applies now, because the secret I'm carrying will have the same far-reaching consequences as yours. But sharing our troubles is a risk I'm willing to take, if the trust we once had still stands.'

The mention of the caravan made Ron feel quite giddy with dread.

'Yes,' Cissy replied. 'The caravan. That's where it all started, didn't it? You and me and Anne and Gracie . . .' Her voice tailed off. 'Now it seems we're all of us in trouble,' she sobbed.

Ron dared to climb on to a nearby barrel so he could look down on the girls who were huddled together in the alleyway. He saw Sandra slip her arm about Cissy's waist, and in the faint light filtering from an upstairs window, noticed they were both crying.

'Come,' said Sandra, 'I know a place we won't be disturbed.'

As they linked arms and walked together into the deeper gloom, the mayor came to the end of his speech and the town crier announced the arrival of Father Christmas to a fanfare of trumpets and drums. They didn't look back, and certainly didn't realise that Ron had overheard every word.

17

'Whatever's the matter, Graham?' asked Gloria, who had been raking it in all evening selling her mulled wine and toffee apples.

'Nothing,' he snapped.

'If it's Sandra yer looking for, she's just gone off with Cissy Reilly. I wouldn't worry about it, Graham, they're mates from way back and were always sloping off somewhere. If you ain't got nothing better to do than stand about 'ere looking miserable, you can go indoors and fill up these jugs from the tub behind the bar. And check on Alfie and Dawn to make sure they're managing all right while I'm out 'ere.'

She watched him take the large jugs and traipse back inside to do her bidding, looking for all the world like a doomed man. 'I dunno, Beryl,' she sighed, adjusting her crown of tinsel. 'This 'as all put the proper mockers on things, and no mistake. I almost wish them two 'ad stayed at 'ome to 'ave their barney.'

'Yeah, I'm beginning to think the same. I'm ever so sorry, Gloria. It ain't much fun for yer.'

'Not fer you neither,' she retorted before catching sight of Rosie and breaking into a grin. 'Watcha, mate. Another top-up, is it?' At Rosie's nod, she ladled out the wine from the big pot she had keeping warm on a butane gas ring. Handing it over, she nodded towards Ron. 'What's up with 'im? Looks like he's lost a quid and found a farthing.'

'I don't know,' Rosie replied with a frown. 'He was fine before he went to collect those crates of mixers for you, laughing and carrying on with his old mates, Chalky, Stan and Fred. I'm hoping this will perk him up again,' she said, raising the glass.

'It'll either perk him up or flatten 'im,' chuckled Gloria. 'There's enough booze in that to stun a sheep.'

Rosie giggled. 'I thought there might be. Oh, well, kill or cure as they say.'

'I'd better have a drop more for Jim,' said Peggy. 'He's gone all quiet too. I can't think what's got into him.'

Gloria grimaced. 'That's men for you, love. Never know what's going on in their 'eads – and they say women are difficult to understand.' She gave a great guffaw of laughter that made the gold baubles in her ears swing, and the tinsel crown slip over one eye. She adjusted the crown and filled Peggy's glass to the brim. 'Mind 'ow you go, Peg. Don't want him falling asleep in church, do yer?'

'I certainly don't, not the way he snores – he'll have the vicar in a proper bate.'

Graham appeared, carrying the filled jugs, which he emptied into the large pot simmering on the gas ring. 'Alfie and Dawn are doing fine in the bar, so if you've quite finished ordering me about, I think I'll take a walk round and see if I can find Sandra,' he said purposefully.

'Leave 'er be, for gawd's sake,' said Beryl. 'She won't want you 'anging about when she's gossiping with Cissy.'

'She's my wife, and I have every right to know where she is,' he replied stiffly.

Gloria watched him march off and wished she'd managed to persuade him to drink some of her lethal concoction, for at the very least it might relax him. She was annoyed that her plans for a lovely family Christmas had been hijacked by Sandra having an affair and causing ructions, and if things didn't improve by tomorrow, she'd be having another word with the pair of them – and, if necessary, banging their heads together.

She looked at her sister and rolled her eyes before dipping the ladle into the wine. 'Let's get stuck into this, Beryl. I don't know about you, but I'm going to enjoy Christmas, and to hell with the lot of them.'

Peggy was fretful, not only because Jim seemed to have lost his enthusiasm for the evening's festivities, and Ron was unusually quiet and well behaved, but because there was clearly something going on between her Cissy and Sandra. She'd caught a glimpse of them disappearing down the alleyway by the Crown, leaving poor Rachel bewildered by their lack of interest in little Noel, who she'd paraded up and down the High Street with such pride.

Peggy didn't know what to make of it all, but was soon distracted from her thoughts as Daisy and the other children swarmed around the horses and dray to receive their gifts from Father Christmas – bought by their parents – before being rounded up for the short walk to the church.

On arriving, there had been the inevitable visits to the church hall loo with the children which seemed to take an age, and finally they'd all managed to squash in together in two of the long side pews. However, Cissy's continued absence was something she couldn't ignore, and it made her even more determined to take the girl to one side as soon as possible to coax her into saying what was wrong.

Despite everything, Peggy began to relax as Daisy, Rose and Emily joined the other children beside the nativity scene to sing 'Away in a Manger' before the service got under way. Although a staunch Catholic, Peggy always enjoyed the Anglican service on Christmas Eve, as opposed to the long-drawn-out and rather solemn midnight mass at her own church. In fact, it – and the tree ceremony – had become such an intrinsic part of her family tradition that the absence of it during the war years had been a heavy blow to already low spirits. But by jingo it was freezing in here.

She surreptitiously pulled up her collar and tucked her gloved hands in her pockets as they sat in the glow of the many candles to listen to the beautiful voices of the choirboys. 'Once in Royal David's City', to her mind, truly heralded the start of Christmas, and the soaring, pure voice of that little choirboy's solo brought the usual tears to her eyes. Glancing across at Cordelia, she noted she too was moved by the beauty of it all, and quickly passed her a spare hanky. Weddings and Christmases always brought tears – but they were happy ones.

Peggy's gaze wandered over the beautiful arrangements of holly, mistletoe and ivy, to the hundreds of candles that had been lit on the window ledges and around the altar, before settling once more on the nativity scene below the pulpit. Baby Noel was warm and safe and much loved now, but what of his mother? Was she safe, warm and loved, or was she alone – cast out from her family, and in the depths of despair for having had to abandon him? She fervently hoped that whoever she was, the girl had someone to care for her and would find peace in her heart, and seek forgiveness from God – who really was the only one entitled to judge her.

The gentle nudge from Jim snapped her from her thoughts, and she got to her feet to join the congregation in the final carol as the vicar and choir began to make their stately exit down the aisle.

'You were miles away,' muttered Jim from behind the hymn sheet. 'Are you all right, Peg?'

She nodded and smiled back at him, relieved that he seemed to be back to his usual self. 'Just wondering how cold one has to get before turning into a solid block of ice.'

He grinned back. 'We'll be home soon by the fire, all warm and cosy with a hot toddy.' He patted his coat pocket. 'Gloria filled a bottle with her mulled wine for us.'

'How lovely,' she murmured. The thought of feeling her hands and feet again was making her impatient to get out of here, and as the singing came to an end and the congregation began to filter from the pews into the aisles, she bustled about, helping Cordelia to her feet and chivvying Daisy to hurry along with her father.

Jim dropped some coins in the collection box, shook hands with the vicar and hurried outside to light a cigarette. Peggy followed him out with Daisy, who was beginning to drag her feet after such an exciting evening. She hugged Anne and her overexcited little granddaughters, and held baby Oscar for a few precious moments while Martin lashed the large pram down firmly with rope on to the roof of the car. Reluctantly handing Oscar back to Anne, she kissed Martin's cheek and wished them a safe journey home.

'Pippa and I are going to the Anchor to see Grandad and Uncle Frank,' said Bob. 'But we'll just stay for an hour and then come back to babysit Daisy so you and Dad can join in the fun.'

Peggy would have liked that very much, but there were too many things on her mind for her to be able to relax at the Anchor. 'That's very sweet of you, Bob, but me and your dad will be just fine at home for the evening.' She checked he had his spare front door key.

'You two go and enjoy yourselves, and we'll see you later.'

Peggy stood beside Jim as Bertie drove them away, and then turned to give Suzy a warm hug. 'It's so lovely to see you again,' she murmured against her cheek. 'How are things with Doris this year?'

Suzy grinned as she stepped back from the embrace. 'Apart from thinking Anthony has been bankrupted by buying my coat, all seems well, thank goodness,' she replied quietly. 'I think she's mellowed,' she added in a whisper.

Peggy chuckled. 'Well, that's something, I suppose, but I wouldn't bet the house on her staying mellow for very long, Suzy.' She deliberately ignored the questioning look from Doris who was too far away to have heard the exchange, and patted the girl's cheek. 'Have a lovely family day, anyway, and we'll see you on Boxing Day.'

Once everyone had driven off, Jim hoisted a drooping Daisy over his shoulder and then took Peggy's hand as they slowly walked away from the church. 'Let's get home and put this one to bed. And as the house will be empty for once, I think we should make the most of it, don't you?'

Peggy actually felt herself blush at the thought. She leaned against him, her heart full of love, her body tingling with promise. 'Jim Reilly, you read my thoughts exactly.'

Ron had hoped Cissy and Sandra would be in the Anchor, but there was no sign of them, and that worried him. He sat in his usual place by the inglenook where a welcoming fire blazed, his thoughts far from the chatter and laughter that surrounded him. He wasn't really in the mood to drink too much, and as Rosie had promised him they'd have an early night, that suited him fine. But even the thought of making love to Rosie had been tarnished by what he'd overheard tonight, and as hard as he tried, he just couldn't shift the awful dread that weighed in the pit of his belly.

'Come on, Ron, do liven up,' urged Rosie, giving him a sharp dig in the ribs. 'You've been down in the dumps for half the evening. Whatever's going on in that head of yours tonight?'

'Probably not a lot,' chuckled Frank. 'Da's mind is more likely addled from all that mulled wine he's been drinking.'

'Aye, that'll be it,' Ron mumbled before taking a long glug of ale and dragging his thoughts back to the present. 'Ruby's got a good crowd in tonight,' he said, looking round the busy room. 'I'm surprised Cissy and Sandra aren't here.'

'They're probably at the Crown, or that new cellar bar in the High Street,' said Frank. 'They get the younger crowd in there – and serve cocktails – whatever they are,' he added with a grimace.

Ron didn't like the thought of his granddaughter in either place, but she'd always been a law unto herself, and was certainly old enough to decide where she wanted to spend her Christmas Eve. But he thought she was being selfish after having lived away from home for so long, and he felt quite hurt that she didn't seem to want to be with her family on a night like this.

He decided to ignore his worry and change the subject. 'I see our young Doctor Darwin has made himself comfortable at the bar again.'

Frank grinned. 'He's a regular visitor according to Brenda, and clearly smitten with our Ruby. But she's keeping him at arm's length and no mistake,' he replied. 'Though Brenda reckons she's starting to weaken as she let him take her for tea at the Lilac Tearooms the other day.' He downed the last of his beer. 'D'you want another, Da?'

Ron shook his head. 'Gloria's mulled wine still lingers in my mouth and makes the beer taste funny.'

Frank left the table and headed for the bar just as Bob and Pippa arrived with Cordelia and Bertie, to be swiftly followed by Danuta and Stanislav. Chairs were shifted to make room for them, and once everyone was settled, Ron and Bob went to join Frank and Stanislav at the bar to order their drinks.

As Ron waited to be served, he leaned on the bar and watched his grandson chatting to Frank. This should have been a special occasion for it would be the first time he could legally buy Bob a pint, but the knowledge that his granddaughter might be in trouble marred any joy he might have felt.

'Ron? Ron, did you want something?'

Startled, he snapped out of his dark thoughts and quickly gave Ruby his drinks order. As she pulled pints and poured sherry, he noted how efficient she was, and how much she reminded him of his darling Rosie who'd once ruled behind this bar.

'I don't suppose you've seen our Cissy, have you?' he asked as he handed over the money.

She avoided his gaze. 'Not recently,' she replied before turning away to get his change from the till.

Ron's suspicions were sparked, and so on her return, he stayed her hand. 'Ruby, I'm worried about the wee girl. If you know where she is, then tell me.'

She eased her hand from beneath his and dumped his change on the bar. 'I'm sure I don't know what you're on about, Ron.' With that, she turned away and began to serve someone at the far end of the bar, her back firmly turned towards him.

Ron stood for a moment and eyed the passage which led to the new lavatory and Ruby's private apartment above the pub. If Cissy was up there with Sandra, then at least they were safe, but what the hell was going on with them that meant they needed to shut themselves away on Christmas Eve? Surely his worst fears couldn't possibly be true?

As he was jostled on both sides by impatient and thirsty customers, he gathered up the tray of drinks and carried them over to the table. His imagination was getting ahead of him, he decided, and he'd clearly got the wrong end of the stick by putting two and two together and making five. They were probably discussing Sandra's affair – which he'd heard about from a very disgruntled Gloria.

Yet that really didn't explain the conversation he'd overheard as he'd stood in the back yard of the Crown, and if his suspicions did prove to be right, then he had to do something about it before Jim and Peggy's Christmas was ruined. But first he had to find Cissy and get her alone – which was already proving difficult.

He sat and simmered as the noise rose in the bar and someone began to play the piano, which made it virtually impossible to hold a proper conversation. Taking his pipe from his pocket, he considered how he might manage to find the girl, let alone manage to talk to her in private. It would have been easy if he still lived at Beach View, but he couldn't very well stake the place out and wait for her to go home – or walk the streets looking for her. Rosie wouldn't let him, for starters, and she'd demand to know why he was doing such a thing – and as it was all supposition anyway, he was reluctant to confide in her.

He gave a deep sigh and drank the last of his beer with little pleasure. Gloria's mulled wine had not only marred his enjoyment of his beer but had affected the clarity of his thought processes, and by the time he had lit his pipe and got it going properly, he was no nearer to a satisfactory solution.

Rosie finished her drink and reached for her coat. 'We might as well go home,' she said loudly in his ear. 'You're clearly not in the mood for a party.'

'I'm sorry, Rosie me darling. I didn't mean to spoil your evening.'

'Is there something on your mind, Ron? Because you've been miles away ever since you went into the Crown for Gloria's mixers.' Her gaze was wide and steady, demanding an answer.

He knew he couldn't tell her, although he could trust her with his life – but this was not his life to discuss – especially not in here. 'Ach, it's nothing really. Just an old man's wandering thoughts mixed with too much of Gloria's wine.'

'Hmm.' She eyed him thoughtfully for a moment, clearly unsure whether to believe him or not. 'An early night won't hurt either of us,' she said lightly. 'At least we're both sober and won't bother the neighbours by getting in late or making a noise.'

'Aye, there is that.' He reached for his hat and coat. 'I'll be with you in a minute. I just need to use the gents before the walk home.'

She shrugged on her coat. 'Try not to get involved in any long chats on the way, Ron. The dogs will need to stretch their legs too after sitting about in here for half the evening.'

Ron nodded. Once he'd checked that Bertie could cope with a rather tipsy Cordelia for the rest of the evening, he said goodbye to the others and headed across the room towards the narrow hallway.

But instead of going into the gents, he stood by the door at the bottom of the stairs leading to Ruby's rooms. He leaned his ear against it but could hear nothing, so after glancing towards the bar, he tried to turn the knob.

The door was locked, which was frustrating, but hardly surprising, for he knew Ruby always kept it so during opening hours. And yet the girl had been decidedly shifty when he'd asked about Cissy, and those upstairs rooms would certainly offer somewhere private to talk. Deciding he had to get to the bottom of this puzzle, he headed back into the bar.

Ruby turned to him after handing over change to another customer. 'Goodnight, Ron. See yer tomorrow.'

'Is my granddaughter upstairs, Ruby? And I want the truth this time.'

Ruby couldn't quite meet his eyes. 'She and 'er mate was up there for a bit, but they've gone now,' she replied.

'Did you get some idea of where they were going after they left here?'

Ruby shook her head and frowned. 'I'm sorry, Ron, but they slipped away shortly after you and Rosie got here, and I assumed they was 'eading for 'ome.' She leaned towards him, her voice just above a murmur. 'Is something up, Ron? You look worried.'

'How did they seem to you when they got here?'

She paused as she thought about how to reply. 'They did look a bit upset, now you mention it, but I thought it was cos Sandra's marriage is going through a rough patch.'

'So you heard about that too?'

'Nothing stays secret round 'ere for long – especially when Gloria's big gob is involved.' She patted his hand. 'I shouldn't worry yerself, Ron, it ain't our business.'

Ron had to accept she was right. 'Thanks, anyway. See you tomorrow.'

Signalling to the dogs, he said his goodbyes to the others and joined Rosie who was waiting for him by the door. 'Sorry to keep you waiting,' he said to her as he let the animals run out to water the lampposts

Rosie made no reply as she stepped outside. Dreading the avalanche of questions he knew were coming, Ron shut the door behind them and tucked Rosie's hand into the crook of his arm to steady her as her high heels caught in the uneven paving. Although she remained silent, he could almost hear her whirling thoughts.

Camden Road was still quite busy with people spilling out from the pub behind them and out of nearly every doorway they passed. Music blared from several quarters, an impromptu party was going on in the Goldman factory forecourt, and as they approached the corner, he could see that a brazier had been lit on the beach and several youngsters had gathered around it to drink beer and mess about, but there was no sign of Cissy or Sandra. Perhaps, he mused, Gloria's hooch had been more lethal than he'd thought and the events of tonight had been an illusion.

'You and Ruby seemed to be having a very intense conversation,' Rosie said at last. 'What was all that about?'

'Ach, it was nothing, wee girl. I was just making sure she wouldn't be late for Peg's meal tomorrow.'

She tugged on his arm and drew him to a standstill. 'Are you sure that's all, Ron? Because you've been be-having oddly all evening, and it's most unlike you.'

'Aye, it is,' he replied. 'I'm just tired and ready for me bed.'

'You're not ill, are you?' she asked sharply.

Ashamed that he'd frightened her, he hugged and kissed her warmly. 'I'm as fit as a flea, Rosie girl, as I'll prove to you the minute we get home.'

'That's more like my Ron,' she murmured, tucking her hand into his arm again and smiling up at him. 'I do love you, you know,' she murmured.

'And I love the bones of you too, darlin', but if we don't get walking again, we'll both be frozen to the pavement.' He strode out with Rosie beside him, his dogs chasing ahead of him, and promised himself he'd never touch a drop of Gloria's hooch again.

Peggy lay in Jim's arms, sated with love, and revelling in the chance to have him all to herself for a naughty hour or two. Daisy had fallen asleep almost the moment Peggy had tucked her into bed, everyone else was still out, and the house was quiet apart from the usual soft groans of the old timbers.

Jim kissed the top of her head and snuggled her more closely to his side. 'Do you want to tell me now what's been worrying you, Peg?'

Startled from her pleasant drowsiness, she tensed. 'I might ask the same of you,' she replied. 'What happened this evening to suddenly make you so silent and morose?'

'It's no use you dodging the question, darling. I know when something's up, so you might as well tell me.'

Peggy was almost afraid to voice her fears, for the glow of their lovemaking was still with her, and she didn't want to break the spell. 'Talk about the pot calling the kettle black, Jim Reilly,' she teased. 'Out with it before I leave this bed and go down to brew a pot of tea.'

'Tea would be nice. Gloria's blasted wine has left a sour taste in my mouth.'

She poked him in the ribs. 'Jim. Talk to me.'

'It was just the noise and the crowd in the High Street tonight. It all got a bit much, and combined with that hot wine, it started to close in on me. I was sorely tempted to escape and find somewhere quiet and deserted, but I knew it would upset you, so I did my breathing exercises and got through it until we left for the church. Once we were away from the crush, I was absolutely fine.'

'You should have said,' she protested, rising on to an elbow to look into his face. 'Of course I wouldn't have minded leaving earlier. Anne could have looked after Daisy and brought her home if you were still feeling pressured.' She stroked his cheek. 'Oh, Jim, you really shouldn't keep things like that to yourself. I'm so sorry you didn't enjoy it.'

He caught her wrist and softly kissed the palm of her hand. 'I did enjoy it – mostly. It was just the noise and the press of all those people that made me jumpy. But six months ago an event like that would have sent me cowering in the nearest doorway, so there is a big improvement. I wouldn't mind betting that this time next year, I'll be the life and soul, and still celebrating after everyone else has gone home.'

'I'll hold you to that,' she replied, kissing his lips. 'But for now, I need tea, and lots of it to wash away the taste of Gloria's wine.'

'Oh no, you don't,' he said, drawing her firmly back to his side. 'Not until you've told me what's been on your mind all day.'

Peggy had never kept anything from Jim before, but something stopped her now from voicing her very real concerns over Cissy, for it could open a can of worms and cause no end of trouble for everyone.

She was about to make some remark about the relationship between Bob and Pippa when he heaved a sigh and said, 'It's Cissy you're worried about, isn't it?'

She couldn't lie to him, but she could still navigate around the truth until she knew if Jim shared her

275

concerns. 'She doesn't look well, Jim,' she said finally. 'And by the amount of luggage she's brought home, I suspect something happened in London and she's not planning to return.'

'Aye, that was my thinking too. No doubt she'll tell us all about it in her own good time, but at least she's had the sense to come home, and that must surely make you feel easier about things.'

Peggy nodded against his bare chest. 'Of course it does,' she said, even though her thoughts were hurtling in a completely different direction. 'But you must have noticed she doesn't look herself – that there's something different about her – something brittle and nervy and not like our girl at all?'

Jim loosened his hold on Peggy and shifted in the bed until he was half-sitting against the stacked pillows. Reaching for his cigarettes, he lit one and blew smoke. 'We haven't seen her for six months, Peg, and girls that age change constantly with their new fashions and silly diets. I agree she looks a bit pasty and tired, but that's only to be expected considering the hectic life she's been leading. I'm sure that now she's home, she can rest and eat properly, and before you know it she'll be as perky as ever.'

Peggy relaxed, relieved that Jim wasn't overly worried about their daughter, and hadn't noticed the small tell-tale signs of trouble that she had. 'I'm going to make that tea,' she said, climbing out of bed to pull on her clothes which were scattered across the floor. 'It's almost closing time, and I suspect Bertie will need you to help him with Cordelia if she's overdone it on the sherry.'

'I'll come down in a minute,' he replied, relaxing back into the pillows like an emperor, the bedclothes barely covering his naked hips.

'And put some clothes on, Jim,' she warned. 'Don't forget we have Pippa staying and it wouldn't be seemly for you to be wandering about in your dressing gown.'

Peggy shoved her feet into her slippers and padded along the landing to check that Daisy was still fast asleep, and then stood outside Cissy's door, wondering if she'd come home while she and Jim had been otherwise occupied. On turning the handle, the door opened and she peeked in to find the room deserted, the bed untouched.

'Where on earth did those two girls get to?' she muttered, closing the door and hurrying down the stairs to the welcome warmth of the kitchen range. She filled the kettle, placed it on the hob and hunted out cups and biscuits.

She was feeling peckish, and suspected the others would be too when they got home. Reaching for the tub of drinking chocolate that Sarah had sent her from America, she read the instructions and realised it couldn't be made with water, so put it back in the cupboard. They'd all have to have tea, as the milk she had would have to last until after Boxing Day, and with so many people expected to arrive over the next two days, it simply wouldn't stretch that far.

While the kettle boiled, she carefully lifted the large, stuffed turkey from the fridge and placed it in the roasting tin, then put it in the range's slow oven so it could cook overnight. She'd already cooked the small ham joint and the vegetables were ready to go on the hob nearer the time. Vi's Christmas puddings would have to wait until morning, when they would be steamed. The potatoes and parsnips would go in the hot oven to roast an hour before dishing up, and Vi's sausages could be fried at the last minute.

Peggy silently went through the list of things she would have to do in the morning, and finally sat down to drink her tea and light a fag.

Ten minutes later, Jim came down in trousers and sweater to sit by the fire and stir it into a blaze just as they heard a key being slotted into the front door. 'Stand by, Peg. We're about to be invaded,' he said cheerfully.

Bob and Pippa were closely followed by Bertie, who had to steer Cordelia very carefully on a meandering route to the other fireside chair. 'I'm afraid we've both rather over-indulged this evening,' he said, fumbling to take off his hat and eyeing them all somewhat blearily.

'That's par for the course, Bertie,' laughed Jim. 'Don't worry, I'll get her upstairs and Peggy will make sure she's tucked in good and proper.'

'I don't need a horse or a prop,' Cordelia protested. 'And you shouldn't be driving, Bertie,' she added, waving an admonishing finger at him. 'You're far too tipsy.'

'It takes one to know one,' said Peggy, trying not to laugh as she helped the elderly woman to shed her coat, hat and scarf. 'There's a bed here for you, Bertie, if you'd like. I don't relish the thought of you driving on those slippery roads, especially if you've had a bit to drink.'

'That's very kind of you, Peggy,' he replied, clinging to the back of a kitchen chair for support. 'I do seem to be feeling rather the worse for wear.'

'That's settled then,' Peggy replied. 'I'll pour you all a nice cup of tea while Jim sorts you out a pair of pyjamas and a toothbrush, Bertie. You'll be on the top floor, I'm afraid, but if you need help, I'm sure Bob will do the honours.'

She set about making the tea as the others dug into the delicious shortbread biscuits that had been sent from Canada, and helped themselves to some of the mince pies Peggy had made the day before. Sitting down, finally, she finished her cigarette. 'I don't suppose any of you saw Cissy tonight?' she asked more in hope than expectation.

'Not since we left for the church,' said Bob. 'She certainly wasn't in the Anchor.'

'I saw her and Gloria's niece outside the Crown,' piped up Cordelia. 'But that was some time before the mayor started his never-ending speech.'

'Oh, well, no doubt she'll turn up eventually,' Peggy said with a lightness that belied the worry in her heart. 'I'd better not bolt the back door as she's probably forgotten to bring her spare key home, and it's not a night to be locked out.'

The tea, mince pies and biscuits were consumed as they discussed the evening and imparted the news that Ruby was slowly warming to Alastair Darwin's determined but gentle courtship. This heartened Peggy, for Ruby needed someone like Alastair to love and cherish her after all she'd been through recently – and they did make a lovely couple.

With the cups washed and left to dry on the drainer, the lights were switched off and Bob escorted Bertie up to the attic bedroom. Jim carried Cordelia to her own room, and Peggy made sure Pippa had everything she needed in the bedroom off the hall before putting Daisy's stocking at the foot of her bed and helping to settle Cordelia for the night.

It was almost midnight when Peggy left her bedroom door ajar and climbed into bed next to Jim, who'd begun to snore the moment his head hit the pillow. She was tired and ready to sleep, but remained wide awake and alert for the sound of Cissy coming home.

18

Peggy and Jim were startled awake by Daisy leaping on to their bed in great excitement.

'Santa came,' she yelled, waving the comic annual into their faces. 'And look, look. I got sweeties too – and an orange and new ribbon for my hair.'

Peggy admired everything and groggily looked at the clock. It was barely five in the morning, but despite the hour and the lack of sleep, she'd have to leave her bed and begin her day if lunch was to be ready by one. The delicious aroma of roasting turkey was already drifting up from the kitchen, so it would need basting, and the puddings would have to go on soon if they were to be steamed through in time. She kissed and hugged Daisy, and left her to chatter on to Jim so she could wash and dress before the rest of the household began to stir.

'Happy Christmas, Mum,' said Bob, leaping down the stairs to give her a hug on the landing. 'Daisy woke me and Charlie up. I take it Santa left a stocking for her?'

'He certainly did and she's plaguing your father with it right this minute – so if you'd like to rescue him while I get dressed, that would be a help.'

'Will do,' he said cheerfully and barged his way into her bedroom to grab Daisy and whirl her about.

Peggy rolled her eyes. Daisy wouldn't last the day with all the excitement, but then her other children had been just the same, and it was lovely to have her eldest boy home. She stopped at Cissy's door as she headed for the bathroom and tried the knob, but this time it appeared to be locked. With a huge sigh of relief, she went into the bathroom and with an easier mind, began to prepare for her very busy day.

Cissy had been woken by Daisy too, and she groaned as she realised how early it was. She would have liked nothing better than to pull the covers over her head and stay in the warmth of her bed for another few hours, but her parents wouldn't stand for such unreasonable behaviour on this special day.

She lay listening to the exchange between her mother and brother, and suspected it was her mother who'd tried turning the doorknob. Thankful that she'd thought to lock the door when she got in last night, she heard Peggy bolt the bathroom door and reluctantly climbed out of bed. She had a challenging day ahead, but with so many people in the house, it should be easy to avoid being cornered by her mother, who would no doubt interrogate her on her whereabouts the previous evening. Grabbing her wash bag and the clothes she would wear that day, she hurried downstairs to the smart bathroom in the basement.

Sandra woke to the sound of her Aunt Gloria clumping down the stairs to the kitchen where she proceeded to turn the radio on full blast, and crash pans about. She looked at the bedside clock and groaned before rolling over and pulling the covers over her head. She'd had very little sleep last night and, after her long and distressing conversation with Cissy, she was utterly wrung out.

She lay listening as her mother greeted Graham on the landing. 'Well, I know she's in there because the door's locked, and from outside, you can see she's pulled the curtains,' said Beryl. 'Probably best to leave her for a bit, as she must have got in very late and is, no doubt, suffering from an 'angover.'

Good grief, thought Sandra. *Is there no privacy to be had in this house?* She buried her face in the pillows, feeling trapped.

A light tap on the door was followed by Graham softly calling her name.

She pretended not to hear, determined to stay in here for as long as her aching bladder allowed her to. But Graham was persistent, tapping at the door like an eager woodpecker, his voice getting louder and more demanding as he ordered her to let him in.

Fed up with his persistence, she crossly flung the bedclothes back, wrapped herself in her thick dressing gown and unlocked the door. 'I was trying to sleep,' she said evenly.

Graham looked positively dishevelled, his handsome face quite ashen with fury. 'Where did you get to last night?' he hissed. 'I waited up but didn't see or hear you come home, so it must have been very late.'

'Mum and Aunt Gloria told you, I went off with Cissy,' she said coolly. 'Now stop fussing and let me get to the bathroom before I have an accident.'

'But I need to talk to you,' he said, folding his arms and barring her escape.

'And I need the lav. Let me pass, Graham.'

'Your mother's in there, so you'll have to use the *lavatory* downstairs,' he replied.

That meant running the gauntlet of Aunt Gloria, but it couldn't be helped, for she was quite desperate now. She pushed past Graham and ran down the two flights of stairs, hoping beyond hope that Gloria wouldn't see her.

'Oy, gel! I wanna word with you!'

'Can't stop. Need the lav,' she shouted back, running down the last flight to the back door. Wrestling with the bolts, she finally managed to get outside and into the lean-to lav that had been built in one corner of the back yard for the use of Gloria's customers. It didn't smell very nice and was probably infested with vermin and spiders, but she was beyond caring.

Sandra emerged a few minutes later to find Gloria waiting for her in the narrow, dimly lit hall that ran between the saloon bar and snug. Her arms were folded and her expression was fierce enough to frighten the hardiest of souls.

'Where did you get to last night?'

Her aunt's voice was deceptively low and reasonable, but Sandra knew this was a sign that Gloria was at her most dangerous. 'I went with Cissy to the Anchor,' she replied calmly.

'The Anchor shuts at half-ten. And you didn't come home then, so where were you?'

'I'm not a child, Aunt Gloria,' she said patiently. 'I don't have to have your permission to stay out late.'

'You do when yer under my roof,' Gloria snapped. The heavily made-up eyes flashed with anger. 'So what were you and Cissy Reilly up to?'

'We weren't up to anything,' she replied coolly, meeting her aunt's angry gaze. 'We went for a drink at the Anchor, and then went on to that new cocktail bar in the basement of Plummer's.'

'So my place ain't good enough for yer now yer so hoity-toity? But I happen to know that closes at midnight, and you weren't home then, cos I checked.'

'They stayed open later last night,' she said truthfully, 'just as you did with your lock-in,' she added slyly. 'I came home through the back way while you were busy chucking the last of your customers out the front.'

Gloria cocked her head and eyed Sandra thoughtfully. 'You got all the answers, ain't yer? But don't for one minute think you're fooling me, gel,' she said flatly, waving a meaty finger in Sandra's face. 'I might not know when yer up to, but I aim to find out what it is before this Christmas is over.'

Sandra stood before her, not daring to answer back. She'd learnt from past experience that Gloria was quite capable of clipping her round the ear if she gave her any lip.

Gloria gave her a gentle push. 'Go on, get outta here and make it up with that husband of yours. You've already put the mockers on things, and I ain't standing for no more of it, you 'ear? I got my friend Albert coming for Christmas dinner, and I don't want 'im thinking my family's at sixes and sevens.'

The heavy thudding on the door jolted Cissy from the relaxing doze she was enjoying in the bath.

'Hurry up, Cissy,' shouted Charlie. 'You can't hog the bathroom all day.'

'But I've only just got in here,' she shouted back.

'There are eight other people in this house, Cissy, and a queue for both bathrooms. If you don't get a move on, I'll keep knocking until you do.'

Cissy realised she was being selfish and reluctantly clambered out of the bath. 'All right, all right, keep your hair on, Charlie. I'll be out in a minute.'

She pulled the plug and as the water swirled down the waste pipe, she gave the bath a quick wipe down, and then dried and dressed herself. The short-sleeved shirt-waister dress of khaki linen skimmed her hips and fell to just above her knees. She pulled on a long-line cream cardigan of the softest merino wool, slipped her narrow, stockinged feet into tan pumps with low heels and clipped on earrings. Once she'd fixed the thin strands of gold around her neck, she was about to start on her make-up and hair when Charlie began to bang on the door again.

'I'm coming,' she shouted crossly, snatching up her make-up bag, nightwear and wash things. She opened the door and was almost knocked down by her younger brother barging past her. As he slammed and locked the door, she shouted, 'And a very merry Christmas to you too!'

Turning, she realised Pippa was standing there watching all this with some amusement. 'Sorry about the shouting, Pippa, but Charlie always was impatient.'

'It's all rather fun,' the girl replied on a chuckle. 'Being an only child, I've never had to queue for the bathroom before or had to deal with oversized brothers.'

'Count yourself lucky, Pippa. This house is always in chaos – as you'll soon find out. It was even worse when there was only one bathroom for the seven of us plus the lodgers we had before the war.'

Charlie came charging out of the bathroom minutes later to take the basement steps two at a time and slam his way into the kitchen. Cissy and Pippa exchanged sisterly glances, and as Pippa shut the bathroom door behind her, Cissy took a breath for courage before climbing the steps to the kitchen.

'At last,' said Peggy, turning from the sink to wipe her hands on her apron and shoot her a playful smile. 'And what time did you get in this morning?'

'Quite late,' she replied, having rehearsed with Sandra what they'd say when the inevitable questions arose. She dropped the small bags and nightwear on a nearby chair and reached for the teapot.

'It had to be after midnight, because I was still awake then, and listening out for you.'

'Sandra and I tried out that new cocktail bar.' She poured tea into one of the many mugs on the table and added a drop of milk. 'I have to say, it's quite sophisticated for dear old Cliffehaven. I bet it caused a stir when it opened.'

'There were objections from the usual quarters,' said Peggy, 'but Rosie said the Council passed the application as it meant bringing back a bit of life to the place.' She sat down at the table. 'So what time did you get in?'

'I don't really know. But it was after one.' Cissy put her hand on her mother's arm. 'I'm sorry if you were worried, Mum. We got to chatting over old times and simply didn't realise how late it was.'

'How on earth did you manage to get up those stairs without me hearing you?'

Cissy couldn't help but smile. 'You forget, Mum, I know every creaking stair and floorboard in this house, so it wasn't difficult.'

Peggy leaned towards her, her dark brown eyes filled with concern. 'Is everything all right with you, darling? You don't seem yourself, and I'm worried about you.'

Cissy was saved from answering by Bob coming into the kitchen with Daisy, closely followed by Charlie, Cordelia, and Bertie Double-Barrelled.

'I won't let this drop, Cissy,' murmured her mother beneath the babble of noise. 'Whatever is wrong, darling, I'll do everything I can to help put it right. But I need you to trust me with whatever it is and talk to me.'

Cissy's hand was trembling as she lifted the mug of tea to her lips. She'd always known her mother could read her too well, but the die was cast and sooner or later she would have to tell her everything – but not before Christmas was over. Her parents didn't deserve to have that ruined.

Ron hadn't slept well, and because he hadn't wanted to disturb Rosie, he'd left their bed before dawn to get dressed and go downstairs. The dogs, of course, were delighted to see him, and after racing about in the garden for a few minutes as he saw to his ferrets, joined him on the couch in the sitting room.

He sat drinking tea and smoking his pipe with Harvey's muzzle resting on his knee, and Monty flopped on his back beside him. He'd drawn back the curtains in the large bay window so that when the sky began to lighten, he could watch the sunrise gild the waters of the English Channel. The panoramic view of the sea and the whole sweep of the horseshoe bay was one of the reasons Rosie had fallen in love with this house, and now the months of hard labour to put the place to rights were over, he too could appreciate it. But his thoughts were still troubled, and he knew he wouldn't be able to truly relax until he'd had the chance to talk privately with his granddaughter.

He watched the rising sun slowly breach the eastern horizon to cast a pink glow on the clouds surrounding it and on the choppy water beneath. The towering chalk cliffs took on the same hue, and long shadows were shortened as the great orange orb rose into the pink and pearly-grey sky to set fire to the firmament in a blaze of red.

'Red sky at night, shepherd's delight,' he murmured, stroking Harvey's velvety ears. 'Red sky in the morning, shepherd's warning. We'd better go for our walk before the weather breaks.'

The word 'walk' had both dogs on their feet in an instant, so he hauled himself up from the couch and went into the hall. There was no sound of life from up-stairs, so he grabbed his poacher's coat and scruffy cap, dug his feet into his sturdy boots and let the dogs out into the front garden. Closing the front door softly behind him, he pocketed his keys, opened the gate and headed for Camden Road.

The dogs were confused, for they usually went to the recreation ground at this time of the morning, but as Ron was striding off, they raced to catch him up in the hope they'd be taken into the hills.

Ron knew he was cheating his animals out of a good run this morning, but he had to satisfy himself that Cissy had gone home last night, and whatever it was that troubled those girls had been resolved. He kept up a brisk pace as the dogs shot back and forth to water weeds and sniff out scents in every doorway and alley. He had to call them to heel when he reached the twitten behind Beach View, for they'd scampered up the track which led to the hills and their usual walk.

He could hear the chatter and laughter coming from the kitchen as he let himself in through the back door, but then stood hesitantly at the bottom of the basement steps, realising suddenly that everyone was up and it would be impossible to get the girl alone. However, he needed to see her, if only briefly, just for reassurance. As he opened the door the dogs bounded into the kit-chen, determined to greet everyone.

He grabbed hold of Monty, who was trying to climb on to Pippa's lap, grinned at Jim, Bertie and his grand-sons and gave Cordelia a wink. 'I see your beau has stayed the night, you naughty girl,' he teased.

'Trust you to make insinuations, you old rogue,' she retorted, playfully swiping at his arm. 'Bertie slept in the attic.'

'Ron, for goodness' sake do something about this hound of yours!' Peggy shoved Harvey away as he stood on his back legs and tried to lick her face, his tail whipping little Daisy so hard it almost knocked her from her chair.

'To be sure, I'm sorry, wee girl,' he said, grabbing Harvey's collar and ordering both dogs to sit still. 'I've just popped in to say happy Christmas to everyone and give my granddaughter a hug.'

He turned to Cissy who was pouring out tea for Cordelia. A swift glance told him she hadn't slept well and still looked pale. 'Ach, Cissy me darlin'. I was beginning to think you were avoiding me,' he said, noting that she didn't rush straight to him for a hug as she would usually have done.

Her smile was bright, but her eyes were wary as she let him embrace her. 'As if I would, Grandpa. You are an old silly billy – but my goodness, how do you manage to look so bright and breezy at this unearthly time of the morning?' She stepped back from the fleeting embrace and quickly returned to pouring out the tea before sitting down out of reach at the other side of the table. 'How's Rosie?'

'She's having a lie-in while I walk the dogs,' he replied, catching Peggy's eye and seeing that he wasn't the only one to have noticed Cissy's unusual reaction to him. 'Everything going to plan, Peg?' he asked. 'All set for one o'clock?'

Peggy nodded. 'Will you stay for a cuppa?'

He shook his head. 'I'd best be getting back to help Rosie with our lunch. We'll see you this afternoon.' He glanced once more at Cissy who was studiously ignoring him as she argued with Charlie over the amount of sugar he was using, and then, with a heavy heart, shooed the dogs out.

Closing the door behind him, he went into the garden and dug into his coat pocket for his pipe. Whatever was eating at Cissy would no doubt make itself clear sooner or later, but it was causing Peggy worry and he could feel the tension building between mother and daughter. There would be ructions, he had no doubt about that, and could only pray that it didn't happen in the middle of what should be a happy family get-together.

However, he knew from past experience that Christmas nearly always proved to be a tricky time, with emotions and expectations running high, and he just wished he could get the chance to speak to Cissy and defuse the time bomb that was clearly already ticking.

19

Gracie had been in a deep, drug-induced sleep when she was woken by the sound of her little Bobby's piping voice. She opened her eyes to find him sitting quietly in Florence's lap at her bedside, clutching the red kite he'd found in his stocking. Seeing the worry on his little face, she felt a pang of sorrow, and although it hurt like blazes to move away from the bank of supporting pillows, she turned on to her side and opened her arms to him.

He abandoned the kite to creep on to the bed, avoiding the drip in her arm, and nestle into her side. 'Is your tummy better now?' he asked tremulously.

She held him close, despite the pain of his weight against her operation wound. 'It's getting better, my love,' she murmured, kissing his curls and breathing in his scent. 'Mummy will have to stay here for a bit until the doctor says I can come home. But when I do, we can go and fly your lovely kite.'

She caught Florence's eye over his head, saw the worry reflected there, and tried to reassure her with a wan smile.

Bobby shifted against her, sharp little knees prodding tender flesh which made her gasp. He looked up at her, his brown eyes shining with excitement. 'Santa brought the kite,' he breathed. 'And Auntie Flo let me open a present early, cos I was a good boy. And it was a fire engine from Auntie Peggy.' He reached for the toy to show her, and then frowned. 'Who's Auntie Peggy?'

Florence could clearly see Gracie was in great discomfort, so she eased Bobby closer to the edge of the bed and away from her heavily bandaged stomach. 'Remember I told you, Bobby. She's the really nice lady Mummy and I work with at the factory. Wasn't it lovely of her to give you such a wonderful thing?'

'Everyone has been so kind,' Gracie whispered. 'I really don't deserve it.' She held Bobby in the crook of her arm, her heart warmed and comforted by his presence, but then he began to squirm, eager to be free to play with his new fire engine, and the tiger of pain stretched and roared through her again.

Florence quickly sat him back on her lap with the fire engine. 'Should I ring for a nurse?' she asked. 'I was worried this would prove to be too much for you, Gracie.'

Gracie was quite desperate for the lovely injection that took away the pain, but she shook her head, her gaze glued to her little boy. She was so lucky to have been given a second chance at life – and to be able to watch him now – so the pain was almost secondary. 'Did you sing in the church, Bobby? Were all your little friends there?'

Bobby nodded, too engrossed in pushing the red fire engine up and down the quilt to talk to her now he'd been assured she was all right.

Florence took her hand. 'Don't worry about Bobby. I'll look after him until you come home. You just concentrate on getting better.'

'I'll do my best,' she managed as the claws of pain took hold again and dug deep. 'Thank you, Flo. Thank you for everything.'

'We'll come again tomorrow,' said Florence, gathering up the kite and her handbag. 'You need to rest. Oh, and I got a note through the door last night. Cissy and Sandra would like to visit if it wouldn't be too much for you.'

'That would be lovely,' she replied, the pain now making her feel sick and woozy.

Bobby leaned on the bed to peck her on the cheek. 'Bye bye, Mummy,' he said cheerfully before clutching his fire engine to his chest and checking to see that Florence had his precious kite.

Gracie's tears rolled down her face as Florence patted her hand. 'Thanks ever so much, Flo. You've been a proper diamond, really you have.'

Florence awkwardly acknowledged this praise and then turned to Bobby. 'Come on, young man. It's time to go home and open the rest of your presents.'

Bobby clapped in excitement before taking Flo's hand and trotting along beside her as they left the room, his chatter fading as the door closed silently behind them.

Gracie couldn't quite quell the spark of jealousy that had shot through her at the sight of her little boy's burgeoning trust and affection for Florence, and was immediately appalled at her lack of empathy. Florence was single and childless – and if she formed a bond with Bobby, then how much better it was for all of them.

Furious with herself, and almost bent double with the pain, she pressed the button to call a nurse. Even as the girl came bustling in to help her, she was well aware that she was only alive because of the kindness and skills of others. If she was granted the chance to heal and begin again, she would make it up to Florence, and be the very best mother she could.

Sandra returned to her bedroom after the presents had been distributed early that morning. She'd been delighted by the creamy silk blouse her mother had given her, and the posh chocolates from her brother and Ivy. The classy real gold and pearl earrings from her aunt had come as a wonderful surprise. However, it was the gold locket from Graham which made her feel quite ill, for he'd clearly taken great care to choose and wrap it, and in the circumstances it was too much. Thankfully, her mother had loved the calfskin handbag she'd found in Harrods, and Gloria was delighted with the fancy bottle of French perfume, which she'd immediately dabbed liberally on her wrists and neck.

Sandra dressed carefully for the day as her mother and aunt squabbled happily over how much longer the turkey should stay in the oven, and Graham was sent off to choose the wines to go with it. The new silk blouse went well with her smart black skirt, and the pearls glowed softly in her ears. She'd decided not to wear the locket as it felt like too much of a bribe, and she'd be expected to show her gratitude. She eyed her reflection in her make-up mirror and gave a sigh. Only a miracle would get rid of the shadows under her eyes, but at least she felt a little better after a bath and was now ready to join the fray again.

Closing the bedroom door, she was greeted by the delicious aroma of roasting turkey, which made her feel quite hungry for once. Hurrying down to the kitchen in search of toast or cereal, she was engulfed by the steam rising from the saucepan that held the muslin-wrapped pudding. She could barely see her aunt and mother, who were ghostly figures busy at the sink, and the window and walls were running with condensation.

'Shall I open the window?' Sandra asked, pushing her way into the cramped room.

'You better 'ad,' said Gloria. 'All this damp ain't doing my hairdo much good.'

Sandra obliged, and as the room slowly cleared, she helped herself to a cup of tea from the pot on the side, wondering if she dared asked if there was a chance of any breakfast. Realising this would probably be pushing her luck, she asked instead if she could help with anything.

'Yeah,' said Gloria. 'You can check on the fire in the dining room and make sure it ain't gone out. I don't trust that cheap stuff what passes for coal these days.' She turned from the steaming Christmas pudding. 'And while yer at it, gel, you can pour us both a large gin and tonic. It's thirsty work, all this cooking.'

It was barely nine in the morning, and far too early for gin, but Sandra said nothing and was glad to escape the busy kitchen. She quickly gulped down the tepid tea and then ran down the stairs to the large dining room that Gloria used for holding functions. The room smelt a bit musty as it hadn't been used for some time, so she opened a window in the hope the cold air might clear it a bit, and took a long, appreciative look at the echoing space.

Gloria had made it more intimate by dividing a third of it off with decorative silk screens that looked as if they belonged to the Art Deco era, and bringing in several easy chairs from the snug. She'd slung paper chains across the ceiling where two crystal chandeliers shot rainbows of colour on to the white walls and highly polished parquet floor, and the Christmas tree in the corner was loaded with tinsel and baubles, the rather grubby angel at the top bearing drooping wings and a bent halo.

The fire in the ornately tiled Victorian hearth wasn't looking very cheerful, so Sandra prodded it with the poker and watched the sparks fly up the chimney until the blaze brightened and the nutty slack settled into a glow. Turning from the fire, she admired the long table which was draped in pristine white damask, with matching napkins folded to look like waterlilies. Silver candlesticks stood in a line down the centre, the creamy candles yet to be lit, and in the middle of the table was a chased silver bowl filled with dark red hothouse roses. Each place was set with heavy silver cutlery and crystal glassware, and the chairs that had once looked very tatty were now freshly upholstered in colourful chintz.

Sandra wondered how on earth her aunt had managed to find roses at this time of year, but then no expense seemed to have been spared for this Christmas, and Gloria had certainly pulled out all the stops – even to the point of unpacking her prized collection of crystal and silverware which she usually stored in the attic.

Quickly, Sandra shut the window and headed to the small bar at the back of the room. She poured out a bottled beer for Graham and two generous gin and tonics and carried them back to the kitchen.

'Ah, that's more like it,' said Beryl, taking a glass. 'You look more cheerful too, Sandra. Feeling better?'

'Yes thanks, Mum,' she replied, passing Gloria her drink.

'Good,' said Gloria before downing half her drink in one swallow. 'Albert will be here soon, so best foot forward and no falling out with Graham – you 'ear?'

Sandra nodded. 'Who is this Albert, by the way?' she asked. 'I never heard you mention him before.'

Gloria's gaze was almost challenging as she looked at Sandra. 'He's my special friend – has been for years – and the only man ever to get past my bedroom door after my divorce, I might add. He warms me bed now and again, keeps me company and makes me laugh; but we decided long ago to keep it private, as it's no one else's business. He's feeling a bit down at the moment, so I invited him over for Christmas dinner. It's about time me family met him, anyway.'

Sandra had to bite the inside of her cheek to keep from giggling, for although her aunt was all mouth and trousers and flaunted herself like nobody's business to all and sundry, she'd never suspected she had a secret lover. How intriguing.

'Did you know about this, Mum?'

Beryl took another slurp of her drink before replying. 'I guessed there were someone before the war, but as Gloria didn't seem keen to talk about 'im, I didn't like to ask too many questions.' She turned to her sister who was topping up the water beneath the steaming pudding. 'How old is he, then, this fancy man of yours, Glo?'

Gloria laughed and slammed the metal jug back into the sink. 'Albert's far from fancy, Beryl – as you'll soon find out – and definitely past the age of consent.' She finished her drink. 'Now, where's Graham got to? His beer's going flat, and the red wine will need to breathe if it's to be drinkable.'

'I'll go and find him.' Sandra left the cramped kitchen, still wondering about her aunt's mystery man, and who he might be. And yet, as she headed for the dining room again in search of Graham, she realised she didn't know the male population in Cliffehaven well enough to guess, and as Albert was a popular name for the men of Gloria's generation, it could have been anyone.

There was no sign of Graham in the dining room, but as she went into the main saloon bar, she saw the floor hatch was open, so went to peer into the gloom. 'Are you down there, Graham?'

'Yes! Mind your head if you're coming down,' he shouted back, his voice strangely deadened by the low ceiling of the underground space.

She negotiated the stone steps, the single lightbulb, and the low-hanging beams to step down into the dimly lit, damp space which sprawled beneath the large building and disappeared into pitch-black darkness. She'd never been down here before, but looking round, she saw that the cellar had been roughly divided into sections. One for the beer barrels, which would be delivered down the chute from the trap in the pavement; two for bits of old furniture and dusty cardboard boxes; and the largest section filled with rack upon rack of wine bottles. The lightbulb was so weak she wished she'd brought a torch, for the dark shadows seemed to close in round her.

Graham appeared from the depths of the wine racks carrying dusty bottles and a flickering torch. 'Hello, there. Gloria sent me to hunt out wines for the meal, but I can barely see anything, and this torch battery is about to die.'

'You've got a beer waiting for you upstairs,' she replied, peering into the distant darkness and wondering what lurked there. 'Gloria never let me down here as a kid,' she said, eyeing the racks of wine bottles, the stacks of rubbish, and the vast barrels of different beers. 'I can now see why.'

'It's not somewhere to stay for long,' he replied with a grimace. 'Too damned cold, dirty and dark.'

Sandra could only agree. She approached the first rack and pulled out a bottle at random. 'Good grief,' she gasped on seeing the label. 'This is very expensive champagne. Where on earth has Gloria managed to get her hands on something like this?'

Graham brushed cobwebs from his hair and sweater, leaving a smear of dirt on his face. 'I wouldn't ask, if I were you, as the revenue would certainly take an interest in this lot. Our Gloria seems to be involved in a very efficient black market. I've found port, brandy and some very good wines down here, and there's more where this came from,' he added, taking the champagne bottle from her and adding it to the collection he'd already placed in an old beer crate.

'Well, we certainly won't die of thirst today,' replied Sandra lightly. 'Come on, let's get that lot upstairs. Gloria's boyfriend is due to arrive any minute, and we'll be expected to be on parade to greet him.'

Graham's eyes widened. 'Boyfriend? She's a bit old for all that, isn't she?'

Sandra bit her lip. 'That was my first thought, but I wouldn't let her hear you say it if you want to survive the day.'

He caught her hand before she could make her way out of the cellar. 'You seem more like yourself,' he said quietly. 'I'm glad, really I am.'

'Things haven't changed even though I'm feeling better,' she replied, squeezing his fingers to take the sting out of her words and avoid an argument. 'But it's Christmas Day and Gloria has put her heart and soul into making it special for all of us, so let's not spoil it, eh?'

His smile faded. 'I'll do my best to forget you've asked me for a divorce and continued to avoid me at every turn – and I'll ignore the fact you've been secretive and out of sorts since coming here. All I ask is that you stop shutting me out, and at least *pretend* we still have a marriage of sorts to cling to. As you say, it's Christmas, and we shouldn't let our troubles spoil it for the others.'

'Oh, Graham,' she sighed. 'Of course I'll make sure the day isn't spoilt.' She eyed the smear of dirt on his cheek and forced a smile. 'You'd better wash that muck off your face before we sit down at the table. You look as if you've been down a mine.'

Taking her by surprise, he snaked his arm round her waist, pulled her roughly to him and kissed her hard on the lips before releasing her. 'If we both go up there with dirty faces they'll think we've made up,' he said coldly. Turning away, he lifted the heavy crate before meeting her startled gaze. 'And I'd appreciate it if you'd wear the locket, Sandra. It was very expensive – unlike those cheap cufflinks you gave me.'

Sandra bit down on a retort and followed him up the steps. She hadn't missed the gleam of determination in his eyes, or the meaning behind that proprietorial kiss. With the pressure of it still lingering on her lips, she was reminded once more of how manipulative he could be, and how he would fight to get his own way – but she'd be damned if she'd wear that locket and chain around her neck.

The presents from beneath the tree had been opened and admired, the fire blazed in the hearth and the BBC Light Programme was broadcasting a lovely service from Westminster Abbey. The atmosphere at Beach View was light and happy as Ruby arrived bearing bottles of gin and whisky, as well as small presents for Peggy and Daisy.

Jack Smith came soon after with a huge tin of sweet biscuits and a long air letter from his daughter, Rita, which Peggy pounced upon the minute he showed it to her. Bertie, having dashed home, brought sherry and cigars as well as the beautiful pearl and diamond brooch he'd purchased for Cordelia – who'd burst into tears with delight and insisted he pin it to her dress immediately. She'd spent the morning gazing at it and admiring its reflection in the dining-room mirror.

Cissy had received a lovely silver bracelet from her parents, which made her feel horribly guilty for what she would do to them once the celebrations were over; a silky scarf in her favourite pink from Bob and Pippa; a bottle of Martini from Ron and Rosie; and a hand-knitted pink beret from Cordelia, which she suspected had actually been made by her mother as there were no dropped stitches and the fit and shaping was perfect.

Charlie had surprised her with a piece of amethyst he'd found on the beach, which he'd cut and polished and set into a thin circle of chrome that he'd salvaged from Jack's garage, to make a pendant. Astonished by his skill and the work it must have taken to make such a thing, she'd hunted out a chain so she could wear it, and thoroughly embarrassed him by giving him a big kiss.

Her own gifts to her family had been received with great appreciation, for which she was relieved. She'd spent ages hunting down just the right thing, and although she hadn't expected Bob to bring a girlfriend, she'd quickly wrapped a pair of her own earrings into a little box for her so she wouldn't feel left out. Peggy and Cordelia had clearly come to the same conclusion, and they'd rustled up bath salts and a small tin of talc.

Now it was almost one o'clock, and while Cordelia and Jack kept an overexcited Daisy occupied with her new jigsaw puzzle, and Bertie poured another sherry for Cordelia, Cissy and Pippa went to help Peggy drain the vegetables into serving bowls. Jim lifted the glistening turkey from the oven and placed it reverently on to a platter. Ruby stacked the golden roast potatoes and parsnips on to another platter; Cissy filled the gravy boats; and Pippa placed the sausages, ham and bacon rashers into individual dishes. Once everything was ready, they formed a ceremonial line behind Jim and, to his rather off-key rendition of 'We Wish You a Merry Christmas', carried everything into the dining room to be greeted by cheers, whistles and applause.

Cissy sat down between Charlie and Bob to watch her father sharpen his favourite knife before he carved the bird with expert ease, spooning out the delicious stuffing to add to the plate as her mother added the vegetables. *It's so lovely to have Dad home again*, she thought, *and to see him and Mum so contented and happy. If only . . .*

She snapped from those dark and dangerous thoughts as the plates were passed down the table. When everyone had been served and the bowls of sausage, ham and bacon were quickly emptied, Jim tapped a knife against his glass to silence their chatter.

'This might not be fancy champagne,' he said as everyone fell silent. 'But who needs posh fizz when family and friends are already bubbling with the joy of being together after so long? Here's to Peggy who has provided this splendid meal, and happy Christmas to you all. May the new year of 1947 bring you peace, joy and much love.'

The toast was repeated by the gathering and then silence fell as they tucked into the delicious meal Peggy had spent so long preparing.

The volume of noise rose as plates were scraped clean and the buzz of chatter rang round the table to drown out the sound of the Bakelite radio Cissy had sent down earlier in the year. It had been brought into the dining room so they wouldn't miss the King's speech at three o'clock. Crackers were pulled and silly paper hats tugged on to heads as second helpings of potatoes and turkey were dished out – mainly to Bob and Charlie, who had voracious appetites. But eventually everyone pushed back from the table and started to loosen belts in preparation for the pudding.

Cissy had discovered she was ravenously hungry for the first time in weeks, and although she was now feeling rather too full, she couldn't resist the rich, dark pudding which was drowned in her mother's creamy custard and soaked in enough brandy to make you quite dizzy.

Not wanting to be spotted by anyone, Sergeant Albert Williams had arrived, as usual, at the back door of the Crown looking very smart in his good suit, his grandfather's watch and chain gleaming from his fancy waistcoat pocket, his shoes and balding pate polished to a shine.

Gloria proudly introduced him to everyone and, once she'd opened his gift of a set of dress jewellery, she thanked him profusely, then sent him off with Graham to get a drink while she organised Beryl and Sandra in the kitchen. However, Sandra suddenly seemed to be all fingers and thumbs, scorching herself on the stove and almost cutting her finger with a knife. When she dropped one of her best plates into the unyielding stone sink, Gloria lost her patience.

'You'd better join the men,' she said crossly. 'You ain't no use to me if yer going to break me best china.'

Sandra apologised and left the kitchen, and Gloria turned to help Beryl get the heavy turkey out of the oven. 'I don't know,' she sighed, reaching for a dustpan and brush to sweep up the broken plate. 'I thought they'd called a truce after they come up from that cellar all mucky-faced and looking guilty – but that girl's a bag of nerves.'

'Yeah, something's up, that's fer sure, but we ain't got time to worry about that now, Glo. This turkey needs carving, and the veg is about to boil to a pulp.'

'Get them saucepans off the heat then, and dish 'em up while I put everything else into the dumb waiter. If I try and carry this lot down in these shoes, it'll end up on the floor, and then where would we be?'

Beryl eyed the scarlet high-heeled shoes and clucked her tongue. 'I dunno how you can even walk in them shoes, Glo. I'd be arse over tit within seconds.'

Gloria loaded the turkey and its accompaniments into the dumb waiter before glancing down at her sister's unattractive brown footwear. 'It takes a lot of practice,' she replied, 'and frankly, Beryl, I wouldn't be seen dead in them things you're wearing – they don't do nothing for yer legs, you know.'

'Well, I ain't about to argue with you, Glo. I'm too hungry, and that turkey will get cold if we stand about 'ere yacking.'

Gloria added the vegetable bowls and gravy boats to the second shelf of the dumb waiter and pulled the ropes which would lower the whole contraption to the hatch in the dining room. She turned the gas off under the plum pudding since it was cooked, closed the kitchen window and, after checking that her hair and make-up were still to her satisfaction, followed her sister downstairs.

As she entered the dining room, she glanced round with pleasure to see that all her hard work over the last few days had paid off. The room looked quite magnificent, even if she did say so herself, and those screens she'd bought from a house clearance made the whole thing look very classy.

Gloria went straight to the hatch where Beryl and Sandra were already unloading the serving bowls and warmed plates to put on the table. Aware that Albert was droning on to Graham about his role in the police force and the task he had to find the missing girl, she tuned him out to reach into the dumb waiter and, with some effort, managed to lift out the enormous turkey. Carrying it triumphantly to the end of the table, she set it down in front of Albert.

'Enough shop talk, Albert. It's time for you to carve the turkey – and don't stint, neither. There's enough there to feed half of Cliffehaven.'

As he rose from his chair to do her bidding, Graham opened the champagne, filled everyone's glasses and also got to his feet. 'I propose a toast to Gloria and Beryl for the magnificent effort they've made to provide such a feast – and to my lovely wife, who is looking quite beautiful today.'

'Blimey, Graham, you don't half go on,' teased Gloria, noting that Sandra had gone a deep scarlet. She raised her glass, the fake rubies and diamonds of her new jewellery sparkling in the light from the chandeliers. 'Cheers all, and happy Christmas.'

The toast was echoed, the delicious champagne slipping down throats with gusto as Graham sat down to shoot an apologetic glance at Sandra – who ignored him.

Albert attended to the business of carving the turkey as Gloria passed the loaded plates round the table and everyone helped themselves from the bowls of vegetables and accompaniments. Eventually Gloria picked up her knife and fork. 'Tuck in before it gets cold,' she ordered.

There was a contented silence for a while, but once the initial pangs of hunger were satisfied, and the delicious meal was eaten more slowly, Graham seemed to feel the need to start a conversation.

'It was most interesting to hear Albert talking first-hand about that missing girl,' he said to no one in particular. 'And I do think it's most unfair that he should be forced to retire just because he hasn't found her.'

'He's not being forced into nothing,' said Gloria, helping herself to another roast potato. 'His service in the police during the war took him past retirement age – or what the police force consider retirement age. They wouldn't keep him on even if he had found her.'

'But Albert still has many good years left in him,' persisted Graham between mouthfuls. 'They should honour the years he worked during the war and permit him to stay until the case is either solved or shelved.'

Albert reached for his glass of champagne and took a sip. 'If it's not solved, it'll be put to one side and kept open – and that could be for years,' he said. 'Once it becomes clear that all avenues have been explored and there's no new evidence to go on, it'll be classed as what's called a "cold case" and will be shoved into the archives. And it could stay there for decades.' He picked up his cutlery again and grimaced. 'Sadly, my time is up, Graham, and I have to make way for the next generation of eager young things.' He stuck his fork into a roast potato and sliced it in half with some vigour.

To Gloria's annoyance, and Sandra's clear discomfort, Graham seemed determined to keep nagging away at the topic.

'But with all your years of experience, Albert, you're far more likely to track her down than some new chap who doesn't know the area – let alone the people living here. And as you so rightly say, the mother of that baby had to be a local, so it goes without saying that someone here must know something.'

Before Albert could reply, Gloria clattered her knife and fork on her plate and glared at Graham who was sitting opposite her. 'For gawd's sake give it a rest, Graham,' she barked. 'You're spoiling me appetite, as well as the mood. We've all heard more than enough about that girl these past weeks, and it ain't the proper topic for Christmas dinner.'

She'd never raised her voice to Graham before, and he stared back at her as stunned and frozen as a rabbit caught in the glare of a poacher's lamp. 'I'm sorry,' he stuttered. 'I didn't mean to offend anyone.'

She picked up her cutlery and waved the knife at him. 'Then change the bleedin' record, Graham, and let someone else do the talking.'

Beryl nervously cleared her throat as a heavy silence fell in the room. 'I forgot to tell you, Glo,' she said hesitantly. 'Our Andy and his Ivy are expecting again. Ain't that lovely?'

Gloria saw the anguish in Sandra's face and turned to her sister in exasperation. 'Yeah, I'm sure it is. But can we *please* find something else to talk about other than babies!'

'I thought I might try fishing as a hobby once I retire,' piped up Albert.

Sandra nearly choked on her wine, Graham started pontificating about his father's prowess with a rod and line, and Gloria gave a deep sigh of defeat before she topped up her glass and proceeded to down it in two gulps.

Once the meal was over and the table cleared at Beach View, Cissy and Pippa helped Peggy to wash and dry the dishes while Ruby put them away and Cordelia gathered up the leftovers and stored them under tea towels in the fridge. Jim swept the kitchen floor, and then saw to the dining-room fire which was smoking rather than blazing. Once this was done, Bob and Charlie entertained Daisy as Jack and Bertie settled down to a game of cribbage and Cissy helped Pippa bring in the cups, saucers and fresh glasses for the afternoon drinks.

Ron and Rosie arrived without the dogs, which was a huge relief to Peggy, and as drinks were poured and presents handed over, Cissy kept herself busy by collecting the table napkins and hunting out the side plates and cake stand for when the cake was cut – although it was doubtful much of it would be eaten as they were all so full.

There had been numerous telephone calls all morning from Peggy's evacuee chicks who still lived in England as well as one from Doreen, and another from Vi. There had been respite over the hour and a half it had taken to eat lunch, but as the time approached for the King's speech, it began to ring again.

'I'll get it,' called Cissy from the kitchen. She lifted the receiver. 'Hello? Happy Christmas.'

'Happy Christmas to you too,' said Anne, although she didn't sound very happy. 'Can I speak to Mum, Cissy?'

'Oh lawks, what's happened?'

'Emily has come out in spots, and Rose Margaret has been grizzling all day, so I suspect she's about to go down with measles too. There's no chance of any of us coming over tomorrow, so I need to talk to Mum and explain.'

'Oh, Anne, that's such a shame. Mum will be so disappointed.'

'What will I be disappointed about?' asked Peggy, coming out of the kitchen armed with a large cake tin and a stack of clean napkins.

'It's Anne,' said Cissy. 'Her girls aren't well.'

'Take these into the dining room,' said Peggy, dumping the tin and napkin against Cissy's chest before snatching up the receiver.

Cissy only just managed to hold on to everything, and didn't linger to overhear the conversation, but she did feel sorry for her older sister and for her mother, who'd planned this Christmas down to the last knife and fork.

She carried the tin and napkins into the dining room, thinking how Anne must have been so looking forward to a day without having to cook or take sole responsibility for her three children. How she managed at all with Martin constantly flying off into Europe to leave her with such a brood, Cissy couldn't begin to imagine.

Peggy returned to the dining room just in time to hear the announcer introduce the King. Everyone fell silent as the King began to speak, but Cissy could tell by her mother's expression that she wasn't really listening to what the King had to say because she was so disappointed that her plans for Boxing Day had been spoilt.

When the King finished talking and the national anthem was played, everyone got to their feet and stood in solemn respect until the very last note.

'To be sure, he's a grand wee man,' enthused Ron. 'But that's enough solemnity for one day, let's have some music.' He crossed the floor to the gramophone and placed the stylus carefully on the record. As Paul Robeson began to sing 'Begin the Beguine', he took Rosie into his arms for a dance.

They were soon followed by Bertie and Cordelia, and Pippa and Bob. Peggy held Jim back to impart the news about Anne, and Charlie rather bashfully asked Ruby to dance with him.

Cissy watched them swirl and sway in the crowded room, remembering all the times over the years that she'd witnessed such a scene. This truly was home – the place she was meant to be – for the bright lights of London couldn't hold a candle to the glow of love in this room.

The record was changed to something livelier, and Cissy was startled by her grandfather suddenly grabbing her hand. 'Well, now, wee girl. We can't have you the wallflower on such an afternoon. Will you dance with your old grandpa?'

She wanted to refuse, but Ron drew her to her feet and held her close in a fast foxtrot. 'To be sure, I remember when you were just a wee thing, and you'd stand on me feet so I could guide you in the dance,' he said cheerfully. 'Those were happy days,' he continued, looking at her evenly. 'But I'm thinking my wee girl is not so happy now, and needs a different sort of guidance.'

'You're talking rubbish, Grandad,' she protested, trying to pull away from him, but finding herself trapped by his strong arm as he continued to glide her across the floor.

He spoke quietly so he wouldn't be heard above the loud music. 'I was in the back yard of the Crown last night,' he said, almost conversationally.

She tensed in his arms. 'Really? And why should that interest me?'

'Oh, 'twas a terrible thing I overheard, wee girl, and it hurt this old man's heart.' He didn't miss a step as he swept her stumbling across the dining-room floor.

'You shouldn't listen to other people's conversations,' she stammered.

His expression was suddenly serious, his blue eyes boring into her. 'Is there something you need to tell me, Cissy?'

Cissy shook her head. 'Of course there isn't. Honestly, Grandpa, you must have had too much to drink last night.'

The record was coming to an end and Cissy was desperate to escape those all-knowing eyes, but as they stopped dancing, he kept hold of her hand. 'I know your secret, Cissy,' he murmured beneath the surrounding chatter.

Cissy was transfixed by his penetrating gaze. 'I don't . . . You can't . . . You're mistaken,' she stammered.

'We both know I'm not,' he replied as the record was changed. 'You know where I am when you're ready to talk – but don't leave it too long, wee girl, or 'twill not be just my heart you'll be breaking.'

Cissy sank into the nearest chair as he walked across the room to dance with Ruby. Her mind was in turmoil, her stomach in a whirl, and then she saw that her mother was watching her with concern.

Did she know too? Cissy wondered. It felt as if the room was closing in on her suddenly – the music too loud, the crush too much, the pounding of her heart threatening to smother her. She got to her feet and managed to get into the hall with some dignity, and then ran through the kitchen down to the basement and locked herself in the bathroom.

Plumping down on the side of the bath, she tried to breathe and get her panic under control. This was no time for tears or hysterics – she needed to stay calm and cool and think straight – if only her head would stop spinning.

As her pulse rate slowly eased and the cold light of reality pierced the panic, she could see things more clearly – and remember exactly what she and Sandra had said. Grandpa knew only that she had a secret – but there was no way he could have guessed what it was from that conversation. If her mother knew or even suspected what was wrong, she would have already said something. As it was, she just seemed to be concerned about her lost weight and lack of energy. She had to trust that Grandpa Ron would keep his suspicions to himself until she found the right time to reveal what was really going on.

The light tap on the door put her on guard immediately. 'I'll be out in a minute,' she called.

'Are you all right, Cissy?' Peggy asked.

Cissy flushed the toilet even though she hadn't used it and checked her appearance in the mirror above the basin, then plastered on a smile and opened the door. 'I'm fine, Mum, really,' she said, giving her a quick hug. 'All that dancing after such a heavy meal was a bit much and I thought I was going to be sick. Luckily it was a false alarm.'

Peggy reached up to tuck a few strands of fair hair behind Cissy's ears. 'You do look rather pale, darling. Are you sure that's all it was?'

'Absolutely,' she replied, taking her mother's arm and firmly steering her towards the stone steps. 'Let's get back to the party.'

20

Once the pudding had been brought to the table wreathed in blue flames of ignited brandy, Gloria served it with lashings of her home-made brandy butter. A very good dessert wine was poured into glasses, more toasts were made, crackers pulled and paper hats donned before everyone moved to the easy chairs in front of the fire and sat back in an over-fed stupor to listen to the King's speech.

As the last notes of the National Anthem faded away, it was time to clear the table and tackle the mountain of washing-up. Gloria was ordered to put her feet up and enjoy her champagne as the others rolled up their sleeves and got on with the task.

Albert seemed to relish delving his large hands into the hot soapy water to wash the plates, pots and pans, and Graham helped Sandra to dry them as Beryl put everything away. Albert then carved the remains of the turkey and ham, and covered the meat plate with a cloth before putting it into the walk-in larder. The cold vegetables would make a lovely bubble and squeak for the next day, and it was clear that Albert expected to be there to enjoy it.

After everything had been cleared and tidied away, they returned to the dining room to find Gloria swaying to the music from her gramophone record, fag in one hand, champagne glass in the other. Albert poured himself a beer, took several gulps, and joined her in a passable waltz as Graham went to hunt through the pile of records for something rather more up to date.

Sandra's girdle was now making her feel very uncomfortable, so she hurried upstairs to rip it off with a great sigh of relief. She was over-full and beginning to feel the effects of all the alcohol she'd consumed, and as the day wasn't yet half over, she decided she'd have to watch what she was doing. Graham always got romantic and soppy when he'd been drinking, and in the past, she would have welcomed the attention, but the idea of it now made her shudder.

She repaired her make-up and was about to go back down to the dining room when she encountered her mother who was clinging to the bannister and swaying rather dangerously at the top of the stairs. 'You all right, Mum?' she asked, taking her arm to steady her.

'Feeling the drink a bit,' she slurred, eyeing her blearily from beneath her paper hat. 'Not used to fancy champagne and all that rich food. But it were lovely, weren't it? Gloria pulled a blinder today and no mistake.'

'She certainly did. Do you want a hand going down the stairs?'

Beryl shook her head. 'Nah. I just got up 'ere, didn't I? Me corsets are killing me, love, and if I don't get them off soon I'll burst.'

Sandra grinned for she knew her mother wore heavily boned, old-fashioned corsets that must be pure torture. 'I had the same problem, and it's utter bliss to get the damned thing off. You go and sort yourself out and I'll wait for you here. I don't want you taking a tumble down the stairs.'

'You're a good girl, Sandra,' muttered Beryl before tottering off to her bedroom.

As Sandra waited for her mother she heard Gloria welcoming more visitors, and wondered who they could be. They had to be trusted friends if her romance with Albert was such a big secret. She'd rather taken to Albert – even if he had been encouraged by Graham to go on a bit about his job and his enforced retirement – for she could see that he was the stabilising and calm influence her aunt needed in the rough and tumble of what must be a lonely, challenging life.

Graham's constant returning to the subject of Albert's search for the baby's mother had threatened to take the shine off the day until Gloria, thank goodness, had told him to shut up. From then on, she'd enjoyed the meal, and the company, and could only hope the newcomers would keep the mood light.

'Are you all right, Sandra?'

She blinked and turned to her mother. 'I'm fine. Better without those corsets, isn't it?'

'Damned right it is,' Beryl said, giving her small belly a good rub. 'I don't know why we women have to put up with it. After all, I ain't no spring chicken and who's to care if I've got wobbly bits?'

Sandra giggled. 'Let's get downstairs. Aunt Gloria's got more visitors, and Graham's probably boring them to death.'

'Well, I hope he don't start on again about that girl and her baby,' Beryl said crossly. 'I saw 'ow it upset yer – and I'm sorry I went on about Ivy too – but I needed to say something after Gloria told 'im off – and it were the first thing what popped into me 'ead.'

'It's all right, Mum,' she soothed, taking her arm. 'Steady as you go, and hang on to the bannister.'

Beryl shot her a look that said she was treating her as if she was ancient, but nevertheless gripped the bannister and let Sandra steady her as they slowly made it down to the ground floor.

'Blimey, I thought you'd done a bunk and were sneaking forty winks,' shouted Gloria from the other side of the dining room where she and Graham were pouring drinks. 'Come in and meet me mates,' she continued, hooking her hand into the arm of a slight, silver-haired man with a weathered face. 'This is Chalky White – he's got a smallholding up in the hills, and this is Stan,' she added, tugging the arm of the tall, well-built, ruddy-faced man standing on the other side of her. 'He used to be the stationmaster, so I expect you both remember 'im.'

Sandra remembered him very well and was delighted to see him again, for he'd always been the first friendly face she'd see as she arrived for her summer holidays, and somehow, he'd become an intrinsic part of those happier times.

Gloria jerked her thumb at the trio by the bar. 'That's Alf who owns the butcher shop, talking to Fred and his wife, Lil, who owns the fish shop. Alf's wife's a bit poorly, so he's only popped in for an hour,' she added quietly, leading them back to the bar. 'More champagne?'

'I think I'll just have lemonade for now,' said Sandra.

Gloria looked at her askance. 'Are you sickening for something, gel? Since when are you turning down proper French champagne?'

'I've already had too much of a good thing, Auntie. I just need to take it a bit slower if I'm to last the day,' she replied.

Gloria rolled her eyes and opened the bottle of lemonade, then handed a glass of champagne to Beryl who took a sip, giggled and had to sit down.

Sandra kept chatting to Stan and learnt about how the railway line had been threatened with closure only to be saved at the last minute – which was more than his job had been, for the line was now automated, and he'd been put out to grass. She also heard about his niece, April, who was working at the telephone exchange and raising her child with his help, as the father had denied all knowledge and gone back to America.

Far from being shocked, Sandra's admiration for the girl rose as she learnt that her child was not only illegitimate, but that the GI father had not been white. How brave she must have been to face the judgemental world – to deal with the inbred prejudices and slights she must have encountered in this small town. And how loving of Stan to take her in when her own mother had rejected her. But then real love always found a way to cope, to shield and support in times of trouble, and she could only pray that, like April, she would be courageous enough to face what was to come – and be similarly blessed.

Peggy was slightly tipsy, but pleasantly tired after the long day, happy that it had all gone so well and Jim had enjoyed it – as well as the wristwatch she'd given him. Now the Town Hall clock was striking eleven, Jack had already left, and Rosie and Ruby were heading for the hall to fetch their coats.

Peggy watched in some amusement as they tried to persuade a very bleary-eyed Ron that it was time to go home, and then glanced across at Bertie who was offering to drive them. She'd noticed that he'd taken great care not to drink too much after the terrible hangover he must have suffered from the previous evening – he was probably looking forward to sleeping in his own bed tonight.

Her eyes misted as he took Cordelia's hand and kissed it softly. 'Goodnight, sweetheart,' he sang to her as the record played on the gramophone. 'I'll see you tomorrow.'

Cordelia struggled to her feet despite his protests, and cupped his face in her hands to kiss him lightly on the lips. 'Sleep well, Bertie, and thank you for my beautiful brooch,' she murmured. 'I will treasure it always.'

Peggy fumbled for her handkerchief and had to swiftly dry her eyes at the lovely little scene before getting to her feet and following them all into the hall.

Bertie pulled on his coat and took Peggy's hand. 'Thank you for allowing me to share your family day,' he said. 'It has been a great privilege.'

'Oh, Bertie, you're part of the family – and always will be.'

His eyes were bright with unshed tears as he nodded bashfully and quickly turned away to hurry through the wind and sleet to get his car started.

'Thanks ever so for a really lovely day, Auntie Peg,' said Ruby, giving her a hug. 'And for my beautiful silk scarf.'

'It was a wonderful day, Peggy girl,' Ron said, barging past Ruby to sweep Peggy into his arms and give her a big kiss on the cheek. On releasing her, he hugged and kissed his large grandsons, Cissy and Jim, and patted Pippa's dainty cheek, before giving Cordelia's hand a gentle squeeze. 'I'll see you all tomorrow,' he slurred, turning rather too sharply and tripping over his own feet.

Rosie and Ruby grabbed him before he fell, and each took an arm to steady him down the steps to Bertie's car.

'To be sure, the old fella's three sheets to the wind,' laughed Jim, slinging a heavy arm over Peggy's shoulder. 'He'll know about it in the morning.'

'I bet he won't,' Peggy chuckled. 'That man can drink for England and still not suffer from a hangover. I don't know how he does it.'

'Years of practice,' Bob replied sagely.

They stood to wave them off, sheltered from the awful weather in the doorway, and once the car was out of sight, Jim shut the front door and steered Peggy back towards the dining room. 'Time for a nightcap and then bed,' he announced, reaching for the whisky bottle.

Peggy worried that with all the drink he'd had today, he'd have one of his bad dreams, and spend what was left of the night shivering and cowering from imaginary artillery fire and bomb blasts. 'I think we've all had more than enough,' she said. 'What I could really do with is a nice cup of tea.'

Jim laughed and turned to his sons. 'Do you hear that, boys? A nice cup of tea indeed!' He drew Peggy into his arms and kissed the top of her head. 'If it's tea you want, my darling, then it's tea you'll have after making this such a special day. You sit by the fire while the others clear up the mess, and I'll put the kettle on.'

Gloria's guests had left the Crown after midnight, and Beryl and the others had gone to their rooms after helping to clear up in preparation for the next day, which would be quieter, with only Albert coming for an early lunch before they all set off for the Boxing Day races.

Gloria lay alone in her large, comfortable bed and listened to the usual creaks and groans of the old building as the rain hit the window and the Town Hall clock struck yet another hour. She fully accepted that she'd had far too much to drink but had hoped it would help her to sleep and perhaps stifle the worrying suspicions that had, at first, seemed ridiculous, but which had slowly begun to make more sense as the last three days had gone on.

She pummelled the pillows and restlessly shifted in the bed, knowing that despite being exhausted, this would be a night she wouldn't sleep. In an effort to stop the images of Sandra's odd behaviour marching through her head, she threw back the bedclothes and grabbed the fleecy and far from glamorous dressing gown her sister had given her this morning and pulled it on. Shivering, she wrapped it tightly around herself, dug her feet into slippers and, without bothering to turn on the light, reached for her cigarettes.

Sleet was rattling against the windowpane as the wind howled around the building to whistle down the chimney, stir the curtains, and send an icy draught beneath her door. Gloria lit a cigarette and drew back the curtains to peer out through the runnels of water streaming down her window to the dark and deserted High Street.

Everything was blurred by the rain, but in the blue glow of the police station lamp she could see that the Christmas tree was being battered against its sturdy tethers by the wind; fallen leaves and bits of paper were bowling down the street to get trapped in doorways and gutters, and the pale moon was repeatedly overshadowed by ragged, racing clouds.

Gloria closed the curtains again and sank on to her padded dressing-table stool. The chill of this winter's night was echoed in the icy dread that slowly engulfed her. Her own life had hardly been easy, but in all her fifty-odd years, she'd never had to contend with what she suspected faced Sandra now. But how to deal with it? And where to even start?

Confrontation had always been her way of dealing with things, but she knew it wasn't the answer this time. There were other people involved – people she cared for and didn't want to hurt. And yet the hurt was inevitable, so all she could do was find some way of getting to the truth and then, when it came, cushioning the awful fall-out as best she could.

She gave a deep sigh and stubbed out her cigarette. Sandra was as precious to her as if she was her own. She'd watched her grow and blossom, had shared Beryl's pride when she'd passed all her secretarial exams and been offered that good job in the City, and had even shed a tear at her wedding to Graham. But now their marriage was in trouble. And if her suspicions were right and Sandra was pregnant by her lover – the lover she'd sworn she'd finished with months ago – it would destroy any chance of a happy reconciliation.

Gloria closed her eyes, her thoughts in a jumble. Sandra had been stupid to have the affair, and then get caught in the family way with absolutely no chance of that barrister leaving his wife and family for her. However, she would have realised that Graham might forgive her the affair, but he certainly wouldn't accept another man's child. He'd made his views very clear on adoption and was unlikely to change them now, no matter how much he professed to love her.

And yet, Gloria knew how devastated Sandra had been when the doctor had told Graham he was infertile and that there would be no babies, so it stood to reason that now she had the chance of motherhood, she would do everything in her power to keep her baby. Which would explain why she was being so cold and distant to Graham – sleeping apart – and insisting upon a divorce.

Gloria opened her eyes and stared at her pale reflection in the mirror without really seeing it as her heart ached for the pair of them. With a deep sigh, she left her bedroom and slowly went downstairs to the kitchen. She switched on the electric kettle, hunted out the bottle of brandy and added a good slug of it to the hot, strong tea. She needed to work out a way to tackle Sandra and coax the truth out of her. It was clear that

Beryl and Graham were puzzled and upset by Sandra's odd behaviour, but she doubted they had the slightest inkling of what was really going on.

Gloria slurped the hot alcoholic tea, her thoughts suddenly flitting to Cissy Reilly who'd also come home looking decidedly the worse for wear. Cissy had been Sandra's best friend and confidante since they were kids and getting into scrapes together, and although the war had kept them apart, it was clear to Gloria that the connection still existed between them.

Cissy had always been the little actress, but Sandra was playing a blinder in the role she'd chosen to cover her tracks, the lies and prevarications glibly delivered as if well rehearsed while she'd kept herself isolated from those who loved her. Gloria remembered how the girls had got into a huddle down the alleyway and then disappeared for hours on Christmas Eve. Had Sandra confided in Cissy that night?

Gloria was surprised that neither Beryl nor Graham had sussed out what Sandra was up to. Surely they must have seen the fear in her eyes – noticed the unguarded moments when her anguish was revealed in every delicate line of her face? She gave a sigh, realising they were all guilty of seeing what they wanted to see and believing what they wanted to believe when it involved those closest to them. It was only because she hadn't seen Sandra in six years that she'd noticed the change, and recognised it for what it was.

Gloria's thoughts veered wildly from one scenario to another as she tried to work out the best way of coaxing Sandra into confiding in her like she had when she was younger. And yet she knew that the war and the years they'd spent apart had changed things, and the intimacy they'd once shared was gone. But she had to at least try to rekindle that trust in the hope they could find a way together to solve the problem – although she had no idea of how they'd do that, as things had gone too far. There really were no easy answers.

Peggy lay next to Jim as he snored peacefully, oblivious to the worries that were tormenting his wife. It had been a lovely if tiring and busy day, and throughout it all, Peggy had been aware of Cissy being too bright and chatty one minute, and then falling into silence, her eyes sad in a drawn little face that was etched with some inner turmoil she seemed determined to keep to herself.

Peggy shifted in the bed, longing for sleep, but aware that her mind was too occupied by all she'd witnessed these past two days to let her rest. Cissy was in trouble. What kind of trouble, Peggy wasn't absolutely sure – but she had her suspicions that whatever it was it had to do with something or someone in London. And if it was – as she suspected – the sort of trouble that only girls got into, then she would have to suppress her own feelings and support Cissy with all the love and calm understanding she must sorely need right now.

Jim grunted in his sleep and rolled over, taking most of the bedclothes with him before he started snoring again.

Peggy shivered in the cold and decided she couldn't stay here wide awake and fretting while Jim's snoring drove her to distraction, and she half-froze to death. She eased out of the bed, snatched up her dressing gown and dug her feet into her new fleece-lined slippers. Softly padding across the room, she slipped through the door she'd left ajar and quietly went downstairs.

The kitchen was warm and welcoming after the chill of the bedroom, and she leaned on the hob covers for a moment to garner the heat and listen to the wind and the rain buffeting the house. There was little doubt in her mind that Cissy had come home to stay – which meant that whatever had happened in London had been serious enough for her to give up her dream and scurry back to her family.

Peggy was profoundly thankful that her daughter still thought of Beach View as home and a refuge in times of trouble – and that she knew her parents cherished her, and would support her through whatever storm she was caught up in. But it frustrated her no end that the girl seemed determined to keep her troubles to herself – which only made Peggy's imagination run riot.

She dug into a cupboard and pulled out the bottle of Camp Coffee that Rosie had left behind a week ago. If she wasn't going to get any sleep tonight, she might as well stay sharp so she could think clearly and try to work out what to do to resolve things with the least amount of fuss.

She made the coffee very strong, added only a drop of milk and sugar and sat down at the kitchen table to drink it. Letting her mind wander over the scenes and conversations of the past two days, the realisation grew that Cissy was not the only one who was troubled, and that when she and Sandra had snubbed poor Rachel and sneaked off during the tree ceremony, they'd shared their secrets the way they always had when they'd been small.

Peggy thought about the other instances where Cissy had made sure she was never alone with her, keeping her gaze averted and her answers short and almost flippant when Peggy had tried to gently ask her what was wrong. And then there had been that strange little scene between Cissy and Ron as they'd danced this afternoon. Had he somehow worked out what was going on, and quietly let Cissy know? It would certainly explain her sudden pallor and the dash downstairs to the bathroom.

Peggy shook her head. How on earth could Ron know anything? He would only have had a fleeting glimpse of Cissy on Christmas Eve, and certainly had very little to do with her until he'd dragged her out of her chair to dance. Perhaps Cissy was telling the truth when she'd said she was feeling sick after being danced too enthusiastically round the floor.

Peggy's gaze fell on the stack of old newspapers she'd kept in a basket by the range to wrap up the food scraps, and use as spills to light the fires.

The headline screamed out at her in large black letters:

ABANDONED BABY FOUND IN CHURCH CRIB

Peggy's heart lurched and fingers of icy dread feathered her spine as certain things suddenly slotted into place. 'Not that,' she breathed. 'Please God, don't let it be Cissy.'

21

Sandra had woken to hear the rain against the window, and the distant crashing of the waves on the beach. Still feeling groggy from the amount of alcohol she'd had the day before, she drew the curtains to discover it was still dark outside. A glance at the illuminated hands of the bedside clock told her it was barely six in the morning, but as she knew she wouldn't get back to sleep, she decided to go downstairs and make a cup of tea while the house was quiet.

Shivering in the chill, she wrapped her dressing gown around herself, dug her feet into slippers and quickly used the bathroom before making her way down the two flights of stairs to the kitchen. She pushed open the door and froze at the sight of Gloria sitting at the small corner table by the fire, in a haze of cigarette smoke, with a pot of tea and an almost empty bottle of brandy in front of her.

'Shut the door, love,' Gloria said. 'It's letting all the heat out.'

'You're up early.' Sandra closed the door and suffered a fit of coughing as the smoke hit the back of her throat and stung her eyes. 'Blimey,' she gasped. 'How long have you been puffing away in here?'

Gloria stubbed out her cigarette and got to her feet. 'Most of the night,' she replied, reaching to fill the kettle. 'I couldn't sleep.' She switched the kettle on and dumped the cold remains of the teapot into the sink.

Sandra experienced a jolt of shock as the cruel bright light from the single overhead bulb illuminated Gloria's ravaged face. Her dyed hair was in curlers and hairnet, her face had been wiped clean of make-up, and without all the usual frills, flounces and bright colours, she suddenly looked her age, and positively frumpy in that hideous dressing gown and her battered old slippers.

Sandra struggled to hide her feelings by going to fetch a clean mug from the cupboard. 'I'm sorry to hear you've had trouble sleeping,' she murmured. 'We probably all overdid it yesterday.'

'Yeah, that could be it,' Gloria replied, spooning fresh tea leaves into the pot and hunting out the milk from the larder. 'Sit yerself down in the corner chair, love. It's nearer the fire and less draughty there.'

She poured the boiling water into the pot, covered it with a knitted cosy and dumped it on the table. 'Let it mash for a bit,' she said, pulling out the other chair to sit down. 'It ain't often you can get a decent cup of tea, so we might as well enjoy it when we can.'

Sandra wished she could open a window, or at least let some air in from the hallway, but Gloria seemed to be oblivious to her discomfort and lit yet another cigarette.

'I'm sorry, Auntie, but I really must open a window.' She stood by the sink as the smoke cleared and breathed in the clean, fresh air that poured in with the rain.

'Yer letting the weather in,' grumbled Gloria, pulling up the collar of her dressing gown.

'It's either that or be gassed,' retorted Sandra. 'I don't know how you can breathe.' She waited a few moments and then reluctantly closed the window and sat down.

Gloria eyed her thoughtfully from beneath the drooping hairnet and curlers. 'Feeling a bit delicate, are you?' she asked.

'It would be surprising if I didn't after all that rich food and wine we had yesterday,' she replied lightly.

'I didn't mean just this morning, Sandra.'

Sandra met her steady gaze even though her pulse was racing, and she had a nasty feeling she knew where this conversation was heading. 'Why on earth should I feel delicate in the mornings?'

Gloria reached across the table and gently laid her hand on Sandra's arm. 'You know very well why, Sandra. I got eyes in me 'ead, love, and enough experience in this world to know what's really ailing you.'

'I don't know what you're on about,' she retorted, moving her arm from Gloria's reach to lift the teapot and fill the mugs.

Gloria gave a sigh. 'You know, when you was little, you always came to me with yer troubles, and whether it was a scraped knee or a falling-out with Cissy or Gracie, we found a way to put things to rights.'

Sandra would have made her escape if she hadn't been trapped in a corner by Gloria having moved her chair in front of the door. 'I'm not a kid any more, Aunt Gloria, and skinned knees are a thing of the past,' she managed.

Gloria blew on her tea and took a sip. 'They certainly are, but of course as we get older, the problems get bigger, and rather more serious.' She eyed Sandra over the rim of the mug. 'Don't they?'

Sandra folded her arms. 'What exactly are you trying to say, Aunt Gloria?

Gloria put the mug on the table and held her gaze. 'You know very well, and we can sit here all day going back and forth, but in the end you're going to have to admit to what's going on. Once you've done that, we can work together to try and sort it.'

Sandra was trembling as she shook her head. 'There's nothing going on apart from me asking Graham for a divorce,' she replied stubbornly.

Gloria impatiently waved her hand. 'That's only the half of it,' she said dismissively. 'So, you had an affair with yer fancy barrister. He's dumped you to go back to his wife and kids – and you're left carrying the can.' Her expression softened, and her tone was gentle. 'Or should I say carrying the baby?'

Sandra could only stare at her.

Peggy stared at that headline for what felt like hours, her thoughts going back and forth over all the clues that Cissy had unwittingly revealed. She'd eventually gathered up all the old papers and gone through them in search of the story of the abandoned baby.

Almost an hour later, she leaned back in the chair, feeling sick at heart. It was all there if you knew where to look and had the name to join up the clues. Cissy was born and bred here; she would have remembered that caravan as it had been a favourite place to go with Sandra during the summers; she'd known Bertie's morning rituals through the letters from home – and the hour when Alan Jenkins would begin his milk round, for it never varied.

Cissy also knew every inch of those hills after all the years Ron had taken her on his poaching expeditions, so would know where to hide the clothes. And despite the flimsy excuses from Clarissa which she'd barely believed at the time, it was clear now that Cissy had disappeared for at least three weeks during the time she would have been giving birth.

Peggy gathered the papers together and put them back in the basket. A dull throb behind her eyes heralded the onset of a headache, so she took a couple of aspirin and poured another cup of tea. Thinking over the past two days, she wondered if Cissy had confided in Sandra when they'd gone missing during the tree ceremony. If she had, then at least she wasn't carrying the burden alone. But it would have been a shocking confession – so shocking that Sandra might have felt unable to keep it to herself – and the thought of Gloria knowing more about her daughter than she did, made her feel heartsick.

Peggy gave an exasperated sigh. It was just so frustrating not to be able to get Cissy alone long enough to get a straight answer out of her.

Cissy heard someone going downstairs and by the light footfall, guessed it was her mother. It was barely six in the morning, and she suspected her father's dreadful snoring had driven Peggy from her bed.

She lay snug beneath the bedclothes listening to the rain and dreading another day of deception and avoidance. With Aunt Doris and Danuta due to turn up this afternoon, it would just about put the tin lid on what was already a tense situation, and she heartily wished she could just escape the house with Sandra, who must also be going through similar torment.

The thought of her childhood friend and the secret she'd shared with her on Christmas Eve hardly eased her own conscience – in fact, it made the whole situation far more stressful. Gloria and Peggy were strong characters, with sharp eyes and a nose for trouble. It wouldn't be long before they put two and two together, and then the whole thing would explode out of control.

Hearing one of her brothers clumping down from the attic bedroom an hour later, she lifted her head from the pillow and waited until she was sure he'd reached the kitchen, before throwing back the bedclothes and quickly dragging on her dressing gown. Now Peggy had company, it would be safe to go down for a cup of tea. Her mouth was parched, and although she'd had very little alcohol the previous day, she had the beginnings of a thudding headache.

After a quick visit to the bathroom, she went downstairs and bumped into Pippa who was just emerging from the small bedroom off the hall. 'It looks like we've all been woken by the wind and the rain,' she said lightly.

Pippa dragged her hair from her face and gave her a sleepy smile. 'And I was having such a lovely dream too. Now I need the bathroom.'

As Pippa climbed the stairs, Cissy hesitated by the kitchen door. She couldn't hear the murmur of voices, which was strange.

'I know you're there, Cissy,' called Peggy. 'I heard you talking to Pippa.'

Cissy squared her shoulders and lifted her chin. Stepping into the kitchen, she saw her mother sitting alone at the table. 'I thought I heard one of the boys coming down,' she said, reaching into a top cupboard for the packet of aspirins.

'Bob woke early and decided to have a bath before the morning rush,' replied Peggy, eyeing her intently before turning her attention to the teapot in front of her. 'I made fresh tea.'

'Oh, good,' she said lightly. 'I'm very dry this morning, and my head's not too clever either,' she added before swallowing the pills with some water.

Cissy sat opposite her and watched as she poured the tea. There were shadows beneath her poor mother's eyes, her face was drawn, and there were lines of worry she'd never noticed before. She hoped wholeheartedly that she hadn't been the cause of those lines. 'You look as if you didn't get much sleep,' she said sympathetically. 'Dad's snoring isn't getting any better, is it?'

331

Peggy put down the teapot and pushed the mug of tea across the table. 'Your father's snoring played its part,' she said quietly. 'But I have a lot of things on my mind.' She lifted her chin, her gaze softening as she looked at Cissy.

Cissy deliberately avoided the questions in her mother's eyes. 'Well, you can relax now, Mum,' she replied airily. 'Cold cuts and bubble and squeak for lunch is far easier than the feast you laid on yesterday. I know afternoon tea for Aunt Doris might be a bit trying, but you'll enjoy catching up with Suzy again, and Danuta and Stan will liven things up.'

'Mmm.' Peggy's gaze didn't waver as she reached across the table for Cissy's hand. 'Doris coming to tea is the least of my problems, Cissy. It's you that's concerning me.'

Cissy's heart pounded and she found her mouth was drier than ever. Easing her hand from her mother's, she picked up the mug and almost burnt her lips on the boiling-hot tea. 'I don't know why on earth you should be worrying about me,' she said raggedly. 'After all, I've come home as promised, haven't I?'

'To stay?'

Cissy hesitated before nodding, and then tried the tea again, but it was still too hot, so she added a drop more milk. 'London has become rather tiresome,' she said briskly, reaching for her mother's packet of cigarettes. 'I've cashed in my share of the business, and once the holiday is over I'll be looking for something else to invest it in.'

She languidly leaned back in the chair, lit the cigarette she didn't really want, and blew smoke as if she didn't have a care in the world.

Peggy regarded her for a long, silent moment and then nodded. 'I guessed as much by the amount of luggage you brought with you. But what I want to know – what I really *need* to know – is where you've been for the past three weeks.'

Cissy's heart missed a beat, and she could feel the colour drain from her face as she squirmed in the chair. 'London, of course. In bed with the flu,' she managed. 'I told you that over the phone, and if you don't believe me, just call Clarissa. She'll confirm it.'

'I'm sure she would,' murmured Peggy. 'Just as she's been covering for you all along. I'm not stupid, darling. I know when I'm being given the run-around.'

'What is it you're suggesting, Mother?' she asked defiantly.

'Nothing, my love,' she replied, reaching once more for Cissy's hand. 'I just want you to tell me what has really brought you home. And don't deny there is something, sweetheart. I've always known when you're keeping things from me.'

The touch of her mother's hand was too much. She snatched away from the contact and made a play of shifting the ashtray closer and tapping her cigarette against it. There was clearly no escape from this conversation, but if she was very careful, there was a way to avoid the darker truths – for now.

'All right,' she replied, mashing the half-smoked cigarette into the ashtray, and then folding her arms. 'Through absolutely no fault of my own – and most unfairly, I might add – I was given my marching orders by Clarissa and her snooty cronies. They at least honoured the contract we'd all signed by giving me back my investment with the interest earned and my share of the month's income.'

She shot her mother a stiff little smile. 'So I'm pretty well set up to start something closer to home. I've absolutely had it with London.'

Peggy's expression was puzzled. 'But I thought you loved London life, and you'd been getting on famously with those other girls?'

'Well, I was. Of course I was,' she replied dismissively. 'But I'd always suspected it would be temporary, and I'm actually quite relieved to be out of it. I never really fitted into their clique, anyway – and that sort of hedonistic life does begin to pall after a while.'

'Oh, I am sorry, darling,' Peggy sighed. 'I wish you'd confided in me earlier. I could have looked around here for something you could invest in.'

Cissy inwardly sighed with relief that she'd got away with it, and took a sip of the cooling tea.

'So, what are you going to do about the baby?'

Cissy froze. The words were stuck in her throat, but she managed to force them out. 'What baby?'

Peggy's steady gaze held her trapped. 'You know what baby, Cissy,' she said softly. 'I so wish you'd trusted me and your father enough to confide in us, because we will move heaven and earth to help and support you.'

Cissy stared at her, unable to move or speak as her mother's words sank in. Then, shoving her chair back from the table, she stumbled to her feet and ran out of the room, blinded by her tears.

Upon reaching the landing she was dimly aware of Pippa emerging from the bathroom to stare at her in shock. She slammed her bedroom door and locked it before throwing herself on to the bed to bury her face in the pillows and give vent to the avalanche of emotions she'd been holding back for weeks.

Sandra got to her feet, aghast at what her aunt had just said. 'I don't know what you're on about,' she snapped. 'But I'd be very careful about what you say in front of the others. Things are bad enough between me and

Graham without your over-ripe imagination making them worse.'

Gloria barred her escape by gripping her arms. 'If you've got a bun in the oven it's going to become obvious to everyone sooner or later, Sandra,' she said quietly. 'So why not admit it now? That way, you can at least share your troubles, and perhaps even find a way for me to help you.'

Sandra wanted to talk to her – to share the truth she'd been carrying for so long – but she couldn't risk it until she had everything in place. She eased from her aunt's grip and kissed her cheek. 'I know you mean well, Auntie Gloria, but you've got it wrong,' she said. 'You'd do better to go back to bed and get some sleep, rather than sitting here smoking and letting your imagination run wild.'

As Gloria looked at her in confusion, Sandra slipped round and ran up the stairs to find Graham standing on the landing.

'There you are,' he said. 'I need to talk to you.'

'Not now!' She barged past him and locked herself into her bedroom.

Gloria stared at the empty chair and the abandoned mug of tea, her thoughts in a whirl as doubts and certainties collided. And then a new possibility hit her with all the force of a hurricane. 'Gawd 'elp us,' she breathed. 'Surely not, Sandra.'

But now the idea was there it wouldn't shift. She looked up at the kitchen clock. It was still early, but she had a feeling that the person she needed to talk to would be awake.

She lit another fag, threw the empty packet in the waste-bin under the sink and picked up the telephone.

*

Peggy was startled by the sound of ringing in the hall. It was a bit early for someone to call and she could only hope it didn't mean there was another crisis looming. Aware that Pippa could overhear everything she said, she listened intently to Gloria, without replying in too much detail.

'I'm really sorry to hear that, Gloria,' she said carefully. 'And yes, I've had a very similar conversation this morning, which ended the same way,' she continued quietly. 'Frankly, I've come to the same awful conclusion and now I'm at my wits' end. Do you have any idea of what we can do about this wall of silence they've put up?'

Peggy listened to Gloria's unusually calm voice as she suggested the one thing that might get both girls to talk and clear the air. 'It's a can of worms, Gloria,' she replied. 'And it certainly won't be pleasant for anyone. I wish there was another way to do this, but I agree, it does seem to be the only solution.'

Gloria outlined her plan in more detail, and Peggy realised she'd given it a great deal of careful thought. Poor Gloria must have been up half the night worrying – but then so had she. What a disaster this Christmas was turning out to be.

Assuring Gloria that she'd do her very best to carry out her side of the plan, she said goodbye and replaced the receiver. Her heart was heavy with the knowledge that by the end of the day, if Cissy and Sandra still refused to talk, she'd have to reveal her suspicions to Jim, and prepare him and the rest of the family for what could no longer be avoided.

'Are you all right, Mum?' asked Bob, on his way back upstairs after his bath.

Startled from her thoughts, she looked up at him and nodded. 'I'm just sorting things out in my mind for later.'

'I thought Grandad, Rosie and Aunt Doris and her family were coming over with Danuta and Stan this afternoon?'

'Oh, they are,' she said hastily. 'I was thinking more about the crowd due to come tomorrow.'

'Would you mind if me and Pippa went out both afternoons if you've got so many visitors? I don't particularly get on with Aunt Doris, and I think Pippa's feeling a little overwhelmed with so many people coming and going. I thought I'd take her for a drive round to see my old haunts.'

'I'm sorry if we're all a bit much for her, Bob. But yes, it's a good idea, and I'm sure she'd like to see a bit more of the place while she's here.'

Bob grinned and ran up the stairs just as Charlie came thudding down. 'Who was that on the phone?' he asked.

'Nobody you need to know about,' she replied rather sharply. 'Go and get your breakfast. I've got another telephone call to make.'

'About this afternoon,' he said hesitantly. 'Would it be all right if I skipped tea and went to see my mate Paul? Only he's been given a load of records to play on his posh new gramophone, and I'd like to hear them as they're the very latest ones.'

She smiled up at him. 'Of course it's all right. You don't want to be stuck here with all the old fuddy-duddies. I'll do an early lunch so you can get off by one. Just don't come home too late, please.'

'Thanks, Mum.' He turned back to her in the kitchen doorway. 'I'll feed the chickens for you this morning,' he said before disappearing.

Peggy had forgotten all about the poor hens amid the turmoil. 'Bless him,' she breathed. 'Thank goodness someone's got their head screwed on this morning.'

Pippa came out of the hall floor bedroom looking very smart in warm slacks and a red and white sweater, her fair hair tied back with a scarlet ribbon. 'I'll get the breakfast going while you make your call,' she said. 'It sounds as if everyone's up and about now.'

'Thank you, dear; that would be very helpful.'

Peggy cocked her head as Jim and Bob exchanged greetings on the landing before Jim locked himself in the bathroom and Bob went back up to the attic. With all the noise going on, she could expect to see Daisy and Cordelia up and about very soon, so she'd have to hurry.

She picked up the receiver and dialled the number she knew by heart. Her pulse was racing as it began to ring at the other end, and she almost wished it wouldn't be answered. But then there was the click of the receiver being lifted, and a cheery greeting from the familiar voice.

22

After talking to Peggy, Gloria had sat staring into the kitchen fire trying to work out how she could manipulate everyone into doing what she wanted the following day. She knew it wouldn't be easy and could only hope that an idea came to her as time went on.

The lack of sleep and too much tea and brandy had begun to take their toll, and she came to the conclusion that it had been a good plan to go to the races today instead of staying indoors. She went upstairs to bath and get dressed, and then went down to ring Albert.

'Hello, love. I hope you remembered we're going to the races today, so put on yer best bib and tucker – and bring yer wallet.'

'Of course I haven't forgotten,' he boomed. 'I was about to check the timetable for the special train they run today.'

'You do that, Albert, and I'll make up a hamper for when we get peckish.'

'But I thought we were having bubble and squeak with pickles and ham.'

'You are, but an afternoon at the races always makes me hungry and thirsty. See you later.' She put down the receiver before he could find something else to moan about.

'Did I hear you say something about the races?' asked Graham, appearing in the hall neatly dressed in slacks, shirt and V-necked sweater.

'You did,' she replied. 'We need to get out of this place for a bit, and a flutter on the gee-gees should cheer us all up.'

'Oh, goody,' said Beryl from the first-floor landing. 'I haven't been to the races in years, and I always enjoy a bit of a flutter.' She hurried down. 'We'll take a picnic, shall we? And luckily I've remembered to bring my best hat.'

Gloria grinned. 'Of course. It'll be quite like old times, Beryl. Remember when Mum and Dad used to take us?'

'Happy days,' she sighed.

'I doubt Sandra will want to come,' said Graham, looking annoyed. 'She's locked herself in her room again and refuses to speak to me or her mother.'

'You two go and make a start on breakfast, I'll sort Sandra out.'

Gloria waited until they were both in the kitchen before climbing up to the top floor. She tapped on the door.

'Go away, Graham!' shouted Sandra.

'It's me, love. I just want to say sorry for earlier, and remind you about the little treat I've planned for today.'

The door opened and Sandra stood there, her face tear-streaked, her arms tightly folded as if to protect herself from another verbal assault.

Gloria gently drew her into her arms. 'I'm sorry I made you cry, love. I really didn't mean to upset you.'

Sandra remained stiff in her embrace, and then pulled away to mop at her face with a handkerchief. 'I'm sorry, too, for storming off when I know you were only trying to help – and sorry for me and Graham being at odds and spoiling your Christmas. I expect you'll be glad to see the back of us tomorrow.'

'I've never been glad to see you go, Sandra, you know that, and I promise I'll say no more about the thing we discussed earlier. Not until you're ready.' She took a breath. 'Now, I want you to dolly up in yer best. We're off to the races after lunch.'

Sandra looked underwhelmed. 'Oh, I was planning to pop round to Beach View and see Cissy this afternoon. I forgot I had all those cards and things Ivy gave me to deliver.'

'I know for a fact that Peggy's got a houseful again today, and as your train doesn't go until five tomorrow, it would be best to leave it until morning.' Gloria stroked Sandra's arm and gave her an encouraging smile. 'Let's just enjoy the day and forget everything else for a while. It's time we set aside all the worrying and had a bit of fun. Now, I'd better get on and sort out a picnic hamper. Do you want to help me make some sandwiches?'

'All right,' she agreed reluctantly and followed Gloria downstairs.

Gloria smiled to herself as she headed for the large store cupboard under the stairs in search of the picnic hamper. Sandra's forgetfulness over Ivy's cards had played right into her hands, providing the perfect excuse for them all to be at Beach View as planned tomorrow morning.

Peggy knew she'd find it difficult to get through the day, but came to the conclusion that the only way was to keep busy. She got Daisy washed and dressed while Pippa and Charlie dealt with preparing breakfast. Once everyone apart from Cissy was downstairs and chattering away like sparrows, she drank down her tea, and then went up to try and coax Cissy into talking.

She tapped on the bedroom door. 'It's just me, darling,' she said quietly. 'I'm sorry I upset you, really I am, but we do need to talk, love. Will you let me in?'

'Go away, Mum,' she replied from the other side of the door. 'I don't want to talk.'

'Then at least come down for breakfast, Cissy.'

'I'm not hungry.'

Knowing Cissy as well as she did, Peggy sadly realised she'd get no further with her in such a mood. But she'd try again later.

The bathroom radiator wasn't particularly hot, and with so many people in the house the water wasn't that warm either. She had a quick strip wash, and as there were really only two rooms in the house that were heated, she decided to wear a pair of tailored tweed slacks and her favourite pale lilac knitted twinset, which she pulled on over a vest. Carefully putting on her make-up, she brushed her hair, clipped on earrings and regarded her reflection in the dressing-table mirror. She looked tired, but that was hardly surprising, and there seemed to be a few more threads of silver in her hair, which glinted most annoyingly in the sun that streamed through the window. She sighed, then turned her back on the unedifying sight and went back downstairs.

The dining room was looking a bit careworn in the bright sunlight, with the cold ashes in the grate and the needles from the tree spilled amongst the presents that had yet to be handed out. The tablecloth from yesterday had been removed to reveal the scratches and scorches from years of heavy use, and a fine layer of dust had settled on the mantelpiece as well as the mirror above it.

She went into the kitchen to find everyone still there, chatting over their cups of tea, as Daisy tried to feed fingers of jammy toast to her rag doll, Amelia. She'd have to put that doll in the washing machine soon, and hope it dried before bedtime as Daisy refused to settle without it.

'Where's Cissy?' asked Jim.

'She's gone back to bed,' Peggy replied as she headed for the sink to fetch her cleaning rags.

'Peggy, will you sit down and be still for five minutes?' Jim pleaded, grabbing her hand as she passed him. 'What on earth are you up to now?'

'I need to clear out yesterday's ashes, give the dining room a good dusting, and sweep up the pine needles under the tree,' she replied. 'You know what Doris is like, and I really don't want her turning up her nose if the place isn't spotless.'

'If she can't accept the house the way it is, then she can stay at home,' retorted Jim. 'I will not have her bullying you, Peg.'

Peggy shrugged. 'I doubt she'll say much in front of John, but then she doesn't have to. I can read every snipe in her expression.' She decided the cleaning could wait and sat down to light a fag. 'At least I've got Mum's best china out, so she can't complain about having to drink tea from a mug.'

'I'll clean out the fire and Charlie can sweep up the pine needles,' said Bob, giving his younger brother a hard stare to ensure he got the message.

'I'll bring in some more wood for the fire,' said Jim, 'and fill the kitchen coal scuttle.'

Peggy smiled. 'When you've done that, Jim, can you slice up the ham and the turkey for our lunch while I sort out the bubble and squeak? There are lots of different pickles in the cupboard to go with it, so once you've all finished breakfast, you can wash up and set the table again for early lunch.'

She turned to Bob. 'Have you decided where you're going to take Pippa on your drive?'

'Along the seafront, and then past my old school before going up into the hills for a visit to Uncle Frank in Tamarisk Bay. Then I thought we'd go on the coast road through Seahaven to the county town for a wander around the cobbled streets and up to the castle ruins. We might find a hotel or something that will give us supper, so don't expect us back too early.'

Peggy smiled at Pippa. 'The old part of the town is full of history, and although the castle is in ruins, it's quite a sight as it's perched on a hill.'

'Are you sure you don't mind us deserting you this afternoon?' the girl asked with a frown.

Peggy laughed. 'I wish I could come with you, to be honest. My sister isn't the easiest person to entertain.' She patted her hand. 'You and Bob must get out and about while you're here, and please don't think I'd mind. I know how daunting it can be with so many people in and out all day, but things should quieten down after tomorrow.'

'Where's Cissy?' asked Cordelia abruptly.

'Having a lie-in,' replied Peggy loudly as she clearly hadn't heard earlier. 'She'll come down when she's ready, Cordelia.'

Cordelia tutted. 'I do hope she isn't sickening for something,' she fretted. 'She didn't look at all well yesterday. In fact, she's been behaving strangely ever since she arrived home.'

'She hasn't had a happy time in London, by all accounts,' said Peggy. 'Actually, she's planning to stay here while she looks around locally for some other business to invest in. I think the change has come as a bit of a shock, but she'll soon settle back in if I know my Cissy.'

'You didn't tell me all this,' grumbled Jim.

'I didn't know myself until early this morning when you were still snoring.'

'Oh, it'll be lovely to have Cissy home where she belongs,' sighed Cordelia. 'It's all very well, these young things dashing off to the bright lights of the city, but they soon realise there's no place like home.' She reached across and squeezed Peggy's fingers. 'I'm so pleased for you, dear. I know how much you've missed her.'

Peggy managed to smile, but her heart was heavy in the knowledge that her daughter's homecoming was far from happy, and might bring heartbreak to their door.

Sandra was glad she'd agreed to go to the races with the others. The escape from the Crown was what she needed after that exchange with Gloria, and it felt good to be doing something new that didn't require a lot of thought.

The racecourse was set in a valley outside the county town, with the ancient ruined castle guarding the hills that rose at the western end, and the railway station set at the eastern end beside a meandering river. The train journey to the racecourse had proved to be jolly as everyone seemed to be glad to escape hearth, home and family for a day out. On arrival at the station, she'd stepped out on to the platform into a crisp, bright day which made all the colours more vibrant, and as the many passengers alighted and began the walk to the course, she felt her spirits rise.

Sandra had avoided Graham as much as possible and stayed firmly with Gloria, Beryl and Albert as they'd spent the afternoon watching the beautiful horses walking round the parade ring before they thundered between the white railings towards the finishing post, the coloured silks of the jockeys flashing as they shot past, the commentator's voice echoing from the loudspeakers placed around the track, only to be drowned by the shouts of encouragement from the punters as their horses approached the final furlong.

She was fascinated by the bookies – or tick-tack-men, as Gloria called them – shouting the odds and waving their arms about in some sort of code before chalking up their boards as they took the bets. As she'd never been to the races before, she had to rely on Gloria telling her how to place a bet, and was absolutely thrilled when her horse won and the bookie handed her ten pounds.

It had been a long time since she'd been able to relax and think of nothing but the present, looking round at the crowds milling between the stands and the course. The women were dressed to the nines in their best clothes and fancy hats, but the men had made an effort too – some in formal suits with top hats and decorative waistcoats, others in tweeds and bowlers, with shooting sticks to open out and sit upon between the races.

And then all too soon the day was over, the straps on the empty hamper buckled up for the short traipse back to the station and the crowded train. The return journey to Cliffehaven had sped by with lots of tipsy singing and excited chatter, and as they'd slowly walked back to the Crown, they were looking forward to warming up by a blazing fire and eating a supper of cold cuts and more bubble and squeak.

Now it was late evening, and Graham was downstairs with Gloria to say goodnight to Albert and help make sure everything was ready for opening the pub tomorrow lunchtime.

Sandra wearily followed her mother up the three flights of stairs and gave her a hug as they reached the landing. 'It's been a happy day, hasn't it?' she asked.

'Yeah, and you did all right, gel,' she replied with a tipsy, lopsided smile. 'What you gunna spend yer winnings on?'

'I haven't decided yet,' she said. 'But I might treat us both to afternoon tea somewhere posh once we're back in London.'

'That would be lovely,' said Beryl. She cocked her head. 'You look a bit better. That outing done you some good, and put colour in yer face.'

Sandra smiled and kissed her cheek. 'Yeah, I'm feeling fine. Sorry I've not been good company, Mum. I know how much you were looking forward to coming down here, and we've spoilt it for you.'

'I've had a good time anyway, and if you and Graham can find a way to sort things out between you, then I'll be even happier.' She caught Sandra's hand. 'Would it help to talk about it with me, Sandra? You know I'm always ready to listen.'

'I know you are, but this is between me and Graham. We'll work things out somehow,' she promised.

As her mother tottered off towards the bathroom, she went into her bedroom and locked the door. Sinking on to the bed, she relaxed her stiff shoulders and gently eased the crick in her neck. The day out had certainly made her more clear-headed, and her weariness came from fresh air and exercise instead of the awful stress which had been plaguing her for days.

Sandra stared up at the ceiling, now almost impatient to get tomorrow under way. She'd been planning how to carry out what she needed to do for the past three weeks, and now every detail was sharp and clear in her mind. As there was still no word from Florence about Gracie, it was unlikely they'd be able to visit her tomorrow, which was a terrible shame, because she liked Gracie and felt deeply sorry for all she must have gone through. However, after meeting up with Cissy tomorrow and making sure she was prepared for the family fall-out that would inevitably come, she would return to London and set about seeing her plans come to fruition. It wouldn't be easy, and people would get hurt, but she knew there was no other option.

Peggy had enjoyed the afternoon rather more than she'd expected. Doris had been on her best behaviour, never mentioning the dust she'd missed on the windowsill, or the fact that the Christmas cake was not home-made. In fact, she'd even complimented Peggy on the beautiful mink collar Jim had given her for Christmas, which went so well with the camel coat Ron and Rosie had bought her.

Once Danuta and Stanislav arrived, the gathering became quite jolly and Peggy managed to put her worries over Cissy aside for a while. It had been lovely to catch up with Suzy and Anthony, and to play alongside Daisy and little Teddy, and get a cuddle with baby Angela, and of course, Danuta and Suzy had a fair amount of catching up to do too.

Stanislav had been his usual animated self, and had encouraged Ron to tell some of his dubious war stories. This had, in turn, led to a friendly rivalry between the two men as to who could find the most outrageous tale to act out, and these got more preposterous as the level in the bottle of whisky went down.

John seemed happy to sit and drink quietly as he and Jim played cards, but Doris was still clearly not at ease with Suzy although she seemed to make a great effort to pretend she was. Which Peggy found very odd, because she couldn't understand what it was about Suzy that Doris found so hard to like. She could only surmise that her sister's nose had been put out of joint because she was no longer the most important woman in her beloved son's life – which really was very immature and short-sighted.

Cissy had eventually emerged from her bedroom halfway through the visit, and had shown no outward sign that anything was wrong. She'd chatted and laughed with Stan and Suzy, played with the children and generally made herself useful and pleasant company. But Peggy had seen behind the bright chatter, and noted how tense she was, and how much effort it cost her daughter to carry on the act she seemed so determined to play. It was there in her repeated, wary glances at Ron; in the unguarded moments when she looked down at baby Angela as she sat in her lap – and in the haunted eyes that held a profound darkness which Peggy had never seen before.

Now everyone had left, and the day was finally over. Charlie had returned from his friend's house and was upstairs in his room sorting through his own small collection of records to take over there tomorrow. Bob and Pippa had come back flushed and happy after their day out and full of their plans for the next day, and Cordelia had gone to bed to read her library book after what had been a heady but tiring two days. Cissy had returned to her room pleading a headache after tea, so Bob and Pippa went to the Anchor without her.

Peggy had asked Ron and Rosie to stay behind, and once the dining room was tidy again, and the dogs had been taken for a short run, she shut the kitchen door and placed fresh bottles of whisky, gin and wine on the kitchen table with bowls of nuts and crisps, and told everyone to sit down. She was nervous and not at all prepared, but the situation could no longer be ignored.

'There are things I need to tell you,' she began. 'And although they will come as a shock, I need you to stay calm and hear me out.'

'Well, it's clear that whatever it is must be serious,' joked Jim. 'You don't usually offer whisky at this time of night – but to be sure it's a more welcome sight than tea.'

Ron poured the drinks and then sat back in the kitchen chair, his intensely blue eyes holding Peggy's brown ones in silent communication. 'Aye, son, 'tis serious right enough,' he murmured.

'What do you know that I don't?' asked Jim with a frown.

'It's not something that either of us really *knows*,' said Peggy. 'It's what we suspect. And it's to do with our Cissy.'

'She just needs feeding up,' said Jim airily. 'The good air down here will soon put the colour back in her cheeks, Peg. You worry too much.'

Peggy looked at him, wondering how men could be so blind.

'I think Peggy's right to be worried,' said Rosie. 'Cissy isn't herself.'

'No, she isn't,' said Peggy on a sigh. 'She's too thin, too pale and too secretive. I've tried talking to her but she's refused to tell me what it is that's causing her such anxiety – some might even call it fear.'

She looked across at Ron who seemed to understand what she was trying to say. 'Her story about leaving London because she fell out with her friends might be true – in fact, I'm fairly sure it is. But I suspect that's only the half of it, and there's something else which drove her home – something far more serious.'

'I agree,' rumbled Ron. 'I overheard her talking with Sandra the night they both went missing for hours – and although they were careful what they said, it was perfectly obvious to me that both of them are in trouble.'

He looked across at Jim who was still clearly confused. 'I'm sorry, son, but when girls are in trouble and sharing secrets, there can only be one reason for it,' he said with a deep sigh.

Jim looked from his father to Peggy, his dark brows lowering over angry blue eyes. 'Are you telling me that our Cissy's pregnant?' he demanded, curling his fists on the table. 'Because if she is I'll . . .'

'Stop it, Jim,' Peggy said firmly, placing her hands over his fists. 'Wanting to beat the living daylights out of the swine that put her in the family way is not the answer. Neither will it help to go shouting at Cissy. She's scared enough, and you getting all het up will just make things worse,' she finished calmly.

'So what do you expect me to do, Peg? Sit back and do nothing? Let the swine who did that to her get away with it?'

'We don't know the circumstances, Jim,' she replied. 'It takes two to tango, as you very well know, and her life and the friends she had in London are a complete mystery to us, so anything could have gone on. But I fear there is something else far more painful happening here than an unwanted pregnancy, and I need you to keep calm and be supportive through whatever happens tomorrow.'

Jim emptied his glass and refilled it. 'You're talking in riddles, Peg. For God's sake, just tell me straight what you think is going on.'

Peggy took a breath and met his angry gaze. 'I think our daughter is the one who abandoned little Noel.'

The words dropped like grenades into the stunned silence.

'She can't be,' gasped Jim finally. 'She wouldn't do that. Not our Cissy.'

'I'm very much afraid she might have done,' said Peggy. She slowly went through all the clues that she'd put together after reading through the newspaper articles, explaining how each one led all too clearly to their daughter.

Jim shook his head slowly, his expression dazed. 'You're wrong,' he managed. 'Not our Cissy. I'd swear my life on it.'

'Ach, Jim, we all find it hard to believe it of her,' sighed Ron. He took a sip of the whisky and placed the glass carefully on the table as he considered his next words. 'I could tell something was wrong the minute I saw her.'

He lifted his gaze to Peggy. 'But you've been so focused on Cissy that you haven't noticed there might be other candidates for the mother of that baby. All those coincidences and clues as you call them could very well point to Sandra – or even young Gracie.'

Peggy stilled and held Ron's steady gaze as the doubts suddenly crowded in. 'It's not Gracie,' she said firmly. 'Florence and Danuta are keeping things very tight to their chests, but what they have said has led me to suspect she's had an illegal abortion which went wrong, which is why she's now in hospital.

'Dear God,' breathed Rosie. 'She must have been really desperate to risk something like that.'

'Sadly, she's paying the price, Rosie,' she replied on a sigh. 'The serious infection had spread too far and the surgeon had to perform a hysterectomy. Now it's touch and go as to whether she'll even pull through.'

Silence fell as everyone absorbed this.

Peggy couldn't bear the thought of poor little Gracie suffering, but her girl and Sandra were suffering too, and that was something she could deal with. 'Moving on to Sandra,' she said, 'from what Gloria said, she's out of sorts and acting strangely, but Gloria suspects she might be pregnant, and is forcing the divorce through because she knows Graham will refuse to take the baby on. An affair he might forgive, but not another man's child.'

She turned to Ron. 'It can't be her anyway. She's not local, Ron. She never went up into the hills with you like Cissy did, and how on earth would she know Bertie's routine?'

'She went up with me and Cissy a fair few times that last summer she was down here,' Ron said, 'and Gloria could have told her about Bertie. After all, it's hardly a state secret. And don't forget, Peggy, all three of them knew about that caravan.'

'Oh lawks,' moaned Peggy. 'Have I got this all wrong? Am I accusing our girl of something she isn't guilty of? But I was so sure. So very sure.'

Ron's expression was grim. 'Sadly, Peggy, I'm of a mind that Cissy seems to be the more likely candidate of the three – especially now we know Gracie's out of the picture. She's certainly living on her nerves, and from what I overheard the other night, the cause of her anxiety has very little to do with her falling out with those other women.'

'You said something about tomorrow,' Rosie said softly. 'Have you come up with some sort of plan to clear this up once and for all, Peggy?'

Peggy rubbed her face and tried to put her restless thoughts in order, for Ron's reasoning had rather thrown her off course. 'Yes,' she said finally. 'I spoke to Gloria very early this morning. She rang to ask if I was having similar problems with Cissy as the two girls have been acting so strangely and virtually jumping at their own shadows. She's also got the idea in her head that perhaps Sandra is Noel's mother.'

'So,' murmured Rosie. 'It really could be either of them.'

'That's why Gloria and I decided to set up something tomorrow.' Peggy poured a finger of whisky into her glass and downed it in one before she told them all what she and Gloria had planned.

23

The telephone rang, as arranged, during breakfast. Gloria picked up the receiver, heard Peggy at the other end, and replied loudly enough from the landing so the others could hear.

'I know she has some cards and things to deliver from Ivy, so that's good timing,' she said. 'Yes, I'll make sure and tell her, she'll like that.' She cut the call.

'That was Cissy,' she lied smoothly as she returned to the kitchen and sat back down at the table. 'She's asked if you'd like to go round for a cup of tea this morning as most of the family seem to be going out. As you were going anyway, I said you would.'

'I wish you'd let me speak to her,' Sandra grumbled.

Gloria shrugged. 'You'll get plenty of time to chat once you get there. She's expecting you at nine.'

Sandra frowned and looked up at the clock which showed it was already eight-thirty. 'It's a bit short notice, isn't it? What's the rush, do you think?'

'I have no idea,' Gloria replied blithely.

Peggy dithered in the hall, the tension growing as she waited until everyone in the kitchen was making enough noise for her not to be overheard. Once she deemed the right moment had come, she picked up the receiver and dialled for the operator.

'Hello, Auntie Peggy. Did you have a good Christmas?' asked April cheerfully.

'Really lovely, and thank you so much for the bottle of scent. And you?'

'Super, thanks. My little Paula was spoilt rotten, and so was I. How can I help?'

'I'm a bit worried that calls aren't coming through, April. Could you please ring this number?'

'I can't see any problem with the line, Auntie Peggy, but of course I will.'

Peggy replaced the receiver and let it ring a couple of times before picking it up again. 'Yes, that came through just fine, April. Thanks, love, sorry to have been a bother.'

'Always happy to help you out, Auntie Peg,' the girl replied warmly.

'Who was that on the phone?' asked Charlie the minute Peggy went into the kitchen.

'It was Sandra for Cissy,' she replied. 'She wants to come round to say goodbye, so I said she'd be welcome to call in around nine.'

'Well, you could have let me speak to her,' Cissy grumbled, clearly not in the best of moods this morning.

'It was just a quick call,' replied Peggy. 'I think I heard Gloria shouting to her for something in the background, so she couldn't speak for long.' She smiled even though she felt awful about fibbing to her daughter. 'Still, it'll be lovely for you both to have a bit more time together before she leaves. It could be another year before you get the chance again.'

'I'd better go and get dressed then,' Cissy said, pushing back from the table and taking her cup of tea with her as she left the kitchen.

Peggy looked across at Jim. They'd both had a restless night, and now the day was here, they were on tenterhooks. 'Jim, could you see to the chickens, please, while I finish putting together a picnic for Bob and

Pippa? They're off to the County Show today, and the price of food there is extortionate.'

'And what are you up to today, Charlie?' asked Jim, getting to his feet to find the chicken feed in the cupboard under the sink.

'I'm going back to my mate's house to play more records, then we thought we'd go and see Martin and the others at the airfield. Martin promised me ages ago that I could sit in the cockpit and he'd show me all the instruments and such, and explain what flying entails. But with school, rugby and Christmas, there hasn't been a chance.'

'That'll be marvellous,' enthused Peggy. 'Do you want me to make you some sandwiches too?'

'Nah, we'll eat at Paul's. His mum cooked a goose for Christmas, and has promised we can pick the carcass.'

Peggy just managed not to roll her eyes at this, for she was relieved he'd be out of the house for most of the day – as would Bob and Pippa. As Gloria had promised to give Rosie her two free tickets from the Council raffle for the lunchtime panto at the Town Hall theatre, Daisy would be occupied, so there was just Cordelia to worry about now, and that might prove tricky.

'Have you and Bertie made any plans for today, Cordy?' she asked casually.

'Not really. We're both a little tired after all the excitement of the last few days. I know he's planning to play golf this morning, and then visit Rachel to look in on Noel. So I thought I might just sit in here by the fire with my library book. It's an Agatha Christie, and very exciting.'

Peggy nodded, satisfied that once Cordelia was installed in here with her book, she'd have her hearing aid switched off and be none the wiser as to what was happening in the dining room. She went to finish the picnic lunch for Bob and Pippa, knowing she needed to get them all out of the house by nine without making it too obvious, but if Sandra arrived early, and they were still here, she'd have to think on her feet.

The telephone rang and Charlie shot to his feet to answer it – no doubt hoping it was the girl he'd taken to the party. He returned some minutes later flushed with excitement. 'That was Martin,' he gabbled. 'He's asked that we get up to the airfield before ten as he's suddenly been booked for a short flight to Leeds, and if we're on time, we can hitch a ride with him! I phoned Paul, and he's meeting me up there.'

Peggy watched with some amusement as he began to snatch up his coat and scarf, and ram his feet into his sturdy boots. 'I'll see you later,' he shouted, already halfway down the steps to the basement.

The back door slammed behind him, only to be opened again within minutes by Jim. 'It sounds as if young Charlie has an exciting day ahead of him,' he remarked, his gaze finding Peggy before he fumbled to put the chicken feed back into the cupboard without spilling it.

'It certainly does,' she replied. 'I just hope he remembers to tie those boot laces, or it'll be a journey to the hospital instead of Leeds.'

The strain was starting to tell on Peggy and she found she was all fingers and thumbs as she put the flask, small tin of cake and packets of sandwiches in the basket and finally managed to fasten the straps. 'Here you go, Bob. There's enough in there to feed you both for the whole day, so don't feel you have to rush back.'

He eyed her quizzically. 'Why do I get the feeling you're trying to get rid of us all?'

357

'Don't be silly, of course I'm not,' she retorted, unable to look at him. 'I just want you to make the most of the day now the weather's improved.'

Pippa left the kitchen to fetch her coat, and Bob eyed his mother solemnly. 'I'm sure you do,' he said, 'but you're on edge, and it's very clear to me that something else is going on here. Is it to do with Cissy? Are you planning some sort of council of war while we're all out?'

Peggy's heart missed a beat. 'Whatever made you think that?'

'I know something's not right with her, Mum, and you've been as jumpy as a cat ever since she came home. I might be a mere male, but I'm neither blind nor deaf, and to be honest, you could cut the atmosphere in this room with a knife.'

'You're right, son,' said Jim quietly. 'There is a problem with Cissy, but your mother and I are dealing with it. You have your day out with Pippa, and we'll tell you all about it tonight, when, God willing, this mess is sorted out one way or another.'

Bob held his gaze for a moment and then nodded. 'We'll leave you to it then. Good luck with whatever it is, and we'll see you tonight.'

'Can I go with Bob and Pippa?' piped up Daisy, who'd been listening avidly to the various exchanges.

'No, darling,' soothed Peggy. 'Auntie Rosie is going to take you to the park and then on to the pantomime.'

Daisy frowned. 'What's a panmonine?'

'It's a show about one of your favourite stories – Cinderella – with music and dancing and lots of singing and cheering and booing,' she replied. 'You'll love it,' she said firmly.

'Why can't you come too?'

'Because Auntie Rosie could only get two tickets,' she replied, her mind already on other things – like whether to offer tea and cake to her visitors – or something stronger.

'But I don't wanna go without you,' whined Daisy, working herself up into what could become a tantrum.

The last thing Peggy needed this morning was a difficult child. She grasped Daisy's small shoulders firmly and looked into her stormy eyes. 'I have already said I can't go,' she said evenly. 'But if you don't behave, you won't either. In fact, Daisy, you will be sent to your bedroom for the day with no lunch – and certainly no cake.'

Daisy thought about this, her bottom lip jutting out, her eyes wide and threatening tears. Once she realised Peggy wasn't about to give in to her, she gave a long sigh as if to highlight the fact she felt much put-upon. 'All right,' she muttered grudgingly.

'Then you'd better put a smile back on that face,' said Peggy. 'Auntie Rosie doesn't want to spend the day with a grumpy puss.'

'Can I wear my best party dress?' she asked slyly.

'Of course,' replied Peggy, prepared to agree to anything if it avoided a row.

Daisy shot her a dazzling smile and happily went off upstairs.

Peggy glanced at the clock and felt the tension rise. 'The others should be here any minute, Jim. Could you check on the fire in the dining room while I clear this table and make sure Cordelia's settled with her book?'

The table was cleared quickly and once she'd found Cordelia's book and glasses, she made her another cup of tea, advised her to turn off her hearing aid as it would probably get noisy, and hoped she'd stay there for the rest of the morning.

She'd just finished settling her when Ron and Rosie arrived at the back door. Peggy hugged them both, seeing the signs that they too had spent a sleepless night. 'We'll be in the dining room,' she said. 'I'll just pop up and make sure Daisy's ready to leave with you, Rosie. Did you get the tickets?'

Rosie nodded. 'I picked them up on the way here. Sandra was just getting ready to leave, so we don't have much time.' She looked round. 'Where's Cissy?'

'In her room getting dressed,' said Peggy before she shot upstairs to find Daisy struggling to get into the lightweight fancy dress she'd worn as a flower girl for Rita's wedding. It was entirely inappropriate for a cold winter's day, but Peggy fastened the buttons, eased a thick cardigan over the top and could only hope her overcoat would keep her warm. She coaxed Daisy into her shoes, and once these were buckled, she grabbed Amelia and chivvied the child downstairs.

Daisy didn't much appreciate being rushed, and was all set to stamp her feet and become mulish when Ron spotted the danger signs and picked her up to whirl her round. 'To be sure, who's a beautiful wee girl this morning?' he said, giving her a tickle. 'Are you all ready for your lovely treat?'

Daisy giggled and looked at her grandfather with adoration. 'Will there be ice-cream?' she asked, batting her eyelashes.

'I think that is quite possible,' said Ron, setting her back on her feet so Peggy could wrap her up in her overcoat, hat and gloves. He caught her eye, saw the tension in her and tried to convey in his smile that he understood and felt as anxious as she did.

'Come on, then, Daisy,' said Rosie, reaching for her hand. 'We're going to have such fun today, and we don't want to be late, do we?' She shot a look at Peggy and mouthed 'good luck', before helping the child down the steep concrete steps to the basement door.

'What is going on?' asked Cordelia querulously from the fireside chair.

'To be sure, 'tis nothing for you to be worrying your pretty head about,' said Ron, giving her a wink.

She fiddled with her hearing aid. 'Now I know you're up to something, Ronan Reilly,' she said, glaring at him over her half-moon glasses. 'What shenanigans are you plotting?'

'Peggy's just inviting Gloria and her family over to say goodbye before they go back to London,' he said, shooting Peggy a pleading look for help.

'That's right,' Peggy said. 'We'll all be in the other room, so you won't be disturbed.'

Cordelia held Peggy's gaze for a long moment. 'There's something going on this morning,' she said eventually. 'But as you've clearly decided I'll play no part in it, I shall ignore you all and get on with my book.'

'I'm sorry if you feel left out, Cordy,' Peggy said as she took her hand. 'But I promise to explain everything later.'

Cordelia eyed her thoughtfully for a moment, then turned off her hearing aid, pushed her glasses up her nose and returned to her book.

'I think we've upset her,' Peggy whispered fretfully.

Ron grimaced. 'It can't be helped, Peggy. She's too old and frail to be a part of all this. We'll break it gently to her later once we know how the land lies.'

Jim returned to the kitchen to wash his hands. 'The fire's going nicely in there,' he said, drying his hands on a tea towel – which made Peggy frown. 'And I've set up the chairs for everyone.' He looked at his father, his nervous smile a mere twitch of his lips. 'This is worse than waiting for the signal to go over the top,' he tried to joke.

Ron was about to reply when someone knocked on the front door. They froze, braced for what was to come, before Peggy broke the spell. 'I'll get it.'

Gloria glanced up at the clock. It was almost nine, and with every tick of those hands moving across the dial, her heart beat a little faster. Sandra had left the Crown shortly after Rosie had picked up the tickets for the pantomime. Now it was time to talk to Beryl and Graham. She wasn't looking forward to it, but it was necessary if things were to be resolved today.

She found them reading the newspapers in the snug. 'Right,' she began, plumping down into one of the leather bucket-chairs and startling them. 'There's things I gotta say, and I'd appreciate it if you'd just listen and don't interrupt.'

'What's bitten your bum this morning?' asked Beryl.

'The same thing what will bite yer head off if you don't shut up and listen,' snapped Gloria. Pleased to see her sister had got the message, she turned to Graham who was looking very wary. 'There's trouble between you and Sandra, and trouble over at Beach View with Cissy Reilly. As both things seem to be connected, and neither girl will talk to us, Peggy and I have decided enough is enough.'

She took a breath. 'We've organised something today which we hope will bring things to a head once and for all. It won't be pleasant or pretty, but I need you and Beryl to come with me to Beach View.'

Graham frowned. 'My private business is not something to be bandied about with strangers,' he said stiffly. 'Whatever the matter is with Sandra, I will deal with it.'

'Oh, you'll have to deal with it all right,' said Gloria on a sigh. 'But do you really want a divorce, Graham?

Because that's where you're heading if this isn't sorted out.'

'I don't know what yer on about, Gloria,' fretted Beryl. 'How can our Sandra be mixed up with Cissy? They ain't seen each other for years.'

'That's exactly why you both need to get your coats on and come with me,' said Gloria, the stress of the conversation making her snappy. 'For gawd's sake, you two, ain't you got eyes in yer heads? Can't you see that our Sandra is dying inside? We have to sort this – now – before she does something really silly.'

Beryl's eyes filled with tears as Graham stared back at Gloria in horror. 'You don't think . . . you can't mean . . .'

'I don't know, Graham, and that's what's really worrying me, now get yer coats.'

Peggy opened the door to Sandra just as Cissy came downstairs. 'I thought you might like to go in the dining room so you'd be private,' she said to both girls. 'Jim's lit a lovely fire, and I've got the kettle on for tea.'

Cissy and Sandra exchanged looks. 'Seeing as Dad's gone to all that trouble, I suppose it'll be all right,' said Cissy ungraciously.

Sandra dug in her handbag and drew out a pile of envelopes. 'I'm sorry, Peggy. Ivy asked me to give you these, and I forgot.'

'That's fine, Sandra, don't worry about it,' she murmured, taking them from her. 'Come on into the warm, and I'll get you that tea.' She stepped aside to encourage them to go into the dining room, and once they'd sat down, she closed the door and hurried back to the kitchen.

'How did they seem?' asked Ron quietly once the kitchen door was closed.

'Sandra's hollow-eyed and clearly troubled by something,' Peggy replied. 'It's no wonder Gloria's so worried. I'm amazed that neither Beryl nor Graham noticed how close to the edge that girl is – much like our own girl.'

Jim stood grim-faced by the range. 'I can't believe I didn't see what you saw, Peg,' he managed through a tight throat. 'How could I have been so blind?'

She kissed his cheek. 'She's been avoiding us both, so it's hardly surprising, Jim. But instead of blaming ourselves, we'll need to be strong and supportive no matter what today reveals.' She smiled up at him. 'And I know we can do that, because together, we can cope with anything.'

They were brave words, but they hadn't done much good for her nerves, which were so on edge, she could barely make the tea without scalding herself. She took a deep breath and placed the pot on the tray she'd prepared earlier.

'The others should be here very soon, and as long as those girls aren't disturbed, I'm hoping they'll stay put.'

Jim opened the door and Peggy carried the tray across the hall. She tapped on the dining-room door and then stepped inside to find the girls ensconced in the fireside chairs, enjoying the cheerful blaze in the hearth. Her hands were shaking so much the teacups rattled in their saucers, and she quickly put the tray down on the small table between them.

'If you need a top-up, I'll be in the kitchen,' she murmured. 'You won't be disturbed again,' she added before leaving the room and closing the door softly behind her.

She was aware of Jim and Ron watching her with concern as she paused for a moment by the dining-room door to catch her breath and attempt to still the fluttering in her stomach. If this plan didn't work, then she had no idea what she might do next.

Gloria had to chivvy and bully them into their coats, and then hurry them along the back alleyways to the main road that climbed up the steep hill from the sea-front. The wind was bitter despite the clear blue sky, and she was glad she'd worn her fake fur coat.

'Right,' she said, pausing to get her breath after the fast walk. 'We have to go in the back way and keep the noise down, cos the girls don't know we're coming and we need to keep it that way until the time is right.'

'This is ridiculous,' said Graham, digging his hands into his coat pockets, his expression mulish. 'Why all the cloak-and-dagger?'

'Because this is the only way me and Peg could think of that might get them girls talking,' snapped Gloria, who was getting fed up with Graham's continuous moaning. 'Don't you want to know what's eating at your wife and making her ill?'

'Well, of course I do, but this all seems rather . . .'

'I expect it does,' she said dismissively. 'But this is a crisis and it calls for crisis measures – regardless of how ridiculous you may think they are, Graham. Now come on before we all freeze to death in this bloody wind.'

'Hold on a minute, Gloria,' ordered Beryl, grabbing her sister's arm. 'This is my girl yer on about. What gives you the right to poke and pry into 'er business and boss us around?'

Gloria took a breath and battled to keep her temper. 'I got the right because you're so wrapped up in yer own misery you ain't seen what I seen, and Graham's blinded by his own ego. That girl needed you both and you let 'er down, now it's time to step up and be there for her – even if it is at the risk of meddling.'

She shook off Beryl's staying hand and led the way down the twitten that ran behind the terraced Victorian houses, and pushed open the gate. Coming to a halt on the path, she turned to glare at them. 'Now follow me and keep quiet. We don't want the girls knowing we're here. Understood?'

Cowed by the strength of her determination, they nodded and quietly followed her along the path, through the back door, and up the concrete steps into the kitchen where Jim and Ron were sitting morosely at the table, Cordelia was dozing over her book by the range and Peggy was pacing back and forth by the sink.

Gloria nodded to Jim and Ron and then, seeing how drawn and worried Peggy looked, enfolded her in a warm embrace. 'You got me now, gel,' she whispered. 'We can do this.'

'But what if we can't?' Peggy whispered back. 'What if we're wrong and make things worse than they already are?'

'I don't think that's possible,' said Gloria, 'but at the very least it might clear the air.'

Peggy nodded but remained unconvinced as everyone sat down and Jim poured tea into cups. She looked up at the clock and couldn't control the tremor of anxiety which shot through her and made her so light-headed she had to sit down. The others would be here soon, and then it would be too late to stop this. Would today's events do more harm than good – and if they did – how would they ever recover?

'Hold yer nerve, love,' murmured Gloria, reaching for her hand just as they heard the back door open and footsteps on the basement floor.

They turned to see Rachel and a grim-faced Solly Goldman at the foot of the concrete steps – and wrapped snugly in a blanket within Rachel's arms was baby Noel.

Peggy went to say hello and quietly introduced them to Beryl and Graham. 'Thank you so much for this,' she whispered. 'I know it was an odd thing to ask of you, but if we're to get to the bottom of things, it was vital.'

Graham almost choked on his tea. 'You think my Sandra could be that baby's mother?'

'Shhhhhhh. For goodness' sake keep it down,' hissed Gloria.

'Oh gawd,' breathed Beryl. 'This is all too much. I don't know what to think no more.'

'None of us knows anything for certain at the moment,' said Peggy, struggling to remain calm. 'We're just hoping that the sight of Noel will be enough to get them to talk. If one of them is his mother, then we'll have to deal with the consequences. If we've got it all wrong – then we'll have to deal with those consequences too – and God help all of us.'

'It's time we got things moving before them girls do a flit,' said Gloria. 'You go first, Peg. Ask if they want more tea and tell them there's someone here who wants to meet them. We'll be right behind you.'

24

Cissy was in tears as she listened to Sandra go over the plans she'd made for her return to London. It would be an ordeal, for she would lose so much – but then Sandra seemed to have found an inner strength and determination to see it through, and Cissy could only admire her. She didn't possess the same drive, never had really, and listening to Sandra, it made her own situation seem so much more straightforward.

They both looked up at the tap on the door and she hastily dried her tears as Peggy came into the room. 'Are you ready for a fresh pot of tea?' she asked nervously. 'Oh, and you'll need another log on that fire, Cissy. You don't want to risk it going out, do you?' she prattled on.

Cissy prickled with suspicion. Her mother was acting very strangely. 'I think we've had enough tea, thanks, Mum. But I'll put another log on for you and Dad. Sandra and I are about to go for a walk.'

'Oh, you don't want to do that,' said Peggy in a rush. 'It's freezing out there, and anyway, you've got a special visitor who's come to see you.'

All of Cissy's suspicions were on high alert now, and as Peggy turned towards the door, she saw Rachel Goldman walk in with Noel in her arms and knew her mother's trap had been well and truly sprung.

Cissy glanced across at Sandra to see that she'd gone as white as a sheet, her eyes burning with some inner fire as she watched Rachel who'd been swiftly followed into the room by Solly, Gloria, Beryl, Graham, Jim and Ron. This had all the trappings of a council of war, and Cissy's first thought was to flee. She reached for her friend's hand and tried to pull her to her feet so they could escape – but Sandra seemed to be rooted to the chair.

'I don't know what you're playing at, Mum,' Cissy said furiously, 'but whatever it is, we'll take no part in it.'

Peggy wrung her hands. 'I'm so sorry if this is distressing you, darling, but you and Sandra are already a part of it,' she said. 'We're all so worried about you both, and this was the only way we could think of to get you here. I know you might see it as meddling in things we have no right to interfere with, but we desperately need you to talk to us so we can help you with whatever it is that's troubling you.'

Cissy glanced wildly at the door only to find that Ron was sitting on a chair right in front of it, arms folded, expression grimly determined. 'We have nothing to say,' she retorted, fear making her sharp. 'So you might as well give this up now. You can't keep us in here for ever.'

'And what about you, Sandra?' asked Gloria softly. 'You going to let Cissy do yer talking, or are you going to tell me what's making you so ill?'

'I don't want to do this – not now,' she whispered, her eyes firmly on her hands which were twisting nervously in her lap, the knuckles white with tension.

Cissy regarded the others who were making themselves comfortable in the half-circle of chairs which effectively surrounded her and Sandra. She sat back down and folded her arms, determined not to say another word. But the baby in Rachel's arms seemed to sense the awful tension in the room, for he began to whimper and squirm, and she couldn't help but look at him as Rachel was sitting right next to her.

'*Oy vey*,' murmured Rachel. 'There now, there now. You must be hungry.' She rocked him in her arms and then suddenly thrust him at Cissy who had no option but to hold him. 'I will need to warm his bottle. You don't mind looking after him for just a little while?'

Cissy did mind – very much. But Rachel was already digging in her oversized bag for the feeding bottle and within moments was bustling past Ron to get to the kitchen.

Cissy held Noel and gently rocked him, which seemed to please him because he stopped grizzling and looked back at her with bright blue eyes. She felt her heart slowly shatter into a million pieces as he nuzzled fruitlessly against her and his precious weight filled her arms. Unhindered, the tears rolled slowly down her face as she regarded every perfect inch of his little face.

'It's upsetting you, Cissy. Give him to me.'

The soft voice broke the spell the baby had cast and she looked up into Sandra's tear-filled eyes, aware that every move they made and every word they uttered was being closely monitored by their audience. 'This can't be easy for you either. Are you sure?'

At Sandra's nod, she gave the baby one last hug before handing him into the safety of her friend's arms.

'He's a lovely-looking baby, ain't 'e?' murmured Gloria to no one in particular. 'His poor little mother must be beside 'erself having to give him up.' She looked from the sad-eyed Sandra to the weeping Cissy. 'A baby like that is a gift to be loved and cherished – not left in a church to die of the cold. He's lucky he's got Rachel.'

'He wasn't left there to die,' said Cissy. 'He was left so Bertie could find him.'

'You seem to know a lot about it, Cissy,' murmured Peggy, who was on the edge of her seat, rigid with tension.

'It was in all the papers, so of course I know about it,' Cissy retorted. 'Look, I don't know what you think you're up to, but this has gone far enough.' She got to her feet. 'Give him back to Rachel, Sandra. We're leaving.'

Sandra shook her head and kept rocking the baby as she sang a soft lullaby threaded through with tears.

Cissy put her hands on her hips and glared at everyone. 'Now look what you've done,' she hissed. 'Sandra's been on the brink of a breakdown for weeks, and I'm not far behind her. If we'd wanted to talk to you, then we would have done. But when we were ready. This *really* is the last straw. Do *any* of you have the remotest idea of the damage you're doing to both of us?'

The ensuing silence was electric. Rachel had returned silently to stand like a statue beside Ron, her face ashen; Beryl began to sob; Graham remained stony-faced with his arms tightly folded across his chest, and the other three men looked bewildered and deeply uncomfortable. Gloria glared defiantly back at Cissy, and Peggy was battling her tears.

Noel broke the silence with a fretful whimper, and Sandra softly soothed him before looking up at Cissy, her eyes dark and profoundly troubled. 'That's enough, Cissy,' she murmured. 'You're upsetting Noel as well as yourself. We always knew this moment would come, so why don't we just tell them, and get it over with?'

The tension in the room was tangible as Cissy sat down and Sandra gently placed Noel back into her arms.

Cissy looked down at him and realised that the moment had indeed arrived, and that Sandra had instinctively known that his very presence in her arms would give her the added strength and courage she would need to talk about what had happened. And although she'd rehearsed what she would say a hundred times over, the words seemed to be stuck in her throat. The truth was ugly and she didn't want it to taint the warm memories of her home, or cast shadows into the hearts of those who loved her. Yet she knew that the suppurating wounds she'd carried inside for so long needed to be cleansed and cauterised if she was ever to heal.

Unable to look into the anxious faces surrounding her, she kept her gaze firmly on Noel and took a shallow, trembling breath. 'I fell in love when I was in London,' she began softly. 'Or thought I had. He was the brother of a friend, and terribly handsome – what they called a debs' delight. He was invited to all the best parties, could get front-row tickets to the theatre and opera, and danced like a dream. He was rich, too, and, stupidly, I thought he was my Prince Charming.'

She paused, seeing him again in her mind's eye, tall, golden-haired, with dazzling green eyes and a smile that could charm even the most hostile old dowager. And then the image faded and she saw the other side of him – the dark, dangerous side that ultimately broke her.

Looking up from Noel, who'd fallen asleep, she regarded her parents and the others, and realised they were going through agonies, so now she'd started, she would have to go on. But they didn't need to know the sordid details of what had happened – she could at least spare them that.

She cleared her throat. 'It happened at a country house party. It was late and I'd left the crowded mansion and gone out into the garden to get some fresh air and to clear my head. He must have followed me.'

Her lip trembled as the memories flooded back to haunt her. She'd been contentedly ambling down one

372

of the meandering paths that led to the lake, enjoying the clean, fresh air and the silence after the smoky, noisy atmosphere in the house, when he'd come up beside her. He was clearly a little drunk, but then she was slightly tiddly too, so she'd let him take her hand for what she thought would be a romantic moonlit stroll down to the lake.

But as they'd reached the small boathouse, he'd pulled her inside, thrown her against the wall and, with his large hand firmly over her mouth, pulled away her clothes and raped her. She'd fought back as hard as she could, but he'd been too strong, too determined to have his way – and when he'd finished, he'd simply adjusted his clothing, told her she'd been asking for it for weeks, and then walked back to the party.

Trembling and appalled by what had happened, she'd gathered up the tattered remnants of her clothes and sneaked round the house to the tradesmen's entrance and made it unseen to her room. She'd then locked herself in the bathroom, where she'd spent what felt like hours in the bath, constantly refilling it with more hot water to scrub away the smell and feel of him on her skin. She'd packed her bag and telephoned for a taxi very early so she could be back in London before the rest of the house party woke.

'I wasn't really ready, but he was persuasive,' she said, her emotions tightly under control. 'Six weeks later I discovered I was pregnant, and when I told him, he accused me of being a gold-digging tart who'd led him on, and that the baby could have been anyone's.'

'Are you telling us he raped you?' rasped Jim, his face ashen, his eyes burning with fury.

'I'm just giving you the facts, Dad,' she replied, stiff with the stress of having to recall the horror and shame of it all.

'Oh, Cissy,' sobbed Peggy. 'Why didn't you come home then? We would have looked after you.'

'Believe me, Mum, I wanted to, but things happened after that which meant I couldn't leave London.'

'What things?' Jim demanded, his fists curled on his knees, the knuckles white with tension.

She passed the restless baby back to Sandra, knowing that her inner turmoil was being transmitted to him. 'I swear on Noel's life that the baby was his,' she said fervently. 'He was the first man who . . . And the only one.'

'We believe you, darling girl,' rumbled Ron.

'We all do,' managed Peggy, her gaze flitting from Cissy to Noel. 'And the baby? Is it Noel?'

Cissy was thankful for their abiding strength and support, and the warmth of love she could see in their eyes, and wondered why she'd ever thought they wouldn't understand. And yet, she wasn't ready to answer her mother's burning question.

'But surely the other girls at the flat must have known it was all lies,' protested Jim. 'Didn't they back you up?'

'They did eventually,' Cissy admitted bitterly. 'But only because they wanted to avoid a scandal and protect the business.'

She fell silent, remembering how she'd plucked up the courage to tell Clarissa on the quiet what her brother had done, but her response had not been at all what she'd expected. Clarissa had at first refused to believe her, and then – after having a furious row with her brother – had coldly told her she'd make arrangements for her to have an abortion.

Cissy decided to keep that nugget to herself as it would distress her parents just as much as it had distressed her. For regardless of everything that had happened to her, and the likely consequences of

374

bringing an illegitimate baby home, abortion was not something she could ever contemplate.

'I was very upset by it all, as you can imagine,' she said with studied understatement. 'And that made me careless. My mind was so occupied by my situation that I wasn't taking any notice of the traffic, and I stepped straight out into the path of a speeding motorcyclist.'

She heard the gasp go round the room, and hurried to reassure them. 'As you can see, I'm fine now, but I'm afraid I did get rather badly hurt at the time, although no bones were broken.' She had a fleeting memory of being thrown into the air only to land heavily on the bonnet of a parked car and cracking her head on the windscreen – after that she'd known nothing more until she'd woken up in a hospital bed. 'Anyway,' she resumed. 'An ambulance was called and I was whisked off to St George's.'

She fell silent, remembering how she'd woken to the news that her barely formed baby boy had been killed in the accident, and despite the fact he hadn't been wanted, she'd wept bitter tears at his loss and saw his death as her punishment from God.

'I lost the baby that night,' she said softly. 'And in the morning I woke to find Clarissa sitting by the bed, clearly determined to keep everything secret. Within hours, I'd been transferred to a private clinic outside London.'

She regarded the stunned expressions, saw how deeply her confession had affected her parents, and tried to make light of it by forcing a smile. 'Clarissa didn't want word of my "unfortunate little indiscretion", as she called it, getting around the city or to the ears of her important clients – and I really was in a terrible state.'

'Not exactly supportive or caring,' sobbed Peggy. 'Oh, darling. I can't bear to think of you going through all that alone.'

Cissy's throat tightened and the tears again began to swell and rise, threatening to choke her. 'She told me I must never mention my baby . . . My poor little lost, innocent baby,' she managed as the tidal wave of emotions broke through the wall of resistance she'd built up over the last months, and she collapsed beneath the weight of it all.

Peggy flew to her side and gathered her into her embrace. 'Oh, my darling girl,' she breathed. 'My poor, sweet, darling girl. I'm so sorry. But you're home now. You're safe and very much loved.'

'Tell me who he is and I'll have the bastard horsewhipped,' stormed Jim.

'You'd have to get to him before me,' rumbled Ron, his face dark with fury.

'There'd be no point,' sobbed Cissy. 'He's too well connected, and no charges would ever stick. And if you did horsewhip him, he'd sue you and see you ruined. He's a dangerous man who has proved time and again to be untouchable.'

'But we can't let this drop, Cissy,' shouted Jim. 'The man should be punished for what he did to you.'

'Don't, Dad,' she pleaded, emerging from Peggy's embrace to dry her tears and attempt to find a modicum of composure. 'It's over and done with, don't you see? If I'm to have any sort of life, I have to learn to live with what happened, and take strength from it, not spend my days eaten up with bitterness and the need for revenge.'

'It sounds to me like you've been spending too much time with some navel-gazing head-shrinker,' snorted Jim in disgust.

Cissy managed a wan smile at her father's old-fashioned way of thinking. 'He was, in fact, very helpful,' she said quietly. 'Just as helpful, I suspect, as the one you've been seeing with your pal, Ernie.'

Jim squirmed in the chair. 'Aye. Well, that's different,' he muttered.

'So, you were in hospital all the time Clarissa was covering for you?' asked Peggy.

Cissy nodded. Clarissa was very good at covering for people. She'd had a great deal of practice covering for her brother over the years if the rumours she'd heard were true. 'She made all the arrangements and paid for me to stay at the clinic until I was well enough to be released. I suspect I was close to losing my mind for a while, for all I can really remember from the first week or so is waking from the heavy sedation, convinced Harry was chasing me, or that my room was on fire. That didn't last for long, thank God, but my mind was definitely troubled, and even now I still get moments of fear that I've had to learn to deal with.'

She fell silent, unwilling to admit that Clarissa had only helped her in return for her silence, and those terrifying episodes at the hospital had left her frail and frightened of her own shadow until the doctor had explained how the trauma of it all had affected her mind, and that, if she followed his guidelines and continued the counselling, she would learn to cope and thereby, slowly heal.

'Dear God in heaven,' breathed Jim. 'Why the hell didn't you let us know what you were going through, Cissy? We would have been up there like a shot to bring you home.'

'She was too scared and ill to face us, Jim,' said Peggy. 'No wonder she's so thin and pale and nervy after such a terrible ordeal.' She stayed perched on the arm of the chair and hugged Cissy to her side. 'But I promise you, darling, no one will hurt you ever again – and if you need further medical help we'll make sure you get it.'

'But why did you go back to that flat in Mayfair? Why not come home once you were well?' asked Jim.

'To be honest, Dad, I wasn't thinking straight. Stupidly, I felt I owed Clarissa something for sending me to that clinic, which proved to be such a lifeline when I felt I was drowning in it all. I'd also put every penny I had into that business and couldn't risk losing it by just walking away. And I suppose I thought things would change, and they'd be more protective.' She shrugged. 'How naive I was,' she finished bitterly.

'Naive, maybe,' murmured Ron. 'But I think you were just a frightened little girl who didn't know which way to turn. To be sure, I wish to God you'd trusted in us enough to come home then.'

'So do I,' she replied sadly. She turned to her mother and clasped her hand. 'But what I don't understand is why you thought Noel was mine, Mum. How could you believe I'd be capable of abandoning a baby?'

'She put two and two together and got five,' said Sandra into the ensuing silence. 'Just as Gloria did.'

'Well, I'm sorry about that, Sandra,' said Gloria. 'But you can hardly blame me when you refused to talk about what was clearly eating you up.'

'Yeah, you can't expect us to know what's going on in yer 'ead, Sandra. It's not like we're mind-readers,' huffed Beryl. 'And you was in a right two-and-eight, and so prickly none of us dared say anything.' She turned to look at Graham. 'Ain't that right, Graham?'

'There's little point in arguing about it now,' said Graham stiffly. 'I just want to know if that is your baby, Sandra – and if so, what you are going to do about it.'

378

Sandra's eyes were clear, her expression cool and calm as she held the baby close and looked back at him. 'What would you say if he was, Graham? How would you feel if I told you I meant to keep him?'

'Well, that's put a tin lid on it,' breathed Beryl, glancing fearfully at Graham.

'I'd say that if you're planning on keeping another man's bastard you'd better make other living arrangements. You'd no longer be welcome in my house, or in my life,' he replied, his face grey and drawn.

Peggy gasped and the room went very still as everyone waited for Sandra's response.

'Bastard is such an ugly word for an innocent baby,' she said calmly.

Graham sneered. 'There are even uglier words to describe its mother,' he spat.

She held his furious gaze. 'I'm sure there are, but it didn't stop you getting some sort of vicarious pleasure out of reading all the newspaper stories and talking about them endlessly. You even pretended to care at one point, reminding me that even though you couldn't give me children, I should show some sympathy for Noel's mother.' Her lips twisted in disgust. 'You can't have it both ways, Graham.'

Angry colour rose in his face. 'I assume that means it is yours. Well, you're welcome to it. Just don't expect me to have anything to do with either of you.'

Sandra very gently passed Noel to Rachel so she could feed him. 'Actually, Graham, he's not mine,' she said quietly into the silence.

Graham stared at her, his Adam's apple bobbing in his throat as he tried to find the words to respond. 'What sort of game are you playing, Sandra?' he finally rasped.

'It has never been a game, Graham,' she replied flatly. 'I just needed you to show your true colours out

379

in the open for once. And I think you've done that today, don't you?'

He looked hunted, his eyes darting from face to face before he replied. 'You always knew my feelings on such matters,' he finally managed. 'You all did,' he continued, his gaze flitting from Beryl to Gloria as if for justification.

'Ah, yes,' said Sandra. 'You've always made it very clear where you stood when it came to babies. Illegitimate or otherwise.'

Graham stiffened in the chair, his eyes suddenly wary as a pulse beat in his jaw. 'What do you mean by that?'

Sandra smoothed her skirt over her knees and looked at Graham squarely. She'd been preparing for this moment, and despite her initial reluctance, was now absolutely ready for it. 'I desperately wanted to have your babies, Graham, and was devastated when I discovered there would be none.'

'That's not my fault,' he protested. 'It's a medical thing I have no control over.'

'But you had control over me, didn't you?'

'Don't be ridiculous,' he blustered. 'I've given you a far better life than you'd ever have had in the East End slums. You didn't complain about the lovely home I provided, or the social circle I introduced you to. I didn't have to force you into anything – in fact, you were only too willing to turn your back on your old life and enjoy what marriage to me brought you.'

'But all that came at a price,' said Sandra. 'And it's a price I'm no longer willing to pay. Because I've realised what sort of man you really are, Graham, and I'm mortified to think I ever imagined I could love you.'

'Sandra,' gasped Beryl. 'You can't say things like that. Graham's been ever so good to you – to me too, offering to buy me the fancy 'ouse and everything – and helping with the 'ouse-keeping when I fell a bit short.'

Sandra took her mother's hand. 'I know you thought Graham was the perfect husband and son-in-law, and so did I at first. But the help and support he gave you was his way of making you depend on him, just as he did to me. He likes to control people, Mum, and if you go against him, the help and support is withdrawn until you fall back into line.'

Doubts flashed in Beryl's eyes. 'You got it all wrong,' she said hesitantly. 'He were being kind to me after yer dad passed away.'

'I'm sorry, Mum, but it's you who's wrong. I realised some time ago that he's been quietly but determinedly moulding me into the pliant little wife who would bow to his judgement and let him take control of everything, from where we lived to what friends we had – even down to the clothes I bought.'

She took a breath. 'But it was only very recently that I discovered what really lay beneath that seemingly compassionate and sincere exterior. And it's ugly, Mum. Dark and mean and rotten to the core.'

Beryl's eyes were bright with tears. 'I don't know 'ow you can be saying such awful things, gel. That man loves you.'

'Does he?' Sandra's eyes were flint as she regarded him. 'Then why, when he knew how much I longed to have children, did he lie about being incapable of giving me any?'

Graham went ashen as his gaze swept the room. 'I . . . I didn't . . . It's not . . .'

'Yes, you did,' retorted Sandra. 'I made an appointment the day before we left to come here. It was to see the doctor. I'm not pregnant – never have been unfortunately, but I needed to see him because of the bout of food poisoning I couldn't seem to shift after getting back from Manchester. We got to talking about the tests we took, and he was puzzled to learn that I thought you were infertile, because you are no such thing. Are you, Graham?'

'Is this true?' barked Gloria as she got to her feet and towered over him.

Graham cowered. 'I thought it was for the best,' he muttered, edging from his seat to back away from her. 'Our lives were ordered and comfortable. Children would have spoilt that, and I hoped that as time went on she'd realise she was better off without them,' he finished weakly.

'You bastard,' hissed Beryl, getting to her feet.

'Leave him, Mum,' ordered Sandra. 'He's not worth the aggro.' Her eyes were arctic as she regarded him in disgust. 'Just go, Graham. Go back to your orderly life. The divorce papers will be in the post as soon as I can see my solicitor.'

Unable to defend his behaviour, Graham eyed them all with seething hatred before snatching up his coat and hat and barging past Ron to get to the door.

Sandra gave a deep sigh, glad it was finally over.

'What I want to know,' said Gloria crossly, 'is why he married you in the first place if you weren't what he were looking for?'

'But I was, you see. He saw this naive, lively young girl from the East End who had ambitions to do better in life. It was all too easy to dazzle me with his charm, his education and position in the City, and make me think he knew everything about everything, whereas I knew nothing about anything other than the price of a bag of spuds. I was an Eliza Doolittle to his Professor Higgins, and for a long while I was content to let him take me over and even pay for those bloody elocution lessons.'

She breathed deeply to calm down and took her mother's hand. 'And then, one day in Manchester, after a long conversation with Margot, I realised how out of control I was of my life. If anything had happened to him, I wouldn't know the first thing about how to pay the bills, what the state of our finances was, or what insurances we had. I had no idea about where the stopcock was, or what to do if the electricity went off. He hadn't even let me take driving lessons because he didn't think I was bright enough to be in charge of a car, for heaven's sake!'

'But how will you get a divorce when it was you what 'ad the affair?' asked Gloria.

'I spoke to Margot about that. The law changed in 1937 so it's easier now for a woman to divorce her husband. And because of that change – and the way he's lied to me over the years – I can divorce him on the grounds of cruelty.'

Peggy dabbed her eyes with a handkerchief. 'I'm so sorry you girls have gone through so much. Please forgive us for putting you through all this.'

'We're sorry too,' said Cissy. 'Sorry for bringing such unhappiness into Beach View and upsetting you all.' She turned to Sandra. 'But we promise never to keep things back from you again, don't we?'

'To be sure, I hope to all that's holy, you never go through anything like that ever again,' rumbled Ron. He got to his feet. 'I don't know about the rest of you, but I need a drink.'

'I'll make a fresh pot of tea,' said Peggy.

'I'm thinking something stronger is called for,' said Ron. 'Fetch the glasses and the whisky from the kitchen, Jim.'

'Yeah,' said Gloria, puffing out her generous bosom. 'I reckon we could all do with a good drink now the air's clear and we know where we stand. Blimey, Sandra, I never took Graham for such a nasty piece of work. It's no wonder you were at yer wits' end.'

She turned to Cissy, who was now looking much calmer, and placed a gentle hand on her slender shoulder. 'As for you, love, me 'eart goes out to yer. I'm ever so sorry for what happened. But yer 'ome now, where you belong, and you'll get all the love and care you need 'ere. Peg and Jim will see to that.'

'Well, I'm glad we could help in some small way,' said Solly, who'd remained a solid but silent presence throughout the drama. 'But we're still no nearer to discovering the identity of Noel's mother.'

'If she doesn't come forward, then I suspect we'll never know,' said Rachel on a sigh. 'Do you think the authorities would allow us to adopt him, Solly?'

'Rachel, my dear, we have to be practical about these things. I know your heart is taken by him, but we are too old for such a responsibility. When he is thirteen and preparing for his bar mitzvah, I shall be in my eighties – if God should grant me such a long life. It is better, my love, to enjoy him while we can and help to see him settled with a young couple.'

'You are wise, as always, Solly,' she murmured over the baby's head. 'Let us go home now and put this little one to bed.'

Ron escorted them to the door and then relieved Jim of the tray of glasses he'd brought in from the kitchen. Once the drinks had been poured, he raised his glass. 'Slainte,' he said, and downed it in one as the others echoed the Gaelic toast.

'So what now?' he asked the gathering. 'The rest of the family already suspect something was happening today. Do we tell them your story, Cissy?'

'I've always hated keeping secrets,' she replied, 'and if we don't tell them it will come between us and get bigger and more destructive as time goes on. They don't need to know the darker details – just that I made some bad mistakes, got pregnant and lost the baby.'

She blinked rapidly and took another sip of whisky. 'I'll tell them, Grandpa, but if you could speak to Rosie, I'd be grateful.'

'What do I say to Doris?' asked Peggy fretfully.

'Just tell her the truth, Mum. If she doesn't like it, then she'll have to lump it. But I suspect even Aunt Doris possesses enough charity in her heart to accept that I was more sinned against than sinning.'

Peggy nodded, her expression giving away her doubts about her sister's charitable side.

The door suddenly opened and everyone looked round. Peggy leapt to her feet. 'Danuta,' she gasped, seeing how pale the girl was. 'Whatever's wrong? What's happened?

Cordelia was standing just behind Danuta, and now she put her arm about Danuta's waist and gently steered her into the nearest chair as a white-faced Bertie dithered by the door. 'Danuta has distressing news,' she said fretfully. 'She has just come from the hospital.'

'There hasn't been an accident at the airfield, has there?' asked Jim sharply.

Danuta shook her head and gratefully sipped from the glass of whisky that Ron had placed into her hand. 'I was called to the cottage hospital very early this morning. The doctor told me that Gracie was losing her battle against the septicaemia and getting very agitated in her delirium. She was asking for Florence, Bobby and me, so I collected them on my way through.'

Danuta dipped her chin as Cordelia grasped her hand in support and encouragement. 'I'm sad to say Gracie died two hours ago,' she said softly. 'We got there in time to see her, but I'm not really sure she knew we were there, for she fell into a coma shortly after we'd arrived. Florence has taken Bobby home, and is sensible enough to realise the child is too young to understand what has happened, but that he will need a lot of love and attention. She will keep him with her until other arrangements can be made.'

'But what will happen to him?' breathed Peggy.

'Gracie must have been aware that she might not get through this, and in one of her clearer moments she had a long talk with Florence and then asked a nurse to write a letter addressed to me and Florence. It was a confession, really, and a plea to take care of her precious children.'

'Children?' Peggy gasped. 'But she only has Bobby.'

Danuta shook her head. 'She also had a baby boy called Noel.'

They all sat in stunned silence until Peggy stammered, 'But you said . . . I thought . . . Oh, my God.'

'I know what you thought, Mamma Peggy, and so did Florence. But the minute I examined her I knew she'd recently given birth. So did Alastair Darwin, which is why he took her straight to the cottage hospital. Alastair and I agreed we wouldn't enlighten you or Florence until it was absolutely necessary because we had to keep Gracie's situation confidential. Neither of us said anything to the authorities either, for it was clear she was extremely ill. Giving birth alone and in such filthy conditions was fatal. Noel was very lucky to have survived unscathed.'

'But surely you and Florence must have seen she was pregnant,' said Sandra to Peggy. 'After all, she works in the same factory, and even shares a house with Florence.'

Peggy mopped away her tears. 'It never occurred to me, and I'm sure it didn't to Florence, either. Gracie actually only moved in with Florence in October and always wore loose dungarees and thick, baggy sweaters, even during the summer. As this last summer has been cold and wet, nobody thought anything of it.

And she's petite and slender too, so her bump was probably quite small.'

She gave a tremulous sigh. 'She was certainly skinny, but I put her weight loss down to that trouble she had with Phil Warner.' She looked back at Danuta. 'I suppose Noel is his?'

Danuta nodded.

'So what's going to happen to them both?' she asked anxiously.

'She explained in her letter that she had discussed this with Florence,' Danuta replied. 'Florence was reluctant to take both children on as a single woman, and they had come to an agreement that I should be approached to adopt them. But of course, first I must get permission from the authorities and ask Stanislav how he would feel about this. It is a big responsibility, and it will mean I must give up my work and find a better place to live.'

'Oh, Danuta. But how do *you* feel about taking on a ready-made family?' asked Cissy. 'I know you've always wanted to adopt, but taking on two at once is quite something.'

Danuta's eyes gleamed and there was high colour in her cheeks. 'I would take them both in one beat of my heart,' she replied. 'To be a mother is far more important than any job or career, and I fell in love with Noel from the moment I took him into my arms.'

'Then grab the chance while you can,' said Sandra. 'I'm sure you'll be a wonderful mother, because Gracie must have known that to entrust you with them.' She reached in her pocket for a handkerchief. 'Oh dear, poor Gracie. I feel so awful that we didn't get to see her.'

'To be sure, there's been enough tears shed today to float the ark,' rumbled Ron. 'I for one will not be sorry when it's over.' He finished his whisky and poured another for Cordelia, who was looking utterly confused.

'Don't you be worrying your head, Cordy,' he said quietly beneath the others' chatter, 'I'll tell you what's been going on later.' He turned to a similarly confused Bertie. 'And if you meant what you said about being Noel's sponsor, then I'm thinking your support would be gratefully accepted.'

'I'll gladly keep my word,' said Bertie firmly. 'I'm just so saddened by the loss of such a young woman and will do my utmost to help and support Danuta and Stanislav in any way I can. It comes as a relief to know that Noel and young Bobby will be spared a life in an orphanage and that they'll both get all the love and care they need.'

A profound silence fell after this statement, for Bertie's heartfelt promise had touched them all.

Sandra dried her tears; finished her whisky and then set the glass down on the table. 'I think it's time we went back to the Crown,' she said to her mother and aunt. 'Hopefully, Graham's caught the earlier train back to London, so I'll stay on if you don't mind, Auntie Gloria. Just until Gracie's funeral.'

'I'll stay here with you,' said Beryl. 'I don't think I can face that journey on me own after today.'

Sandra embraced Cissy and kissed her cheek. 'I'll see you tomorrow.'

Peggy swept Sandra into her arms. 'I'm sorry this has all been so painful,' she said softly. 'Just remember you're always welcome here,' she added, pulling from the embrace with a warm smile. 'Good luck with the divorce, my dear, and pop in anytime while you're here.'

Sandra awkwardly shook Danuta's hand. 'It was nice to meet you, Danuta, although I wish wholeheartedly it was under better circumstances. Please stay in touch. I'd love to know how things turn out for you and the children.'

Jim gave Sandra a hug, was swamped in fake fur and perfume by Gloria, and pecked on the cheek by Beryl before he escorted them all to the front door. 'We'll see you soon, I'm sure,' he said as they stepped outside.

They walked away arm in arm, Gloria in her ridiculous high heels and fake fur coat, Beryl in her sensible shoes and gabardine mac, and Sandra in her smart overcoat and low-heeled pumps. Jim shut the door and turned to Peggy. 'Did I detect a spring in Sandra's step as they were leaving?'

'I think you did,' she said, putting her arms about his waist and leaning her head on his chest. 'And I expect it's because she's feeling a freedom she's never had since marrying that Graham. The freedom to be true to herself, and to forge her own path through life.'

'But it won't be easy for her to start again as a divorced woman – it could affect her reputation, and her career.'

'She has her family to love and support her, and I suspect the strength and purpose she found today in telling us her story will grow now she can truly believe in herself.' Peggy looked up at him. 'Love will always find a way, Jim. Just as love for those children will make our little Danuta whole again to become the mother she was always meant to be.'

She gave a sigh and hugged him. 'It's been a sad day, but I get the feeling all those tears will bring a rainbow tomorrow.'

WELCOME TO

Cliffehaven

ELLIE DEAN

A Map of Cliffehaven

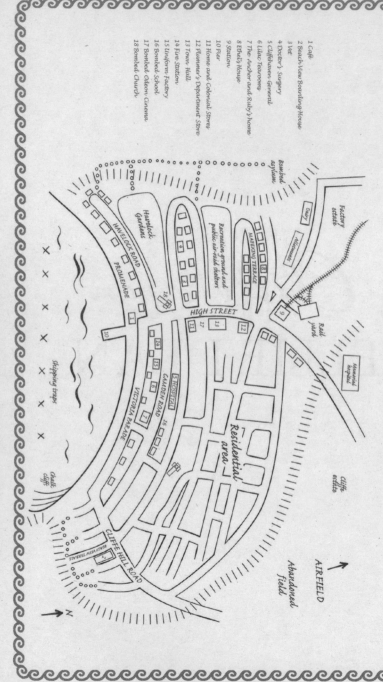

1 Café
2 Beach View Boarding House
3 Vet
4 Doctor's Surgery
5 Cliffehaven General
6 Lilac Tearooms
7 The Anchor and Ruby's home
8 Ethel's House
9 Station
10 Pier
11 Home and Colonial Stores
12 Plummer's Department Store
13 Town Hall
14 Fire Station
15 Uniform Factory
16 Bombed School
17 Bombed Odeon Cinema
18 Bombed Church

MEET THE CLIFFEHAVEN FAMILY

PEGGY REILLY is in her late forties, and married to her childhood sweetheart, Jim. She is small and slender, with dark, curly hair and lively brown eyes. As if running a busy household and caring for her youngest daughter, Daisy, wasn't enough, Peggy is now the manager of a local clothing factory, yet still finds time to offer tea, sympathy and a shoulder to cry on when they're needed. She and Jim took over the running of Beach View Boarding House when Peggy's parents retired. During the war years when her family were scattered and Jim was fighting in Burma and India, Peggy took in numerous evacuees who remain to this day an intrinsic part of her life.

Peggy and Jim have three daughters, two sons and three grand-children, and their permanent lodger, Cordelia Finch, has become a surrogate grandmother to them all. Peggy can be feisty and certainly doesn't suffer fools, and yet she is also a romantic at heart and can't help trying to match-make.

JIM REILLY is in his late forties and was a projectionist at the local cinema until it was bombed, and he was called up to fight for King and country in India and Burma. He had previously seen action in the last few months of the First World War with his older brother, Frank, and father Ron, and the experiences he'd gone through in both wars are now affecting him to the point where he needs help. Returning from the Far East, he is now employed by the British Legion and finds great solace in the fact he's doing useful work.

Jim is handsome, with flashing blue eyes and dark hair, and the gift of the Irish blarney he'd inherited from his Irish father, which usually gets him out of trouble. He likes to flirt with women and although he would never be unfaithful to Peggy, he enjoys the chase. Now he's returned home, Jim is finding it hard to settle even though it was all he'd dreamt about while away – but there have been too many changes and Peggy has become far too independent for his liking.

RONAN REILLY (Ron) is a sturdy man in his late sixties who led a very secretive life away from Beach View during the hostilities as a member of the highly secretive sabotage and defence arm of the Home Guard. Widowed several decades ago, he's recently married Rosie Braithwaite who used to own the Anchor pub. They now live in the posh end of Cliffehaven in a detached house in Havelock Road.

Ron is a wily countryman; a poacher and retired fisherman with great roguish charm who tramps over the fields with his dogs, Harvey and Monty, and his two ferrets. He doesn't care much about his appearance, much to Rosie's dismay, but beneath that ramshackle old hat and moth-eaten clothing, beats the heart of a strong, loving man who will fiercely protect those he loves.

ROSIE BRAITHWAITE is in her late fifties and is extremely happy to be finally married to Ron, even if he does drive her to distraction with his shenanigans. Having sold the Anchor to Ruby Clarke, she is now a local town councillor with a passion for improving the lot of those who have been left homeless after the war. Rosie has platinum hair, big blue eyes and an hour-glass figure – she also has a good sense of humour and enjoys sparring with Ron when he's got himself into yet another tangle. And yet her glamourous appearance and winning smile hides the heartache of not having been blessed with a longed-for baby, and now it's too late. Peggy is her best friend, and the people living in Beach View have taken the place of the family she'd never had.

HARVEY is a scruffy, but highly intelligent brindle lurcher, with a mind of his own and a mischievous nature – much like his owner, Ron. His pup, Monty, is the product of an illicit courtship with a pedigree whippet, and the pair of them like nothing more than being out on the hills with Ron. Harvey adores everyone but Peggy's elder sister, Doris.

DORIS WHITE was once married to the long-suffering Ted who'd secretly been having an affair for years. They used to live in a large house in Havelock Road until it took a direct hit from a doodlebug and she was forced to move in with her sister Peggy. She has always looked down on Peggy and despite having recently married the gentle and loving retired colonel, John White, is a terrible social climber and snob.

Doris is a leading light – or would like to be – in Cliffehaven society and enjoys being married to John who is captain of the golf club and on the committee of the Officer's Club. They have converted their two bungalows into one grand house in Mafeking Terrace. Doris insists upon calling Peggy, Margaret, because she knows it winds her up like a clock and loathes Ron because he calls a spade a shovel and refuses to change his nefarious ways. Yet, despite her snooty attitude and her refusal to unbend, Doris has realised that her marriage to John is in danger if she doesn't change.

ANTHONY WILLIAMS is Doris's much beloved only son. He was a teacher in a private school before the war and worked for the Ministry of Defence during it. He still works for the government and is now married to Suzy, who was a lodger at Beach View Boarding House during the war and was a theatre nurse at Cliffehaven General. They have now moved to Oxford and are the proud parents of baby Angela and little Teddy.

DOREEN GREY is the youngest Dawson sister and although she loves Peggy, cannot stand Doris. Doreen has long been divorced from her ne'er-do-well husband, Eddie, and after the tragic death of her lover, Archie Blake, is raising their baby boy along with her two young girls. She works as a school secretary in Swansea.

FRANK REILLY is in his early fifties and has served his time in the army during both wars, but at heart, he's a fisherman. He was married to the very difficult Pauline, who left him for a job in London, and now he lives alone in Tamarisk Bay in the fisherman's cottage where he was born. Free of Pauline who has demanded a divorce, Frank is now courting Brenda – a childless and very attractive widow who works at the Anchor pub with Ruby Clarke.

CORDELIA FINCH is a widow and has been boarding at Beach View for many years. She is in her eighties and is rather frail due to her arthritis, but that doesn't stop her from bantering with Ron and enjoying life to the full. She adores Peggy and looks on her as a daughter, for her own sons emigrated to Canada many years before and she rarely hears from them. Everyone who lives at Beach View, including Peggy's youngest, Daisy, regard her as their grandmother. Cordelia's close friendship with Bertie Double-Barrelled has come too late in their lives for romantic potential, but they're content in each other's company.

BERTRUM GRANTLEY-ADAMS (Bertie Double-Barrelled) is a re-tired army officer in his eighties. Raised in an orphanage and numerous foster homes, he found his family in the army. Old habits die hard and he's a stickler for time-keeping and efficiency, and his daily routine is unvarying. He lives in a bungalow which overlooks the golf course and acts as church warden. He adores Cordelia, but knows friendship is really all he can offer her now they are so elderly.

RITA SMITH came to live at Beach View after her home in Cliffehaven was flattened by an air raid. She worked for the local fire service as a mechanic during the war where she met an Australian flier, Peter, who shares her love of motorbikes. Once the war was over, she married Peter and went with him back to Australia to set up home in Northern Queensland.

FRAN is from Ireland and is a talented violinist who worked as a theatre nurse at Cliffehaven General. She was one of Peggy's evac-uees until she married Robert – a Ministry of Defence colleague of Anthony Williams. They now live in London with their baby.

SARAH FULLER and her younger sister, **JANE**, came to England and Beach View after the fall of Singapore. They are the great-nieces of Cordelia Finch who welcomed them with open arms. Having worked in the Timber Corps and for the government's secret service, both girls returned to Singapore to search for their father and Sarah's fiancé, Philip, and to reunite with their mother and much younger brother. The tragic news that neither man had survived was tempered by the fact they had their mother and Jim Reilly to help them through. A double wedding in Singapore saw both girls finally settled with the men they'd met during the war years. They now live in America.

IVY is from the East End of London and was billeted for a time with Doris where she was expected to skivvy. Now married to Fire Officer Andy Stevens, they have moved to Walthamstow, and have a baby boy and another on the way. Ivy and Rita are best friends and are still in touch despite living on opposite sides of the world.

DANUTA is in her early thirties. Originally from Poland, she managed to escape Europe and come to England in search of her brother, who was a pilot. She arrived at Beach View to learn that he was killed during the Battle of Britain and, after losing the baby she so desperately wanted, tries to make the best of things by using her nursing skills at Cliffehaven General. But she is soon recruited to the Secret Service where she meets Dolly Cardew who becomes her mentor and guide during the dangerous missions into war-torn Europe. Following her capture by the SS and a miraculous escape, she meets the Polish flier and amputee, Stanislav, who she eventually marries. She is now the local district nurse and midwife in Cliffehaven.

RUBY CLARKE is in her late twenties and has taken over the Anchor pub from Rosie Braithwaite. She met and married a Canadian soldier in Cliffehaven and went to live in the wilds of Canada but never settled. When her husband was killed in a logging accident, and she lost her baby during a brutal winter, she returned to Cliffehaven and the only family she ever really knew at the Beach View Boarding House. The memories of what happened in Canada still haunt her, and although she is being very sweetly courted by Dr Darwin, the local GP, she is not yet ready to make a commitment.

DOLLY CARDEW is in her sixties, married to retired American General Felix Addington, and living in California. She is mother to Pauline – from whom she's estranged, and Carol, who lives in Devon. Dolly is a live-wire and spent the First World War working with the resistance in France – and the Second World War training girls like Danuta in unarmed combat and sabotage. She spent her lonely childhood holidays roaming the hills surrounding Cliffehaven and her first love was Ronan Reilly – a man she will always think of as the one who got away. But she is very happy with Felix – Carol's father – and thoroughly enjoying the liberating life in the warmth of the Californian sunshine.

PEGGY'S CHILDREN

ANNE is married to Station Commander Martin Black, a retired RAF pilot. Together they have two girls, Rose Margaret and Emily Jane, as well as newly born Oscar. Martin is now a partner in Phoenix Airfreight Services and Anne is a full-time mother since giving up teaching at the local primary school.

CICELY (Cissy) was a driver for the WAAF and stationed at Cliffe Aerodrome. She once had ambitions to go on stage but found great satisfaction in doing her bit. She invested her life savings into a private hire chauffeur company with three other young women she met during the war years and for a time was enjoying the bright lights of London. But when things turn sour, she returns home to Beach View and her loving family.

BOB and **CHARLIE** are Peggy's sons of eighteen and sixteen who spent most of their childhood in Somerset because of the war. Bob is serious and dedicated to running the farm, while Charlie is still mischievous and, when not causing trouble or playing rugby, can usually be found under the bonnet of some vehicle, tinkering with the engine. Charlie has plans to join the RAF, and is proving to be quite a scholar, while Bob is making his life in Somerset on the farm which he will inherit.

DAISY is Peggy's youngest child, born the day Singapore fell. She found it difficult to relate to Jim on his return home as he was a stranger, but is now a real daddy's girl, and can wind him round her little finger. She has just started school and is in the same class as Anne's Rose Margaret.

Lose yourself in the

The Sunday Times Bestselling Author

Will a new home provide the fresh start she needs?

Ellie DEAN

There'll Be Blue Skies

Far From Home

Will she ever see her loved ones again?

Ellie Dean

Ellie DEAN

She swore she would never lose heart . . .

Keep Smiling Through

The Sunday Times Bestselling Author

Can love survive in a time of war?

Ellie DEAN

Where The Heart Lies

United by love, separated by war . . .

Ellie Dean

Always in my Heart

It was a time of friendship, family, love and loss . . .

Ellie Dean

All My Tomorrows

The Sunday Times Bestselling Author

War can bring hope as well as heartache

Ellie DEAN

Some Lucky Day

The Sunday Times Bestselling Author

When war reveals a family secret, it can only bring trouble . . .

Ellie DEAN

While We're Apart

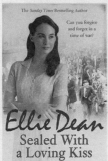

The Sunday Times Bestselling Author

Can you forgive and forget in a time of war?

Ellie Dean

Sealed With a Loving Kiss

world of Cliffehaven

Discover the new novel from

Ellie
DEAN

With Promises To Keep

Coming March 2025

Part of the *Percy Street* community